I0690344

DAIKAIJU!2

REVENGE OF THE GIANT MONSTERS

Other Titles by Agog! Press:

AustrAlien Absurdities, Edited by Chuck McKenzie and Tansy Rayner Roberts, 2002/2006

Agog! Fantastic Fiction: 29 New Tales of Fantasy, Imagination and Wonder, Edited by Cat Sparks, 2002/2006

Agog! Terrific Tales: New Australian Speculative Fiction, Edited by Cat Sparks, 2003/2006

Agog! Smashing Stories: New Australian Speculative Fiction, Edited by Cat Sparks, 2004/2006

Daikaiju! Giant Monster Tales, Edited by Robert Hood and Robin Pen, 2005/2006

Agog! Ripping Reads, Edited by Cat Sparks, 2006

Daikaiju!3 Giant Monsters vs the World, Edited by Robert Hood and Robin Pen, 2007

DAIKAIJU!2

REVENGE OF THE GIANT MONSTERS

EDITED BY ROBERT HOOD AND ROBIN PEN

Daikaiju!2: Revenge of the Giant Monsters © Robert Hood and Robin Pen 2007

Cover art by by Todd Tennant
Design and layout by Cat Sparks
Typeset in Bookman Old Style and Footlight MT Light.

All stories © 2007 by their respective authors, printed by permission of the authors.

All rights reserved. Without limiting the rights under copyright above, no part of this publication may be reproduced, stored in or introduced into a retrieval system, or transmitted in any form, or by any means (electronic, mechanical, photocopying, recording or otherwise), without the prior written permission of both the copyright owner and the above publisher of this book.

Published by Agog! Press:
PO Box U302
University of Wollongong
NSW 2522
Australia
www.catsparks.net

In partnership with Prime Books:
www.prime-books.com

ISBN:
978-0-8095-7230-4 (hc)
978-0-8095-7231-1 (pbk)

CONTENTS

PREFACE

Some would say that producing one sequel to a successful themed anthology is pushing one's luck. But two? *Daikaiju! Giant Monster Tales*, which appeared in 2005, proved to be a pleasant, and often enlightening, surprise to many readers. Critical opinion was positive. It won an Australian Ditmar Award for Best Collection. It was reprinted in partnership with Prime Books in the US.

Things were looking up for giant monster stories. Our belief had been vindicated. There was a definite market for them, albeit a niche one.

Following our final cull for that anthology, we had already determined that we would like to produce a sequel, one that would include those stories that we would have liked to include in the first volume but simply couldn't, logistically. As it was, *Daikaiju! Giant Monster Tales* was "over-sized". More would have been catastrophically excessive.

So we decided, with the authors' blessing, to produce an e-anthology—an electronic sequel that could simply be downloadable, thus avoiding publishing costs. However, as time passed, circumstances arranged themselves in such a way that we had the opportunity to produce the sequel as a physical book. Why not take it? This was exciting—except we discovered that, as envisaged, the e-book sequel volume was too long for a print version. So we did the logical thing; we decided to publish the single obese e-anthology as two separate svelte books. The space gained allowed us to solicit extra material from assorted more-than-willing contributors. After all, one can never have too many giant monsters. Right?

Thus, *Daikaiju!2: Revenge of the Giant Monsters* and *Daikaiju!3: Giant Monsters Versus the World* were born. The first of these you hold in your hand. The second follows closely on its heels.

As editors, and in hindsight, we can detect similarities and differences between the first volume and the sequels. The stories in both are varied and inventive and enthusiastic. There are lots of giant monsters and they tend to trash the trappings of human society. Both anthologies contain stories of a kind you might expect, as well as the odd tale that proves to be totally left-field. Both are lots of fun.

But what about differences? Possibly, *Volume 2* contains more stories of a traditional monster-trashes-city kind, though generally the approach is rather less traditional than you might expect. Many of the stories refer to aspects of filmic giant monster lore that weren't touched upon in *Volume 1*, such as revenge as a motivation, Monster Island, conglomerate monsters and the monster as victim. You will also find planet-sized monsters, giant zombies, human giants, human–kaiju cross fertilisation, giant monsters from the folklore of non-Japanese cultures, and space-borne apocalypse.

Where the first *Daikaiju!* contained some very *very* short work —haiku, in fact—this volume in contrast contains one story that is virtually a short novel, or at least a short story that has grown to *daikaiju* proportions. In this case the author offered us a shortened version; but we decided to stick with the bigger one. After all, what are *daikaiju* all about, if not excess?

Before wishing you well as you undertake this second foray into the world of the gigantically impossible, we would like to thank a few people. First and foremost, there are the authors, who not only offered us their work, but tolerantly waited an inordinate amount of time to see their stories in print. Their patience was much appreciated. Secondly, we'd like to acknowledge the wonderful Todd Tennant, whose excellent artwork adorns the cover. Todd has a boundless enthusiasm for all things gigantic and we think you'll be seeing much more of him in the future. Thirdly, we'd like thank Sean Wallace of Prime Books for making these volumes available to an international audience. Lastly, there's Cat Sparks, who not only put up with Rob's obsessive-compulsive behaviour but was responsible for designing and laying out *Daikaiju!2: Revenge of the Giant Monsters*. Thanks, Cat, as always.

Robert Hood
Robin Pen

June 2007

Where Have All The Monsters Gone?

Robin Pen

There are no monsters. As much as we wish it were not so, there are no monsters. No monsters slumbering in our dark lakes. No monsters in ice caves high up on our tallest mountains. There are no monsters far underground beneath our remotest deserts. No winged monsters soaring above our white clouds. No monsters knocking down trees in our green jungles. No monsters in the deep dark oceans …

Well, okay, maybe there are. We don't know for sure. We have explored so little of our oceans and we have yet to extend our reach down into the great rifts. So maybe monsters do lurk there—creatures lying dormant in the black, once in a while extending a mandible of some kind to snatch up a Colossal Squid for breakfast.

The deepest darkest waters are the last places on this world into which our consciousness has yet to extend itself—in person or remotely. But perhaps our unconscious mind may see, or at least sense, what is there. And if we can sense it, maybe, just maybe, the monster *is* there. For the monster, the giant monster, the *Daikaiju*, needs more than fresh calamari to exist.

The giant monster needs to be believed in.

Far more often than not, people these days say they don't believe in giant monsters. Why? Because the giant monsters don't exist, they say. They are impossible. They are foolish fictions.

But the truth is, monsters don't exist because those very people won't believe in them, denying their existence with every breath, every scornful laugh. Modern skepticism is the monster's greatest enemy. Yet in times past people *did* believe in giant monsters, believed in them because they saw them, were killed by them, rhapodised over them. And we know this because it is in the records. In fact, giant monsters appear to have existed up until quite recently, just beyond our living memory.

According to the records—records we can all readily access— they were prancing around in ancient times in great numbers. You couldn't go for a walk to anywhere particularly far before you were stepped on by one of them. There were big boys like the Kraken and the Colossus of Rhodes when he decided to have a stretch. Even that bloody big horse that kicked the shit out of Troy is well documented. The proof is clear. Odysseus, who was riding the thing, still holds the record for sitting tallest in the saddle. And the dumping of a big load of manure on King Priam's palace may not be sung about all that often, but roses still grow spectacularly upon the buried ruins of Troy.

The records tell of many more monsters. Siegfried fought the dragon and bathed in its blood. This act was still celebrated well into the twentieth century in the form of song and dance, even entering modern media through the art of the talking picture. Most people would not have seen any of the Siegfried Follies live, of course, but glitzy dance spectaculars featuring rows of chorus girls pervade our collective consciousness even today, along with images of sparkly blondes in top hats and stockings, kicking high just as the buff guy in golden loin cloth, wielding a big shiny sword, runs in covered in bright red party blood. Many a scholar debates the holy origin of George and the Dragon, arguing that it is the overlay of a Christian deity onto the history of the pagan Siegfried. Indeed some see little difference between the Feast of St George and the Follies—except for the fact that the girls wear fewer sequins and the guys more blood. And of course the dragon doesn't get much look in at all.

The truth is, religion is responsible for many a monster's disappearance from our belief systems. Consider, for instance, Noah's Ark. Rationality has gone a long way in deconstructing this myth; building a boat to take two of every animal is quite an impossible feat. Yet many a fundamentalist Christian believes it regardless. So what ancient reality lies behind the story? Sure, there was a huge flooding of the Dead Sea at that time, probably when an earthquake temporarily joined the sea with the great oceans. And, yes, many animals were saved. But salvation did not come by way of some man-made boat—such conjecture is sheer folly (though nothing like Siegfried's, I assure you). The truth is much more astounding—that the animals were saved by hitching a ride on the back of the crocodile god *ARC!*—named after the loud screeching he made that would reverberate along the high desert walls. *ARC! Friend of Animals!* The giant creature did tend to eat stupid humans who strayed near the water, however, which is how the place came to be known as the Dead Sea. Many a Crypto-Paleo-Archaeologist believes *ARC!* is still out there somewhere, lying dormant in the mountains. To date, however, any reported sightings have been followed up to no effect or have revealed themselves to be based on mounds of clay.

Elsewhere clay is what researchers hope to find. Somewhere in the permafrost under the Siberian tundra ended the journey of the last golem to escape from the Clay Wars of 16th Century Poland. As with the Woolly Mammoth, there are dreams of finding the golem and restoring it to life. Madonna has funded such an operation and rabbi mystics wait on standby. Current science says it's impossible yet thankfully there are those who still have faith.

Similarly, there are those who still have faith that the Sphinx's nose, lost during the battle with the Turkish army in the 18th Century (not shot off by Napoleon's gunnery battalion as some would believe—we must keep to the facts) will one day be found. Or those looking for the lost inkwell used in signing the peace treaty that brought the North and South of the United States together; it is a little known, and even less believed, fact that this historic bottle contained the dried ink of a Hundred Tentacled Super-Squid that swam up the Mississippi during the final days of the American Civil War. In 1862, Grabomarri, as it was named, grabbed and sank both the ironclads *CSS Virginia* and *USS Monitor* while they were in mid-battle. Upon learning of this Robert E. Lee and Ulysses S. Grant ordered their guns away from their enemies and toward the river. The joining of the opposing armies and the long battle to drive the beast back to the ocean brought about a lasting truce. It is believed in esoteric circles that besides the many tentacles that caused endless casualties Grabomarri also squirted huge columns of ink to knock over soldier and cart. In one wheel groove was found a puddle of ink; this was scooped into a bottle and presented to the now unified generals. Researchers hope to find this bottle one day—but will we ever again see Grabomarri, Giant Monster of the Mississippi? Perhaps, one day, we'll meet it down in a rift of the deep, dark ocean.

Of course, there are those so-called experts who want us to believe we'll never meet monsters again, anywhere, if indeed we ever did. It is stunning to conceive of people who refuse to accept the reality of giant monsters, particularly in the light of the archaeological evidence. Yet there are many who maintain that stories of stupendous beasts roaming this earth are merely stories—folklore, myth, an excess of the imagination.

Some confusion in the fossil record allows the odd religious hick to claim that it was man and dinosaur, not man and giant monster, that lived contemporaneously. Any true scientist knows this is nonsense, but time and time again such religious extremists point to controversial footprints—a fossil record of human feet and dinosaur feet together in an ancient dried riverbed. They say these footprints show man being chased by a dinosaur or man chasing a dinosaur. But let me assure you of this: the footprints are not true rock and not true fossil, but very hard clay that dried back in 1928 and are a record of Bumba the Jungle Boy and his giant lizard companion Brutar running together during one of their many adventures, protecting villagers from the continually attacking Wasp Men. Bumba and Brutar disappeared soon after that time, returning to their jungle home and spurning man and his modern technologies.

Brutar may well have been the last giant monster to

encounter man's mechanical world, except for one who held out amongst our encroaching civilisation. Indeed, this monster of which I speak embraced it for awhile. But after only a short time as a big Broadway star and having made only one film, King Kong retired to Hawaii and to his private Skull Island. The King never made another appearance to any human soul and his island was found empty by an expedition of anthropologists and movie buffs in 1965. How Kong lived his last days we can only speculate, but it is important to recall his final statement before he entered into his self-imposed retirement:

> "To be alone is only sad if you had good company. I am happy to retire to a solitary existence. Other than to entertain or to terrify, we monsters have no place with humans."

So why did all the monsters leave us? King Kong's last statement to the world may well provide an answer. Monsters have no place with humans. As humanity expanded in numbers so did the technologies of civilisation, most particularly the technologies of war.

But it wasn't the ability to fend off these monsters that spelled their demise. Monsters are natural forces, yes, but they came into existence with the express purpose of interacting with mankind. They are Gaia manifestations intended to remind humanity that it is but a small part of this complex Earth. Giant monsters were created to force man to know his place. The monster was meant to terrify, to awe, to be run away from before stopping at a safe distance and looking back in amazement at the spectacle of tooth, claw and destruction. By its mere presence the giant monster showed us where we fit in this plane of existence. We would measure the value of our own humanity in the presence of the giant monster. The monster was to be feared and respected. To be worshipped. One who sees *Daikaiju* and lives is one to be blessed.

Now there are no more blessings to be had. For man made the monster redundant. Monsters have been usurped by man's own terror, by man's own mad destruction. Technology took away the monster. The firebombing of Dresden once would have been the result of summoning a Hell Demon. By replacing the monster with a squadron of bombers and incendiary bombs, man had no further need for such a creature and the priests, the believers, who controlled them. No new generation of summoners replaced them and as summoning was entirely an oral tradition, no colossal Hell Beast will ever be summoned again. But then no one needs to when a warhead of destructive force beyond imagining can be more precise and controllable.

Mind you, not all monsters have been replaced by weapons of mass destruction. There are less technological replacements. These days a Japanese village doesn't need a giant statue to come to life at the hour of need. A call to a lawyer can be just as effective and no one need lose their roof.

So the monsters have gone. What few monsters remained toward the end, like King Kong, departed of their own volition. The Loch Ness Monster left the lake and Quetzalcoatl departed into an alternate world where I hope many a monster now frolics.

What about the remaining dregs of humankind? What about those of us left to fend for ourselves, with no monsters to keep us warm? For we need the monsters. We need them to protect us. Protect us from ourselves. Protect us from our own pride, our own arrogance, our belief that we determine our own destiny and the destiny of the whole planet. As a result of such self-delusion we are destroying the world and will destroy ourselves along with it. We have lost our humility and will make ourselves extinct because of it.

We need to know we can't control everything. We need to know that we are insignificant compared to the natural laws of the universe. Indeed, only the universe can break those laws. Only nature can defy reason and raise up insanely huge colossal beasts that bellow and screech and walk through man-made constructions and blast holes through mountains with radioactive breath. Sure we can nuke something but we can't get it to do a victory dance afterwards or decide to trash a city but first make sure all the children are safe.

We need our spirit back, our spirit of being one with the universe. We need to feel we are a part of everything rather than separate from it—to feel our nature, our Gaia, souls again. The giant monster is the bridge. The *Daikaiju* is the way and the truth and the radioactive light to our salvation. We must have faith in the monster again. We must believe in the monster again. We must dream of the monster again. And dream big. Dream the biggest monster we can. We must believe once more and with hope and with time maybe whatever is down in the deepest darkest trench at the bottom of the deepest darkest ocean will begin to rise to the surface and move toward shore.

And as our hearts fill up with true humanity again, the *Daikaiju* will proceed to terrorise shipping and pull down a bridge or two.

And we shall exult!

SEE ME THROUGH YOUR EYES

DAVID BOFINGER

Whether you're large or small, it's hard to be unseen. It's much easier to be recognised as something you aren't— something for which your watcher is looking, because they've seen it before. I am half-buried in sand, and so my skin becomes the colour of sand. The water is not still, and so my skin ripples gently like sand grains shifting in the current. The fish is still too far away.

I know a lot about how other creatures see. The eyes of a fish, for instance, are very different from mine. The peripheral vision of a fish is very good at picking up motion, and triggering an instinctive response to flee. But the peripheral vision is too stupid to see things that aren't there, so when the fish looks away from me I blend in, not trying to trick it.

The fish's mind is not like mine either, and not nearly as good. The fish's mind looks out through the middle of its eye. It's just dumb enough to fool, and just smart enough to be fooled.

I wait until the fish's eye looks toward me before I move. I send faint pulses of darkness down my mantle and all eight tentacles. I call this pattern *look at me*. The fish looks at me, but all it sees is the pattern.

I change the pattern to *come to me*. The patterns of light and dark on my skin talk to places in the fish's small, simple brain and change the way it sees the world. For the fish, only directions that lead to me exist. It is free to swim in any direction it chooses, as long as it comes toward me. The closer it comes, the more of its field of view my tentacles fill and the more control I have over what it sees and what it thinks.

When it is within a quarter of the length of my body I wrap it in my tentacles. Even now its mind does not realise there is danger, but it struggles regardless: a lot of the things a fish does don't involve its mind. I draw it in to my beak and inject venom, and it quickly weakens. Holding the fish so it has no choice but to watch me, I flash another pattern through its eyes into its brain: *die now, die now, die now.* Soon it is dead and limp.

I could eat the fish here, but it will be safer to go back to my home, a cave in the rocks. I swim close to the rocky bottom so I have cover from passing dolphins and sharks. A dolphin's mind is much better than a fish's mind. Maybe as good as mine, though very different from either. That's one thing that makes a dolphin dangerous; it's too smart to be easy to trick. A shark's mind is like the mind of a fish but simplified. That's one thing that makes a shark dangerous: it's too stupid to trick.

But a shark or a dolphin is a bit larger than I am, so as long as I stay close to small gaps in the rocks I'm reasonably safe. I remember sharks and dolphins used to be much larger than I was, not so long ago. That's true of a lot of things; I had to move out of my old home, for instance, because it was too small, although at one time it had been quite comfortable and I'm good at getting into small places. Since I moved to my new home, though, it seems to be happening faster.

It comes to me that rather than everything else getting smaller it might be that I am getting bigger. I wonder why I've never thought that before. Perhaps my mind is getting better, as I grow bigger, and I've only now become smart enough to have that thought. If I become larger and smarter, perhaps some day I won't need to fear sharks and dolphins at all.

My new home is an interesting place. It is one of several caves, each a perfectly circular and very long tube. I went looking once for the end of mine but gave up. The walls are made of a different kind of stone from most of the rocks around here; it is like coral mixed with sand. A current flows out of each cave, and the water tastes strange. That used to bother me a little, but I've got used to it. I suppose my body has adapted. At night you can see that the water coming out of some of the caves glows a faint blue.

I eat the fish and go to sleep to digest it. When I wake my home is even smaller and I feel ravenous. It's night and low tide, which means there will be lots of pools in the rocks just above the ocean's edge. I leave the ocean and walk across the rocks on my tentacles. I'm getting better at this; I used to just sit on the rock and drag myself, but now my tentacles are much stronger and I can support my body clear of the rock, which is much faster. Also I can breathe air for much longer than I once could.

I almost don't see the rock pools. They're tiny, and the creatures that live in them are far too small to be worth catching. In the distance I see rocky pillars thrusting up into the air like coral, covered in glowing spots. It's interesting, and I'd like to look at it, but it's too far away to go tonight.

But just above the rocks is a flat expanse of land with green vegetation on it, and there are four-legged animals grazing. I stop before I frighten them and try *look at me*. It seems to work, so I pick out one I think I can drag home and use *come to me* on that one. I don't even have to drag it down to the water; I just let it follow my *come to me* out to sea until it's tired and starts to sink. I wrap it in my tentacles and inject venom—it hardly struggles at all, less than a fish would.

When I wake I'm hungry again. I go back to the same place and call the rest of the four-legs out into the water, and eat them all. When I wake from *that* I'm almost too big to fit in my home. If I had hard bones inside me, like fish, I would be stuck, but fortunately all my body is soft and I can squeeze my way out.

The land seems an easier place to get food than the ocean. So I decide to swim along the coast until I get to the land coral I saw in the distance. I'll find a home there, and there must be animals living amongst the coral so I won't have to travel far to get food. On my way I see a couple of sharks and a dolphin, so I make *come to me* patterns and eat them all. But even together they're too small to be a filling meal.

The land coral colony turns out to be built around an inlet, so I swim in and raise my body above the water to see what it looks like. By daylight the land coral looks a lot like the rock from which the long caves were made, and it's full of little cavities. I reach inside one of the cavities and pull out a small creature. It walks on two legs and waves the other two in the air. I wonder if it's making a sound—my hearing hasn't really adapted to air yet. Perhaps these creatures made the land coral, by secreting it or something—but they could just as easily be parasites, or harmlessly sheltering in it. I'll have to understand these things if I'm to live here, but there'll be time for that after I find a home. So far none of the cavities has been large enough.

The two-legs is too small to be worth eating so I drop it and walk on, stepping between the coral pillars or climbing on them as seems most convenient. There's a lot of dust—tiny pieces of land coral suspended in the air like sediment in turbid water. I'm wondering why when all at once I know because I see the dust being made. A pillar ahead of me tumbles against the one next to it, and both shatter into pieces. Through the gap where the pillars had been I can see water—it's another arm of the inlet I've been following. And in the water is a creature.

It's bigger than I am, which makes it vast compared with any other animal I've seen today. It's long and slender—streamlined—and its skin looks rough. It opens its mouth to take a bite out of another land coral pillar and there are rows and rows of brutal triangular teeth.

I've got a good mind, but right now I'm only thinking with the most simple part of it. And it's screaming *shark.*

Of course the creature's not exactly like a shark. It's much bigger, and it has learnt to walk on land by changing its pectoral fins into legs. But I know what it once was, and as it looks at me I think it knows what I once was. Probably it chased me, or would have liked to, when we swam together in the blue glow of strange-tasting water. It's changed as much as I have, but a piece of each of us is still what we once were.

The shark takes another bite from the land coral. Small

two-legged creatures drop from it to the ground below—without water to support them they drop very quickly and don't move afterwards.

If this goes on the shark will destroy all the land coral and I'll have nowhere to live. I decide to try to scare it off. Spreading my tentacles to make myself look big I slip into the water. The fins look slow and clumsy; I'm confident I can dodge it if it comes for me.

Mistake.

It doesn't even use the fins. The big tail propels it forward faster than I expect and its mouth closes on a tentacle. If it were smart it would take me into a death roll, spinning me over and over the way a moray eel would. But it isn't smart enough to do that. Instead there's an instant of agony and it shears off two-thirds of the tentacle.

The mouth is open again, for a second bite. I squirt out a jet of ink and dodge to one side. This trick works well against predators that track by sight, but I don't know if the shark really does. Mixed with the black cloud of ink there's a blue cloud of my blood, and the shark can probably follow me by that. My hearts are racing and I try to calm them down, to give the amputated tentacle a chance to stop bleeding.

The shark breaks through the cloud of ink not far away and spots me. It turns fast and I realise that if I stay in the water I'm going to be shark food—it's a better swimmer than me as well as bigger, and it has those mineralised teeth that can bite so much more effectively than my beak. I scurry up a hillside beside the water. It's covered in low growths of land coral and I run around them. The shark runs after me on its belly, ploughing through some coral and sliding over the others.

Ahead the pillars are taller and the shark begins to lose interest. I can see it doesn't like going very far from the water, or in amongst land coral too high to slide over. I stop at the edge of the taller area, and spread my seven surviving tentacles wide. *Look at me. Look at me. Come to me. Come to me.*

The shark comes closer and I step back, deeper into the coral. It's an easy pattern to make, because the shark half-wants to chase me anyway, but I have to improvise for the missing tentacle. I notice two-legged creatures falling from the nearby pillars, as the *come to me* makes them step out of the coral. But I can't worry about that at the moment—one mistake in the pattern and the shark might be on me.

There are long gaps between the pillars, straight or mostly so. They are filled with two-legs: either live and scurrying or dead and broken. And there are larger crawling creatures: small ones of many colours, larger ones coloured dull green-brown with a long arm or eye stalk. A few have been broken open and I see dead two-legs inside. The land seems almost as complicated a place as the water: how long will it take me to understand it?

We're deep into the tall coral now and the shark is feeling unhappy. It can move all right as long as it follows the gaps, but it can't turn around without demolishing all the pillars and that takes time. I sense the shark is about to give up, despite the *come to me*. I dodge to one side, using a small gap it can't fit through and come at it from the side where it cannot bite. I hang on and try to inject venom, but the skin is tough and hurts my suckers.

It turns on the spot, trying to get at me, but it can't turn fast enough to throw me off. Pillars tumble around us; dust is everywhere, coating my mantle grey and making it hard to see, and a great chunk of falling coral misses me by half the length of my body. I hang on, looking for a weak point.

The shark makes for the water, travelling in a straight line downhill. Its labours have tired it, and it gulps air, expelling through its gills. I wait for the gills to open and thrust my beak inside, injecting venom into the first soft tissue I find. Now the shark rolls over, trying to crush me, but I am soft and cannot easily be damaged in that way. I pump all the venom I have into its gills, hoping that the good blood circulation there will take it quickly to the creature's heart. The shark continues down the hill toward the water, moving more slowly. I try to slow it up, dragging my own body along the ground.

At the water's edge it becomes so weak that it cannot continue on against my resistance. I hold my tentacles in front of its eyes and triumphantly tell it, *die now, die now, die now*. It's a long time before it does.

I slowly look up. My body aches from bruises and cuts, and the missing tentacle hurts even where it isn't any more. I've left streaks of blue blood on pillars all through the colony. I need to find a home, in which to lie and recover, and regrow my tentacle.

All the two-legs I can see are lying on the ground broken. I suppose that's because of the *die now* pattern. But a stream of the larger brown-green creatures is crawling down the hill toward me. The arm of every one is pointing at me.

No matter how good your mind is, it's hard to see something as it really is. It's much easier to see it as another of something you've seen before. I wonder what they see, when they see me. I suppose I'll find out, sooner or later. They're quite close now.

SURVIVOR:
MONSTER ISLAND 2025

MICHAEL BOATMAN

Salvatore, the blind bus driver from Brooklyn, screamed while Queen Jombodrah ate his legs. Queen Jombodrah, the biggest mutant tarantula on Earth, swallowed. Then she fired a burst of her stun-webs at the bleeding green mountain behind her; Borgo the Brobdingnagian disappeared beneath ten tons of incandescent energy webbing.

Queen Jombodrah uttered her infamous "spider-shriek", snatched up the now unconscious Sal and waddled into the shadowy forests of Monster Island. Borgo's mangled, multi-tentacled corpse would last, preserved, until the Queen returned for dinner. Sal was lunch.

A lone pteronodon glided across the clearing.

A moment later, four tiny human figures climbed out of a hole in the trunk of the Prometheus tree that stood at the edge of the Northern Clearing. Mercedes, the blonde real-estate agent and former *Miss Boca Raton*, spoke first.

"This ... is ... *Bullcrap!*"

"Let's keep calm, guys." This from Geoffrey, the black Wall Street broker from Manhattan. "If we lose focus—"

"Lose focus!" Mercedes snarled. "Lose ... freakin' ... *focus?*"

Ken Obotu studied the other survivors.

Mercedes ran seven miles every day, and followed a daily calisthenics routine that would have ruptured Sylvester Stallone. Their first hour on the Island, before the eyes of the other six original contestants and millions of couch potatoes watching at home, Mercedes had single-handedly torn the suckers off a giant leech that had battened onto their landing craft.

And later, while the other contestants were resting before dinner, Mercedes had slipped one of the poisonous suckers into the communal dinner pot, sending Eva, the personal trainer from Holland, off-island for emergency medical treatment, and making everyone else too nauseous to compete in the 'Challenge Round'.

Everyone except Ken Obotu. He'd simply commanded his nervous system to convert the venom into a cocktail of harmless proteins. Mercedes had won millions of fans, ensuring her survival until the next episode.

"Sal just got eaten by a giant motherhumping *spider*, people," Mercedes raged. "I think we should *focus* on *that!*"

"Typical female response," Geoffrey drawled. "Careful, Marissa. Whole world's watching."

The broker pointed languidly to the closest 'game-cam'. a glittering silver ball of 21st century nano-optics that flitted above their heads. The game-cam zipped down from its standard operating height to capture the conflict.

"Wouldn't want the folks back at Hog Piss High to see a crack in the Amazon armor," Geoffrey crooned.

Mercedes shook her sweaty-blond ponytail.

"Screw ... you," she said in her thick Florida twang. "And for the last time: It's Hoggsberg High School. *And my name is Mercedes, idiot.*"

"Whatever," Geoffrey sang.

Like Ken's host, Geoffrey was of mixed African descent, lighter in skin color, with a build the news-vids had described as "pugnacious". Ken had considered forming an alliance with Geoffrey, who possessed the sheer ruthlessness required to win the ten-million dollar prize.

But Geoffrey's ego was as monstrous as the Island's mysterious inhabitants.

"You tricked Sal," Ken said.

"What?" Geoffrey replied.

"You led him into one of Queen Jombodrah's web traps. I saw you do it while the others ran for cover."

Geoffrey smirked and said, "Prove it, loser."

Shouldering his backpack, he sauntered over to the river to wash his hands. Ken followed him.

"You maintain an air of confidence," he said. "But a challenge to your ego, say, by a vastly more dominant personality, would shatter the illusion like so much coloured glass."

"Get away from me, freak!" Geoffrey hissed.

Ken nodded and moved away. He'd made the right decision. On Monster Island, foolhardiness was tantamount to hanging a dinner bell around your neck and painting "Come and get it!" across your backside.

"What do *you* think, Ken?"

Cindy Meinelschmidt, the narcoleptic redhead from Winona Minnesota, trotted up to him. Small but fit, Cindy's freckled skin burned easily in the tropical sun. She was forced to cover herself in gallons of sunblock to keep from roasting to death. As a result, she always glistened, her skin a perpetual lobster-belly red.

"I think *you* should lead us up the trail," Ken said.

He listened to the stream of pheromones that wafted over him, propelled by Cindy's joy at his confirmation of her leadership skills. He also detected a vaguely acidic *undertrail* accompanying her normal emissions.

They'd enjoyed sexual congress last night, heedless of the game-cams and the roars of giants crashing through the dark. At the height of that experience, Ken had been barely able to control the tiny organic information packets that burst from his body to invade Cindy's reproductive pathways. It had taken all his focus to guide the packets, mentally selecting the most suitable ones while dead-ending the rest.

His efforts had not been wasted. Three months from now, Cindy would give birth to three fine offspring, a male and two females. They would look no different from the locals. In time, they would rule galaxies.

Ken released a burst of psycho-kinetically engineered pheromones to incite feelings of well-being in Cindy while bolstering her courage for the next challenge. Then, because he knew the folks back home were watching, he spread a plume of slightly different pheromones over the clearing.

A second later, Mercedes kicked Geoffrey in the balls, and decked him with a hard uppercut to the chin.

While the game-cams bounced, Cindy's smile widened. She laid a hand on Ken's shoulder.

"I've never known anyone like you," she said.

Ken Obotu arched one eyebrow, a gesture he'd learned from Geoffrey the night before.

"I know."

☆

The Island had been discovered ten years earlier. It lay two-hundred nautical miles off the west coast of Japan, at the farthest edge of a cluster of little-visited islands known locally as 'The Dumps'. Its official name was lost in the tsunami of publicity that followed in the wake of its discovery: an unexplored atoll the size of Manhattan, inhabited by carnivorous creatures the size of skyscrapers.

The first of the "Titanoids" to greet the news cameras was Vyperion, the gigantic, bat-winged rattlesnake.

As the heli-vids buzzed around its wedge-shaped thirty-metre-wide head, trying to capture footage for the global info-net, Vyperion spat burning lances of hydrochloric venom at them, incinerating the heli-vids along with their human crews. Fifty-two brave broadcasters lost their lives that day.

Vyperion had tracked the twelve survivors to a large cave on the Northern half of the island, and would have flensed them from the face of the jungle had the atoll's most terrifying resident not appeared at that moment.

"Thanodon Rex's lair is just over that rise," Ken said. "The producers stashed the Dragon's Horde there."

"We *know* that," Mercedes drawled. "How'd this jerkweed escape the vote-off?"

"Ken's a natural leader," Cindy snapped. "Unlike two other people I could name, he'd never betray a team mate."

Ken Obotu shrugged. As the others argued, the bundle of optic cells he'd left in near-Earth orbit high above the Island issued a high priority alert.

'We'd better hide," he said. "Something's coming."

"I don't hear anything," Geoffrey said.

A second later, the trees and shrubs around them burst into flames, and a second after *that*, Pyros the Fire Maggot slithered into the clearing.

"Quick!" Geoffrey shouted. "Into the lake!"

The survivors scuttled toward the glimmering northern shore of Lake Urquhart. Mercedes hit the water first, dove in and struck out toward the center of the lake.

Along with her stress-related bouts with involuntary unconsciousness, Cindy Meinelschmidt had also acknowledged a powerful fear of water in her videotaped pre-interviews. But now, fortified by Ken's subtle enhancements, she dove in after Mercedes.

Geoffrey the broker, mere steps from salvation, screamed, and exploded in an oily gust of flame.

Ken Obotu recalled what he'd learned about the Maggot.

Pyros's territory lay over the Spinning Turtles (a mountain range that separated the northern and southern halves of Monster Island like the ridge down the back of a sleeping stegosaurus), but Pyros foraged for food on the northern side, which was far more lush with vegetation.

Pyros was the only herbivorous Titanoid known to science. The only reason it ever came this close to the lair of its mortal enemy was to dowse its legendary thirst at the largest freshwater source on the northern side.

Pyros was headed for the centre of Lake Urquhart.

Ken Obotu scanned the rocky soil at his feet until he found what he sought. As one of the game-cams zipped toward him, he bent and selected a thin flat rock about the length of his palm.

His primary mind shifted its perceptive mode and the world became a swirling kaleidoscope of energy matrices, bound together by ethereal lines of force. Facing the camera, he reached out with one of the many bio-electric enhancements he'd installed prior to his arrival and tickled one of those lines.

The game-cam zipped away to film a giant dung beetle pushing its boulder-sized burden up a grassy slope on the southern side. It would only be a matter of moments before the game-cam's onboard computers corrected the mistake and sent it back.

But a moment was all Ken needed.

"Ken!" Cindy cried, unaware that death by Maggot was mere seconds away; Pyros, though a staunch vegetarian, was notoriously territorial in regard to its water supply. He'd been known to boil entire rivers down to the bedrock to destroy a single trespasser.

Ken Obotu studied the flat rock with that special dimension of perception. He sent a pulse of energy along the atomic pathways that held the rock together, agitating molecules, loosening their bonds. Then he surrounded the rock with a thin shield of force. In three seconds, the flat rock was hot enough to burn through concrete.

On the far shore, Pyros reared up in a searing plume of wrath preparing to incinerate Cindy and Mercedes. Ken Obotu threw the rock. It flew three-hundred yards, punched through the sound barrier, skipped seventeen times over the surface of the lake and exploded, sending up clouds of steam.

Fire Maggots navigated using the glowing ring of sky-blue eyes at their anterior ends. The steam would confuse Pyros, but, more importantly, it would conceal Ken's movements from the game-cams.

As his companions faded from view, Ken turned and raced along the embankment toward the Maggot. Pyros ignited a square mile of lakefront real estate in its confusion; Ken dodged explosions, somersaulted over whirling tornadoes of fire, leapt high into the air, and landed on Pyros's head.

A dozen blue eyes the size of manhole covers swiveled to glare up at him. The air around him grew uncomfortably warm.

Ken opened his mouth and sang.

He'd learned the call of the Fire Maggots in preparation for this very moment. Using the formal tone/speech intended to address one of tremendous weight (a sign of high social standing among Maggots), Ken respectfully stimulated certain pleasure centres in the Maggot's brain, while implanting the suggestion that Pyros visit the cave of Infernis, the heaviest female Fire Maggot on Monster Island.

Convinced, Pyros shuddered, turned, and slithered back the way it had come. Ken pitied his companions; by tomorrow, this half of the Island would be infested with twenty-foot-long, radioactive larvae.

But he would be out beyond the Pleiades by then.

☆

They were a mile from Thanodon Rex's lair when an earsplitting hiss announced that someone was about to die.

"Sweet Jesus," Mercedes moaned. "That freakin' snake."

Vyperion.

Ken Obotu was communing with his optic cells, so intent upon perusing the latest audience surveys that he ignored his peril: ninety tonnes of mutated reptilian fury hurtling straight toward them.

"Over there!" Mercedes shrieked, pointing toward the Western sky.

"Where? Where?" Cindy tried to look in all four directions at once. Mercedes planted a foot in the small of Cindy's back and shoved. Cindy stumbled out of the forest and sprawled face-first into the clearing.

The Lord of Serpents struck the ground with the force of an earthquake.

While Cindy screamed and fainted, Mercedes bolted toward a cave several yards to the east. She dove toward the mouth of the cave, her face contorted by the naked lust for survival that had made her the "Number 1 Real Estate Superstar in Broward County".

Drawn by her erratic movements, Vyperion flew *over* the unconscious Cindy and impaled Mercedes on its fifteen-foot-long fangs, skewering the blonde Floridian like a Southern shish-ke-bob. The Lord of the Naga regurgitated a cloud of toxic waste that flash-fried the former beauty queen alive, and swallowed her whole.

Cindy climbed woozily to her feet, her bare shoulders glimmering with X-tra-strength *Sun 'n Fun.* Vyperion half-flew, half-slithered toward her, encircled her in thirty-foot-high coils, its rattle hammering the air like rapid–fire dynamite charges. Cindy clapped her hands to her ears.

"It's just a stupid reality show!" she screamed. "It's not even in the top 10!"

Ken Obotu felt the Alpha-pod throbbing where it hung from his belt clip. No telepathic trick would deter Vyperion. If he died here, in this body, he would stay dead, at least until someone from the old neighborhood could come and back-engineer him, perhaps from whatever remained of him in Vyperion's droppings.

Ken grasped the Alpha pod and raised it above his head.

"Kyaputen ...!"

But a sound like the death-cry of planets froze the words on his lips. The shattering roar was repeated. Ken's eardrums ruptured with a wet *pop!* And the world went silent.

Ken turned to face his prey. Even he was forced to admit: Thanodon Rex was nightmare given flesh.

The Father of All Monsters stood nearly six hundred feet tall. His skin, which had withstood a direct hit from an ICBM, was a deep greenish gray. Thanodon was part dragon, part Tyrannosaur and somehow, horribly, part human.

Cindy fainted again. Ken caught her and lay her down behind the trunk of a nearby Prometheus bush.

Pity, he thought. Cindy would miss whatever happened next.

Vyperion launched itself at Thanodon, its fangs raining venom upon the earth. Thanodon smashed the Naga out of the sky and slammed it to the ground. From where he stood, Ken felt the earth tremble.

Vyperion drove its fangs into Thanodon's right forearm and began to chew. With a heave of his mountain-wide shoulders, Thanodon Rex slammed Vyperion's head against the Northern peak of the Spinning Turtles until it let go.

A yellow flash ignited in Thanodon's eyes as he prepared to unleash his Omni-blast, the one power no living creature could resist. But the Serpent King whipped itself backward and spat death into the Death God's burning eyes.

Half-blinded, Thanodon dropped Vyperion.

The Lord of the Naga wrapped its tail around Thanodon's legs and snatched his feet out from under him. Thanodon toppled backward and crashed into the forest, crushing acres.

Vyperion reared high above the Island, jaws agape, and unleashed a molten gout of hydrochloric venom. The burning fluid splashed Thanodon's face, scorched flesh and exposed bone.

Thanodon Rex howled.

Ken Obotu moved. He'd come more than ten trillion miles and he wasn't about to let the trip go to waste. He raised the Alpha-pod above his head and shouted his mantra:

"Fushigi Kyaputen!"

A tremendous thunderclap shook the island as a flash of lightning blasted the spot where Ken stood. When the smoke cleared, he was gone. The shining silver figure that stood in his place bore little resemblance to the man who'd been selected as a finalist for the most popular reality gameshow on Earth—the dead man whose body Ken Obotu had 'rebooted' three months ago.

Alpha Man performed a lightning *kata* to activate the weapons chakras which formed the basis of his offensive capabilities. Cosmic power filled his limbs, expanded them until he was as large as the struggling giants before him. In a flash, the Alpha Pod became the deadliest weapon in the known multiverse: The Red Requiem Blade.

Alpha Man plunged the Blade through Vyperion's rattle, pinning it. Forged in the heart of a newborn star, the Requiem was sharp enough to carve a path to the planet's core. Ken Obotu summoned a fraction of its power to stun the Serpent into submission.

Vyperion spat a torrent of venom into Alpha Man's face.

Ken released the burning hilt of the Red Requiem and staggered backward, the living metal of his helmet screaming in agony, while Vyperion grasped the Requiem in its fangs and tore it from his body.

Ken tried to summon the Red Requiem to his side, but his armor's agony created too much psychic static. Its screams disrupted his connection to the Blade.

Vyperion struck. Alpha Man raised his right arm to block the Titanoid's attack, but Vyperion's jaws slammed shut and severed his arm at the shoulder.

A black burst of power blew the opponents apart. The servitor-class nano-organisms that inhabited the pocket dimension contained within Alpha Man's armor scrambled to staunch the energy bleed before it could ravage the planet. The servitors sealed the breach with a screech of molecular fire.

Alpha Man climbed to one knee, his defensive shields flickering. Vyperion's eyes were blackened pits; its tongue lashed out, tasting, searching the air for its foe.

Alpha Man raised his left fist. And the skies over Monster Island turned black. A snarl of lightning gouged a crackling circle of elemental fire around Vyperion.

Ken Obotu was loathe to destroy such a magnificent specimen. Monsters like Vyperion were rare in the universe. *Can't be helped,* he thought, as the smell of barbecued reptile filled the air.

The force of Vyperion's takeoff blasted the surrounding forest into matchsticks. The King of the Naga rocketed through the air and stabbed its fangs into Alpha Man's chest.

Behind his silver faceplate, Ken's vision failed as neurotoxins flooded his nervous system. The nano-servitors in his blood refocused their energies against this new assault. His primary brain closed off access from his circulatory system, shutting the poison out. His limbs grew leaden as his reserve brain, the techno-organic cluster of cells in his right chest cavity, redirected energy reserves toward neutralising the river of venom.

The lightning storm broke apart. Without Ken's mental influence it swept out to sea and disintegrated. The crimson light of the Red Requiem flickered and went out.

Is this death? Ken thought.

He wasn't certain. No one he knew had ever died permanently. Desperate, he peered into Vyperion's mind and attempted to shut it down.

eat. blood. crush. burn.

In response, Vyperion's fangs ground deeper into his throat, scouring his veins with molten lava.

Then, abruptly, the pain stopped.

Ken's vision grew sharper as both brains came back online. His blood cooled as the hydrochloric venom was converted and absorbed. His right shoulder began to throb; if he survived he would have a new arm by nightfall.

Alpha Man leapt to his feet.

A hundred yards away, Vyperion grappled with the Dragon God of Death. Thanodon Rex was dragging the Serpent into the churning waters of the Pacific Ocean.

Thanodon extended both arms, six-fingered hands splayed. Retractable claws, sixty-feet long and razor sharp, burst from his flesh. The Dragon became a whirling blur. Chunks of snake meat the size of small houses rained down on Monster Island. Vyperion roared. A luminous eruption of hydrochloric venom lit the night like the wrath of Vulcan.

Ken Obotu summoned the Red Requiem Blade. It rose, singing, and flew to its master's hand. Half gutted, the Serpent reared, even as Alpha Man swung the Requiem in a shining scarlet arc. The Blade bit into Vyperion's neck and passed through. A moment later, Vyperion's head fell into the boiling sea.

Its body remained upright, the lethal, fifty-metre tail thrashing the waters. A moment later, twenty malodorous stalks burst from the bloody stump of Vyperion's neck. Each waving stalk sprouted a bulb-like nodule roughly the size and shape of an English double-decker bus. Each bulb grew murderous fangs, opened two luminous emerald eyes ... and roared.

Bloody Hell, Ken Obotu thought. *Twenty heads.*

Regenerated, Vyperion lunged.

And Thanodon Rex struck.

His eyes took fire from the storm, projected twin streamers of heat and force, flash-fried Vyperion with the full fury of the Omni-blast, a soundless detonation that lifted Alpha Man off his feet and slapped him onto his back in the churning surf.

When his senses returned, Vyperion was gone, a four-hundred-foot line of ash the only evidence to suggest that the Serpent had ever existed.

Ken Obotu stared up at the King of all Monsters.

Thanodon stood, wounded but defiant, bright echoes of a terrible power flickering in the amber depths of its remaining eye: power that might destroy even Alpha Man.

Ken Obotu talked fast.

☆

Thanodon Rex left the Earth an hour later.

It would take the transport nimbus five hours to reach the artificial wormhole that seethed on the far side of Earth's sun. Once inside the wormhole, Thanodon's voyage across the universe would be much quicker.

The air shimmered as Ken Obotu sloughed off the Alpha Man persona. As he shrank down to his borrowed six-foot frame, he realised that he would miss being human. He'd developed a fondness for eating and drinking, even sex.

But there were billions of planets out there—talent pools dotting the night sky. Few worlds, however, would host the kind of talent he'd discovered on Earth, talent that would make him the most successful Producer of Entertainments his race had ever spawned.

He'd gotten the Dragon to sign off: a three-millennia-deal that included broadcast rights to both local and neighbouring universes, as well as any ancillary income from merchandising, publishing rights to Thanodon's autobiography (both actual and telepathic), and a host of other perks. In exchange, Thanodon Rex desired only a warm cave to regenerate in and a good brawl once a month or so. Ken Obotu could scarcely believe his luck.

Thanodon Rex was a supernova, a hideously powerful star who also happened to possess nobility, even compassion—the perfect centerpiece for Ken Obotu's latest multi-reality-based entertainment: *Monster Wars ... Live!*

☆

Cindy Meinelschmidt lay dreaming behind her burning Prometheus tree, her head filled with images of custard-filled bear claws and hot cocoa. Looking at her, Ken Obotu experienced a twinge of regret; he would never see the mother of his future children again.

We will care for her, they giggled from the depths of Cindy's womb. Ken nodded. He was a Producer, and there was a big multiverse out there awaiting his next Production.

All seven game-cams were circling now, fighting for the best close-up. Ken waved at the cameras, imagining the uproar sweeping the planet. Earth had officially made the Big Show. From now on, humanity would never be "alone".

After a fond last look, Ken Obotu folded the contract bearing Thanodon's mark and shoved it into a pocket universe for safekeeping.

Then he smiled, and sprang into the sky.

DEAD FOLK HERO
DOES INTERSTATE TRAVEL

MP JOHNSON

It says here some folks are concerned that zombies are being mistreated. They're getting together to do a protest," Earl summarised the front page of the newspaper for the table full of his fellow truckers.

"Goddamn tree-hugging, vegetarian faggots!" Big Ted shouted, drawing the attention of everyone else who happened to be slurping down the swill served in Edna's Family Restaurant, a greasy spoon just off Highway 29 near Wausau, Wisconsin. He continued his rant, "It's probably a bunch of fucking college kids who just want something to protest. Liberal assholes. College is great for making boys into bitches and bitches into witches."

Earl looked around and saw everyone nodding in unison. He decided to hold back on reminding them that he had gone to the University in Madison for a couple of years, for fear of the conversation turning on him.

His route overlapped with Ted's once a week. On those days, they got together for brunch. Usually, they were joined by a random group of fellow truckers they knew from here and there. The food was hideous, but the camaraderie couldn't be beat.

"Let me tell you, there are few things I love in life more than when one of those creeps stumbles in front of the grill of my truck so I can plow through him at seventy-miles per hour. The sight of my wipers scraping off the bits of dead brains from my windshield just fills my heart with joy."

"You might feel differently if it was somebody you loved crumpled up against the front of your truck," Earl tried to reason, licking a spot of bacon grease from the back of one hand while holding the newspaper with the other. As he loaded up another mouthful, he realised the significance of what he had just said. He looked up and caught the pissed-off look in Ted's eyes.

"You know damn well what I'd do. Corpses got no business walking around, family or not."

"Well, I don't know if I'd be as eager as you," Earl said.

"It's not about eager. It's about getting done what's gotta be done. That's what nobody understands."

Earl knew Ted meant what he said. They had been hanging out one Sunday afternoon, grilling, shooting the shit, and downing a few cans of beer, when Ted's dead Uncle Pete wandered into the yard. They followed the corpse into the kitchen, where he tried to grab a box of Fruit Loops from the cabinet, part of a daily breakfast routine that Ted explained involved heartfelt ruminations over life and love. The routine had ended six years before, when Pete was crushed in a car accident. Ted didn't hesitate to drag the corpse outside and use a shotgun to remove whatever it was in the old man's soggy brain that made him move around again. Together, they buried Pete and did a Jack Daniels memory purge to get the whole scene out of their minds.

As the men sat around mumbling their complaints about the walking dead and stuffing hash browns into their mouths, Earl noticed his fork shaking as it sat unused beside his plate. Soon, the table started shaking, too. He realised the whole place was rumbling like his guts after a plate of Edna's chilli cheese fries.

"It's a damn volcano! Holy shit! Rib Mountain is erupting. It's a goddamn volcano." Big Ted pointed out the window toward the mountain, which was a skiing hotspot during the winter, but not much of anything on a warm summer day like this one. In fact, it wasn't a mountain at all, but a large poorly named hill. It rumbled and the top began to split, sending boulders of dirt and debris down the slopes, flattening the pine trees that lined the hill.

"It's not a volcano," Earl said as the mounted head of a buck fell from the wall above him onto the table, its antlers messing up his plate of eggs and bacon. "That's not physically possible."

"Well, college boy, you just glance out the window and tell me that doesn't look like a volcano to you." Ted grabbed Earl by the neck and aimed his eyes to the hill. "It's going to shoot lava any minute!"

Earl stared in anticipation as the top of the hill completely fell away. Ted's thick hands on his neck prevented him from looking away even if he'd wanted to. He realised he was holding his breath as he watched a hand push its way out of the crater.

The appendage was massive and rotting. Flesh had been stripped completely off the pinky finger, leaving only bone. More of the hill gave way as the hand was followed by an arm, which was wrapped in a thick red-and-black flannel sleeve. Another hand and arm appeared; the flannel covering this one was tattered, revealing gaping holes in the dead flesh. This arm was more bone than meat.

The two huge arms reached out and planted themselves on the sides of Rib Mountain. Slowly, they pulled the rest of the body out from under layers of dirt and rock.

Where a hill once was, a giant man now stood. The gravelly remains of the popular tourist attraction rolled off his messy lumberjack clothes. Under a worn green hat, the man's sunken face was mostly hidden by a puff of brown beard. The little flesh that was visible was gray. Around the giant's hollow eyes, it looked like thin paper sheets clinging to his skull.

"It's Paul Bunyan!" Earl whispered.

"Damn right it is," Big Ted agreed, finally releasing Earl's neck.

"Well, take that Kelliher, Minnesota. Turns out you put his tombstone in the wrong place after all," stated Earl, pleased that one of the least popular battles between the neighbouring Midwest states had been settled. Minnesota still had all those tiny lakes they bragged about, but Wisconsin had the Green Bay Packers, the best football team in the world. Who needs lakes anyway?

"Amen," Ted said, before adding the triumphant chorus of the state song, "On Wisconsin!"

Paul stood still over the rubble of Rib Mountain, surveying the landscape that, according to legend, he had helped form. After some minutes of turning his head from side to side and scanning the area, he took his first tentative step west. The ground shook and Earl could only imagine what kind of havoc was wreaked in the spot where that boot touched the ground. Another step followed. Bunyan covered major distance with each stride. Earl realised that the giant would soon be out of sight and felt a sense of relief. He sat down at the table to finish his eggs.

"I'm going after him," Big Ted announced.

"What the hell for?" one of the other truckers asked.

"He may be big and a legend, but he's still a corpse and he's out there causing a mess of trouble."

"And what are you going to do about it?"

"I'm not sure yet, but in Wisconsin, we say 'Forward.'" He marched out of the restaurant to a round of applause.

Earl followed close behind. "This doesn't make any sense, but I've got shotgun."

Big Ted gave him a grin as they jumped into the orange truck and took off on 29.

"What about your load?" Earl asked.

"I've got a bunch of crap going to a carwash factory in Green Bay. They can live without it. I mean, look at this—this is more important." Big Ted pointed out a batch of smashed cars. People tried to pry doors open, running around and crying as their loved ones' arms hung at strange angles from shattered windows. This was the damage caused by one step.

"You know you're not just going to be able to plow him down like the rest of them, right?" Earl asked.

"We'll see."

They cruised west down, watching Paul in the distance. Every time the giant took a step, the ground shook, causing Earl to cringe and check his seat belt. Since the highway was filled with mangled and abandoned vehicles, they spent most of the drive on the cramped shoulder.

Silence prevailed as Big Ted concentrated on the road. Earl

stared out in awe at the fields they sped past. Driving never gave him much of a chance to enjoy the view. Everyday, he got up bright and early, locked his eyes on the white lines and hardly turned his head until he stepped out of his truck in the evening. For the first time he noticed how the yellow flowers seemed to blanket the small patches of grass along the road. He took note of the various types of barns: the old ones, the really old ones, and the weird new ones that looked like they were made out of tin. All were red, to some extent. On the old ones, a war raged between the red and the brown that crept slowly over it, turning what was once a colourful standout into a weathered object that seemed to grow out of the ground like some kind of warped, square tree.

Earl looked over at Big Ted, whose eyes were locked on the bouncing green hat of the giant far ahead. He decided to break the silence by whipping out his stock joke, the one he told to pretty much everybody he came across. "You know those deer crossing signs? Where the buck is rearing majestically against that yellow background?"

"Yeah."

"Well, imagine if that was the first panel of a comic strip. What would the next few panels look like? Blood spraying everywhere, cars driving into the ditch, pretty much full-blown chaos. If they showed one of those panels people would be a lot more wary. As it is now, it almost looks exciting."

"Makes sense to me," Big Ted agreed. After a moment of thought, he asked, "Can you imagine what happened when Bunyan had to shit?"

Earl tried to picture the big guy squatting somewhere, his fellow lumberjacks blinded by the pale white ass.

"It was probably bigger than most of the trees he cut down," Ted continued. "I'll bet he had a sense of humour about it. Probably decided to pretend one was a log and send it down river with the rest of the day's harvest. Can you see that? A big turd floating down the river, stinking to high heaven? If that fucker dissolved it would turn the whole works into a poop slide."

Earl laughed. "Nah. I bet he was polite about it and went behind a hill somewhere. He probably dug a hole and buried it. Maybe it turned into oil. Supposedly, he created the Grand Canyon. Maybe the truth is, he had to piss really hard and that's how he made it. Kind of like when you piss in snow and it cuts a nice line in it."

"Shit, I'd take a hurricane over standing around while Paul Bunyan pissed any day." Big Ted laughed.

"In the stories, he could whistle so hard that it would blow down twelve acres of jack pine. Every time he sneezed, he blew the roof off his bunkhouse," explained Earl.

"Well, I'm really fucking happy that he ain't breathing now, if that's the case."

Paul kept following highways, eventually merging onto I-94.

Around Menomonie, he paused and squatted down by a patch of trees.

Earl looked at Ted and they giggled like they hadn't since they were teenagers when they used to run around and smash peoples' lawn ornaments.

The giant's inactivity gave them a chance to catch up, which was nice since they had fallen behind. In a half hour, they were on top of him again. Big Ted stopped the truck and they stared at the huge boot that covered most of the road. Unlike in a typical traffic jam, where people waited patiently, everyone now abandoned their cars and ran in the opposite direction.

After a moment of staring into a nearby barnyard, Paul leaned over and picked up a tractor. The red machine, with its big wheels, looked tiny cradled in the giant's massive rotting digits.

He scooped up a pile of cars in his other hand and gazed into the horizon. His dead eyes showed no sign of intrigue or curiosity. They just stared. He didn't move for five minutes. Suddenly, he clamped his two hands together. He pushed metal against metal. It creaked and squealed as he worked at it. Bits of engine and door flew out of his grip and crashed through windshields of waiting cars. Eventually, he formed the metal into a club. From afar, Earl noticed that it looked like it could have been made of crushed soda cans.

With one massive horizontal swing of his new tool, the giant felled the small patch of trees that rested between crop fields. Satisfied at a job well done, he nodded his bearded head, dropped the hunk of metal and continued his trek west.

"He's moving pretty slow. If I hit the gas and cruise down the shoulder at top speed, maybe I can ram his foot." Big Ted's tone wasn't as sure as usual.

"I don't think that's a good plan."

"Well, we gotta do something. Do you have anything better, college boy?"

Earl hadn't learned crap at the University. He'd taken some basic classes, but had primarily focused on getting drunk. Yeah, he was smarter than a lot of guys, but it wasn't because of college. It was because he used his free time to read books and watch public television. Hell, that's where he saw stuff about Paul Bunyan and his buddy, Babe the Blue Ox. He laughed to himself about the closing of the show, which explained that, not only was Paul not real, he wasn't even a real myth. They proposed that he was actually an advertising ploy thought up by some creative executive at one of the logging companies. As Earl watched the giant lumberjack moving toward Hudson, it occurred to him that somebody should fire their fact-checker.

"Let's just follow him for a while longer. Maybe an opportunity will present itself as we go," Earl proposed.

"Okay, but if it comes down to it, I'm ramming him."

"Sure, just let me out first." Earl looked over at Ted, who

shook his head.

They trailed the giant down 94 toward Hudson. "Well, at least he's staying on the highway, so the Market is safe," Earl said, referring to the 24-hour grocery store that he had a habit of stopping at when he made runs through the area. It was more efficient than spending time at one of the various family restaurants, and he could use it as an opportunity to make himself one of his favourite foods. He would run in, grab a loaf of bread, a jar of pickles and some mustard and make himself a pickle sandwich. It was something he couldn't do in front of other people. He had tried to once, but the rest of the guys ribbed him so bad he ended up throwing it away before he could finish it. After that, he learned that it was more enjoyable to eat his sandwich while sitting down against one of his big tyres, in the shade of his truck.

"Look at that." Ted pointed to Paul as, for the first time since emerging from Rib Mountain, the giant veered from the beaten path.

"Please don't stomp the Market. Please don't stomp the Market," Earl chanted. It wasn't official, but it was the closest he came to saying a prayer. Unfortunately, it didn't work. While he couldn't see what happened from the highway, he could tell that Bunyan's foot had landed right on the grocery store. He groaned.

Big Ted let out a hearty laugh. Earl turned to him with a furrowed brow, trying in vain to indicate that it was a sensitive moment. Eventually, he just joined in on the laughter.

They stayed on the highway and watched as the giant moved closer to the border between Wisconsin and Minnesota. When Bunyan put a foot in the St Croix river, it caused water to splash so high it seemed like they had driven into a thunderstorm, albeit one that lasted only a few seconds.

"Wait a second! I've got a plan!" Earl shouted. "Look how close he is to the bridge as he's wading through the river."

"So what?" Ted asked, stopping the truck.

"So, his head is right next to the bridge. It's just a few feet. If you pick up enough speed on the shoulder, you can probably veer off the bridge and send your truck flying into his skull! We can jump out quick and fall into the river."

"That is the craziest idea I've ever heard," Ted stated, shaking his head. "Even if the rest works, I'd probably drown."

Earl looked at Ted, surprised to hear hesitation in the man's voice, the man who had been aiming to ram the giant in the foot for the last hour or so. "It's your call. If you don't think you can make it, then screw it."

Big Ted took a deep breath and clicked his tongue against the roof of his mouth.

"You know what? Let's do this fucker." Grinning, Big Ted reached out and grabbed Earl's shoulder hard, before letting out a "Woohoo!"

Ted paused before starting the truck. "Only one of us needs to be in here for this."

Earl nodded his head and climbed out of the truck. "Good luck."

"Ain't no other kind," Big Ted replied, jamming the truck into gear and pulling away.

"That doesn't make any sense," Earl whispered as he watched the semi pick up speed as it made its way to the bridge.

Paul moved slowly across the river. It had taken him a while, but he had made it to the halfway point, which was optimal for Ted, as that was where the bridge was the highest, a few feet above the giant's head. Earl watched as Ted opened the door of the cab and hung out, still holding the wheel. The trucker yanked and the vehicle swerved hard into the wall of the bridge. As it flew over, it knocked pieces away.

Ted jumped clear of the truck, flailing his arms. As far back as he was, Earl could still hear his buddy screaming. For a second, he thought Ted wouldn't make it. He would drown or be crushed. Instead, Ted landed on Bunyan's arm and clung to the scrappy flannel shirt.

The orange truck had smashed into the giant's face, which easily gave way, the dried-up skull turning into a cloud of dust. Bits of bone and beard flew into the river where they were washed away with the current. The giant zombie's head slowly collapsed. His green hat sank into the dried-out skull.

After a moment of swaying gently on the weakened neck, the remains of the head fell backwards. A stubborn piece of flesh kept it attached, hanging awkwardly against the giant's back.

Earl kept his eyes on Ted, who held on hard, dodging bits of dried-up flesh and brain. The truck had fallen quickly after impact. The rear had twisted with the momentum of the crash and pulled clear of Ted. All in all, the insane maneuver had been perfect.

Earl realised he was squeezing his hands together very tightly. He wondered what the zombie would do without his head. Typically, they went down like a stack of pancakes in front of a table of truckers, but Bunyan just stood there, arms at his sides, as his crushed head flopped loosely behind him.

Earl walked from one abandoned car to the next, trying to find one with the keys in place so he could drive closer to the scene or to a gas station and phone for some firemen with a ladder to rescue Ted. Nothing.

Finally, Paul began to wobble. His knees shook and after a moment, he collapsed backwards into the water with another heavy splash. Big Ted righted himself and hopped over to the chest of the corpse island that Bunyan had become. He yelled for help as the current pulled the two of them down the river and out of Earl's line of sight.

Earl stood still for a moment, trying to decide what to do.

His thoughts were interrupted by a thudding sound. The ground shook. At first, he thought the giant zombie must have recovered and was coming back. Then he turned and looked east down 94, the direction they had come from. Stomping in his direction was a huge ox. It was the color of the sky, except for the bits where the fur hung from its bony structure like someone had taped mud flaps onto it.

He looked around for an abandoned truck. On second thought, he decided against it. The Ox would be across the river and over the border before Earl could do a damn thing about it.

"Fuck it," he said out loud. "Let Minnesota have him. He can piss in all their precious lakes."

CURIOSITY UNVEILED

TONY PLANK

Slowly she wended her way across the harsh terrain. If she moved over rough, grey basalt she became rough, grey basalt, and on black mud she became black mud. Jagged shards did nothing to impede her, and when she cast her senses upward she felt cold, unrelenting ice above. Ahead, twin orbs of light swept an ocean floor that until now had known only darkness, and their curious brightness awakened outlandish feelings within her. The Intruders had come from somewhere beyond understanding, spewing heat and light into perennial darkness as they descended to settle above the mantle. At first they confined themselves within hastily hewn igloos, but soon were followed by entities of unimaginable power, who gouged labyrinths deep in the ice. Had they hewn their igloos above the cold, barren places where no heat filtered through the seabed to warm the domains then all might have been well. Instead, they chose to settle above the volcanic vents where waters were warmest and Kin most abundant. Magic followed. Heat, light and sound filled the labyrinths, and as their side-effects penetrated the waters beneath, they instilled anxiety into its dwellers.

Intrusion followed. The first breach in the mantle heralded a fear that wafted into every rift, trench, and canyon to disturb places that had long been sacrosanct. Fear became horror as the first Intruders entered and, descending to the seabed, seared those caught in its blazing orbs with an energy they neither saw nor understood.

Uncountable Kin succumbed in that first onslaught, yet their numbers were insignificant in the light of what followed. Intruder after Intruder dropped into the Kin domains until they hummed with the voices of juggernauts raining death over ever-widening grids. And for what purpose? Why did these things bore through the ice and impose death on the innocent? Were they not aware of the carnage they wrought, or could it be that they knew, but didn't care?

☆

Lenny Groves stared unblinkingly at the screens, eyes scouring the seabed through the lens of Bot-5. There it was again, a flash across his field of vision, gone almost before he saw it. Was it light bouncing off rocks on the ocean floor, or a reflection of things that moved? He shivered. The feelings were coming again—the tingles, the light-headedness, and the crawling perception that he was being watched. They were stronger now, much stronger, and he wriggled in his seat to ease tension and dispel the outlandish images ploughing through his head. Bot-Five reached the end of its sweep, turned for its next run, and as it came back online he saw the flash again. There was nothing down there except mud … mud as black as a coal scuttle. So what could there be for light to reflect off?

They'd been on initial approach to Jupiter when he'd first felt uneasiness germinate in him. Europa was no more than a billiard ball etched in hairline scratches, but as the scanners displayed the ice moon's ever-increasing detail, his apprehension had grown. Hour by hour he'd watched the scratches enlarge. Cracks at first, then rifts, and finally hundred-kilometre-deep canyons sculptured haphazardly across the frozen surface. Then nausea had hit and he'd questioned his reasons for being here.

The first week was Hell. No one had anticipated the effect Jupiter would have as it hung over them, utterly intimidating and looking down with a swirling, bloodshot eye that made their skins crawl. It seemed to Groves that it watched every move they made, its swirls belching a warning that threatened terrible consequences should they desecrate one of its children. Like most of his companions he hadn't felt safe until an igloo had been blasted in the ice and they'd crawled inside to become troglodytes. That had been nine months ago; now those igloos were a honeycomb of caverns half-a-billion kilometres from Earth.

Later, as heat probes melted the first bores through the mantle, Groves prayed they wouldn't find the sub-ice ocean that scientists had predicted. His hopes were dashed, however, when at eighty-three kilometres they burst through into the sombre blackness of liquid ebony.

There it was again! A quick flash, almost too fast to see. Dizziness swirled in his head as in his scanners he watched patches of carmine and ivory spin into catherine wheels of blood and bone— bright at the centre, yet fading to black at the rim. He knew what would happen next and, as if it had read his mind, Bot-5's lights extinguished, leaving him staring into inky, unplumbed fathoms.

☆

When the intruders had first broken through, the realisation that other entities existed above the mantle had thrown the Kin into confusion. When the attacks came, terror had run riot. Yet despite this an affinity had grown and alliances never before thought possible had been nurtured. The process was long and arduous, but resolve grew, and as it spread its message was clear. *Resist!* Many volunteered, yet for most the training was too much and they succumbed. The price was horrifying, not only among those who exposed themselves to the attackers to distill a few grains of knowledge, but also among the millions who rose from the warm depths into the freezing upper regions to form thick layers of phlegm beneath each bore to lock Intruders out.

As a chosen one she'd lain beyond the bores and been tutored in the ways of purpose. Her will was strengthened and her resolve hardened until all that mattered was her mission. Painful though the training had been, it had not compared to the anguish of leaving her family and placing herself in the path of an Intruder. As it approached, fear hazed her senses, and as its glare washed over her she expected death. But it didn't come. Intruders swept in grids, and as she waited for the next pass she widened her perceptions. When next it came she felt only the briefest disorientation. Her spirits soared. There had been no pain, and without pain she could mesh. Moving swiftly she matched speed with her quarry, slid into its beam, and allowed its glaring light to bathe her in feelings beyond belief. A deep, steady thrum entered her consciousness, and again her spirits soared. The Intruder's rhythms were fast, but not so fast that she couldn't meld. Long, difficult hours followed, hours in which she synchronised with an alien resonance; hours in which she felt discordant and lost, but also hours in which she learned much about Intruders.

Their ingenuity was bottomless. For every bore the Kin blocked they drilled another. From where did they come? What did they want? And why were they so intent on carnage? Volunteers perished willingly, each passing what little knowledge they'd gleaned back to the broodmind before cessation. For months the butchery raged, but they were months of arousal, months in which dormant abilities awoke and knowledge accrued. They were now aware that the mantle was not infinite, and that the Intruders came from far-off domains—domains of power and magic, but above all, knowledge. Where were these places? As data accumulated, questions abounded, and the need for answers became paramount.

☆

"Have we found what's blocking the bores yet?" asked Daley.

"Not yet, Boss," replied Harrison. "Nor do we know why the Bots keep breaking down. Groves swears there's some sort of intelligence working here, but I think it's interference from Jupiter."

There was a snigger around the room.

"Where's Lenny now?" asked Daley.

"Probably staring into his scanners again," replied Harrison. "He's weird, Boss, really weird."

Daley bleeped Groves, but got no answer. "Go and get him will you, Fred? He really ought to be here."

Harrison left, only to return ten minutes later, pasty-faced and barely holding his astonishment together behind a veneer of calm. "He's gone, Boss," he stammered. "Groves has gone, and so has the submersible."

☆

Word spread through the ever-growing broodmind such that all heard it at once. A live thing had come to visit. Wise ones came from everywhere, some from so far away their existence had only been rumour. Now a different kind of Intruder had come, one containing a living being, and only their best negotiators would be allowed close enough to make contact. A thousand layers deep they formed a bubble around the submersible while the wise ones moved in closer. Could this thing converse? Could it tell of places outside their domain—places it had been, and things that it had seen? Most of all, would it tell why it was here, and why it wrought carnage among them? They crowded around the submersible, apprehensive, yet with abounding curiosity. Many thought that if they could communicate with the being, then things could return to the way they'd always been. Their leaders, however, realised that never again could things be the same.

☆

Inside the submersible, the living thing was terror-struck. Enshrouded in a bubble of phlegm and desperately seeking escape, Glover found that panic dulled his wits and hampered his movements. Didn't those things out there understand paralysing fear? Didn't they know how it causes humans to scream, and that sometimes, the louder the scream the quieter it gets. And they obviously failed to hear the thunderous noise in his head. And when the blood vessels burst, and a massive stroke terminated his life, they just hovered, staring, and still unaware.

☆

Daley gazed into the liquid amber of his glass and saw tattered hopes and shattered dreams. He was drunk, but right now, he didn't care about anything much. Out on the great Mare Serenitatis Plain shuttles stood tall and majestic, waiting to supply the Mars orbiters. Trains of machines fed the shuttles, and a thousand human ants guided their actions. He'd been back a week, yet still couldn't look people in the eye. They were nice enough to his face, but he knew what they were saying behind his back. Got the kiss of failure on him, they'd whisper, and he'd shiver at the memory of thick, green phlegm bursting from the bores and filling the labyrinths so quickly they'd barely made good their escape.

☆

The spoked wheel of Orbiter-3 emerged from the dark side of Mars. In the observation turret David Bollard had made a discovery. His first impulse was to report it, yet he hesitated. If he was wrong he'd be the laughing stock of the ship; better to sleep on it and check it out next orbit. He was back in the turret two hours before Orbiter-3 again entered the dark side. Focusing on Europa he found the bubble was bigger now—much bigger. It seemed to have grown to almost the size of Europa itself, but even at max mag he couldn't make out exactly what it was. He raised the alarm and people tumbled into the turret. Soon, the whole of Mars knew about the Europan bubble, and not long after, the whole of Earth. They called Daley from the Moon. He took one look and realised exactly what it was. When the phlegm had roared up through the bores they'd had to scramble out of the labyrinths and up to the ships. They'd escaped only minutes before the sludge would have engulfed them, and as they pulled away they concluded it was sub-oceanic slime forced upward by pressure from beneath. Now he realised they were wrong. This wasn't pressure, this was design. There was a lot more happening here than anyone realised. Seven weeks later the bubble broke free of the Europan surface and hung motionless in space—a massive, wavering balloon seemingly unsure what to do next.

☆

That the first Intruders were no more than mechanical devices was now clear. Beings like the one who'd come to visit were living things much like themselves—bigger, more advanced, but more importantly, the ones who controlled the killer machines. The Kin had tried to communicate with the visitor, learn his ways, reason with him, ask why his kind wrought carnage among them. Yet when he saw them swarming in his light beams his shape had contorted horribly. Why had he thrashed around so furiously inside his bubble? Was he trying to escape? Was he in some sort of pain? Couldn't he understand that their gestures were ones of friendship? And then he'd suddenly become inert and his rhythms had ceased. Long after he'd become still they breached the hull of his vessel and examined him. He was biological like themselves, had a large brain, and obviously possessed knowledge far in excess of their own. How were beings like this able to exist above the mantle? The killer machines had awoken the Kin from their abstract existence and forced cohesion among them, but now there were other beings who, by their very existence, implanted seeds of curiosity, seeds well sewn, and which could not be ignored.

When they'd rushed up the bores to confront the Masters their leaders had led the way, but the Masters had fled. The Kin had felt cheated and hadn't known what to do next. For a while they stared out the labyrinths at unimaginable scenes, and as a swirling red eye stared back it seemed to confer approval. Finally they decided that wherever the Masters could go, they could go, and the knowledge possessed by these strangers could also be learned by the Kin. No reason was found why they shouldn't follow, and no reason found why they shouldn't learn of these things for themselves.

☆

Something odd was happening out there. The bubble was not only expanding, but changing shape. Thousands of eyes focussed on it twenty-four hours a day, but those on Mars had the best view and were first to see it take human form. Many weeks later it started walking, mimicking human gait, long, bumbling strides that went nowhere, just ambling on the spot. Other things were also happening; details were forming that for a long time could not be resolved. Jenny Robson, a cook who couldn't keep her eyes away from the 'scopes when she was off duty, was the first to realise what it was, and she let out a bloodcurdling scream.

"It's Groves," she yelled in panic. "It's Lenny bloody Groves! The bastard's come back to life and he's comin' to haunt us for leavin' him behind."

Daley eyed her coolly. What must it be like to suffer from cognitive anorexia, he wondered? But when he took another look he was staggered to see she was right.

A week later Groves was clearly identifiable, a huge figure walking toward Earth. The terror etched on his face made Daley shudder. What sort of hell had he been through under the ice? With arms held forward, palms turned outward, and fingers spread wide he looked like he was defending himself against some unknown horror. Over following weeks he moved closer, and it was obvious to watchers that it was something other than walking that propelled him. As detail became clearer he appeared partly transparent, a network of pulsating nodes held together by a web of nerve-like strings that formed elaborate gossamers of twinkling flashes. Radar put him at 380 million kays from Mars, and estimated his height at 3100 kilometres. It took months to get accurate readings of his velocity; most predicted that at a million kilometres per day he'd be on Earth's doorstep shortly after its next solar orbit.

Panic didn't begin until he was within range of amateur telescopes. Full colour photos appeared in the press and on TV, accompanied by highly emotional headlines designed to attract viewers and earn brownie points for the newscasters. Jupiterman, or Jupe, as he'd been named, could only be bent on destruction—why else would he be heading for Earth and not any other planet? Nine months later, as Earth swung back into Jupe's path, he was walking unscathed through the asteroid belt, and a few months after that, as he neared Mars, Phobos and Deimos were evacuated. A little later, as the evacuation of Mars itself began, Daley stood atop Olympus Mons and gasped at the sheer size of the approaching monster. Even back on Earth he was huge, and each night at sunset millions of eyes turned eastward to watch a massive green head appear over the horizon and rise into the night sky. First the tousled hair, then the wrinkled forehead, and worst of all two, wide, fearful eyes. Throughout the night, as more and more of him appeared, people around the world ran for deep, dark places: subways, cellars, sewers, caves, anywhere where out-of-sight was out-of-mind. After the eyes came the nose, followed by a wide-open mouth, teeth bared and lips drawn back as if in mid-scream. About midnight the matted beard rose into view, followed by outstretched arms that looked like they were fending something off, and finally long, striding legs that made the figure sway and bob as though it really were human. The likeness to Groves was astonishing to those who knew him, which only added a further dimension to their unease.

☆

Now only thirty million kays distant and well inside the orbit of Mars, the figure's detail was uncanny. Astronomers tried to keep as much as possible from the public for fear of increasing panic, but in just over a month he'd be here. What would happen then?

Several days later the missile was fired. Who launched it no one knew. The military of most countries denied all knowledge, yet were relieved at not having to reveal plans to do it themselves. It was thought to have been one of the Middle Eastern countries, most of whom had declared Jupe an affront to Islam and Allah. Once in space the missile accelerated to half a million kph and would hit its target in two days—two days of nail-biting tension for an entire planet. Churches, synagogues and mosques became packed with faithful and not-so-faithful alike, suicides flared, crime prospered, and mobs took control of cities. Mecca overflowed with Moslems trying to complete their Hajj, the once-in-a-lifetime pilgrimage to the Ka'ba before Allah called them. Christians flocked to Rome and the Vatican City, some declaring Jupe to be the second coming of Christ, and Jews from across the world thronged the streets of Jerusalem, fighting to reach the Wailing Wall and worship at the Temple Mount. Small wars erupted around the globe in last-ditch efforts to even old scores, and attempts to hijack space vessels became so commonplace they hardly rated a mention.

The missile was off-target. It exploded ten miles to the left of Jupe's waist, bringing about an apparition even more terrifying than before. From the waist up his torso careened crazily to his left while his left arm detached at the shoulder and trailed behind on a long, sinewy thread. His left leg, seemingly broken at the knee, jutted outward, its foot dangling from a wayward ankle. Yet he kept walking. Still he kept coming.

☆

It had been difficult at first, so very difficult. Feelings of release and sudden freedom coupled with the knowledge that one huge ecosphere existed above the mantle was hard to absorb. How strange to have no ceiling above and be free to go wherever they wished! Under the watchful eye of Jupiter they expanded and probed their new surroundings. Very far off, rhythms like those of the visitor emanated from an area of small worlds near a great central light. Surely they must come from the homes of the Masters, the strange beings who had knowledge of these domains and how to survive in them. The Kin needed such knowledge, and needed it quickly, if they were to adapt. The need to send a sign became apparent, a sign to let the Masters know they were coming, a sign that would be recognised and not misinterpreted. What better than to use the shape of the visitor. Not only would the Masters recognise him, but more than likely would welcome him home. Mimicking the walk became second nature within a short time, and without the pressure of an ocean to contain them, duplication became easier and their increased numbers boosted broodmind power to a level far higher than anyone had thought possible. And so their journey began—a facsimile of the only Master they'd ever met—walking through space... going home.

☆

When the second missile hit it entered the side of Jupe's neck where the carotid artery should have been, exited under the skull just above the second cervical vertebrae, exploded, and blew the head clean off its shoulders. It tumbled over and over on a path toward Earth. Down on the planet, unbridled panic took root and as the head careened Earthward; confusion erupted into open warfare as crowds fought for deeper and darker places in which to hide. Cities became ghost towns while rural areas overflowed with refugees believing they had a better chance of survival in the country. Victory to the strongest became the norm as human populations descended into savage competition for food and shelter. Astronomers calculated that the head would enter the atmosphere over China, travel eastward across Europe and the Atlantic, and plunge to earth in the vicinity of Baffin Island. It was going to be a terrifying spectacle, a human head six-hundred kilometres from chin to brow traversing a highly populated area of the world. Although it was not solid, no one knew what effects it would have when it hit.

It struck on September 23rd 2108 at 22:40 hours. The chin hit first, toppling the face forward so that it bit deeply into the atmosphere. Facial hair on its chin was the first thing to ignite, followed closely by eyebrows and eyelids, and as it skidded across the night sky it left in its wake a trail of flaming debris that fell like burning rain. As the skull rotated it flared furiously, first the forehead, then the crown, then the nape of the neck, and when next it looked down on those below it was with bottomless eye sockets below which yawned a cavernous mouth containing a flaming tongue. It moved over northern hemisphere landscapes, gradually falling closer to the surface and sending shrieking populations across the length and breadth of Europe stampeding for cover. It didn't reach Baffin Island as predicted but plunged into the Atlantic just short of Greenland. The impact was an anticlimax; no explosion, no tidal wave, just a hot, shrunken lump that sizzled violently as it hit the water, leaving only a vapour trail high in its wake to show that it had ever been. With the immediate threat over, the whole planet looked skyward to see what kind of havoc Jupe's headless body would now wreak upon them. It did nothing. Much to everyone's surprise it stopped walking and stood forlorn, a headless human shape wavering in space, disoriented and knowing not what to do next.

☆

Why had the Masters done this? The question rattled through a broodmind devoid of answers. Had they not sent a clear signal that they were coming? What were the Masters afraid of? Were not the Kin weak and childlike compared to them? They'd been gratified when the first gesture of friendship had risen from the Master's planet and moved out to greet them. When visiting the Kin domains the Masters had been cruel, even murderous, but here, in their own territory, they were friendly and were dispatching a message of goodwill. And then the message exploded. Millions died in the blast, and many more would also die if they were unable to re-establish contact with their brothers in the nearly severed section. Although the blast had been hideous, it was nothing to the shock that coursed through the rest of the network. Those on the right kept walking while those on the left struggled to effect repairs and limit damage. So intent on maintaining system integrity were they, they forgot how precarious their position had become. A second "gift" was on them before they knew it. Tearing its way through the uppermost part of the network it exploded and detached the complete top section.

This time all activity stopped as they watched their brothers spin toward the Master's planet, scud sickeningly across its atmosphere, burn and vanish. Their situation now became shockingly clear. There were no friends here, no learning was to be had in this place. There was no empathy or compassion, only death delivered by a race of beings who wanted nothing to do with them. For the first time in their existence they felt anger, yet there was little they could do for they had no defence against such barbarism, and even less did they comprehend it. Finally, with feelings of despair, they turned and walked away.

☆

It took a year to re-establish law and order, a year in which the apparition in the sky became smaller as it receded. When it had first turned away the question of whether to finish it off had been considered; it might, after all, return later. Whether it was ethics, morals or just plain sympathy for the bedraggled creature in the sky, the answer was no. Whatever it is, agreed authorities, let it go. Observers in the Martian orbiters watched it return to Europa, but much to their surprise it kept going, out past Saturn, out past Uranus and Neptune, and out past Pluto. Walking ever deeper into space, it vanished somewhere near the Kuiper Belt, never to be seen again. What was it? What had it wanted? Could they have communicated with it? In later years humans regretted never having tried. Global terror had prevailed and the politics of fear had guided actions; actions of which they were now thoroughly ashamed. Should the creature ever return, then next time they'd try harder, a lot harder. Perhaps, next time, the logic of the few could overcome the fear of the many.

☆

The Kin returned home. Many wanted to re-enter the sub-ice ocean and be left in peace to live as before, but the majority, now having had a taste of freedom, disastrous as it had been, wanted to continue on and see what else lay out there. They stopped at Europa while those who'd remained behind for the first journey chose whether to join them or whether to stay, and those who'd had enough of freedom returned to the sanctity of their homes. When all was settled, the broodmind moved outward toward the eternal darkness, out toward the twinkling lights that somehow seemed to beckon them. Were they the homes of other Masters— more understanding Masters; Masters able to teach them the wonders of these domains and many other unknown things?

And so their second journey began ... a headless shape with left arm trailing, leg shattered, left foot dangling, yet brimming with optimism. One day they too would be as clever as the Masters, they too would understand the laws that governed these places. Out there in the blackness there'd be someone who'd teach them, someone who'd help, someone who'd be their friend... there would... there would... they just knew there would.

Born of Woman
(A Warning for Youji-Yajuu)

Lyn Battersby

Dali's *Leda Atomica* hangs on the bedroom wall. It's not a very good print. The colour rendering has tinged the picture green, making Leda and her swan appear quite ill. A crack in the glass runs a horizontal line across Leda's left thigh while the yellowed pine frame has started to bow. Flawed as it is, I love the picture and can't bring myself to throw it away. It reminds me of a time when Japan was ruled by monsters.

Please, my darling, don't consider my comment to be a slight against you. You are my son, perfect, beautiful—my pride if not my joy. I have raised you as best I can. Now you must find your own way in the world. These are my final words to you, a gift from mother to child.

I proposed to your father at a picnic. I fancy Michael would have asked first, but February 29 was made for women such as me, so I pressed my advantage. We spent the rest of the day giggling into our champagne and making plans for an unspecified day in the future.

Then the war erupted and our plans changed.

"Follow me," your father begged when the draft letter arrived.

I couldn't help but agree. A foreign wedding wasn't ideal, but we didn't have time to plan one here. We kissed our families goodbye and made our separate journeys to Tokyo.

The city was a mess. Those buildings not burning were reduced to rubble under the trampling feet of successive monsters. Streets were littered with the dead, the living having fled west to the mountains. Nobody was left to keep order, or to stop me sneaking through the combat zone. I found your father with his troop, penned in against the banks of the Tamagawa River.

"I've found a priest," I told him as we huddled before the onslaught. "He will marry us tonight in the Buddhist temple."

"And the licenses?"

"Here." I patted my handbag then ducked as concrete debris rained down from above.

Somewhere to my right a Japanese man shouted orders. I couldn't understand his words, but your father jumped to his feet with the others and charged the prowling enemy. Planes roared overhead, adding bombs to the bullets. I huddled behind an overturned car and waited out the battle.

You have his feet. It may seem strange to draw your attention to a body part you can't see, but you have to remember that at ground level, you are still human.

Michael's feet were strong and broad, made for running beneath the legs of monsters, dodging giant claws that gouge holes into the bitumen and sidestepping shrapnel—not intended for him, but every bit as deadly.

He didn't see the danger until it was too late. The monster sent forth two bolts of lightning from its forked tongue. Instinct drove Michael to the left, away from the first bolt, throwing him directly into the path of the second. I held my breath as your father hung there, suspended in air by the blue current that ran from beast to earth.

And then it was over. The allies saved the day, driving the monster back to the sea. Just one battle out of many, but it's the only one I ever witnessed.

I ran to your father and checked his wrist. I found the merest pulse, faint, but discernible. I kissed Michael's forehead, his cheeks, his lips. I held him close, my nose embedded within his hair. The stench of ozone clung to the strands. I breathed him in and prayed for his life.

In time Michael came around. He smiled into my crying eyes and asked, "Will you marry me?"

There is nothing to show we ever married. No certificate, no photos, no ring. All I have are my memories, and you.

We made love afterwards in an area cleared of rubble. The men of the garrison gave us a wedding present of three blankets and an hour of privacy.

All mothers have pregnancy worries. I sometimes look at Leda and wonder what she thought of her seduction and the resulting children. Was she proud of Helen, or did she cower in shame at Troy's destruction?

Japan honoured your father and flew him home a year later in a coffin crafted from daikaiju bone. He never saw you, but he was proud of what you would become. I sent him letters, detailing your development, how strong you were and how you grew more quickly than any of the other babies at the clinic. By the time he died you were only three months old, yet you already towered over me. Other infants your age let out mewling shrieks to say they are hungry or tired or in pain. You let loose with mighty roars that shook the neighbourhood. The police would come to silence you but I'd show them your sweet baby face and what could they do? Arrest you for having a wet nappy?

Today you turn thirteen. Some would say an unlucky number and I admit it hasn't always been easy. What mother ever thinks she'll use secateurs to trim her child's toenails? But here you are and I am not ashamed. You are your father's son, a fine young man with your powerful legs, broad shoulders and enormous tail.

And your father's feet. Use them well, my son. Dodge the enemy's bullets. Flee from their bombs and their tanks and their nuclear missiles.

Don't apologise for what you are. You are the son of a war hero. Go in pride. Make something of yourself. But remember:

Be kind to other children. Nobody likes a bully.

THE REIGN OF WORMS

DARREN GOOSSENS

The rain of worms began on a mild August evening in 2016, and now here we are, cooking over a campfire and eating possum. I was spiralling down into the carpark of the new Oakleigh shopping centre when it started, and I was safe. I did not hear anything unusual until I turned off the whining motor, switched off the movie player and climbed out of my GMBMW $1\frac{1}{2}$ series. A couple of the fluorescent lights of the carpark buzzed and flickered.

The noise from outside sounded like hail, only less frequent and louder. A car swooped around the spiralling carpark ramp, past me, deeper into the underground. Cracks radiated out from a bullet hole in its rear window. I wondered if the noise was the Queensland Army Against Federation (QuAAF) laying siege to Big W. The sounds could have been bullets striking walls and windows, I thought; but I could hear nothing that sounded like guns being fired.

A second car raced past me, and a third. The fourth decided to park on the same level (blue triangle) as me. A sleek crimson two-door, probably a Toyota-Tupolev TT25, slotted into place and the roof clamshelled open. A fit-looking young woman in a black fedora and a red Adidas tracksuit stepped out. Ignoring me, she examined the rear of the vehicle and tsked over a small hole in the boot lid.

"What's going on?" I said, venturing towards her.

She looked up nervously. She wore bright red lipstick, the colour of a tomato, and wraparound sunglasses; they looked like the kind you could pick up for seven dollars at Dimmeys.

She spoke quickly. I could tell she was on edge, as you might expect from someone who just had a near miss on the roads. "Don't go up there. It's raining nails or something."

She poked at the hole in the boot lid, then uttered a cry and drew back. Something pointy poked through the hole and waved back and forth, like a centimetre long snake tasting the air.

"What is that thing?" she said.

I leaned forward for a closer look. Cars whooshed past behind me. "Some kind of miniature robot? I hear they're using them to treat sewage now."

"Be careful!" she said. "It might shoot out and poke you in the eye or something."

It looked like a shiny legless millipede, only pointy. As we watched, it crawled fully out of its hole and raised its head (I guess that's what it was) again and swung it about. The steel creature settled on a particular direction and began inching across the sheet metal, leaving a shallow scratch in the paint as it went.

"That's enough!" The girl hopped on one leg long enough to pull off a sandal, then used the sole to flick the worm off her car. "Scratches as well as a hole? I don't think so."

It skittered to a stop near one of the blue induction paint lines demarcating a parking space, tasted the air again, and began methodically working its way across the floor, upwards and out of the carpark.

"And these things are falling out of the sky?" I said.

She nodded. "Yes, and I don't think my insurance will cover this. Damn damn damn!"

I could still see the worm, although it had almost vanished up the spiral. I didn't want to follow it too closely lest some panicking motorist run me down. I watched as cars flew over the top of it. It merely hunkered down while they passed then continued on its way.

"I guess a rain of metal worms from outer space counts as an act of God," I said. We still stood near the rear of her vehicle.

"Some god, anyway. I bet it was the Americans. I bet it's some kind of weapon they've set off accidentally. Like that weapons dump that's been burning in Nevada since '09."

I nodded sagely. "It's always the Americans."

"Well, they better pay for the panel-beater."

"You've got a better chance getting God to cough up ..."

She snorted, but the joking seemed to settle her down a little. The metallic pattering continued.

I opened my car door and turned on the news channel. The repeaters in the carpark were still working and we had some signal. The rain of worms dominated every channel and the more we saw the worse, and the weirder, it got.

The worms had been linked back to a cloud of interstellar debris astronomers had noticed approaching earth late in 2015. In a hyperbolic glide the swarm of rocks, none bigger than a marble, had swung down into the plane of the ecliptic from on high as if in an extreme polar solar orbit. Telescopes had tracked the swarm easily, and point-by-point plotted out its orbit until the intersection with Earth could not be denied. Newspapers had carried the story and told people to watch for a glorious lightshow in the sky; scientists commented that, while none of the incoming bodies were large enough to even reach the ground, we must learn from this lesson and continue to fund the search for near-Earth asteroids—for surely one day the Earth killer would come ...

The first rocks and dust motes hit the exosphere at approximately 7:45 pm on August 6th 2016—today. The expected shower of sparks did not materialise, for the motes failed to burn. Instead, radar showed us that they braked—braked—and skipped across the thinnest layers of air, losing speed and dropping lower all the while. At the time this was thought odd, but merely odd and interesting. Theories suggesting highly pressurised pockets of trapped gas that acted as braking rockets when released were put forward in explanation.

The marbles hit the ground, the water, the ice all over the world. They thudded like bullets into grassy banks, they crashed through window panes and into office walls. They buried themselves in whatever they hit, be it an ocean wave, a Buick or an acupuncturist. Then they uncoiled into shining metallic worms, each less than three centimetres long and segmented like the elbow joints in a fifteenth century suit of armour.

Then they moved, just as we had seen, with some definite, inscrutable goal in mind. And they continued to rain down. No one could estimate how many had fallen so far. Millions? More likely billions.

Hospitals filled up with the wounded, mortuaries with the dead. Cars ground to a halt with holed fuel tanks and smashed fuel cells.

Aeroplanes fell out of the sky or at the least suffered rapid depressurisation.

Then the news started to repeat.

"We're under a shopping centre," I said. "You could go shopping."

She shook her head. "I've been. Shit."

My eyes followed her gaze down to the flat rear tyre on the TT25. She thumbed the driver's window open; the tyre surged like a breathing beast as the car woke, but the inner-inner tube must have been holed as well and the reflate never happened. Presumably a flying worm had driven through all three layers of rubber. The gas reservoir would have kept the tyre up for a while—long enough for her to get out of the metal rain, anyway.

"Can I help?"

She looked at me through the mirrorshades. Her mouth pursed up for a moment.

"Yeah, all right. I live in Cheltenham."

We transferred her shopping—I noticed it was all gluten-free, lactose-free, meat-free and dairy-free—into my car (she made a face as I packed it in beside the carton of VB and the large packet of BBQ sausages) and then watched the news cycle through again. As the bulletin finished with footage of the smashed windows of Chartres Cathedral, the drumming noise slowed and quite quickly cut off.

We left hurriedly, taking a punt that the rain would not start up again.

"Bill," I said as we spiralled up into the night streets.

"Cassy."

No cars moved, but vehicles of all types littered the roadside. Suddenly I could see what carnage the worms had caused. Cars on footpaths, trucks through windows; mostly old models without autopilots. An erratic trail of streetlights lit a roadbed mosaiced with shattered glass and scrawled with skid marks. Blocks of flats stood, gap-toothed in the darkness above to either aside.

I put in a call to Emergency Services—I had to leave a message in the queue—then pulled over near a tangle of vehicles and street lamps plastered against the partly-lit front of a clothing shop. When I opened the door, I heard nothing but breeze stirring the plastic bags in the gutter. No cries for help. Cassy stayed in the GMBMW while I had a look around. I walked past an empty Boeing SolarScooter (ugly damned thing) and looked at the other four vehicles. Of the three on the street and footpath, two lay empty—it appeared the drivers had made it safely to cover—and the third contained two dead bodies beneath a roof as waterproof as a colander. The driver looked about forty-five; his mid-life crisis convertible had cost him dearly. The woman beside him might have been his wife or his daughter—or not. Fluorescent lights flickered around me, their harsh white light making the round, bloody holes in the two bodies all the more plain. I saw a metal worm crawl out of the woman's ear and turned away to vomit.

I think oysters are one of the worst things you can vomit up. The mere sensation of an oyster sliding up your throat is enough to prolong the vomiting bout. I retch just thinking about it. But I eventually recovered and, breathing as deeply as I could, approached the last car, parked in the menswear section of the shop. The unbreakable windows had not broken, but I could see a couple of holes in the roof. I pulled on the driver's door but could not get it open. Cupping my hands around my eyes I looked through the glass and saw a figure slumped over the console. My head pulsed in time with the clicking lights, but I forced my breathing into regularity and looked more closely; the man's chest rose and fell. The visible bits of him showed signs of crash injury but not worm damage.

I tried all the other doors but none budged. I left another message with the SES, noting down the shop and saying that some sort of cutters, or failing that a teenager, would be needed to break into the vehicle. I tried smashing my way in with a section of display rack knocked loose in the crash, but could not make an impression on the windows or the magnesium alloy body.

Cassy looked at me blandly from the passenger seat when I got back. I reported what I had seen.

Everywhere it was the same. People either made it to safety or were killed by the hail of bullets from the sky.

We looped over the railway tracks and headed south, then

turned right, towards the city. I slowed down as I noticed shiny, lumpy balls rolling along the road.

"Clumps of those worms," said Cassy.

I slowed down more. We passed through a length of road that had lost few streetlights. In the brighter light I saw that the balls weren't really rolling; the worms crawled over each other and in doing so worked like the tracks on a tank or a bulldozer, each worm a link in the belt. It looked like a pile of caterpillars only with more purpose. We came to an intersection. Similar clumps rolled out of a couple of side streets and crashed—no, melted—into the clump we were following. It became as tall as a car tyre. In fact, it was a car type in shape if not in construction or colour.

We passed a pharmacy and a fuel stop and crossed into Cheltenham. A tyre made of worms rolled along the footpath. It rolled right over a letterbox and when it moved on nothing remained. It then rolled up the driveway and a monolayer of worms spread out across the family car. The car shape slumped then vanished behind us.

"Which street?"

"Are you going to keep following it? After you drop me off?"

"I guess so."

I looked across at her. The shades lay in her lap. Her face was quite plain; she had kept her freckles.

She smiled at me. "Don't drop me off, Bill."

"OK."

We drove on in silence. I liked driving, so I tended to have the car in safetynet mode most of the time, but switched it over to fulliautomatic when we reached the Nepean Highway. Highway driving bored me.

We cruised up the left lane. A few other cars had ventured out onto the streets now, but all cruised about slowly, tentatively.

And up the right lane, overtaking us slowly, drove a Holden Commodore—made entirely of shining, segmented grubs slithering endlessly over each other. Stippled, broken, lamplight bounced off it. It made a strange tinkling, chittering sound as it rolled up the road. For some reason I found the lack of headlights as disturbing as anything else.

"I guess they're trying to fit in," said Cassy.

"Well, it's not the Americans," I muttered.

Her voice fell. "No, it isn't. I guess they're from a little further away than that."

"Canada? I doubt it."

She laughed, sounding less strained than at any time since we had met. "Sirius? Betelgeuse?"

"They're made of metal, aren't they? I'd guess they're from Tin Cannus Major."

She laughed at a joke that deserved a groan. I felt my wobbly nerves steadying, although I kept seeing the dead couple in the convertible. I knew that from now on every time fluorescent lights flickered in my vision I would see them. Of course, I haven't seen many fluorescent lights since then.

We continued along the highway and soon caught a glimpse of the CBD. No lights shone there. We drove amongst many vehicles now, almost all of them stippled masses of quicksilver worms. We crossed onto St Kilda road, passed the green slopes of the gardens. The new bat-like sculptures out front of the NGV lay in tatters across the road. The new, even higher, even more desperate-for-attention spire on the arts building still stood but its hologrammatic projection of the current Premier's welcoming visage, normally projected onto the clouds above (artificial clouds being produced if necessary) could not be seen.

Neither could the ruins of Federation Square. A bomb had gone off there only a few weeks earlier and the site remained a skeleton of blackened, twisted girders and charred cladding. The forensic studies went on; but not now, because the ruins lay beneath a seething mass of silvery grubs. I pulled to the left and stopped the motors in front of Flinders Street station. Parking had never been so easy. The chittering, rustling sounds of the worms became audible as the last of the GMBMW's momentum drained into the reservoir.

We watched the worms converge on the Square. They came from all directions and in all shapes. Most came as cars, a few as motorcycles, busses, trucks. The layer of silver grew higher. I noticed the tallest ribs of the Federation Square structure fold in and vanish into the sea of worms. I saw a tin foil humanoid figure plough into the mass and become absorbed, its component worms dispersed through the larger agglomeration.

We watched, mesmerised. The pile became higher and higher, its sides flattened and formed little details—window frames, scrollwork, buttresses.

"St Paul's," said Cassy. She seemed to shrink into her seat. "It's mimicking St Paul's."

She was right. The original cathedral sat on one side of the road and a rustling, pulsing, glistening copy of it on the other. And somehow her calling the worms 'it' rather than 'they' seemed to make sense. They were many, but ultimately they were one.

The mock cathedral rose higher as more ersatz cars and people (and dogs and possums) threw themselves into it.

As we watched, a glistening arm, or perhaps tentacle is more accurate, extended out the side of the cathedral of worms. A funnel formed at the end of the tentacle and it came down on top of a parked car—a real one this time. A metallic curtain surrounded the car. And then the car shape began to collapse as if melting. Another tentacle reached out and did the same to another vehicle, and another; and then one by one the tentacles lifted up and we saw piles of fine grey dust where the cars had been. And I fancied that the pile of worms grew bigger after the meal.

I grabbed my receiver out of its socket in the dashboard. "Out!

Get out!"

We leapt from the car just as a tentacle descended. A sound like a million dentist drills vibrated through my body. Instinctively I tensed up and felt around my mouth with my tongue. Then the tentacle rose up and I was the proud owner of a 2014 GMBMW pile of grey ash. Pulverised plastic, glass and rubber made up most of the mass. The worms could eat their way through anything but only did so to get at the metal beneath.

The sight which greeted us was like a vision from Dali, Geiger and Paul all rolled into one. The shape of the cathedral could still be discerned but now dozens of arms sprouted out in all directions. They worked their way across the faces of buildings like some kind of vacuum cleaner, leaving a thin trickle of dust, rejected atoms and molecules in their wake. They crawled along the railway tracks, soaking up the rails and the catenary and the handrails and everything metallic.

A teardrop of worms shot straight up out of the pile with a boom, wrapped itself around the hovering Channel 7 newscopter and fell back with a hissing splash. A small tentacle extruded from the mass and planted three dazed, rumpled men on the footpath. The same thing happened to a couple of cars that raced past.

I turned on my receiver and it scanned through the bands. TV stations were down. A few netcasts braved the aether and a couple of shortwave stations. We picked up a BBC World Service bulletin. The story was the same wherever they crossed to; giant silvery shapes were eating their way through all the biggest cities on Earth. The Statue of Liberty had been eaten by a copy of itself; a mutant Eiffel Tower feasted on Paris, Big Ben rampaged along the banks of the Thames. It went on, with smaller accumulations of worms roaming through suburbs and across the countryside, consuming anything metal they came across, converting it into more and more worms, which then consumed anything metal they came across ...

"Bill, I think we have to get out of here," said Cassy.

I pulled my attention away from the universal receiver.

A tentacle weaved back and forth in front of me like a snake charmer's cobra. I turned and ran, but squirming metallic ropes grabbed me. One curled around my wrist and ate my watch. Another enveloped my receiver. I felt my trousers sag as my belt buckle disappeared. The worms crawled over me, a sickening sensation. They crawled everywhere—and they were not warm. They ate the eyelets from around my shoelaces. I remember being glad my fillings were ceramic and that I had had the screws removed when my broken finger healed. Then they withdrew and my jeans fell down. I hoisted them up (at least I was not naked amidst a pile of denim dust; I thanked the worms for that) and looked around. No hint of the mock cathedral remained. In its place stood a tree, its branches winding tentacles spreading ever further afield. The tentacles started burrowing into the ground, following cables and pipes. Ragged furrows in the concrete and bitumen showed where tram tracks had lain. The tree loomed as tall now as any building except maybe the Rialto. If that still stood.

The giant metal tree writhed in the moonlight. No artificial lighting remained, but we could see the groups of worms still converging on the central mass.

A lump of masonry crashed onto the road a few metres from us. The tentacles were eating away all the metal brackets and bracings in the surrounding buildings. We ran across the bridge towards the gardens and watched. Lights swooped through the sky but did not come close. Reconnaissance, I guessed. Suddenly, thunder rolled across the gardens from all directions at once. Spears of fire streaked towards Federation Square and slid into the creature like skewers into a cake. It roiled and bubbled as it absorbed the explosions and expelled the gases. A cloud of metal snowflakes puffed into the air and fell back to be reabsorbed. The tentacles did not waver but continued stripping the city. They ran through the streets like a network of pipes—we could see one travelling down St Kilda Road, methodically consuming a row of parking meters, change and all.

The squadron of jet fighters screamed away at low level. Faster than the helicopter but not fast enough, three of them ran into iron curtains and were no more; and again thin tentacles extended and delicately placed tiny figures on the ground, unharmed. One came down on our side of the river. Cassy and I ran to him. We found a young man standing, bewildered, on a grassy rise. He held his trousers up with one hand and his flight jacket closed with the other, all the metal fasteners gone.

"What's going on?" said Cassy.

He looked at her blankly for a moment, then blinked a few times. "What's going on?"

"Yes, what's going on?"

"We're at war and we're losing."

We looked at the city. A building sloughed off its top few floors. The rumble of continuously tumbling masonry reached our ears.

He looked at his wrist. "I have to get back to my unit."

"How?" I said.

"It's my duty. A shot-down pilot is to resume the battle as quickly as possible. I—"

"In case you didn't notice, you weren't shot down. You were pulled out of the sky by a giant alien squid tree monster thing."

"Yeah, I was, wasn't I?"

I could see his mind scrolling back through the recent events, as though only now could he believe them to be real and so only now could they put fear into him. On cue, he shivered, although I must admit the night air held a chill.

"What's going on?" I asked him, as much to distract him from his personal experiences as anything else. "Around the world?"

He swallowed and sat down on the grass. "These things are all over the country, all over every country. They're eating up metals, fossil fuels, radioactive elements, all sorts of stuff. They don't bother with oxides or sulphides, or don't seem to, and they're not attacking our bodies. We can't talk to them, we can't stop them. We're trying to blow them up but the energy of the explosions gets dissipated in blowing the mass apart. The worms just crawl back together. Broken ones get swallowed up by the rest of them and we guess reassembled into new ones." He talked quickly, as if giving a report. The routine nature of such a thing helped him calm down. "The US is getting ready to use nukes. They hope that the electromagnetic pulse will fry whatever electronics the worms use; if that doesn't work out, then we're stuck."

"If they head for the metal in the Earth's core, we're more than stuck," I said.

All night the silver tentacles spread out across the city, all night clusters of silvery worms converged in greater and greater numbers on the pulsing mass across the river. It grew into a cylinder that dominated the sky and towered over what little remained of the city. It spilled out onto the streets, wider than a city block, taller than the most grandiose dream tower of western civilisation. I imagined its tentacles draining the oil refineries of their black blood then consuming the refineries themselves.

A couple more sorties threw themselves against the monster, but to no avail. They merely fed it that little bit faster.

I watched through the night while Cassy and the pilot dozed in a flower bed. Just before dawn the tentacles withdrew along the roads around us, retracting into the central mass. The mass started to shift shape again. A point formed at the top, a flared section at the bottom.

I grabbed Cassy's arm and shook. "Get up! Both of you! It's going to take off any minute." Lord knew how far the blast from a rocket of that size would travel. "Run!"

We ran. For all I knew we had ten seconds or ten hours to get away. We ran and ran. Over concrete paths, over grass, past an old bandstand made of stone and wood, past old trees who had lost their metal plaques explaining which Royal had donated them and when, across roads, past brick gateposts without gates, past the ruins of Government House and through its pretty gardens. No obstacles blocked our way. The pilot's training and Cassy's careful diet let them outrun me, but I fought on with my muscles screaming at me and the cold air rasping through my throat—until I heard the roar from behind and leapt into the lee of the broadest tree I could find.

No wall of fire scorched the earth or sucked the oxygen out of the air around me and I turned to watch a vast silver missile standing on a stream of fire as wide as a stadium. The missile gathered momentum impossibly slowly. I pushed my fingers into my ears and squinted into the sky. Looking to the left, I saw another, more distant pillar of exhaust gas, I guessed from somewhere near Geelong. Flames curled up from the remains of the city, now no more than a giant launch pad.

"I'm hungry," said Cassy.

"That could be a problem," I murmured.

The young pilot handed her some sort of military ration.

"Thanks. My name's Cassy."

"Simon."

I noticed one of the tame possums watching us nervously in the dawn half light. It hardly knew less than us about the night's events.

We roamed around the gardens as the sun rose. For now, they were still pretty, with a broad selection of plants and a range of handsome trees.

"What do you think that thing was?" said Cassy as we crossed a torn-up street.

A handful of people milled about in side streets and glanced nervously at the sky and each other.

"Some kind of mining expedition," said Simon, ripping a planting stake out of the ground.

Cassy said: "Maybe aliens who didn't like the way our technology was going."

"An organism," I said. "One that lives off civilisations. It'll get up into space then blow itself apart and spread its little metal grubs across the whole universe. That's why it didn't destroy us completely—it wants us to build up again so its descendants can come back and feed off us again."

"Whatever," shrugged Simon. He lunged with the stake; a possum squealed in agony and twisted for a moment on the point, then sagged. "We better head back towards the city. There seems to be lots of fire there. We'll need to cook this and I don't want to waste my matches."

THE SPACER AND THE
RED HOT MONSTER

TP KEATING

Lights please, Simon." Blinking in the sudden glare, she struggled out of bed, took a quick shower and got dressed. Damn, but the wall chrono gave her barely ten minutes before the midnight rendezvous, ship's time. The whole shenanigans wreaked havoc with her sleep cycle. "Conveyor belt please, Simon."

First came the purple Spacer boots. No, Betty-Lou didn't need their poison dart capacity today. They trundled by. Next, the Day-Glo lemon pair with the flower pattern, complete with a toe-driven 3D holo-recorder. As it wasn't an undercover operation, these too she ignored. The silver boots. Perfection. Not for any hidden agenda, but because they fit her the best.

"We have entered orbit over Keskinel, captain," Simon the computer informed her, in his usual melodious bass tones.

Her boots tugged on, she sashayed over to the full-length mirror. Silver Spacer boots, a brand new cherry red Spacersuit, long blonde hair, green eyes and glittery orange eye-shadow. "Transit-o-matic me now," she ordered.

A microsecond later, she stood in a gigantic marble hall, where seasonal rain tapped against the square windows.

"Good afternoon, space-lane trader Betty-Lou Perkins." For a moment, his Nu Terran blue suit and yellow tie masked his phenomenal alien height. She looked up at the thin, mauve face of a man-like being of who-knew-what age. She estimated him at around 70 feet tall.

"Good afternoon, store master C.T.X. Have I pronounced that correctly?"

"Yes, that'll do. Over there is your cargo." A long mauve finger, with a yellow fingernail, pointed to a stack of wooden crates. She decided that asking if his nails were naturally yellow, or painted that colour, contained a high risk of being taken the wrong way.

"Are you ready to take payment?"

"Always."

She held up a puce plasticon oblong, which he delicately took and slotted into a hand-held computer. A pleasant chime told of a successful credit transfer. C.T.X. dexterously returned the oblong and accompanied his action with a courteous nod, which briefly masked his fine features behind a flop of long, black hair.

"A safe journey then, space-lane trader Betty-Lou Perkins."

"Right back at you, C.T.X. Is there a Mrs C.T.X.?"

"Like I said, have a safe journey." So much for small talk.

"Simon, transit-o-matic me and the crates." Following the almost-instant transition, she found herself momentarily lost. She wasn't on the Arrow. Instead, she'd arrived in a huge cave. In the distance, unseen, a machine produced a regular dull thud. A woman entered through a rock arch: a vermilion-skinned woman, equal in size to store master C.T.X. She wore thigh-high leather boots, a mini-skirt and a bikini top, all in leatheroid.

"Firstly, Betty-Lou Perkins, please accept my apologies for intercepting your transit-o-matic process."

"Simon, can you hear me?" shouted Betty-Lou. The machine kept thud, thud, thudding.

"Down here, you're beyond sensor range."

"How far down?"

"Two miles."

"By the lost bones of the great galactic kings." She whipped out the thunderstick from the synthomesh holster on her right thigh. "You're after my cargo, aren't you?"

"Captain, the Volcano People are immune to thundersticks."

"Huh? What's a volcano person?"

"Our correct name is the Volkas, though Volcano People is an acceptable, if somewhat literal translation. But you're right; we've confiscated your cargo. Though we're willing to give you very reasonable terms for it."

"Terms, my recycling unit. It's credit or nothing."

"Then you'll get nothing."

"Terms, you say? Well, I am a space-lane trader. Carry on, you've got my undivided attention." Plus, if the thunderstick really doesn't work on these people, my bargaining power is zero, thought Betty-Lou, returning the weapon to its holster. Also, even if it did work, where could I go? Simon would be working out what happened during the transit-o-matic sequence, but how long would it take him to locate her? If he could at all. "Actually, if you're Volcano People, how come this is a leatheroid clothes environment?"

"We're not barbarians, captain. Our air conditioning is very advanced." Betty-Lou recognised a trading opportunity when she heard one.

"Have you ever exported that technology?"

"Only through our own outlets. That's why we're confiscating your cargo. If the Surfikas, or those you call the Surface Dwellers, were to get hold of it, the consequences would be dire in the extreme."

"Dire? What, getting some decent air-conditioning. How could that be dire?"

"Because we sell sealed units which self-destruct if tampered with. To be blunt, ours is an economy dependent on one export, air-conditioning. Without that monopoly, well, we'd face a very uncertain future."

"Curious. The Surface Dwellers aren't dullards when it comes to science and technology."

"True. It's a cultural matter."

"Excuse me?"

"And neither people will discuss cultural matters with an Outerkas, or Off Worlder."

"Great. Go on then, what terms can you offer me?"

"A deluxe, cutting-edge air-conditioning unit for deep-space flight. Small and highly portable, it can turn a close brush with a star into the cold between galaxies. If the cover is removed, all life in the vicinity gets obliterated. Understand?"

"Completely. That's it?"

"Passage out of here is included in the terms."

"If I don't accept?"

"Non-acceptance means death."

"Then I accept your gracious offer. Can I choose the colour of the air-conditioning unit?"

"No. This season's shade is taupe."

"Taupe? Yuk." The vermilion face glared at her. "That is, *yuk* that there's only one unit in the deal."

Back on the flight deck of the Arrow, it took a few seconds to adjust to surroundings of a human proportion.

"There you are, captain." For a computer, Simon sounded mighty relieved. "What, no cargo? Ah, I see you've exchanged it for that sealed ultra-plasticon whatever. What is it?"

"A portable air-conditioning unit."

"Wow, it must be extremely good, because you're allergic to taupe and you've swapped it for several crates full of diamonds."

"Diamonds? Our contract was for calculators. What are the Surfikas up to?"

"When Surface Dwellers indulge in a little smuggling, 'calculator' is their standard euphemism. You did study the Spacer training vids on their culture, didn't you? So tell me, what's a Surfikas?"

"We'd call them Surface Dwellers." As if Simon couldn't work that out for himself.

"So, your trade really was intentional. In which case, I can't wait to see the air-conditioning in action." On the com panel, she flicked a switch to the position labelled "Off", which silenced the computer. With a few twists of a blue dial, together with the pressing of a blue button, she erased his memory of events since her return. Captain's prerogative, on a one-woman ship. She swivelled in her chair and gave a look of bad intent at the taupe monstrosity. Hell, it filled fully a quarter of the flight deck. She returned the switch to the "On" position.

"Ah, there you are captain," said Simon. "Didn't see you arrive. Where's your cargo?"

"I sold it while on the surface. Got the plasticon credit right here in my pocket." She tapped the left breast pocket of her cherry-red Spacersuit.

"What's that? Isn't it taupe? What's inside? Here, I'll open it."

"Nooooo," she screamed. But a golden ray from the ceiling made a complete circuit of one side in seconds, which clattered to the floor. She remained disturbingly unexploded. Inside, it was hollow and empty.

"Well, I can't say I'm not disappointed. Why the outcry, Betty-Lou?"

"Tension headache. Think I'll retire to my quarters for a rest."

Yeah, hollow and empty. That summed up how she felt about being duped out of her precious cargo. What fool said that space-lane trading consisted of one thrill after another? Her, chatting up a handsome space-freighter captain at a party last week.

Before she reached the door, goosebumps appeared on her arms and rapidly spread all over. Brrr, but she'd never sleep with the ship's thermostat set so low. She must've knocked it by accident on the com desk. No, apparently not. A faulty air vent then? She followed her outstretched hand, as it grew colder, tracking the source of the chill. Which led her to the ultra-plasticon box. At six feet from the open side, it felt like being thrown outside naked in a polar region.

Her plucked eyebrows shot up. "I'll be zapped into atoms, the Volcano People really do specialise in air-conditioning." They specialised in excellent sales pitches, too. When it began to wear out, you'd buy a new unit, rather than risk an explosion. "Simon."

"Hiya, Betty-Lou."

"Any planets suffering from global warming recently?"

"The nations of Follian are holding a series of emergency summits."

"Then set a course for Follian, best speed."

In her quarters once more, she tugged off her silver Spacer boots and dumped them on the conveyor belt. Wearing her favourite silver pyjamas with the kitten motifs, she flopped down onto the red silk sheets of her bed. Best speed would be followed by best sale for best profit, she considered. So, hollow and empty can provide a full experience after all. Cool.

"Lights please, Simon."

☆

The red warning light blinked like an irritated eye above the bedroom door, while the ship's alarm wailed as if goaded by the same discomfort. "And good morning to you, too," said Betty-Lou wryly. "Simon, report please." He didn't reply to that or several further requests. Swiftly donning her Spacersuit, she rushed to a com panel. "WARNING, CRASH LANDING IMMINENT!" screamed the large red letters. She opened a closet door and wedged herself in amongst the variety of different coloured Spacersuits, while the ship lurched violently. A particularly severe jolt pushed her deeper into the closet. The Arrow fell still again, the alarm and the warning light halted. A collapsing shelf had broken her com screen during the landing, scattering books and glass all over the floor. She escaped her quarters.

Fires raged, blocking every route to the flight deck. Thick smoke threatened to choke her. The uncontrolled conflagrations, coupled with the lack of a computer, meant that she had no choice. She had to assess the damage from outside, and an airlock lay nearby. Reaching the airlock within a minute, she slipped on a cherry-red helmet and oxygen backpack, which matched her Spacersuit. Through the door panel she saw sand, stretching all the way to the horizon, beneath a cloudless blue sky. She pushed the control lever up and stepped out.

The intense heat on her back forced her away from the ship, until she turned in response to an explosion behind her. Fire engulfed the vessel, all along the external silver fins on the sleek, black fuselage. Her view shifted to her left, her attention caught by a large object: one of numerous tall buildings, including pyramids, towers and spheres, ankle deep in sand. Inside the helmet, the readout told of a moderate temperature and a breathable atmosphere.

"Helmet-com, are you there?" She sounded rather plaintive.

"Don't worry, Betty-Lou, I downloaded myself to the helmet-com system when the ship was an obvious goner."

"Simon, thank the great galactic planet crusher, it's you. Where are we?"

"At the abandoned city of Havenville, on planet Voci."

"Yeah, I remember. The Surfikas left it to rot about 55 Standard Galactic Years ago. An attempted pleasure city, but shipping enough water here proved uneconomical." A shadow fell over Betty-Lou. A huge shadow. She turned to find a giant creature on fire. No, it didn't writhe or cry out in pain. Rather, it was *made of* fire. A flickering, burning humanoid, fully 100 feet tall, which snatched up a piece of the Arrow to examine in its blazing right hand. Then it dropped the molten debris, to scoop up another piece.

"Simon, is that monstrosity a native?"

"Negative. It sprang from the air-conditioning unit. It was all I could do to down-load myself before the ship's computer fried."

"The Volkas take their threats seriously, it appears."

"Meanwhile, I strongly suggest that you take refuge in Havenville."

"What, run in that sand and ruin my favourite boots?"

"You've got a better plan, have you?"

"The thought of scampering along with a fire-being on my tail doesn't exactly enthral me. You've seen the monster holo-movies. Creatures like that tend to climb tall buildings, if not devour them, while fending off whole armies. No, I'd be trapping myself, like some stuntwoman playing a dumb sap about to get squashed. An extremely attractive stuntwoman, mind you, who the holo-camera lingers on. If I've even got a minor chance of success, I've got to make a stand right here."

"Bravo, a most stirring speech. But what action do you propose?"

"You're one sarcastic computer."

"Like programmer, like machine."

The creature thrust its arms skywards and from each massive digit emitted a jet of fire, each of which raced towards the heavens. The arms dropped down and it turned a head of flame in her direction, regarding Betty-Lou from two charred-black eyes with a somewhat contradictory coolness. Before bellowing "Roarrrarrrrgh!"

Betty-Lou unsheathed the thunderstick and set it at "Overdrive", then pointed the ashen rod at the wreckage of the Arrow. "Let's compare your firearms with mine, hot stuff. Simon, tell me when I'm aiming at the hyper-secure storage compartment."

"But captain, that's where we keep the oxybombs, remember? Ah, of course, you do remember. Right eight degrees. Up four degrees. Fire!"

The wildly pulsing yellow light of the over-concentrated negatron beam hit home, turning a small circle on the storage compartment wall to ashes. An intense blue flash heralded the destruction of the entire compartment, producing a shock wave that knocked her onto the sand. A ferocious roar accompanied it.

Painfully, she lifted her head up. Of the fire-creature, no sign. "Simon, did I succeed?"

"Betty-Lou, your plan worked perfectly. The explosion temporarily removed all the oxygen from the atmosphere, so asphyxiating our friend from the air conditioning. It's extinguished, if you will. Now you can breathe."

"Yeah, extinguished, just like Havenville. Send the standard Spacer distress message, Simon. I'm done trading here."

BREAKING THE ICE

MAXINE MCARTHUR

The footsteps stopped. Huddled under the low bridge, Kaoru stuffed his fist into his mouth to stop the whimper escaping. *Please, go on. Don't find me.*

More giant footsteps ground on the rusty girders and vibrated into Kaoru's shoulders. He was jammed into the tiny space. Surely they'd think he couldn't fit in here ...

A shrill buzz drilled into his ears. What ... no, it couldn't be ... He scraped his elbow painfully against the concrete support as he jammed his hand in his pocket and thumbed the 'Off' key. The thing kept ringing. Desperately he thumbed the 'Receive' key ...

A hand grabbed his sleeve. With a satisfied "Got him!" the enemy yanked Kaoru out of his refuge.

He struggled feebly against the grip on his arm. "Leave me alone."

The two worst bullies in his class: Ariyoshi and Nakata. *Bastards, oni, demons,* Kaoru spat at them in his mind. But his body just stood sullenly beside Nakata. He'd learned the futility of fighting back years ago.

Ariyoshi jumped down from the footbridge and wrinkled his nose at the mess of beer cans, cigarette butts, and dried vomit in the ditch.

"Stinks down here." He slapped Kaoru casually across the head. "You stink."

Kaoru's ears buzzed and he staggered against Nakata's wide chest. Nakata shoved him back.

Ariyoshi lit a cigarette with his special silver lighter and tucked the lighter away carefully in the pocket of his non-regulation scarlet shirt. Nakata lit up, too, using an orange plastic 100-yen lighter. They grinned at each other and both blew the smoke into Kaoru's face.

Kaoru squeezed his eyes shut and tried not to cough. *They'll finish soon they'll finish soon they'll* ...

"Where's your weekly contribution?" Ariyoshi puffed. "You're two days behind."

"I ... I didn't get any lunch money," Kaoru heard his voice

squeak. "My mum made lunch for me."

"'My mum made it for me,'" mimicked Nakata. His livid, pimple-filled face clashed with his carroty dyed hair.

A housewife carrying bulging plastic bags from the supermarket glanced over at the unused footpath and bridge, but hurried on when she saw the black uniforms. Kainan Junior High students were to be avoided.

"No excuses." Ariyoshi shoved his face into Kaoru's.

The burning eyes and nicotine-heavy breath filled Kaoru's universe. He scrambled backwards but Nakata was in the way.

"I'll get it, I'll get it. Tomorrow. I promise I will, I'll get it." He was sobbing with fear, apprehension, remembered pain.

"You better." Ariyoshi leaned back, smoothed his gel-slick hair and lit another cigarette. "Check his bag."

Kaoru choked off another cry as Nakata dragged his school bag from under the footbridge and upended it. The contents hit the ground in a shower of textbooks, notebooks, lunch box, calculator, loose paper, MD player and gym t-shirt. His pencil case burst and pencils rolled everywhere.

"Hey, that's a better calculator than mine." Nakata pounced. "The MD's too old, but."

"You oughta get some new stuff, stink-arse," said Ariyoshi. "This lot's not worth stealing."

That's the point, moron. Kaoru kept looking at his feet. His pencil sharpener had come to rest beside his right toe.

"What's this?" Nakata grinned ferally. "Still playing with toys, are we?" He held up the small plastic figure of a monster, one of the daikaiju who battled superheroes of TV and manga.

"It's not mine," protested Kaoru. "It's my kid brother's." Masaki had given it to him to fix at school in his craft class, because one of the legs had snapped off during too-strenuous aerial manoeuvres between kitchen table and sink.

"Playing wiv liddle bruvver's toys, now?" Nakata cooed.

On the other side of the footbridge adult voices rose in a real altercation.

Ariyoshi's handsome face blanched and he turned away. "Let's go."

Nakata kicked as much of Kaoru's stuff under the footbridge as he could, then followed. As they sauntered away, Nakata stopped and, obviously so Kaoru could see, broke the monster figure in half. Or tried to—the hard plastic resisted. With a curse, Nakata chucked it away. The little monster hit the concrete with a crack, and ricocheted off at an angle.

Kaoru bit back his moan. At least this time he wasn't going home with half the skin scraped off his face. Coming up with explanations to fool Mum was worse than the pain.

He squatted in the ditch and collected everything, not bothering to brush off the dirt as he stuffed things back in his bag. The pencil case's hinge was broken. It didn't matter—he'd given up carrying things that mattered.

The two men quarreling on the other side of the footbridge had calmed down a bit. One of them, a sharp-faced gangster type in a faded floral shirt, patted the other over-familiarly on the chest as he made a point. The other nodded sulkily. No wonder Ariyoshi had headed off so quickly; the sharp-faced man was his dad. Ariyoshi said he worked as muscle down at the pachinko parlour. The other kids thought he just lazed around.

The little monster wasn't there. He crawled over the stained concrete for what seemed like hours. His knees ached from crouching. He would be late for juku. Why was he bothering? He should just tell Masaki he left the toy at school. Or say it had been stolen. It was only a cheap plastic model, after all.

But in the end he found it, half inside a hollow concrete block, grey-camouflaged where once the shaggy moulded fur had been ice-white. The raised claws and snarling teeth once glowed yellow, the bulging eyes had been blood red. Three … four years ago, he'd wasted some of his New Year money on a 'bargain bag' at the local toy store. Even though he'd bought a '12 years and over' bag, it was full of junk like the plastic monster: a leaking water pistol, and character cards he'd thrown away in grade one. He gave the monster to Masaki, who loved it.

As Kaoru picked it up, the leg fell off again. He flushed with anger at the bullies. Dickheads. Fuckwits. Now he'd have to go through all the hassle of smuggling the monster into craft class and secretly gluing it again. He didn't have any proper glue at home.

The autumn sun was already off the narrow lane and all the buildings on this side of the street. The grey canyon was damp and chilly. Most of the shop signs were old, the colours faded. Nobody shopped along this road any more, except the old people who didn't have obliging grandchildren to drive them out to the superstores.

As he climbed out of the ditch and trudged home beside the rumbling traffic, his phone vibrated in his pocket. That's right, it was because of the stupid phone he'd been discovered. He was sure he'd had it turned off all day. This call would be his mother, demanding to know where he was. Or somebody selling things.

Strange. The activate light was off but it still buzzed. He pressed 'Receive' automatically.

The screen said simply, <Do you want revenge?>.

He sighed and pressed the delete pad, then slipped the phone back into his pocket. Whatever hot new product 'Revenge' was, he didn't want any. He'd made the mistake once of answering an online sale, and they pestered him until he had to dump the phone and tell Mum he'd lost it.

At home on the ninth floor of the apartment block, Masaki played a game on the big TV screen. On the old TV, half the size, a rerun of *Ultraseven* spooled on slowly. Both the *pico-pico trrrilll* of the game and the tinny music from the TV were running at full volume.

"Where's Mum?" shouted Kaoru. She wasn't here, or Masaki wouldn't have the sound so loud.

Masaki pointed at the kitchen with the controller, his eyes not leaving the screen. His round, six-year-old features were set in concentration.

There was a note on the kitchen table beside a tray with covered bowls. The note read, 'Kaoru, I've gone to the P&C meeting. Make sure you lock the door behind you when you go out. Masaki isn't to keep watching TV.'

"Mum says turn the TV off," Kaoru yelled.

Masaki kept his eyes on the screen. "Okay." But he made no attempt to do it.

Kaoru sighed and peeked under the lids of the bowls. Hamburgers, with steamed cauliflower, potatoes and carrots. And rice. The soup bowls each held a turd-like brown curl of instant miso, ready for hot water.

He wished Mum would hurry up and finish this 'home-cooked' fad. He preferred the defrosted microwave gratins and fried rice of old.

In the bedroom he shared with Masaki he took the plastic monster out of his bag and managed to prop it between two boxes of ninja cards in his desk drawer. He needed some proper tools —a clamp, for a start ... but why bother? When would he build models—in his ten minutes of free time after dinner? He used some glue he'd found in the kitchen drawer and held it while the glue set. It wasn't as good a job as he'd done at school—he'd have to scrape the overflow of glue away after it set properly—but Masaki wouldn't notice. He shut the drawer carefully.

Shit. He was late for juku. He grabbed his second bag and ran full-tilt out the door, forgetting to check the lock so he had to sprint back and then missed the lift down. By the time he reached the cram school, which was in a building near the station five blocks away, sweat was stinging in the corners of his eyes and his heart pounded shamefully in the certainty of humiliation to come.

He tried to sneak into the classroom, but the teacher, a hearty bully concerned with his own popularity points, made a big thing out of his lateness.

"Perhaps our clock-reading skills need revising?" he boomed. All the students turned to stare and the two girls sitting directly in front of Kaoru's back-row seat giggled.

Kaoru sat, his face burning. Smart quip, come on, you can think of a comeback if you try ...

"The elementary classes are in the next building, you know." More girls giggled.

Just as the teacher lost interest, Kaoru's phone rang. He froze in disbelief, then plunged his hand in his pocket, letting go his textbooks to do so, but the textbooks cascaded onto the floor and he had the wrong pocket and everybody was giggling this time ...

The teacher loomed over him. "You know the rules about phones, Hoshino?"

"Y ... yes. But I turned it off, I did ..." he stammered, which was a waste of time and only prolonged the agony of more sarcasm.

The teacher finally turned back to the whiteboard. Kaoru stacked his textbooks, trembling. *Leave me alone, leave me alone leave me ...*

"Don't let him get you down." The girl next to him, Emiko Tada, leaned over slightly and muttered out of the corner of her mouth. "He's a prick. And a small one, at that."

Shocked, Kaoru flicked a glance at her. Tada was known as a slob. She came to juku in old sweaters and stained jeans. She didn't style her hair like other girls, or use lip gel, or carry a fluffy phone case, or even use a phone at all. And now she'd been nice to him and he didn't know what to say, and it was too late because Tada was looking back at her books thinking he was a snob for not even acknowledging her kindness. He was hopeless.

And why had the stupid phone rung? He had definitely turned it off, but the screen still said, <Do you want revenge?>

Yes! a voice inside him screamed.

<Yes> he typed.

The screen went blank. Oh great, he'd probably accepted a virus that would screw his address file. With all of its two or three names.

The teacher's drone faded. The hunched beetle-backs of his fellow students faded. White light surrounded him.

Good, maybe he was dead.

If so, he had come to a frozen part of hell. He was striding across a plain of ice that reached to the horizon on all sides except one—when he looked behind, a jagged white mountain range pierced grey sky. A wind solid with sleet played around his ears, but it didn't feel cold. Must be a dream. His feet crunched on frozen snow ... *his* feet? He stopped striding and looked down.

Long dark claws poked out of toes covered with a carpet of thick, yellow-white hair. The rest of the feet, the legs, the ... he was completely covered with pelt. No wonder he wasn't cold. His arms ended in stubby fingers tipped with the same claws as his toes. It all seemed familiar.

He laughed out loud, and a roar was whipped away by the wind. The ice-monster. He'd stared at that little model for so long he was dreaming about it. He started striding again. It felt good. The snow subsided like crusted sand under bare feet; when he swung those long arms his whole body rocked from side to side, and he roared again, just to hear how loud it was and then to hear how even that loudness disappeared into the frozen wasteland. Best of all, he was completely and utterly alone.

Something glinted on the ice nearby. He stopped and bent

over to see better, growling in annoyance at the effort this took. Kaiju bodies weren't very flexible.

A lighter? He laughed at the incongruity. Nothing to light here.

A silver lighter. Like the one Ariyoshi used. As he stared, anger surged up in his throat in a snarl that heated his entire body. He scooped up the metal sliver with his claw and crushed it in his palm.

It was so easy.

"Hoshino-kun. Hoshino-kun!" Tada's whisper replaced the howling of the wind.

Kaoru blinked at the sight of the teacher sauntering down the line of desks, checking homework. He fumbled his notebook open and glanced at Tada.

"Thanks," he whispered back.

Tada shrugged, but her eyes laughed.

What a weird dream! Not very symbolic (he had read all the books about dreams, it was the fad-before-last, and he knew symbolic dreams should be obscure and preferably involve food or sexually significant objects), but definitely therapeutic. He felt better than he had for ages. A pity he couldn't smash Ariyoshi's real lighter.

☆

"Stay away from the gang of three," warned one of the few boys in Kaoru's class who bothered to talk to him. "Ariyoshi's pissed off big time."

Kaoru nodded thanks. It was the day after his daydream at the cram school and he wanted to stay away from everyone, not just the gang. He had dutifully studied until 3am for today's math test, but still hadn't answered all the questions. He didn't even want to be a doctor, he was going to make a terrible doctor ... Mum gave him lunch money, but not enough for the gang. And the plastic monster's leg fell off again when he took it out of the drawer. A rod would be the best way of making sure the leg stayed on, but every method he thought of required more time and tools than he had.

"What's going on?" said one of the others. "Ari's dad been beating him up again?" There was a general guffaw, hastily muffled.

"Someone smashed his lighter," said the first boy. "Ran a car over it, they reckon."

Kaoru didn't hear the rest of the conversation. A chill spread from his stomach over his whole body. It must be a coincidence. His dream couldn't possibly have picked up on an event in the real world.

I'm glad Ariyoshi's hurting, gloated a small voice deep inside him. It sounded like the ice monster's voice.

No, you're not, Kaoru shot back. He's going to make life hell for the rest of us. More like hell, he revised.

☆

This time, the dream seemed to take much longer. Kaoru raged across the frozen land, each roar a protest at his roar-less existence in the real world. The monster's body felt comfortable to him now, and he loved the sensation of power.

The juku sign hung in the air. He didn't question why it was there. He just ran his fist through it. Didn't even sting. Crunch. That stupid teacher. Smash. Couldn't get employed at a real school, so he taught at juku. Crack. Always using the weakest kids to make himself look smarter. Splinter. Keeping us late so we have even less of a life than we would anyway ...

The sign shattered completely.

There, that feels better, doesn't it? chuckled the ice-monster.

☆

"Tanaka-sensei phoned. You're to finish the workbook exercises," his mother called into his room later that afternoon.

Kaoru jumped and shoved the drawer shut on the plastic monster. He couldn't work out a way to drill a hole small enough for a wire rod.

"What are you talking about?" he yelled back.

"You know, the juku teacher." Mum stood in the doorway of his room, spatula in hand. "There's no juku tonight. Vandals trashed the place, apparently."

"What, the whole place?" Kaoru heard himself ask, and immediately wondered if she'd notice the strangeness of the question. The sign in his dream, he'd only smashed the sign.

It couldn't be another coincidence.

What have I done?

I didn't mean to.

"Kaoru, are you all right? You look peaky." Mum placed her hand on his forehead. "I'll get you some multivitamins. You know how important your grades are this year. We don't expect you to pass the uni exams first time, but you know you'll have to get into the top twenty to get into the supplementary school—" He tuned out, and finally she left.

He didn't mean to smash everything. What was going on? Maybe someone was playing a stupid joke on him, messing with his mind. The phone! He'd turned it off, though, hadn't he? He might have typed 'Yes', drowsy and stupid, then slumped back to sleep with his head on the desk. Only for a minute or so, at the end of home-room time this afternoon. Nobody took any notice—kids stole a few minutes of sleep at school all the time, it meant they were fresh for juku in the evening.

Maybe the phone message caused the dreams. That must be it. Some company was trialling a method of implanting subliminal suggestions in people's minds. So they couldn't hold him responsible for trashing the juku.

Anyway, a sneaky thought prompted, they'd never know it was him. Nobody would suspect or be able to find out. He could get away with murder. Not literally, of course. He'd never hurt anyone ...

He stared across the open workbook to the faded movie poster on the wall above his desk. The boy hero confronted an insect monster bigger than a house, the proboscis longer than the boy's body. Wavy lines in sunset colours surrounded the two figures, indicating the event was happening in an alternate dimension. He'd had that poster since he was in grade one. Until now, he'd always identified with the boy.

So what if his dream of the ice monster was connected with reality? It wouldn't help him keep away from Ariyoshi and his sycophants, not unless he could metamorphose into the creature when he wanted to. It wouldn't help him finish this stupid math that he couldn't understand and never would.

"I'm going out for a walk," he yelled on his way past the kitchen. The sizzle of frying onions competed with the burr of the exhaust fan.

"Take a jacket," called his mother.

Masaki waved at him from in front of the TV, eyes reflecting *Gundam*.

☆

He regretted coming out as soon as he left the building. What if Ariyoshi and the gang were hanging around?

The sky was blue with coming night and the shadows between streetlights were dark. He looked up and down the street, but could see only a few people hurrying home from the station. In the park, elderly walkers chatted as they followed the path around the fenced baseball ground. Around and around they went, unworried and unflurried. Past the age of having to get family dinners, evening was a good time for them. Kaoru thought of his father, off to work before the family woke, home after they were asleep. I suppose I'll have to wait until I'm old before I can relax.

"Hey, Hoshino," a voice called from the swings.

He tensed, ready to run, but it was a girl's voice. In the gloom he could just make out Tada, rocking the preschool-low swing with her knees almost dragging on the ground. The swing creaked rustily each time she pushed it back.

"No juku, so I thought I'd get some fresh air," she said cheerfully. "You going somewhere?"

"No," said Kaoru and, greatly daring, sat on the other swing. It squeaked.

They creaked and squeaked for a while without saying anything. If this were a manga, he'd tell her his problem and she'd offer him sympathy and say something smart to solve it. But of course manga were never like real life. Who'd read them if they were?

"What do you want to do with your life, Hoshino?" said Tada suddenly.

"Wha-at?" Kaoru stared at her in disbelief, but it was too dark to see her expression. The question was so alien to his thoughts that he would have been more comfortable if she had asked him how yellow smells.

"You know," she went on in that abrupt, confronting manner of hers. "What did you always want to do when you were a kid?"

Kaoru laughed uneasily. "Same as most boys, I suppose. Be a baseball star, a pilot, game designer, I dunno." Monster-slayer, he added silently.

Tada's swing creaked a bit more. "What about now?"

He should get off the swing and go home. Tada was strange in the head. You didn't ask questions like this of someone you hardly knew. He never asked them of himself.

But he answered. "It doesn't really matter, does it?" He would spend the next five or six years struggling to get into a mediocre medical school because, sometime during his childhood, somehow it had been decided that he would become a doctor. He didn't even think he could pass the supplementary school exams, let alone medical school ...

"Of course it matters." Tada stopped her swing with the scrunch of sandals dragging through dirt. "No wonder you look so wet if you think like that."

"What about you, then?" retorted Kaoru, stung by her scorn and emboldened by the darkness.

"I'm going to breed dogs," she said contentedly. "I'll get a day job, then when I've got a bit of capital I'll buy a place to build runs. It'll have to be in the country, of course, you can't do things like that in Osaka. I've got a budget and everything."

Kaoru felt his mouth opening in awe.

"It's because I like dogs," she said. "What do you like?"

Being left alone, he wanted to say, but didn't.

"What's the most fun thing you've done recently?" she pressed.

Stomp and roar and smash things, grinned the ice-monster voice inside him.

"I ... I'm fixing a model," he said hastily, anything to avoid the thought of lighters and signs crumbling in his fist.

"There you go, then." Tada stood up, her jacket rustling. "You'll probably be an engineer or something. See you tomorrow." She ran lightly across the park and vanished in the gloom of the camellia hedge.

☆

He was nearly asleep when the phone rang. He rocketed upright and snatched it off the bedside table before it woke Masaki. Found it, pressed 'Receive', stared uncomprehendingly at the message that shouldn't be there because the battery was drained.

<Do you want revenge?>

<Who are you?> he typed. Nothing happened. He stayed hunched over the little blue screen in the dark, the only sound the shush-shush of the air-conditioner.

<Shall I show you?>

Kaoru hesitated, then typed <yes>.

The screen's blue light flickered, then glowed brighter and brighter until it filled the whole room with blue-white radiance. Kaoru flung up his hand to protect his eyes then realised the light didn't hurt. He *liked* the brightness. He liked being strong and fearless and invulnerable.

The wind blew across the ice plain with a wail like all the spirits of the dead. He didn't care. No wind could blow him over.

A flat rectangle tumbled over and over through the air. He reached out an arm longer than a telephone pole and caught it. Elaborate characters ran from top to bottom on one side of a wooden board. He recognised the name of the local gang. This was off the door of their headquarters, a narrow building squashed between the butcher and a funeral parlour. Ariyoshi's dad was a member. He cocked his head at the board, then, remembering the juku sign, ripped the wood in two with the fingers of one hand and flipped away the pieces. That would teach those loudmouthed bastards, always swaggering around, thinking they could get away with anything.

He noticed the ice plain nearby was covered in irregular bumps tracked through with darker lines. He peered at the bumps and saw they were snow-covered squares and rectangles. Houses? They looked like they were made of blocks or cardboard cartons, a kindergarten playscape. He remembered the daikaiju movies and roared lustily. All those boring lives: bullying teachers, moronic little brothers, nagging mums, work-sodden fathers ... He roared again. Who needs them?

He stomped, and was gratified to see the nearest houses shudder. Stomped again, closer. The roof of one house rose upwards then broke in the middle, exactly like a cardboard carton house. He blustered and stamped his way through the town until he came out the other side, back to the ice plain. It was only a small town, he noticed with disappointment.

☆

Kaoru jerked awake, sweating on top of his futon as though he'd run a marathon. The digital clock glowed 4:00. He lay there for a while, not wanting to think about the dream. On the other side of the room, Masaki lay in a mound with the futon over his head, as usual.

One way to find out if the dream was connected with the real world. Kaoru slid his legs over the side of the bed, tottered to his little TV, and flicked through the muted channels. Porn, gossip, sport, gossip, game show repeat, porn, samurai drama ... on the bottom of the screen, hiding the wicked merchant's dying gasp, ran a line of text: *Earthquake in Hokkaido at 0300 hours magnitude 6 town in ruins.*

The remote slid out of his palms, which were suddenly slippery with sweat. I don't want to hurt anybody, he thought pathetically.

His stomach heaved and he clamped his teeth on the threat of
vomit. It didn't seem like a real town, it was only cardboard...
    The phone buzzed. He grabbed it.
    <Do you feel better?>
    <Go away> he typed.
    <I can make you feel better.>
    He flung down the phone, pulled on a pair of tracksuit pants
over his pajamas, grabbed his jacket, and went to leave. But what
if the phone kept ringing and woke Mum? Or worse, what if it
woke Masaki and he answered? With a helpless gulp, he picked
up the phone and dropped it in his pocket.
    Outside, the cool air dried the sweat and tears on his face. He
crossed the park where he'd met Tada earlier, not bothering to be
nervous of dark shadows. He trudged past the primary school,
with its high open fences. Opposite the school, a light shone in
the window of the newspaper delivery office. Everywhere else was
dark.
    What if people had been killed in the earthquake? Did that
make him a murderer? But he didn't know it was real. Tears
blurred the darkness.
    He kept walking, around the corner and past the kindergarten.
On his right, behind a wire fence, ran the railway tracks. He'd
have to go to the level crossing to get onto the tracks themselves.
At this time of night there'd be nobody to notice or stop him. The
first train would pass through at about four-thirty.
    There was someone lying on the footpath. A hunched bundle
that made a snoring, slobbering sound.
    As soon as he noticed, he stood still, hoping he hadn't been
seen. A drunk? In case the drunk reached out to grab him, he
edged past on the other side of the narrow street.
    A voice wheezed, "Help me."
    Keep going. He was only a kid; he couldn't carry a drunk
home or go and report it to the police because they'd want to know
what he was doing wandering the streets at 4am and he couldn't
say, it's because I have this problem with turning into a monster,
could he? It wasn't his job to clean up after irresponsible adults.
He just wanted to stay out of trouble. Then he realised he knew
the voice.
    His heart thudding, the phone in his pocket forgotten, he
edged closer. One of Ariyoshi's eyes blinked back at him. The street
light on the corner gave enough light to see that the other eye was
swollen shut. Most of his face was swollen or bloodstained, and he
lay curled up as though it hurt too much to move. But he could
still raise his head slightly and groan, "Stinky."
    "What happened?" Kaoru's shocked voice sounded high like
a child's.
    "The ol' man ..." Ariyoshi forced the words through cut and
puffed lips. "Thought I took the gang's door ... sign ..."
    Kaoru's phone buzzed and jiggled in his pocket.

"Go ...'way." Ariyoshi shut his good eye.

Kaoru didn't want to look at the screen, but his hand held the phone of its own accord.

<Get rid of him>

What?

As if he'd typed a reply, the screen said, <Everyone will think the father did it. You'll be free. No more bullying>.

<I can't do that> he typed, shocked.

<I can do it for you>

The ice monster would enjoy it. The ice monster would help him get his own back for all the years of torture and misery and playing humble. Nobody would ever know. After all this time, he had power. He could destroy whole towns. He looked down at Ariyoshi, and it was as if he looked down from a great height. All around them blew wind full of icicles. All he had to do was reach out his hand and close it around Ariyoshi's neck. This time he knew what he was doing. There would be no excuses.

And when he'd got rid of all the bullies?

He'd be alone on the ice plain.

What do you want to do? whispered Tada's voice in the wind.

He looked down, this time at the phone in his hand. He didn't want to stay alone on the ice plain, even if he was the greatest monster ever.

The first train would come through at four-thirty.

He ran back around the corner to the newspaper delivery office and pounded on their door. A bleary-eyed man in layers of cheap sweatshirts opened it cautiously.

"Someone's been mugged," Kaoru panted. "On the path. Outside the kindergarten. Call an ambulance."

The man narrowed his eyes. "Is this a joke?"

"It's no joke!" Kaoru yelled.

The man flinched and turned to a phone on the wall. "Okay, okay."

Kaoru waited until he heard the man say the street number then ran again. Down the streets of sleeping houses, through the urine-dank underpass, past the shuttered grocery store to the level crossing. The barriers were raised, and he slid down the edge of the road and ran about a hundred metres along the tracks, left the phone and dashed back to the crossing.

There he waited, shuffling his feet and peering anxiously at the tracks that curved east, glinting under the line of lights. The tracks ticked. In the distance he heard the cling-clang of the level crossing in the next suburb. At the same time, the phone on the tracks started ringing, with a sound all out of proportion to the source, rising until it drowned out the clanging of this crossing, rising until Kaoru put his hands over his ears and screamed with agony.

<You can be strong>

The words glowed on the screen of his mind.

<You can show them ...>

Under the wheels of the train green sparks flared once, then vanished. The only sound was the fading growl of the engine.

☆

"I fixed your model."

A week later, Kaoru placed the plastic ice monster on Masaki's desk, already crowded with robots, aliens, spaceships, rangers and racing cars.

Masaki actually put down his game screen and stood up to take a proper look. "Hey, you can't even tell where it broke." His goggle eyes regarded Kaoru with new respect.

"Pretty good, hey?" Kaoru grinned, but a bit uneasily. He still felt horrible about the earthquake and concentrating on fixing the monster had been a way to forget that for a while. The wire rod idea had worked. He'd spent a week's worth of lunch money on new tools, but he still didn't have enough time to use them.

So he'd made a decision. Engineers fix things. Things like ruined towns.

"I'm not going to juku tonight, Mum." He poked his head around the kitchen door. His mother stopped in the middle of stirring a pot of stock, a recipe book held in one hand.

"Are you sick?" she said.

"No." He kept going on his way to the door as he spoke, otherwise he'd end up in a debate that would last till bedtime. He'd tell her about not going to med school later. "I'm only going twice a week from now on."

"Kaoru! Your grades ..."

"I'll manage." As he shoved his feet into his shoes he could hear the spoon being dropped into the sink, the gas being turned off, and the recipe book slamming down on the table.

"I'll be back later," he yelled. Tada was waiting for him in the park.

Beneath Southern Waves

Shane Jiraiya Cummings

S trange stuff's been happening in these parts for a few days now," the ranger drawled around a piece of chewing gum. She pondered the scene with exaggerated calculation before taking the gum from her mouth and stuffing it into the pocket of her khaki shorts.

"What do you make of it, Rhonda?" Bill Markham directed his question to the side of her weather-beaten face.

"I don't really know, Mr Markham. Dead whales is not really my thing. I'm just holding the fort until the boffins from the aquarium get down here."

"When will that be then?" Markham tried to hold the impatience from his tone.

She shrugged.

Since Rhonda knew next to nothing, he dropped any pretence of interviewing her. Like Rhonda, he found it almost impossible not to look at the spectacle on the sliver of sand that lined Esperance's Bay of Isles. The grassy foreshore offered a clear view of the sperm whales.

The pod had beached itself the previous day. More than twenty carcasses formed a ghastly parade of sun-blistered blubber on the otherwise pristine beach.

Crowds of beach-goers, mostly tourists, were held at bay by two police constables and a handful surf lifesaver volunteers. They were cordoning off the area with tape in the hope the gawkers wouldn't contaminate the site for the scientists.

"They died so quick, though, as if they were already exhausted when they beached themselves," Ranger Rhonda mused, loud enough that Markham caught it on his digital recorder. "It was like they were in some kinda hurry. Like they were running from something."

"Yeah. Strange," he answered with distraction. "Do you think it had something to do with the icebergs being so far north? Some kind of polar shift throwing the whales off track?" Two iceberg caps glinted on the southern horizon, no more than a few kilometres from the West Australian coast.

"I don't know much about icebergs but I do know that scares the living daylights out of me." She pointed to one of the whale carcasses. The corpse she singled out had washed up not long after the others beached. Only its head and left fin remained. The beach and the lapping waves were awash with its crimson-black blood. "I don't wanna meet whatever could do that."

"I've got to go, Rhonda, but thanks for your time." He paused long enough for her reply, his eyes darting all the while, searching for a better angle on this story

"My pleasure, Mr Markham. You sure you'll put my story on the front page?"

"Just keep your eye out for the paper in a few days."

With a brief wave, he headed back to the air-conditioned sanctuary of his motel room. Having been in Esperance almost a week now, he had secured a room in the Isle's Bay Motel, right on the esplanade that looked out onto the bay. With all that was happening, he was lucky for the head start on the curiosity seekers who now poured into the seaside town daily.

He flipped his laptop open and it hummed into life. He reviewed his notes and the real reason he was here. The last week or two had been hellish. He was due to meet his brother, who was sailing into Perth on the HMAS Victoria. The last report the Defence Department gave him was that the Victoria had hit an iceberg and Luke was missing, presumed drowned.

The news stunned him for days. He'd only recently made peace with his younger brother after their parents had died, but Luke had been in active service in the navy and based in Sydney. Luke's new posting in Fremantle offered them a chance to reconnect—a chance dashed by an iceberg.

When icebergs appeared in the Great Australian Bight, he pestered his boss to let him check it out. When the icebergs drifted towards Esperance, near where they picked up the last transmission from Luke's ship, he took the chance to seek understanding for his brother's strange passing. And here he was.

After standing in the hot spring sun interviewing eyewitnesses for most of the day, weariness had settled in. He folded up his laptop and dropped onto the over-soft bed. His head was filled with fragments of dead whales, unseasonal icebergs, and Luke. His last thought before sleep took hold was of the expected marine biologists. Maybe they could supply some answers to these mysteries. He'd catch them in the morning.

☆

Bill awoke mid-snore, certain the earth had shuddered. The clock told him it was after midnight. He buttoned his shirt, ignoring the stickiness caused by the evaporative air-conditioner, grabbed his room key, and headed for the beach.

In the distance, the venerable Esperance jetty snaked more than a kilometre out to sea on timber legs. Three figures were on the jetty, caught in the amber glow of intermittent light poles. The fishermen carried their gear in slow procession toward shore.

He crested the foreshore rise to find a small group of people wandering between the whales. The rest of the town slept; the esplanade stood silent.

"Hey there," he called to the nearest person as he descended to the beach.

"Can I help you?" a woman answered. She pushed back the hood of her water-sealed parker to reveal thick short-cropped black hair.

"The name's Bill Markham. I'm a journalist from the West Australian."

"Hi, I'm Dana. You keep late hours, Mr Markham."

"I'd say the same of you."

"Yeah. We're down from Perth, from the Aquarium. Just arrived."

"I've been waiting for your team. The locals know next to nothing about what's going on. I was hoping you'd uncover some answers."

"Just more questions at the moment, Mr Markham, but it's early days yet. We've only been here a few hours."

"Call me Bill." He extended a hand.

"Bill," she smiled, and took his hand after rubbing the slime from her own. "Dana."

"Look, I don't have my gear with me right now, but is there any chance I could interview your team tomorrow?"

"Sure. I'll run it past Dr Matheson but I don't see any problems."

"Great." He caught himself smiling like a teenager. He cleared his throat for composure and pointed to the whales. "So, what do you think could have done something like this?"

"Whales beach themselves all the time. Their motives are often a mystery. It's rare such a large pod of sperm whales would do it though." She hesitated.

"Go on."

"Well, one of the most contentious theories is that whales are affected by strong sonar signals. The US Navy has been condemned for the experimental sonar devices in their newer submarines. They've been linked to several mass strandings around the world."

"There were Australian navy ships in the area recently," he said. "The HMAS Victoria."

"I don't think that's the answer, but it could be part of a lot of little things that drove these poor whales into this bay." She sighed. "I normally love coming to Esperance. My family have holidayed here a few times now. I love taking the cruise around the islands. It's a shame I have to come back here under such tragic circumstances."

"Yeah."

Together, they looked out across the bay, united in different forms of grief, marvelling at the islets that dotted the coastline, the glittering blanket of stars, and the dark expanse of ocean beneath.

☆

"Dana!" Bill waved to her as he pushed through the throng of curious tourists. The morning sun added dimensions to her face only hinted at by the starlight.

"Hi again, Bill. I enjoyed our talk last night."

"Me too." He ducked under the perimeter tape. His eyes were bloodshot from talking with her most of the night.

"Hey, I didn't ask you last night, but do you have any idea what could cause damage like that?" He pointed to the bodiless whale.

"That's what concerns me. At first Dr Matheson thought it might be Orcas, you know, Killer whales. I thought perhaps a pack of sharks, maybe even Great Whites. We were both wrong. The whale's body seems to have been taken in one bite. I really don't know what could do that to a forty tonne whale. It's kind of freaking out the team a little bit."

"A new species then?"

"It would have to be. But don't quote me on that. Not just yet anyway."

"Okay, off the record then, but I'd be grateful for something more definite soon, for the story—even if it is 'species unknown'."

"Sure."

"What about the icebergs, have your guys come up with anything on them yet?"

"Not much. Faxes came in from the Bureau of Meteorology and a few other sources. They confirm an Antarctic current is carrying the icebergs. We don't know what that means yet or why it's happening."

"Thanks. I'll check with the Bureau and see if they know ... hey, look! The dolphins over there. Does that look right to you?"

Half a dozen brightly coloured yachts skirted along the bay, all racing to corner an orange buoy close to the jetty. Nearby, several dolphins were leaping out of the water in a frenzy.

"They do that, although they're normally a little more timid and playful. They look a bit stressed."

"What's that beyond them, Dana, next to the large island on the left?"

"Just a smaller island. Strange. I haven't noticed it before."

"Yeah, I don't remember seeing it either. What the hell is that, where it meets the water? You see the bubbles and whitecaps?"

"It's like something is chopping and churning the water underneath the ..."

"Oh shit, is that—"

"It's moving," she whispered.

Bill grabbed her arm and turned his back to the bay.

"Everybody run!" he screamed. "Run!"

The crowd looked at him in confusion as he pushed through their ranks. Even the scientists, busy studying the whales, turned at his shouting with stunned faces. Soon others on the beach and the nearby jetty pointed and screamed. Within seconds, they all saw it.

Moving slowly at first, the rounded islet bobbed on the surface and then rose out of the water, with a widening split across its centre. Dull brown plating receded to reveal a black the shade of the abyssal depths. It ascended from the water, fully the size of an island—a gargantuan eye.

Propped up on a stalk the width of a grain silo, the huge orb soon towered over the town. Bubbles churned the water a few hundred metres away. Within moments, a second monstrous eye broke the surface and propelled upwards.

Screams of panic echoed through the town. On the jetty, which was uncomfortably close to the first eye, dozens of people jostled one another in a stampede to escape. A handful of the crowd were bundled over the unrailed side of the jetty, where they floundered in panic in the wash near the pylons. The nearest eye was drawn to the sudden movement. Swivelling with ease on its titanic stalk, it regarded the crowd with inhuman dispassion.

Along the esplanade, scores of cars had slowed to a crawl as they gaped at the spectacle playing out in the bay. Distracted, several cars ploughed into the tail bumpers ahead of them. Squeals of brakes and crunches of metal provided only momentary distractions for nearby drivers and joggers.

The crowd on the beach jostled for safety. At their head, Bill and Dana crested the rise. They turned as one to the sound of splintering wood.

"Bill, look!"

Bill couldn't tear his eyes away even if he wanted to. "Holy shit."

"This can't be happening," Dana muttered.

People streamed around them as they stood rooted to the spot. Like ants dashing to safety, the jetty and beach throngs swarmed across the esplanade and scurried around crashed cars, dispersing amongst the houses and motels that lined the road. Only a few hardy souls remained to watch with Bill and Dana as a writhing mass of colossal tentacles broke the surface.

The splintering continued as one of the creature's tentacles ripped the jetty's supports apart piece by piece. Other tentacles uprooted the pillars from their foundations, sending planks of wood crashing into the water. In the clutches of the tentacles, the robust pylons looked like match sticks. The jetty's metal rail popped free, buckling like a piece of wire. A tentacle brushed the rail aside as if it were an inconvenience, tipping it into the sea.

"Come on!" Bill pulled Dana along as he ran toward the disintegrating jetty.

"Why? What are you doing?" She tugged his arm. Her shout was muted by the cracking and tearing.

"There are people still on that jetty." The last of the crowd in the water floundered onto the beach and were out of imminent danger. However, a woman in a yellow dress, cradling two children, huddled beneath a bench about a third of the way along the jetty. Dana caught Bill's eye; they nodded in agreement, and then sprinted down the beach.

Out on the water, the small fleet of yachts had scattered. Some had beached themselves and the sailors had promptly fled. A few poor souls were still out on the water, vying for the dwindling breeze as more tentacles seemed to taunt them. One of the yachts was caught and hoisted high in the air. The two terrified sailors leapt from their boat and thrashed for the shore.

Another tentacle slithered out of the water and draped itself over the retaining wall that sheltered the port. It dislodged boulders before clutching at the tanker-ship half loaded with containers. The tentacle pushed through the containers stacked on the ship's deck, knocking many into the water. The tanker bobbed on the water under the tentacle's weight, tugging at its anchor. Content to let the ship rock on its keel, the creature eased its tendril along the hull like a blind man reading Braille.

"Faster, Dana, the squid's getting too close!"

The pair mounted the ramp onto the jetty. It came down to a race, as the giant tentacles steadily tore through the planking.

"Lady! Get up and run! Come on!" Bill screamed. The huddling woman covered her ears and propped her elbows on the children's backs.

"Come on!" Dana echoed.

The jetty was fast disappearing. In the wake of the creature's rampage, a line of boards and flotsam, hundreds of metres long, floated on the water like an oil slick. Only fifteen or twenty metres of usable jetty remained before the woman and kids were pulverised.

"This isn't real," the woman babbled as they hauled her and the children from their hiding spot.

"Run," Bill screamed in their faces.

The woman blinked at him but found her strength as Bill dragged her towards the shore. Her children, puffy-cheeked and on the verge of tears, fled with speed fuelled by terror. Dana stayed with them, herding them to safety. Tentacles loomed only metres away, tearing out pylons they had just passed.

Another tendril rose from the water, darting for the section of jetty between them and freedom. It crashed into the jetty just behind Dana and the children. The impact drove shards of wood and steel high into the air. Only a sliver of the jetty remained, supported by a single, unsteady pylon. Bill and the mother were caught on the wrong side of the devastation. Dana paused but the kids didn't look back as they sprinted for land.

The tentacle heaved itself into the air directly above Bill.

He threw the woman across the gap in the jetty with all his strength. She bundled into Dana, who stumbled from the impact. In desperation, she carried the woman forward.

The sky darkened as the monstrous tendril plummeted.

Bill glanced up. He wasn't going to make it.

He dived for the water as the monstrosity slammed its weight into the jetty, shattering the timbers to pulp.

The tentacle slowly withdrew.

Bill surfaced in the shallows, concealed by the floating debris, in time to see Dana escape the jetty and lead the family beyond the carpark. To his horror, the tentacle lashed at them a final time, missing, but flattening a beachside gazebo instead. As it reeled back into the water, Dana and the others disappeared beyond the line of foreshore houses.

Drained of energy and adrenalin, Bill dragged himself ashore and picked his way through the shattered remains of the jetty. The incessant Esperance wind froze him inside his wet clothes. He shivered and hugged himself to keep the worst of the chill at bay. His world was reduced to rubble and brine and struggling to stay warm. He huddled in the sand amid the driftwood.

The carnage was widespread. The jetty was no more than a few snapped pylons. Yachts were capsized—a flotilla of broken butterflies floating face down in the bay.

Along the port, shipping containers were upended and strewn about like discarded Lego blocks. The tanker still bobbed as though it were a rubber-duck, with smoke rising from its bowels.

The port itself was completely wrecked. One of the factory-sized sheds was reduced to rubble. Another bore a huge hole in its roof and billowed with thick black smoke. Cranes were snapped—one had fallen into the bay while another pinned a berthed tugboat to the dock.

The marina also bore the beast's brunt. Many of the moored boats were now half-submerged, including the big island cruiser. Its aft section was rammed up onto the concrete pier, while its nose was wedged underwater. The picturesque tea house, bustling with people only minutes before, had become a pile of rubble.

The tentacles withdrew as Bill watched. It took several surreal minutes for them to disappear from view, leaving only the huge distended eyes hovering above the bay on their stalks. Soon they too withdrew, dipping down below the water, but not entirely out of view. Where the Bay of Isles was alive with slithering tentacles moments before, only the plated crest of one eye remained.

"It's not going to leave just yet," Dana called from behind him.

Bill shot her a weary smile, too tired and drenched to throw his arms around her. "Why do you say that?"

"It hasn't fed."

☆

"The sun's coming up," Bill gently prodded Dana. He stood by the window, scanning the horizon for any signs of danger.

Through the twilight, searchlights swept their beams across the water; a sign the military had established their presence.

"What's the time?" Dana stifled a yawn and rose from the bed.

"Just after six."

"Any sign of it?" she asked.

Bill didn't have to ask what 'it' was, but the casualness of the remark disturbed him. In other situations he might have laughed, but not in this one. "No, but the army has been raising hell for most of the night."

"We better go check out the situation then," she leered like a shark.

As she made her way to the bathroom with sleep-addled steps, Bill couldn't help but admire her awkward beauty. The previous twenty-four hours had been tense, with the gigantic squid creature lying dormant off the coast after its initial attack. Laying up in Bill's motel room, the pair had kept vigil on the bay, while sharing their pasts and thoughts on the creature.

Once Dana was done, Bill grabbed his coat and keys and led her out onto the esplanade. Camouflage-clad soldiers were setting up guns and equipment where joggers once greeted the sun. The dawn wind whipped at the soldier's clothes, adding a degree of difficulty to their tasks.

It was clear that very few of the residents were still in town.

"Excuse me." Bill approached a pair of men erecting a tripod-mounted machine-gun.

"Who are you?" challenged the younger of the men, whirling from his task. "You shouldn't be here."

"Bill Markham, with the *West Australian*," he replied, flashing his media ID card. "This is Dana Sorenstrom, from the West Australian Aquarium. We need to speak with the officer in charge."

"You still shouldn't be here," said the soldier.

"The Brigadier is down there." The other soldier pointed along the street.

"Thanks." Bill was already striding away.

A few minutes later they arrived at the army's operations centre, passing several knots of soldiers along the way. A heavy tarpaulin marquee was set up in the carpark of the local Centrelink office. Streams of soldiers passed in and out of the main building. Bill and Dana joined the procession and slipped inside.

The reception desk was decked out with telescopic viewing equipment. The other desks had been cleared and were piled with military computers and communications gear. A group of soldiers stood in the centre of a brightly-lit room at the rear of the open-plan office, around a table with maps laid across it.

"Can I help you?" An imposing soldier stepped in their path, shifting his Steyr-Aug rifle for emphasis.

"Yeah, we've come to sign up for the dole," said Bill.

"Bill. You're not helping." Dana jabbed him with an elbow.

"Seriously, I'm a journalist. We need to speak with the Brigadier. We have information about the creature."

"Wait right here. I'll check." Before leaving, the soldier nodded to two other men who shuffled closer. They also held their assault-rifles at the ready.

A minute later, the hefty soldier emerged from the back room and motioned for them to come forward.

Bill stepped through the doorway first and met the grey eyes of the man at the furthest end of the room. His confident air, service pins, and characteristic brim-up hat gave Bill the impression this man was in charge.

"Good morning. I've been told you know something about the enemy," the Brigadier said.

"Yes."

"Well, before you waste my time. Who are you?"

"Bill Markham, a journalist with the *West Australian*."

"And I'm Dr Dana Sorenstrom, deputy head of marine research at the Western Australian Aquarium. Whale specialist." From her tone, Bill knew she would take no further pomposity from this man.

"And you are?" Bill added, just to stir the pot.

"Brigadier Marcus Stannard. This is my operation. Now what do you have for me?"

"First of all, Brigadier Stannard, do you know the scope of what you're dealing with?" asked Dana.

"A giant sea monster. Yes, yes, I've heard all the hoo-haa. Let me assure you, I have four hundred men mobilised along the shoreline, with dozens of machine-gun and AW50 anti-material gun placements. I have three 105 millimetre howitzers already in position and six heavily armed ASLAV assault vehicles. As we speak, mortar placements are being established along the foreshore and at the lookout on the head. Six Leopard tanks are on their way, as well as two Collins-class submarines and air support from Perth. I have the situation well in hand."

"Is that all?" Dana asked with absolute sincerity.

"Look, Brigadier, this thing is enormous. It must be kilometres long. Kilometres!" Bill waved his hands for emphasis.

"That's ridiculous. How can something be that big?"

"I think it took down the HMAS Victoria. I don't buy some bogus story about hitting an iceberg. If the Victoria couldn't stop it, a few men and pop guns won't do the trick."

"Brigadier." Dana re-focused the conversation. "Have you ever heard the legend of the Kraken?"

"No."

"The Kraken was said to be a monstrous giant squid. One that roamed the northern oceans, capsizing ships and eating their crews. Historians have put these tales down to exaggerated sightings of regular giant squid. However, the Bishop of Bergin, in Norway, wrote in 1752 that the Kraken was a floating island, more than a mile and a half long."

"If that's true, then the good Bishop saw a baby," added Bill. "This thing is colossal."

"I don't need campfire stories," Stannard said. "I need hard data on this thing. What are its strengths and weaknesses?"

"It appears to be a squid or a cuttlefish," answered Dana, "with around eight arms or lesser tentacles and two greater tentacles. These are hundreds of metres long and can easily reach onto land. The strange thing is its eyes; they're on stalks. That isn't typical for a squid."

"Well, what is typical for a squid? Strengths and weaknesses specifically." The Brigadier's eyes narrowed.

"They normally have cylindrical shells that protect their bodies. They swim by jet propulsion—you know, squirting water. The related Cephalopod family have well-developed brains and circulatory systems; three hearts and all. When in danger, they often have ink-sacs they squirt at enemies."

"Weaknesses, Dr Sorenstrom?" prodded Stannard.

"Nothing obvious. They're not great swimmers and their natural enemies are larger predators. The giant squid is hunted by the Sperm whale, but nothing could come close to threatening something this size ..."

"Thank you, Doctor. Captain Ross," Stannard turned to a tall officer to his left. "Disseminate this information to the men ASAP and take your position at the lookout."

"Yes, sir." He snapped a salute and then stepped from the room.

"Now, as for—" the Brigadier started.

"Sir!" A soldier barrelled into the room.

"What is it?"

"We have movement in the bay!"

"Places, gentlemen. Instruct the men to fire at my command!" Brigadier Stannard swept from the room. The cluster of officers trailed behind him.

"Why did you space out there, Dana?" Bill could feel his pulse pounding.

"I'll tell you later. We need a better view," she said.

"Right, let's get my car and we'll go up to the lookout."

☆

"I want that BlackHawk in the air yesterday," Stannard bellowed at the corporal sitting at the radio.

"Yes sir, they're taking off now."

"Good, and are the mortars set?" He turned to another corporal.

"Yes sir. Sergeant Fielder says the wind will make accuracy unpredictable."

"Bull," scoffed Stannard. "I've hit a teacup at four hundred yards in wind stronger than this." He looked to a slender-built corporal tapping at a laptop. "What's the wind speed now, Grimes?"

"Fourteen knots blowing East NorEasterly, sir."

"Good. Tell Fielder to pull his socks up. Fourteen knots isn't so bad."

"Sir, look!" called one of the lieutenants congregating at the glass doors.

A huge orb, supported by a flexible stalk, jutted from the water close to the nearest island. Before it, gigantic, sinuous tentacles broke the surface and flailed in the air. Soon the bay was filled with writhing tendrils, each coil more than a kilometre long, whipping the water in a frenzy. Waves crashed from the tentacles as they dipped into the water and emerged again.

The tip of its shell crested and rose ever higher. In moments, the titan overshadowed the islands, and the bay, and the town itself. Dragging its bulk forward, it scraped its shell over a rocky atoll and fully into Esperance Bay. The displaced water swallowed the beach.

"Sir, I think the lady was right," muttered an officer. "We need more firepower."

The living dreadnaught raised its face out of the water, exposing a jagged, beak-like maw. It hissed like ten thousand enraged snakes before plunging forward.

The tide surged over the shoreline and flooded the town.

Hundreds of soldiers clung to their positions along the row of pine trees on the esplanade as the water surged around them. Several of the smaller gun emplacements were carried off by the backwash or turned about. As the water subsided, many of the soldiers prayed to their Gods or whispered messages that would never be heard by loved ones.

A voice buzzed from the radio. "This is Sergeant Fielder. Permission to fire?"

"Sir?" the radio man called to Stannard.

The Brigadier stood transfixed by the mythical creature in the flesh as it loomed over Esperance. "Fire at will."

The corporal relayed the command into his microphone.

Gunfire erupted from the esplanade, overshadowing another monstrous hiss. Scores of tracer lines lit up the morning sky, trailing their bright orange spray into the creature's limbs and carapace.

The writhing giant wasn't slowed by the onslaught. It lunged toward the town.

Heavier sprays of fire streamed from the eight-wheeled ASLAV assault vehicles as they joined the fray and unloaded their fifty millimetre cannons. More than four hundred soldiers opened fire with machine-guns and Steyr assault rifles. The soldiers huddled along the sodden foreshore parks and trees.

More waves slammed over the beach and into the streets beyond each time the creature moved.

A handful of mortar-propelled grenades trailed smoke as they arced skyward. They exploded on contact with the Kraken's arms and armoured shell but left only scorch marks or tore away the tiniest chucks of flesh. More plumes of smoke trailed in the wind as mortar shells were launched from the hill overlooking the ruined port. Explosions bloomed across the plating of the creature's oval head.

They were nothing but pyrotechnics.

In response, a powerful tentacle crashed across the first few coastal blocks of the town. A burning ASLAV vehicle and several buildings lay demolished in its wake. Another giant tentacle thudded into the town, shaking the ground with its impact. Dozens of soldiers fled.

Waves of gunfire raked the creature over and over, most bouncing off its tough shell. Thousands of bullets scored themselves into the creature's barbed and rubbery tentacles—all too insignificant to affect it. With every lash of its appendages, fewer and fewer streams of gunfire rose from the town. The earth convulsed with each assault.

The BlackHawk helicopter was now in the air and buzzing high above the Kraken's head, unloading its side-mounted cannon into the creature. One of the beast's eyes swivelled to regard the helicopter as it circled its head.

The remaining ASLAVs and machine-gun placements renewed their attack with vigour, bolstered by blasts from the howitzer cannons. Every blast from the howitzers rattled the Kraken. Mortar shells continued to bombard its carapace.

Stung by another cannon blast, the Kraken slapped at the town and wiped out one of the howitzer placements. It continued its rampage, crushing whole blocks at a time. It then swept a tentacle across the town, tearing through the line of pine trees and shattering many to pulp. Most of the soldiers were either injured or killed by that one terrible swipe.

"Where's my air support?" screamed Brigadier Stannard, as he watched the telling blow. The attack narrowly missed the command centre. "Damn it, concentrate on that eye! Get the howitzers repositioned, now!"

The soldiers were slow to respond. The BlackHawk was the first to pinpoint an eye. Circling lower, it strafed the plated eye with machine-gun fire. There was no obvious damage on the pitch-black iris, but the eyestalk flinched and pulled back into the creature's body.

A further round of mortar shells exploded near both eyes, but with the swirling wind and moving orbs, accuracy was near-impossible.

The BlackHawk pilot came in low, her gunner strafing the retreating eye again.

The Kraken heaved its bulk into the air. The helicopter's blades smashed into the creature's armour. An instant later, the BlackHawk exploded and slid off the Kraken's body, crashing into the sea.

Through sheer luck, its rotors clipped the eye, slicing the iris to pieces. The creature convulsed and pulled back from battering the foreshore. Gelatinous ooze wept from the now-closed eye.

Both eyes, one open, one closed, bobbed low in the water as the monster drew into itself and retreated behind the archipelago.

☆

"Faster, we've got to get up that hill," Dana said from the passenger seat.

With the Kraken's savaging of the coast, Bill was forced to take the backroads. Even so, the way was not clear; a military truck had blockaded the last section of the road, forcing them to abandon Bill's sedan and jog up to the lookout.

Captain Ross watched the battle with binoculars atop the metal scaffolding of the lookout structure. A few other men stood beside him and called coordinates to the mortar crews. The four teams of soldiers were busy firing and reloading mortar launchers in the carpark immediately below.

Bill and Dana ascended the lookout tower stairs. No one tried to stop them; all eyes were on the battle.

"How are we doing, Captain?" asked Bill, a little breathless from the climb.

"Losing." Captain Ross didn't lower his binoculars.

The Kraken had returned to the battle, flailing its tentacles across the town. Few of the pine trees that lined the coast were left standing. Only pockets of resistance remained, including a single howitzer. Still, the soldiers fought on, raking the creature with the pittance of ordnance remaining.

A low boom rose from the western horizon. The roar of jet engines approaching at supersonic speed.

"Signal the Brigadier. Tell him the air support has arrived," the Captain called to his radio man.

A tremor rocked the earth—the Kraken smashed at the town again.

"Sir, I've lost HQ's signal. I can't raise them."

A massive tentacle withdrew from the spot where the command centre had been only seconds before, leaving a pile of smouldering debris embedded in shattered concrete.

Captain Ross shook his head.

The jet roar intensified as two FA-18s shot past the headland and overflew the monster. They swung around hard, hugged the horizon and disappeared from view, the dull roar of their engines the only sign they still lurked in the area.

The Kraken turned away from the shattered town to face the incoming jets, bringing it in line with the lookout and the people standing atop it.

Again the roar intensified as the FA-18 Hornets rocketed past, even lower. Their cannons ablaze, they strafed the Kraken, etching lines of black scorch marks across its shell. Too quick for the monster to react, the Hornets shot over the top of it before turning for another run.

Out of habit more than determination, the mortar crews below Bill loaded up and shot off another volley. More scorch marks pocked the Kraken's hide as the grenades struck true. The observers no longer called new coordinates—the creature was unmissable, yet despondency stole their voices. No further resistance came from the town below, the drone of the jet engines had mesmerised the remnant of the ground forces.

All hope rested with the two jet fighters.

Bill and Dana flinched as the Hornets roared overhead again, so close they felt they could almost touch them.

The monster pulled itself from the water, an island incarnate. Massive plated leg joints erupted from the sea, either side of its carapace and tentacles. Eight chitinous legs, encrusted with barnacles, propped up the mass of its body. As the creature continued to rise, an armoured lobster-like abdomen and tail emerged from behind its head cone. Two towering pincers, barbed and jagged, also surfaced. These claws were stubbier, deadlier, than the squirming bunch of tentacles they straddled. The Kraken flexed and unflexed its pincers in near-human anticipation.

As the jet fighters streaked in low above the bay, the creature arched its face forward, allowing its tentacles to billow like hungry serpents.

A missile spiralled from the lead Hornet, followed by one from the wingman. The warheads streaked forward, trailing smoke and fire in their wake.

The monster lurched toward them. A geyser of black tar erupted from near the creature's beak. The gush was monumental, a rain of untold tonnes of sticky tar.

The missiles wedged themselves into the black fountain, exploding in muted coronas. An instant later, the Hornets ploughed through the geyser. The lead Hornet spiralled into the Kraken's upraised claw. The resulting explosion sprinkled fire and metal across the bay. A second fighter veered away, but ladened with the black tar, it couldn't pull up and crashed as a black glob into a flattened caravan park on the coast. The fiery debris of its demise spanned hundreds of metres.

The Kraken loomed over the town like a demented god. Black tar covered everything for kilometres. Every building within five hundred metres of the shore was flattened. The port, already smashed by the first assault, lay in a heap. Dozens of whip-like craters lined the town. Few buildings remained standing and nothing had survived intact. Nothing at all.

Like the town, the bay was covered with black scum that bobbed on the surface like an oil-slick, choking the waves. The hill and lookout were similarly coated, the mortars silenced by the tar.

Smoke billowed from a dozen places in the town not covered in tar, clogging the sky with a ruddy-charcoal haze. The sun remained a tiny red ember trapped behind the haze as morning blurred into afternoon.

Esperance, along with her defenders' spirit, was broken.

☆

"Bill, are you okay?" Dana whispered.

"Yeah, just sticky and a little bruised is all."

The force of the Kraken's geyser had knocked everyone from the lookout tower. Men wriggled like black larvae and groaned, nursing wounds hidden beneath the sludge, but all were still alive. Like them, Dana and Bill were blanketed in the black morass.

"Come on, we've got to talk to the Captain."

"Why? We've lost, Dana. Didn't you see what happened? That thing is damn near impossible to kill."

"You'll see."

Bill hobbled to his feet and joined Dana in her search for Captain Ross. Identification proved difficult; everyone appeared the same covered in a layer of tar. So it took a while to find the Captain, who sat at the base of the metal stairs, lost in thought.

"Captain, do you still have a radio?" Dana can barely suppress her excitement.

"In the truck. Why?"

"I think I know a way to get rid of this thing."

☆

"Damn. The phone's dead." Dana threw Bill's mobile to the truck floor.

"Hey! Careful with that! It's on a two-year plan." Bill bent to retrieve his phone from beneath the bench seat. The jostling of the truck made the task difficult.

"How will we contact the Aquarium without a phone?"

Bill returned to his seat and waved his phone nonchalantly. "I don't think mobiles work if mine's anything to go by. The creature must have taken out the towers."

"And it's a seven- or eight-hour drive to Perth from here, maybe longer in this truck," Dana added. "We need to get instructions to those subs before they get here."

Bill banged on the cabin wall. The soldiers seated with them in the back of the truck, covered in black tar, kept their gaze on their boots. Within moments, the cabin window slid open to reveal the tar-streaked face of Captain Ross.

"What?" he asked.

"Our mobiles don't work. The network must've been smashed by the Kraken. Do any of your men have satellite phones?" Bill said.

"Sure. There were two at the command centre. You know what happened to that."

Bill nodded, his mouth a tight line.

"There might be one or two out in the field. We can radio any survivors and check. Don't hold your breath, though."

"We have to try something, Captain." Dana pushed her face to the window next to Bill's. "Hundreds, maybe even thousands, of people could die if we don't get word to those subs in time."

"You're right," he sighed. "I'll try to raise someone. We'll be on the far side of Pink Lake in a few minutes. You can stretch your legs and I'll update you then."

The cabin window slid closed, muting the engine and road noise outside.

"So what's your take on all this, Dana?" Bill leaned his head on the wall and closed his eyes.

"On what exactly?"

"The Kraken. The icebergs. All of it."

"There's a lot science doesn't know yet. There are whole sections of the ocean we haven't explored. My guess is this thing came from Antarctica. Maybe it was trapped in the ice and finally escaped. I've no idea how something so big could exist, let alone flourish and grow like it has. The amount of food it'd require just staggers me."

"Maybe science is to blame," Bill pondered. "I mean, the thing looks like a genetic freak—a chimaera. Maybe twenty years ago this thing escaped from a gene-splicing lab that was combining marine DNA. A squid-crab-osaurus."

"It's all just speculation. I don't think we'll ever really know. I'd love to study it, but I doubt I'll ever get that chance. Anything that threatens to knock humanity from the top of the food chain won't be allowed to exist for long."

"Yeah. This could be the first battle in a war of extermination. I just hope there aren't any more of these things."

The truck's halt interrupted their discussion, bringing the soldiers back to life. They all piled out to find a roadside picnic area with a tap, where they took the opportunity to clean themselves. After a few minutes, a much cleaner Captain Ross approached the pair.

"Good news. We've made radio contact with a unit carrying a working Sat-phone."

"Great!" said Dana. "Can you relay what they need to tell the Aquarium?"

"Well, that's the problem. The radio reception is fine but they say they can't get a signal on the phone. They're trapped down near the beach without transport, so they need to get to higher ground."

Bill's face darkened. "That means we have to run the gauntlet past the Kraken to get the phone, somehow reach higher ground, and then hope it gets a signal through to Perth."

"Sounds about right."

"I'm in." Dana stepped forward. "Pass me the keys."

"If you're going, I'm going," Bill said.

"Alright, let's saddle up. This truck is too slow to run a gauntlet as you say, Mr Markham. I'll drop you at the edge of town and we'll requisition a vehicle."

"You mean steal a car?" Dana smirked.

Captain Ross grinned.

☆

Navigating the road into town was difficult. Rubble and debris clogged the streets, even kilometres inland. The truck pulled up in the outer suburbs when they spied an older model Land Rover abandoned on the street.

The Captain opened the car's door, leaned inside, and did something to the steering column. Seconds later, the engine revved to life.

"They teach you that at Duntroon?" Bill raised an eyebrow in mock disapproval.

Captain Ross smirked. "Get in. I'll rendezvous with the men back at Pink Lake. If you find any survivors, tell them to meet me there. You remember where to find the Sat-phone?"

"It's under control, Captain," Dana said.

"Good luck." Captain Ross farewelled them with a wave before jumping in the truck and taking it back the way they came. The rumble of its engine lingered, and dwindled, long after the truck left their view.

"This is it." Bill caught Dana's eye from the driver's seat and offered his hand. She squeezed it for a moment. Then he put the vehicle into gear. They picked up speed and bounced over the rubble littering the streets. As they crested the rise near the centre of town, the Kraken loomed into view.

Bill stopped the car between the ruins of a supermarket and a seafood shop on the main street. The engine hummed as they paused to observe the monster.

"Calamari ring, Dana?"

"Not appropriate right now."

"I know, I know. It's just ..."

"What?"

"This thing probably killed my brother. If I don't try to find the funny side to all this ... Even if we do survive this crazy plan, I don't know if I'll ever be the same old Bill again."

"Come on." Dana placed her hand on his as he gripped the steering wheel. "Let's take care of this and work the rest out later."

Bill shifted into second gear, rubbed his hands together, and then guided the four-wheel drive through the obstacle course streets.

The Kraken probed the port's wreckage, oblivious to their drive through town. Its tendrils plunged through warehouses and withdrew containers and barrels, drawing them in close until they disappeared below the waterline.

"It must be feeding. Chewing right through the steel and eating what's inside," Dana whispered.

Bill took the last few hundred metres of road with extra caution. Exposure might attract the Kraken's attention. The Land Rover clambered over planks, tree branches, and chunks of brick. The tar coating added complexity to the drive. Most road obstacles were amorphous black lumps.

"I hope none of those lumps are people," Bill muttered.

"I don't want to think about it."

As they crossed a thick pine branch, a wheel spun for a second, spitting mud and tar into the air.

"Bill! It's looking this way!"

The monster shifted its bulk and whipped tentacles in their direction. Its movement triggered a wave, flooding more sea water onto the foreshore.

Bill slammed the accelerator, threw the Land Rover into overdrive and tackled the sodden, rubble-strewn foreshore streets in a sudden rush.

A titanic tentacle crashed to the ground right behind their car, throwing them into the air. The Land Rover bucked before settling into the rhythm of driving once more.

A shadow crossed the windshield, a harbinger of their oblivion. Tearing the wheel to the right and slamming the brakes, Bill banked the Land Rover hard amid the squeal of tyres. The tentacle thudded into the earth, another earthquake, and missed the car by centimetres.

Bill veered back onto his original course as the tentacle withdrew and cascaded down the trench left by the Kraken's handiwork. The Land Rover shot up the incline on the far side, launching into the air before crunching onto the street.

"You're gonna kill us before that thing ever does!" Dana hissed.

Bill bashed debris out of the way, pushing the vehicle to the limit. The scrape and denting of metal was a constant companion.

The Kraken withdrew a little. Its single good eye bobbed around, trying to focus on the car.

Flame pockets and jagged metal filled the road ahead. Amid the crashed fighter's wreckage, they bore down on a solitary man running towards them. He was covered in the Kraken's tar. The four-wheel drive screeched to a halt alongside him. Dana flung the rear door open.

"Get in!" they screamed in unison.

He clumsily dived in, spilling a bundle across the back seat.

"Hang on!" Bill wrestled with the steering wheel.

The car wheels spun on the spot for a second, throwing out plumes of grime and smoke.

A tentacle whipped across the land, a vengeful thunderclap shattering the spot occupied by the Land Rover only an instant before. It left another trench-like crater in its aftermath.

Bill pushed the car to its limits, barrelling along the ruined esplanade toward the lookout at the top of the headland.

Dana turned to the tar-soaked passenger.

"That's the Sat-phone," the man said.

"Thanks."

"The name's Fielder. Sergeant Max Fielder."

"Dr Dana Sorenstrom, pleased to meet you." She clasped his sticky hand. "This madman is Bill."

Sergeant Fielder nodded and then grabbed the pitch-spattered bundle and handed it to Dana. "It works like a normal phone." He removed the phone from the backpack and pointed to one of the buttons. "Press that button to dial."

"Hold on!" Bill turned hard to the left.

A tentacle battered the street ahead, barely missing them.

Dana grabbed the phone, fumbled it because of the tar, and then stabbed her finger at the buttons. "It's ringing!"

The Land Rover sped past the port entrance, crossed the railway tracks and began the uphill climb. Bill maintained momentum by flooring the accelerator.

"Hello, it's Dana," she called into the phone. "Dana. Dana Sorenstrom," she shouted. "Damn. The signal keeps fading out. We need to get higher, Bill!"

"Watch out!" yelled Sergeant Fielder.

Bill banked into a sharp corner and slid against the gutter, narrowly avoiding another swipe. The tentacle sheared away the remains of a two-story cottage.

"Yes! Dr Sorenstrom," Dana shouted down the phone. "I need you to transmit those Sperm whale recordings to this number." She recited a number Captain Ross had given her. "Yes, now! It's life or death!"

She listened to the handset for a moment, her brow creased in concentration, before repeating her instructions.

All three of them were jostled as Bill reached the headland summit.

"Good," Dana said into the phone, "now transmit them straight away. You're sending those recordings to the Navy."

A tentacle groped along the streets, flattening anything in its path. But it was blind now. The headland sheltered them from the creature's direct sight.

"Get us out of here, Bill." Dana terminated the call and dumped the phone to the floor.

They plunged down the steep streets and scurried further inland, veering away from the Kraken's reach.

☆

Lurking off the Esperance coast, the submarines *HMAS Sheean* and *HMAS Rankin* coordinated the execution of their instructions.

"Have the modifications been completed?" asked Captain

White.

"Aye, sir," replied a young technician.

"Prepare to release sonar bursts on my mark," said the Captain. "Rankin, are you ready?" he called into the comm.

"Affirmative Sheean. On your mark." The response filtered through the speakers.

"Standby ... Three. Two. One. Mark."

At approximately four thousand metres apart, holding a parallel course, the *Sheean* and *Rankin* released a series of intensified sonar bursts, in imitation of the recording sent through by Naval Command in Perth. The short bursts, sounding like underwater clicks, resonated sonic surges through the water towards Esperance.

☆

"Look!" called Dana. "It's reacting."

Nestled in a collapsed garage on the outer fringes of town, Bill, Dana, and Sergeant Fielder kept a distant watch on the Kraken, willing Dana's tenuous plan to work.

The creature thrashed its tentacles at the water as it turned from the town to face the expanse of the Southern Ocean.

"It must be detecting the sonar signals. If I'm right, it should be hearing the hunting call of the world's largest Sperm whale!" Dana's excitement was almost palpable.

"Look at that," Bill murmured.

The Kraken heaved its body out of the water and propped itself up on its eight massive crustacean legs. It lumbered across the islets that spanned the outer bay and hauled itself into the open waters beyond. A huge wave rippled out in all directions. Its cluster of tentacles writhed as it flexed its gargantuan claws.

"Was your plan to piss it off, Dr Sorenstrom?" asked Fielder.

"Hmmm. It does look a little aggressive," Dana pondered.

"It won't attack the subs, will it? I mean, it's supposed to run way in fear, isn't it?" Bill said.

"That was the plan." Dana exhaled a deep breath and pressed her lips tight.

"Wait. What's it doing now?" Sergent Fielder leaned forward.

As the Kraken floated further out to sea, it abruptly stopped and then veered to the east. It sank beneath the waves, disappearing amid white caps and turbulence.

"It must have realised it's overmatched. Maybe its bravado has faded," said Dana.

Ripples trailed the creature's wake.

"It worked, Dana! Your bluff worked! We scared it off!" Unable to contain himself, Bill leaned across the gear stick and embraced her. The embrace turned into a lingering kiss.

The shrill ring of the satellite phone pulled the pair apart. Dana disentengled from Bill to retrieve it.

"Hello. Dr Sorenstrom speaking."

"Dr Sorenstrom. This is Captain White of the *HMAS Sheean*.

I was ordered to call you on this line if anything went wrong with the operation."

"Yes?"

"We transmitted the sonar signal as we were instructed. We picked up the creature on the scope coming towards us. Then, out of the blue, we picked up another signal."

"What do you mean, another signal?"

"Well, it didn't come from us, or the creature. It was an exact replica of the noise we were transmitting. Except it was stronger. Much stronger."

"Look!" Bill pointed to the ocean.

On the edge of the horizon, beyond the peaks of the icebergs still floating off the coast, a vast black ridge churned through the water at tremendous speed. A towering plume of exhaled air and water shot into the sky, an immense geyser reaching into the heavens and catching slivers of fading twilight.

Dana lowered the phone. "That's from a blowhole. A whale's blowhole."

The sea chopped and churned, and the icebergs bobbed with the whale's passage.

It was headed East after the Kraken, and into the gloom of the approaching night.

STOMA

PAUL A TOTH

Glass from Wilshire Boulevard buildings shot through the streets like sand bullets. "Stoma," Martin shouted, but what did Stoma know of mercy? And from whom would it have learned it? At that moment an explosion sent roots and chutes one mile high, another bomb-strapped terrorist immolating himself in a hot-finger pinch Stoma never noticed. Then another and another. What seemed wind, but was really the exhalation of oxygen, sent a wave through the business district. Ties ruffled, then disappeared along with their wearers. All these protestors in their starched white shirts would soon disappear. Their more radical friends had learned that black clothing allowed an easy approach, and they flung themselves for family and country into the moving jungle. No eyes looked down upon them; Stoma was blind, by human standards, but it could see in other ways.

Martin knelt in his green robe and chanted, "Stoma, Stooo-ooomaaaaaaa, Stoooooooooooooommmmmmmmaaaaaaaaaaaaa."

He was not alone, Los Angeles humming like a Buddhist temple. Stoma ignored these Greenies, chimney-stack pores inhaling smog, the sunset already less impressive, desaturated, made purely yellow like whipped yolk. The techno-organism lashed buildings with leaves. Below, the Insistent Ones in white shirts and ties defied the dictatorship of photosynthesis and, when recognised, disappeared in plant pores, sucked like elongated flesh-bales of glucose. Memories ...

"Forgive me," Martin said between chants.

He had been just one programmer among thousands of geneticists, biologists, artificial intelligence gurus, chemists, botanists and more. All had landed for the first time years before on a weed-cracked landing strip deep in the lush of some Pacific island seized in World War II. This secret response to greenhouse would allow the US government to flick a switch and say, with ten thousand red, white and blue balloons drifting from the humid sky: "And you thought we didn't care about the future." Corporations foot the bill, cheaper than lawsuits in some international court. Besides, no black budget could lay enough fog for Stoma's creation, and the patents would repay financiers like deregulated energy stocks. The only problem was that Stoma, when awakened from techno-sleep, walked on water like supermagnified phytoplankton—but not before developing a taste for white shirts and ties.

Too much emotion had been stimulated, and the chanting calmed Stoma's nerves. The Insistent Ones, suits who rejected this permanent Earth Day, refused to wear the green garb. Stoma sucked up pollutants, but it sucked up civilisation, too. Despite its memory chips, it grew: a walking weed. It had crept many miles across the Pacific on the way to LA. And with smog went the movies.

Martin was already bored. The Greenies had a lot of sex in the refreshed air, but there wasn't much else to do. Some went swimming, but they all feared the day Stoma would take to the beach on the way to Japan. It had plenty to do. It wasn't dying anytime soon. It might never die, in fact.

If only, Martin knew, Stoma could be planted, frozen on some mountaintop instead of lunging at the light, moving on roots, then they and it would survive.

How quickly the bizarre had become normal. How soon the churches had emptied into the streets for a new religion of plant worship ... or at least for placation. How soon people had stopped driving after realising that to Stoma a car was zooming molecules rich for absorption. Yes, a Porsche still streaked down LaBrea every now and then, a one hundred mile per hour act of suicide. Some just couldn't take the new Zen protocol. To simply stay quiet and out of the way was too much for them, and so they barreled into inhalation and planted themselves forever. They became flowers for their own funerals and contributed to the future they abhorred—soldiers who somehow stumbled into the wrong army and died for its cause rather than theirs.

The empty focus of meditation parted for a quick shot of analytical thought. It had been so long since Martin had enjoyed his jigsaw formulations, the eroticism of trigonometry and calculus. This was a simpler deduction. If Stoma could be lured— to Malibu, perhaps—they might bathe it in artificial light, poking holes in the side of a giant tent that no doubt would fill and sag like a patient's oxygen bag. They had built the thing; could they not build it a home?

He called the commissioner of the project, but was informed that same commissioner had been buried for self-inflicted gunshot wound the previous day. Offering the secretary only abbreviated comfort, Martin asked for the vice-chairman.

"Busy," the secretary said.

"Busy doing what?"

"At the desk with his boss' gun to his head."

"Put him on."

Martin breathed. His asthma had almost been vanquished. No

more dilators, no more antihistamines. He felt the ocean breeze clarify every nasal passage until it seemed his pores would soon leak mentholyptus.

Then came the voice. He knew the tone of soon-to-be suicides, a heavy resignation with the occasional lift of heaven-bound dreams.

"It won't work," said the vice-chairman.

And then came the bullet and a cry from the secretary. Martin clicked off his cell phone just as a satellite spun from a skyscraper. As usual, the police came and shot at a weed as though it were a runaway pitbull. The bullets scattered greenery. Stoma moved on, unable to laugh but possibly feeling the urge.

That night, as Stoma lurched toward the moon, Martin gathered a few friends. His little green army searched for surviving rebels. It took a lot of talking, words in the night so full of oxygen they lifted away like hot-air balloons.

Martin begged. "We will march. I'll join you. I'll go home, if I still have one, and put on my old clothes, my mission control outfit. We'll retreat to Malibu, me, you, as many friends as you can gather. It's supposed to rain tomorrow. We'll play the part of the sun. Come with us. Please."

The bizarre became normal by assuming a movie-like plot. With nothing better to do, the Insistent Ones adopted the town's industrial spirit and became would-be actors, extras on an outdoor set, climbing, climbing, as Martin directed them through the canyon. When they reached the peak, all, including Stoma, were too exhausted to do anything but gasp. Meanwhile, the trucks rolled as close as they could, and then began another climb. The giant walls were erected as the moon distracted Stoma. Soon, Stoma could not reach for the lunar. Inside the tent, lamps provided rays. Through the porous tent flowed air in need of all that Stoma was meant to do.

Martin retrieved his green robe and changed clothes. He ordered the others out and chanted. Stoma seemed to sigh, and Martin was glad it had no gun.

As everyone else streamed down the mountain, Martin realised Stoma was already dying. Below, civilisation resumed, the population already laughing at the robes in their garbage cans. But deep inside Stoma, lights flickered even as its breath laboured. Martin hoped it was the flickering of some virtual heaven. He said, "Stoooooooooooooommmmmmmaaaaaaaaaaaaa" one more time, and then fell asleep. By morning, his asthma had returned, a limp leaf covering his mouth.

Kadimakara and Curlew

Jason Nahrung

I 've heard of corrugation but this is ridiculous." Steve changed down a gear as the Land Rover bumped over another waist-high furrow in the gravel road.

Sarah held onto the dash with both hands, wincing at the thought of what the jolting was doing to the equipment rattling in the back of the vehicle. "I've never seen anything like this. This could be our big break."

"We'll find out soon enough," John said, leaning forward from his cramped nest amid luggage and gear on the rear seat. "I can see Kadimakara, over there." He pushed his glasses back into position on his nose, then pointed ahead through the dusty, insect-spotted windscreen towards an ochre monolith on the horizon. It seemed to float on a bed of heat haze; the plain around it was scrunched like a tablecloth.

Sarah stared at their destination, inwardly cursing that she'd worn a tank top. But it was so damn hot, and she'd expected to be riding in the back, not having John perving down her cleavage every time he wanted to say something. Poor guy, he just couldn't help himself, however much he tried to fight it. And with those Coke-bottle glasses, he could probably see every damn freckle on her chest.

"The satellite photos didn't do it justice." Sarah retrieved a folder from a bag at her feet, doing her best to swivel away from John's telescopic lenses. "It's bigger than I thought."

"I bet you say that to all the boys," Steve said, flashing a knowing leer.

And the shorts had been another mistake, she realised, as Steve's eyes continued their roving circuit from the dirt track to her knees, thighs, chest and back to the road. "Never, unfortunately, but I live in hope."

John spluttered with laughter, spraying her shoulder with spittle. She flinched and he fell back in his seat, stared out the window. She swore under her breath. It was like being on a high school excursion. This was the first time she'd been out in the field with Steve since, well, that last time, but if he thought they were picking up where they'd left off, he was sadly mistaken. Hopefully, with John joining them on this trip, past errors of judgment wouldn't be repeated. Maybe it would all be worth it, if this seismic event turned out to be as unusual as she suspected. Yes, there could be a paper or two in this; a promotion, even a real job overseas where the earth really moved.

The road stretched towards the western horizon, vanishing into the haze somewhere between Kadimakara and a smaller outcrop to its north. A few scrubby wattle trees had been uprooted; others leaned at crazy angles, all facing away from the huge rock.

"Just incredible," Sarah said. "I don't think anyone's encountered anything like this before." She held up the pictures as she tried to compare the satellite images with the world around her. "It's like the rock was dropped in a pond."

The photos clearly showed the rings of disturbed earth radiating out from the monolith in rough concentric circles. They were broken only where they hit the buildings of the Aboriginal community nestled near the only other natural feature in the area, the Sentinels, whose twelve granite towers looked like jumbled flagstones when seen from above. She could just make out the wavering line of a dry watercourse jagging down the western side of the settlement from the Sentinels towards Kadimakara.

"If only," Steve said, flexing his shoulders against his sweat-soaked shirt. "I could use a dip and a cold beer about now."

Sarah swiped the air-conditioning outlet in the dash with the photographs. "I'm sure this bloody thing isn't working." Her back was stuck to the seat and her bra itched.

"Maybe it needs re-gassing," said Steve.

"Not long now and we'll be able to cool off," John added, without leaning forward. "We should be at the township well before dark."

"I hope they've got a bar." As he spoke, Steve steered off the road to avoid a particularly nasty uplift of earth. The ground didn't seem any rougher than the road as small bushes thwacked against the vehicle and rocks dinged off the underside.

John squeezed Steve's shoulder and settled back. "Sorry, mate, it's a dry camp."

Sarah sighed. "We talked about that last night." How had she ever thought going to bed with Steve was a good idea? How many days was she going to be stuck out here with these two boys?

"Oh yeah, I forgot," Steve said with a mischievous grin. "Better empty this then." He reached into his shirt pocket for his battered flask and let go the wheel while he unscrewed the cap.

"Steve, I don't think you should—Watch out!" Sarah shouted, but Steve was already braking hard and jerking on the wheel, the flask sloshing liquor as it clattered to the floor.

"Where the bloody hell did he come from?" Steve yelled as the Rover rocked to a stop, boxes sliding in the rear as dust billowed around them. "Jesus!" He leaned forward, fighting his seat belt as he groped for his flask.

"Did you miss him?" Sarah asked. "He came from nowhere... I think you missed him."

"Who?" asked John, trying to extricate himself from the avalanche of gear.

"Didn't you see him, John?" Sarah glanced back. "A blackfella... It must've been close." She peered out the side window, squinting through the sun and dust.

She shrieked. The men jumped.

An elderly Aborigine stood next to her window, staring at them through the glass, his wide nose twitching with dust, apparently oblivious to the half-dozen flies crawling around the corners of his moist, brown eyes.

Sarah, one hand on her thumping heart, wound down her window. The fresh dirt smell rolled in on a blast of hot air.

"Jesus," she said. "You scared the shit out of me."

"Not as much as you mob scared me, missus." He smiled, revealing a few dark gaps in his wide, white grin.

"Are you all right?" Sarah asked. "We didn't even see you."

He wore faded, stained jeans and a dirty singlet. Rings of grey hair framed his dust-caked forehead. Dots of dark red paint flecked his cheeks.

"I'm all right, missus." He pointed at them with a knobby finger. "It's you mob should be worried."

"Us?" she asked. "We didn't hit you, did we? I'm sure we didn't." She looked at him more closely but couldn't see any injuries. Bare feet, she noticed, and he was thin, his skin the deepest black, and the eyes—old, but not dulled by age.

"No, missus, you didn't run into me. I come to warn you. This isn't a good place. You should all go back where you belong."

Steve snorted. "We spent three days driving out here. We're not going back now."

"'Im no good for climbin'," the man said with a gesture over his shoulder to the monolith.

"Are you talking about the climber who died last week, just before the first quake?" Sarah asked.

"We're not here to climb it, old timer," Steve said. "We're here to study it. We're scientists, from the government."

"Guv'ment? Guv'ment don't come out 'ere."

"Well, we're bloody well here now," Steve said.

"Are you from the camp?" John peered across Sarah's shoulder at the man. "You want a ride?"

The man cast an eye over the four-wheel-drive. "Better to walk, eh."

"At least tell me your name," Sarah said. "I need to talk to you about the tremors. About what you saw, what you felt."

The old man stepped even closer, staring into her eyes, and his voice dropped to a hard-edged whisper. "I told 'im, that fella that died. I told 'im, Kadimakara's no good for whitefellas to scramble on. He's no good for any mob." He wagged a finger at them. "You better stay away from 'im, missus. You don't wanna end up like that other fella."

"What are you saying?" Sarah asked. "Are you threatening us?"

"I've had enough of this bullshit," Steve said, crunching the Rover into gear. "See you there, old fella." He drove off with a lurch that sent John flying back into his seat.

"You didn't need to be so rude," Sarah said, "even if he was a bit creepy. I needed to talk to him."

"You can chat all you like when he finally gets back to the camp," Steve said, and shook his head. "Not that he made much sense. Pissed, probably." He caught a glimpse of John between jolts in the rearview mirror. "I thought you said it was a dry community?"

"Oh, it is," John said.

Sarah fired a dirty look at Steve, then reefed her gaze away. Disgusted, she bit her lip, tasting dust. Through the window, the monolith shimmered in the haze, waiting patiently.

☆

The houses of the local community seemed baked in the sun. Paint had faded on the windowless walls; tin roofs wavered with the heat rising from the unsealed roads. There wasn't even breeze enough to stir the plastic bags and food wrappers that littered the bare, dusty yards. People and dogs lounged under scrubby trees shading the open space in the middle of the township.

Hope hadn't died here, Sarah thought as they passed yet another rusted car body. It hadn't been game to slow down, let alone stop. No, hope had taken one look and headed for the coast where at least it could live out its old age in comfort. The urge to follow it welled inside her. Maybe the encounter with the old Aborigine had spooked her more than she realised. He'd been right on one score, though—she didn't belong here. Maybe that was what was really bugging her; the realisation that her world had, to whatever degree, contributed to the state of this one.

Sarah shelved her disquiet as they pulled up outside the canteen. One thing she could be sure of—an unusual, perhaps unique, geological event had occurred here, and it held enough promise to override any apprehension she might be feeling.

She flashed a nervous grin at two Aborigines seated on a warped bench. The pair swatted at flies as they watched the three scientists get out of the four-wheel-drive.

"Uncle's inside. He's bin waitin' for you mob," one of them said with a half-hearted movement of his hand.

"Is that right?" Steve replied. "Hope it's his shout."

The man's expression didn't change, but Sarah sensed the hardening behind his brown eyes. She could've kicked Steve, she really could've.

They went in, blinking in the sudden dimness until their eyes adjusted. The screen door clunked behind them with a scratch of tired hinges and an aluminium rattle. There was the clink of someone taking a shot on the threadbare pool table, and a tinny radio played country music. A little girl in a white dress danced to it with unselfconscious grace as two others played with sticks on the floor. Everyone stopped what they were doing as the scientists entered.

"Holy shit," Sarah whispered, gesturing towards the bar.

"How the hell?" asked John.

"Tricky bastard," Steve said, and led them over. The old man leaned against the bar, his hand wrapped around a cold can of soft drink that had left a puddle on the polished timber. He raised it in salute as they reached him.

Sarah licked her lips as thirst fought with curiosity. She pulled up a stool, the cracked vinyl creaking under her, and decided she could satisfy both—if Steve would let her.

He had walked right up to the old fella and, as John asked the teenage girl behind the bar for three cans of lemonade, Steve poked the air in front of the man's face and said: "So how'd you do it, granddad? You have a bike stashed out there? A horse? What was the idea, jumping out like that? We could've hurt you."

"No bike, no fancy four-wheel-drive. I told you blokes, out 'ere, these are better, more comfy." He pointed to his bare feet. "Got good air condition' too, boss." He waved a hand, sending a few flies buzzing.

"You're crazy," Steve said, and walked back behind Sarah to get his drink.

Sarah introduced them. "And you're...?"

"You can call me Jimmy Curlew. You mob shouldn't be 'ere. This isn't your place."

"Jimmy, what can you tell me about the earthquake? It doesn't seem to have damaged the community."

"How the hell could you tell?" Steve snorted behind her, and again she had to quell the impulse to slap him.

"John, maybe you and Steve should go set up the camp? Where's a good place, Jimmy?"

"Brisbane's not far, missus. Not with a good car like your one."

She laughed. "You're persistent, I'll give you that." Then she got serious. "We're here to study the rock, Jimmy, but we don't want to offend anyone. So please, where do you think is a good place for us to camp?"

He studied her, then nodded. "All right then, missus, if that's what you want. There's a little billabong, over by that creek there." He pointed out the back door. "Not much water, but he's got good shade. Close to Lumaluma. You mob will be safer there."

"Thanks, Jimmy. You boys go on, I'll catch you up."

"You be all right, Sarah?" John asked, wiping the dust from

his glasses.

"Yeah, I just want to find out more about what they saw from here and how it affected them."

Sarah's teammates left, promising her a fine meal of baked beans on toast, and again she asked Jimmy about the tremor.

"Lumaluma, what your mob call Sentinels, they look after us, missus. They might look after you, too, if you don't upset 'em."

"And how would we do that, Jimmy?"

"Just keep away from Kadimakara, that's all, missus. Don't go climbin' on 'im. Too many died up there already. That fella, he's got too much blood in 'im."

"Yes, I know. The latest one only last week. A heart attack, wasn't it?"

"That's what they say, missus. But it wasn't no 'art attack."

"So what was it, Jimmy? Why don't you want us here? Because we are staying. This upheaval is amazing. It could make a person's career."

Jimmy shook his head. "Could cost you plenny, this career of yours. Kadimakara is the spirit of this place, older than old. We keep 'im quiet, keep 'im dreamin'." His voice rose, so it carried through the shed, and he swept the rest of the building with his gaze. "But these young ones, they aren't innerested in the old ways." He looked over to the pool table where two young men in football jerseys had resumed playing. Sarah felt their eyes on her, measuring her like she was another ball in the game. "They don't wanna stay 'ere an' sing to Kadimakara. They want money an' them fancy cars."

One of the lads threw his cue on the table. "You're mad, Uncle. And you're mad, too, missus, if ya listen to 'is stupid old stories."

He stormed out, leaving his mate to flash an apologetic grin and a shrug before he, too, sauntered away.

Jimmy shook his head and took another swig. Sarah smiled as his throat bobbed, reminding her of a frog as he gulped down a few mouthfuls before he resumed talking.

"And the guv'ment, they aren't innerested neither. They want tourists to come an' climb 'im, carve their names on 'im, piss on 'im. They don't unnerstand it's the land, missus. People forget where they come from, people forget where they are."

"And where are we, Jimmy?"

"We're in the land of Kadimakara, missus. We're livin' in 'is shadow." He grinned, without amusement.

The ground shook. Bottles rattled on the shelf. Sarah grabbed at the bar as her stool wobbled. A pool ball bounced off the table, cracked across the concrete floor.

Jimmy grabbed Sarah's arm, so hard it hurt. He put his face next to hers so she could hear over the din. "You should go," Jimmy said, eyes hard, face set. The little girl cried and the barmaid whimpered. A dog howled. "It's not safe 'ere any more, not for whitefella or black."

☆

It was almost dark when Sarah reached the camp, which the men had erected in the shade of a small, tree-lined waterhole hidden in a patch of scrub within sight of the community. The monolith glowed red in the fading light, the last rays of sunset tipping the pillars of the Sentinels with pink. She identified the dry creek bed she'd seen in the photos, and could just make out where it once might have joined up with the billabong before a movement of the earth or perhaps just sediment had cut the waterhole off. Now the only thing coming down from the pinnacles of grey stone were the haunting calls of curlews, but Sarah blamed the increasingly cool night air for her goose pimples.

The men had pitched the tents. Sarah had her own, though she would be sharing it with a good deal of equipment they had unpacked from the four-wheel-drive. John was squatting by the campfire he'd built inside a circle of water-smoothed stones on a sandy patch near the bank of the waterhole.

"Did you get it?" she gasped, out of breath from her stumbling jog from the township. "It had to be two, maybe three points."

John, looking over his shoulder, shook his head. "Sorry, Sarah. We were still unpacking when the aftershock came. But Brisbane will have recorded it. And yeah, I'd say around 2.5 on the Richter scale. Shook some of the dust off the Rover."

"Shit." She stood, legs apart, bent over with hands on knees, the sweat cooling on her back and forehead. "I can't believe we missed it."

"But you're just in time for dinner."

She could see he hadn't been joking about the beans. They were simmering, fresh from the can, on the fry pan.

"Where's Steve?" she asked, moving over to warm herself by the fire. She breathed deeply to inhale the fragrant wood smoke. Already, she could see through the branches stars twinkling in the clear, darkening night. Out here, with no city lights or pollution, the star field would stretch from horizon to horizon. Maybe she would go for a walk later, get out of the scrub so she could enjoy that vista.

"Watering the horse," John said, and then in a low voice: "He didn't dump the booze."

Before she could say anything, Steve stepped into the campsite, one hand still working at his fly, the other holding a bottle of rum.

"I thought we agreed to leave that at the motel last night," Sarah said.

"You agreed. It's almost a third full, no point leaving it for the maid." He offered her the bottle.

She shook her head. "You know they can throw us off for bringing that onto their land."

"Their land? Since when?"

She clenched her teeth, aware of John motioning with his

eyes for her not to get into a brawl.

"Jesus," she muttered. "I'm going to get my coat." She rubbed her arms with anger, not cold, as she headed for her tent.

"Better get the first-aid kit, too," Steve shouted. "Get a bandage for that bleeding heart of yours."

"Fuck you," she yelled through the canvas as she angrily rummaged for her sweater.

"You wish," he shouted back. Before she could retort further, she heard John calming Steve down.

Still, she didn't go outside, just lit her lantern and started to check and prepare equipment for the next day. Damn Steve. Damn that he'd been more interested in getting pissed than setting up the equipment. Damn that they'd missed the aftershock. Their first chance to get some real data, rather than Jimmy Curlew's mumbo jumbo... The old man's thinly veiled warning made her shiver. Not that she thought he would actually harm them. How could he? But he had suggested that the climber had not died of a heart attack—what did he know about that? She swore again as she hauled equipment from boxes, powered up her laptop. Old Jimmy wouldn't have to poison them or arrange any accidents to end this expedition. He'd just have to catch Steve boozing.

A beep from the laptop announced it was ready. Sarah was particularly interested in downloading the latest satellite pictures, and any new data from the earthquake monitoring centre in Brisbane. She'd set up as much of her own equipment as she could tonight, to make sure she didn't miss any other aftershocks. The two men couldn't do much before morning, when they'd start taking soil samples and checking for damage as part of a safety assessment.

John brought dinner to the door and she took it gratefully. Sarah could see Steve, sitting by the fire with his back to her tent, staring out in the direction of the monolith, barely visible through the trees.

"Don't pay him any mind," John said. "He gets loud when he's on the piss."

"The arsehole will ruin our trip."

"Don't let him. It's a beautiful night, why don't you come out? Birds are loud."

"They give me the creeps."

"Just birds, Sarah. Anyway, I'm going to turn in soon. We want to do as much as we can in the morning before it gets too hot, eh?"

"Sure."

"Will you be all right?"

She smiled.

"Well, if you want anything, just holler."

She thanked him and finished her meal, soaking up the juice with a piece of bread, with a chocolate bar for dessert. John, bless him, had brought her coffee as well. His heart was in the right place. If only she could transplant it into Steve's body... She zipped up the tent and retreated with the brew to her sleeping bag on the camp bed. But she'd only just picked up her laptop when Steve stumbled into the tent door.

"What the hell do you want?" she shouted as he clawed at the canvas then finally found the zip. He loomed large and dark at the door, his face bright red, eyes shining in the gas light.

"I wanted to shay I'm shorry," he lisped, kneeling in the doorway, one hand on the tent pole, the other around the neck of the nearly empty bottle. "Y'know, I really like you, Sharah. Been thinkin' about you lots since that last trip."

"Well, thanks Steve." She hoped her voice was suitably sarcastic. "I'm just about to get some sleep." Then she regretted it; she didn't want to antagonise him further. "Maybe we can talk about it in the morning, eh?"

"Why not now, Sharah?" He lurched to all fours. "Y'know, it could be a cold night ..."

She felt a chill run through her and pulled the blanket higher. "I'm sure I'll be warm enough, thanks. Why don't you turn in? Early start and all that."

"Ah, shoulda known ya wouldn't be intereshted in a real man. Not lefty enough for ya, eh?"

She flinched in the face of his sudden anger, drawing up her knees as he waved the bottle. "It was a mistake, I told you that."

John called out, his voice sounding hesitant and thin. "Hey Steve, you finished with the fire? I'm gonna put it out."

Sarah held her breath, wondering if the interruption would distract Steve or just annoy him.

"You bitch," Steve muttered, and drained the bottle.

"Steve?" John called. "I'm, ah, putting the fire out. You gonna hit the sack?"

Sarah's grip on her blanket relaxed as Steve backed out of the tent. She jumped as he whacked the bottle against the fly, then hurled it into the bush. It must've hit a rock, because she heard it smash. The sharp crack made her flinch again. "Yeah, I heard ya the firsht time. Put yaself out, why don'tcha? I'm gonna take a leak."

Then Steve was gone. She heard his shambling footfalls in the gravel, then a few cracks of branches and leaves. For a moment she thought she should go after him. Stumbling around in the dark, he could get hurt. She sighed. Serve him right if he did. A night out in the cold would do him the world of good.

John stood outside her tent. "Everything okay, Sarah?" he asked quietly, as though afraid of being overheard.

"It's fine, John. Thanks."

"Ah, okay then. I'm gonna turn in."

"Sounds like a plan."

She heard him walk away, then called after him: "John?"

He stopped. "Yes, Sarah?"

She paused, not sure what she had meant to say. 'Thanks' seemed pretty weak. "Sleep tight, eh?"

"Yeah. You, too."

A moment of silence, then he resumed walking. She heard the zip of the other tent open and then shut.

Damn, she would have to go out. Her bladder wasn't letting her go to bed just yet. Maybe she could blame Steve for causing a nervous reaction.

It was cold outside, even in jeans and jumper. The fire was dead. The tent John shared with Steve lay in darkness. Poor John; he would have to spend the night with Steve's drunken snoring and bad attitude, once the obnoxious geologist returned from his nocturnal stagger.

Clutching her toilet bag under her arm, Sarah turned on her flashlight and headed down to the waterhole.

Business done and teeth cleaned, she started back towards the camp. Then she heard something. She froze. The sound of crickets rose up, and the damned curlews of course, and other birds she didn't know. Then she heard the noise again—hushed voices.

"I can take ya there," a young man said. "It's not far, boss."

"How far exactly?" Steve asked. "I'm not in the mood for a bloody midnight hike."

"Not very far, boss. Plenny of drink there. No one knows about it. Just us young fellas."

"Well, I dunno."

Sarah saw movement, a flash of pale skin as Steve ran a hand through his hair and turned towards the camp. She couldn't see the other man clearly; he was just a dark shadow among many.

"C'mon, boss, you'll be back in plenny of time. There'll be girls there, too."

"Yeah? Ah, what the hell. Lead the way, sport."

And Steve lurched off into the trees.

When Sarah was sure he was gone, she ran, fast as she dared, the short distance to John's tent. A few shouts and he came stumbling out, wiping his face and fumbling with his glasses.

"What is it, Sarah? What's wrong?"

"It's Steve. The bloody idiot's gone off with some blackfella to get drunk." She tossed her head and rolled her eyes. "Drunker," she amended. "He'll be bloody useless tomorrow. Christ, he might even get us kicked off. We can't afford to let someone else get to this, John."

"Ah, shit, all right. Let me get my boots on and we'll go get the bugger."

"Thanks, John. Hurry."

It took only a few minutes before they were both dressed and ready. She showed him the way she thought Steve had gone.

"Are you sure? That's not towards the community."

"No, it's towards Kadimakara, I know. The bar must be in a

cave or something. Damn him." How typical, she thought: finally a chance to get some professional attention, and Steve was going to louse it up in a drunken fit of pique.

John eyed the Rover, shrugged, then started walking. "Steve's got the keys."

"That'd be bloody right," Sarah huffed, and trudged along next to him.

It wasn't long before they cleared the scrub and emerged onto the plain. A half moon threw everything into light and shade, making the footing treacherous, especially since the quake had thrown up deep runnels. They tried to keep their torches pointed at their feet so the beams wouldn't alert Steve and give him time to hide. They could just see his white shirt, bobbing in the wan light as he wove around rocks, spindly bushes and his own inebriated sense of direction.

Despite the cold, Sarah was sweating when they finally approached the monolith.

"For a drunk, he makes good time," she wheezed. They stopped near the base, trying to find Steve and his almost invisible guide as they gathered their breath.

"Yeah, he's a big bastard," John said, and she thought she could hear doubt in his voice. Neither had broached the subject about just how they were going to convince Steve to return to camp.

"Christ, it's big, too." She stared up at Kadimakara looming above them, silvered in the moonlight.

"Yeah," John muttered. "I would have preferred to see it in daytime. It looks a lot bigger in the dark."

"Yeah, and of course, bloody Steve has gone to the shadowed side. How the hell are we going to find him?"

"I guess we'll just have to keep looking."

Pebbles crunched underfoot, loud enough in the still, quiet night to make them wince as they worked their way around the base. An incredible lip of earth surrounded the rock. It made Sarah think someone had simply dropped the monolith from a great height. How much of it was still underground, she wondered? How deep did it go?

They couldn't hear the curlews from here, but occasionally something would scrabble in the dark, or small rocks would clatter on the stone mountain before them. She walked close to John, enjoying the sensation of another body within hand's reach, however reedy.

John checked his watch. "Christ, we've been out here for hours."

"Where the fuck could he be?"

"Oh shit," John said, and pointed up.

"Oh shit indeed." Steve and his companion were scaling the side of the rock, already half way up the slope. "I'm sure that's the boy from the canteen."

John looked at her blankly.

"Never mind," she said. "What do we do now?"

"Follow them, I suppose."

"At night? That's crazy."

"What else can we do? Look for his body in the morning and try to explain what a geologist was doing staggering around half pissed in the middle of the night?"

She trembled.

"You all right?" he asked, touching her sleeve.

"Yeah, I was just thinking about what Jimmy Curlew told me back at the canteen."

"And what was that?"

"He said the rock killed that tourist the other day."

"What the hell does that mean? You didn't believe him, did you?"

"I dunno. It's just crazy, the way the quake seemed to be centred here, and then the ground's all ruffled like this."

"I'll grant you Mother Earth's got a few tricks up her sleeve, but that's why we're here, eh? One way or the other, though, we have to get Steve down from there before we all get into serious trouble. Not a lot of jobs for washed-up seismologists these days."

They scrambled onto the rock surface. It still felt warm, as though all the heat of the day was still leaking out. The rock was pitted with age and weather. Tufts of hardy spinifex protruded from among the cracks. It was a steep climb that made their legs ache.

Sarah's apprehension mounted as they worked their way higher. She felt like a burglar, climbing across someone's roof. How long before she got caught?

"No wonder people die up here," John gasped when they called a rest stop at a place where the rock flattened slightly before curving up towards the apex. "Christ, I've got to work out more."

Sarah nodded in sympathy. Her shirt was soaked with sweat; her ankle smarted from when she had slipped. She would have felt stupid about it but John had been tripping a lot, too, as they tried to find solid footing on the smooth stone and puddles of scree. At least the moon had risen farther, was giving them some extra light. They used their torches, but often the wavering beams were more a menace than a help, and in places they needed both hands to crawl up the steep slope.

Finally they neared the top, the star-filled sky arcing over them. Sarah had forgotten how many there were; how big the world was. A cold wind froze the sweat and made her shiver.

"There they are," John said, pointing.

"Oh Christ, he's passed out," Sarah said. "We'll never carry the bastard down."

Steve was on the ground, his guide standing over him. The teenager saw them, waved.

"What the hell happened?" John shouted as they got closer. He played his torch beam over Steve. There was a dark splash of blood near his head.

"He tripped over, boss. I think he's hurt pretty bad."

John swore as he knelt beside Steve and felt for a pulse. "He's still alive," he told Sarah, his face washed out in her torch beam. "But he's bleeding plenty." John turned back, studying Steve. The teenager stepped up behind him.

Sarah screamed. Too late. John, looking puzzled, was still turning towards her as the knife plunged into his back. She saw his face contort with pain as the blade rose and slashed down once more. He fell across Steve's body. John's torch rolled away, bouncing and flashing until it broke with a crack.

"What the hell are you doing?" Sarah tried to keep her torch beam on the teenager as she backed away. Splashes of blood glistened on his arms and face.

"Kadimakara, he needs more blood. Just a bit more. Then he will wake up and drive you mob from our land."

"That's not what Jimmy said," she stuttered as the youth approached, the gory knife held loosely in one blood-soaked hand. "He said it didn't care who it killed, black or white."

"What does that fella know? He's old an' soft."

"And you're a murdering sonofabitch," she shouted, and then cried out as the rock lurched under her. She lost her balance, fell, dropped her torch. It bounced metallically over a lip and out of sight.

The youth swayed, but kept his feet, like a surfer.

"Kadimakara awakes! Your other mate must be dead, too. All Kadimakara needs is a little more." He held his arms out, as though into a breeze. "Can you feel it?"

Oh yes, she could feel it. Trembling up through the rock, making her teeth rattle. Tears burned hot in her eyes.

The rock heaved again, even more violently, and gave a mighty crack like a glacier splitting. Sarah, already on hands and knees, fell sideways. Her head smacked on rock. She heard the boy cry out as he fell with a heavy crunch.

"No, Kadimakara," he screamed. "I'm your servant!"

A shape blotted out the moon. Dust fell over them like mist. Pebbles dinged off rock. A thundering grating sound filled Sarah's ears, penetrated by the boy's cries.

Then what seemed like a huge boulder smashed down. Sarah sprawled on her stomach. The boy flew sideways, tumbled, then vanished, flailing, into the same darkness as her torch.

Sobbing, she tried to hold on as the rock shuddered. It vibrated with the sound of a huge tree being torn from the ground, one desperately resisting root at a time. Pain shot through her fingers as she sought purchase, shredding skin and nails as the movement worsened, the rumbling increased. The moon vanished again. Shadow fell over Sarah. Something black, seeming as big as the sky, rushed towards her. She might have rolled; maybe the rock's movement threw her. The descending boulder smashed down next to her. The rock under her heaved like a bucking horse, tilting on crazy angles. Screaming, Sarah slid over the edge, plummeting, bashing into bushes and rocks, until finally a jarring thump stopped her fall.

When she could see, through the blood and fear and pain, she couldn't believe her eyes. Dust rolled from the flanks of Kadimakara; pebbles and stone cascaded down its sides. It was alive, heaving itself up on massive legs, a lumpy head rearing from the south on a long, turtle-like neck. The earth trembled, jarring her broken bones. Too huge, too incomprehensible. What had been above the earth was but a piece of its armoured spine. There was so much more, still emerging, pushing the soil back in a wave that carried her, rolling her like surf. A tail of rock lashed at the ground, sending trees and boulders flying.

She dragged herself backwards, using her good arm, her good leg; tried to ignore the agony in her ribs, the myriad stabbing wounds.

Another sound penetrated Sarah's fearful daze. A whooshing sound, low and rhythmic, like a fan blade or some deep, bass siren. She turned in the direction, to see Jimmy, dressed only in jeans, his scarred chest daubed with paint. He swung a bullroarer, the painted piece of timber flying around in a circle at the end of a piece of string, making that ghostly noise.

Two other men ran towards her. They too were half-naked, wearing mostly paint. They picked her up and carried her back, ignoring her groans of pain and terror.

Jimmy started chanting, and the massive creature turned towards him, blotting out so many stars, its feet hidden in clouds of dust and soil. When it took a step, the ground quaked with a resounding crunch, but Jimmy kept his feet, and the sound of the bullroarer didn't falter.

The two men hauled Sarah back, and all she could do as she clung to consciousness was watch Jimmy facing off the beast armed only with a piece of wood on a string. She could hear the curlews, calling out in a multitude, like cicadas, and the bullroarer whining and Jimmy chanting. She could hear—feel— the thudding of the earth as the creature stepped forward on its towering limbs.

Movement caught her attention. Tearing her gaze from the spectacle before her, she saw, from the direction of the Sentinels, a flitting line of dark shapes—birds winging in the thousands from the splintered outcrop towards the monster. It turned to face them, bellowing, and again the ground shook and it seemed even the stars vibrated with the call.

The birds plunged into the rock, and Sarah screamed at the thought of them mashing on the thick, rocky hide. But they emerged unharmed from the creature's side and sped towards

Jimmy. As they approached, Sarah could see a faint red glow around the birds. And then they hit Jimmy, vanishing into his body. He kept chanting, even as he jerked with each impact, and the bullroarer kept swinging, its siren call unbroken. Bird after bird, impact after impact, ploughed into him and was absorbed. And then from the bullroarer came a welter of tiny, white shooting stars, shrieking like fireworks as they scribed a brilliant arc across the sky before landing somewhere inside the dark, silent spires of the Sentinels.

The beast roared, then turned and lumbered towards Jimmy once more as the incredible flock plunged into its back, then tore from its chest, only to dive into Jimmy. And the sparks flew from the bullroarer, the glimmering arch so bright it made Sarah squint to look at it.

Sarah saw Jimmy stagger, and the beast fall to one leg, and she heard it bellow one last time as her body and mind finally yielded.

☆

Sarah awoke in her camp bed. Any thought, any hope, that the horror of the previous night had been only a nightmare was vanquished a moment after she opened her eyes. Someone had taken off her clothes and daubed her wounds with a chalky white ointment. Her body, what she could see of it before the pain made her rest her head back on her pillow, was more ointment than skin. One arm was tied in a splint, as were both her legs, though one not as extensively as the other. Outside she could hear chanting and the rhythmic clacking of sticks, and some murmur of conversation.

The girl from the canteen entered shortly after, carrying a bowl of brown creek water and a piece of pink-stained cloth.

"How you feelin'?" she asked.

"I've been better." Sarah risked a smile, was rewarded with only a twinge of pain. "Thank you."

The girl bobbed her head. "The flyin' doctor, he's comin' for you. Won't be long, now. You should rest, eh."

Sarah nodded.

The girl gave her water and checked the worst of her cuts and bruises, the tightness of the splints.

"So what happened?" Sarah asked.

"Some men, they climbed Kadimakara. They fell. Maybe they were drinkin'. There's no drink allowed 'ere."

The title of a research paper flashed in Sarah's mind: Supernatural phenomena and their causal relationship to seismic activity. She smiled, shook her head carefully, so as not to set off any more pains.

"I do believe you're right. But what about Jimmy? The creature?"

The girl just smiled.

"Help me then."

The girl gave her a puzzled look.

"I want to see."

"You can't from 'ere, missus. Too many trees..."

Damn.

She heard the hum of an approaching aircraft.

"Doctor's comin'," the girl said.

Sarah nodded, the thought of being carried to the plane and then flying out not particularly appealing. Although they would have morphine. The plane made her think of something else, but she would have to hurry.

"Help me, can you please? Before the doctor gets here?"

The girl gave her a suspicious look, but nodded hesitantly.

"Great. Can you get that box? Yes, that one. Can you set it down here, so I can see it? Next to my good arm."

The girl did as Sarah asked, and then Sarah talked her through connecting the relevant wires. Fortunately she'd done most of it the night before, before Steve ... She concentrated on her equipment, trying to fight off the sudden shaking that made her hand quiver over the laptop's keyboard.

"What time is it?"

The girl shrugged. She wasn't wearing a watch, just bangles of coloured beads and leather. "Late afternoon. You slept all day. It's good, it'll help you get better."

"Sure. Now, let's see if it works." Sarah gritted her teeth as she operated the computer. "Bingo," she muttered as the uplink finally connected.

Raised voices outside told her the doctor had landed. It wouldn't be long now, just a short drive from the bush airstrip; like the community, the landing field had also been shielded from the quake by the twelve needles of the Sentinels.

Sarah swore. She needed just a little more time. There, the latest satellite photos, from this morning...

"I'll be damned," she said.

The girl moved around to look at the screen as Sarah zoomed in, the area around Kadimakara drawing exponentially closer.

"Jimmy," the girl said.

Sarah stared at the screen. Kadimakara was buried once more, but out of place and tilted slightly, its base still showing signs of massive disturbance. She could see the settlement, its buildings still standing. Even her campsite showed up.

"What?" she whispered. "That can't be." She panned the image and homed in on the Sentinels. She looked at the girl, who didn't seem surprised at all.

"There's thirteen," Sarah said. Outside, a curlew called.

ATTACK OF THE 50-FOOT COSMONAUT

MICHAEL CANFIELD

The desert shimmered.

Most people in Henderson, Nevada, ignored it—as Jack had been advised bluntly to do. He would've ignored it too, if he hadn't been, as Sheriff Hubbins put it, "damned contrary by nature."

That, and maybe if his Dad hadn't shot and killed himself in his patrol car one night seventeen years ago, out there investigating the glowing hills.

Jack stood in the front room of their mobile home, watching the glow and thinking about these things. The glow seemed to get bigger every summer and every summer he went out to investigate—or try to anyway, stopped by electrified fences and heavy security patrols surrounding federal lands.

That night the glow was brighter than ever before. The horizon seemed to pulse with it so strongly and rhythmically the hills might have been breathing. The moon basked in its green reflection.

His old Mom came in out of the kitchen, looking drawn. "Why are you just standing there—gazing out the window again? What are you always dreaming about?" she said.

He shook his head. School would start pretty soon. Other concerns would take priority. If his next season's performance was even close to matching his previous season's he was sure to win a scholarship somewhere. And he was probably supposed to marry Janniffer eventually. The next few years were mapped out for him based on the expectations of others ...

Jack went outside and put on his track shoes. He sensed his Mom behind him.

"Where are you going?"

"To run, Mom," he said seriously, and of course that wasn't really a lie as far as it went.

As he trotted off he looked back at her, pretty sure that she knew the truth, and sure she didn't like it.

Their mobile home was the last in the row and beyond it lay nothing but the desert, or as Sheriff Hubbins would say, "Nothing that's nothing to nobody."

Jack moved into the darkness, picking up a little speed—not too much, as he didn't want to get winded before he reached the green foothills.

☆

Janniffer answered the phone and it was Mrs Jaffe calling for her Dad. It was about Jack, of course. Janniffer turned down the television. The news was over anyway; Ted Koppel announced that tomorrow night Peter Jennings would broadcast live from Berlin. Her friend Paige and Paige's idiot boyfriend Doggart, who were over to watch TV with her, howled in protest.

"Shut up! It's Jack's Mom on the phone!"

"It's always Jack's Mom," whined Doggart, cranking the television volume back up, "I wanna hear the Nightline theme. I love the Nightline theme." And he was supposed to be Jack's best friend.

Janniffer put a hand over her ear. "I'm sorry, Mrs Jaffe, could you say that again?" Apparently Jack had gone out running about six and still wasn't back. "No, he hasn't been over here ... do you think he ...?"

Doggart and Paige turned their attention from the TV to Janniffer.

"My father's not here, Mrs Jaffe," said Janniffer, "but I can beep him ..." She hung up after promising to call Mrs Jaffe back if she heard anything, and getting Mrs Jaffe's promise to do the same.

Doggart raised his arm. "Not this time. He's on his own—I'm through getting busted by the feds."

And then Paige, who was supposed to be her best friend, said: "Don't you think Jack's caused you enough trouble already, Janniffer?"

Janniffer looked out the picture window. It was a clear night and she thought maybe she could see a little something different, way off there, over the blocks and blocks of suburbs. Maybe. "It's getting brighter lately, don't you think?"

"No," said Doggart with conviction. "You're imagining that. It's the reflection of moonlight off black sand. If it were radiation, the anti-nukers would have some evidence by now. Which would be okay with me, 'cause I wouldn't say no to a fat settlement. But it just didn't turn out to be anything. So don't worry, girls," he added typically, "you won't have no two-headed babies."

"Not if we stay away from you, you inbreed." Janniffe picked up the phone again and dialed her father's pager.

Paige looked up seriously. "You just gonna call your Dad, and that's all. Right, Janniffer? Janniffer?"

She said nothing, just stood thoughtfully, waiting for her Dad to call back. True, she hadn't seen much of Jack lately, and probably he didn't like her any more, but if he got into trouble again his friends should be there.

"Doggart," she said, "I need to borrow your jeep."

"No way," said Paige, jumping in before Doggart could say anything. "I thought we agreed not to chase after these sexist losers."

"He might get busted—" And anyway, she thought, looking at Doggart, Paige had no call to talk about losers.

"And maybe he's not even in the foothills—did you even think of that?" said Paige.

Janniffer paused. "Well, where do you think he is?" she said defensively.

"That's not the point and you know it."

The phone rang.

Janniffer filled her father in and he told her he would take a run out to look for Jack. He made her promise to stay put. "I don't need more than one crazy teenager running around a one-time H-bomb site," he said.

She hung up the phone. "My Dad's gonna look for him."

"That's good, isn't it?" said Paige.

"Doggart," Janniffer said, "I can't take my Honda into the foothills—I need the keys to your jeep."

It surprised her how easily he gave in, reaching into his jeans to pull out his keyring.

"Doggart, what are you doing!" said Paige.

"She's made up her mind," he said coolly, moving the keys away as Paige tried to take them from him.

Janniffer almost grabbed them from the opposite direction, but Paige yanked Doggart's arm away.

"Girls, girls, please," said Doggart and everything stopped. "Don't fight over me!"

Paige slapped Doggart on the shoulder and Janniffer took the opportunity to snag the keys. She bolted out the front door. "See ya!" she yelled triumphantly.

Paige chased her. "Hold up! We'll come with you."

"We will?" said Doggart, surprised.

"Yes, stupid. Still think you're so funny?"

That was good, thought Janniffer, who, having jumped into the vehicle, suddenly remembered she didn't know how to drive a stick.

☆

Sheriff Hubbins took the patrol car and headed toward the foothills as soon he got off the phone from his daughter. He turned off the dirt access road into the sagebrush, bumping his way through the desert around the chain-linked barb-wired perimeter of government land, looking for a way in.

Damn skinny kid, he thought, just like his old man. A skinny kid could have slipped under the fence just about any place.

Hubbins looked to the foothills, only a few hundred yards off, and they were pretty damn green—greener than he'd ever seen them, and there hadn't been a night in the last seventeen years when he hadn't looked at them. No doubt about it—the kid had gone for it. Again. Crazy, contrary, inquisitive kid. Trying to get into the foothills, trying to get them to give up their secrets.

Sheriff Hubbins knew more about those secrets than most.

And he knew that it was better for it to stay that way. If anybody found out what he knew then somebody might get themselves really hurt someday. That wouldn't happen to Jack if he, as Sheriff and family friend, could help it.

Then again, there was a pretty good chance he wouldn't be able to help it. Not if Jack kept poking.

Hubbins had the patrol car's lights off—necessary in case helicopters showed up. He searched by the beam of his flashlight aimed out the window and the green glow—and that made for damned hard searching. Still, he didn't have to remind himself that he'd fifty and more years experience in these hills: three times as much as the kid.

The patrol car's tyres scrunched the dry earth slowly. There was only that, and the soft rumble of the engine.

His front tyre hit a rut and Hubbins directed his flashlight onto the fence. That was it. There was the spot where Jack had scooped out the dirt and slid under the fence. Damn skinny kid.

After cutting the engine, Hubbins got out and appraised the depth of the opening. It was nothing. There was no way he was going to get his fifty inches of long-accumulating gut through that mouse hole, so he had two options: either blow the whistle and radio the military—which he didn't care to do—or widen the hole.

Reluctantly, hating to break a damned sweat in the cold night air, Hubbins popped the trunk and took out a little camping spade.

There was nothing like manual labour, enforced and at a late hour, to put a man in an unreasonable mood. Especially when he hadn't had dinner yet.

☆

Concluding the job at last, he tossed the spade aside roughly; then, head first and belly skyward, he scooted under the fence. Dirt got down his collar and in his pants.

Pushing himself to his feet again, both knees ached. That was par though. They always ached when he stood up these days. The price you paid for letting yourself get old. Old, aching, with dirt down his arse did not put him in a better mood for the hike to come.

Just as he stood there getting his wind, he heard sounds coming out of the silence.

Not the wind and not the quiet hum of nature—but some other kind of sound. A pulsing, pumping noise—deep and rhythmic. It appeared to him as he looked across the desert that the pulsing rhythm of the glow was in sync with it. Funny. The sound was new, he thought—at least he'd never noticed it before—not even that first night seventeen years ago, when he'd driven the now restricted dirt road all the way up to the foothills looking for his fellow deputy, who was hours late reporting in.

The glow had been a lot dimmer then, just a sheen on the horizon after the meteorite's bright flash. Of course, there was speculation even at the beginning that it hadn't been a meteorite, but a UFO that crash-landed. The speculating only got worse when Deputy Angelo Jaffe turned up dead that night, a hole in his temple and his service revolver in his hand.

But then—perhaps because government was better at keeping mouths shut in those days—nothing more was heard about the incident. And what with people moving away and new folks coming in all the time, talk died out after a while.

Hubbins began walking toward the foothills. There was nothing much up there for Jack to see, even if he made it without being picked up by the military—just blackened metal. But he'd never been able to convince the kid of that, even though it happened to be true.

☆

Jack's skin hadn't actually turned green, but it looked like it when he got close enough to bask in the glow.

The light permeated the wasteland, coming from everywhere and nowhere at once. He was frankly a little surprised to have made it all the way without getting caught. Probably the talk about budget cuts was true; the whole empty test site might be unguarded. It looked that way. Nothing was around. Not a thing grew above ankle height, nothing scurried across the ground or buzzed in the air. There was only the sound: the drub drub drubbing under the foothills. Eerie. Strange.

But it was nothing to kill yourself over, he thought harshly.

He sat there, thinking about it, for how long he had no idea. Indeed, he might have sat there all night if an earthquake hadn't hit the area.

It began as a rumble in the hills—and before he could move, the ground slid away underneath him, carrying him along like flotsam.

Then the hills stood up.

Jack grabbed hold of an exposed clump of root to stop his slide. The hills shook dirt off themselves and Jack saw what he thought was a man. A giant: fifty feet tall at least, naked—but a man nonetheless. It towered over him.

Jack realised the roots he'd clung to were snarled hairs at the base of the giant's calf. When the giant started walking, Jack didn't know whether to let go and risk getting crushed under a heel—or to hang on for the ride.

The giant took no notice of him in any case, but seemed intent on moving. With a few strides, it spanned metres and continued to quicken its pace. Displaying deliberate purpose, it headed back the way Jack had come. Jack could no longer let go even if he'd wanted to for fear of being kicked twenty feet into the air by the hurling of the giant's legs.

Dirt choked Jack's throat and filled his eyes. He tried but couldn't see the giant's head from his low vantage point—just locks of matted hair clumped with dirt hanging below its shoulders. The giant's arms swung in monstrous arcs, the monstrous fingers curled. And something else as the clouds of dust began to settle—Jack could see that the giant itself was the source of the glow.

Not that the giant's skin glowed; rather it was encased in the glow, a green aura.

The giant came up to the perimeter fence and Jack watched as the ground passed below.

He saw Sheriff Hubbins' patrol car and watched as the giant's other foot crushed it indifferently. If the Sheriff was in it—well, that was the end of him.

The giant took to the highway and moved toward town.

The ropey hair that Jack coiled himself in was cutting his flesh. If he had to hang on much longer his arms would be shredded.

Far off, Jack heard the wupping of helicopter blades.

☆

Sheriff Hubbins saw a figure coming out of the hills. Damn hard to miss, considering it was fifty feet tall and blocked out of good chunk of the sky.

Hubbins ran for the fence, throwing himself under it. His belt caught on something and pinned him. He struggled, finally unbuckled it, losing his holster and revolver in the darkness. A few bullets couldn't hurt a thing that big anyway, so he didn't waste time feeling around for his weapon.

Freeing himself just as the giant loomed over him, he was on his hands and knees when he saw his patrol car collapse under the thing's foot like it was made of kitchen foil.

By the time he got upright again the monster was already a half mile away. "I'll be," he said aloud. It was something his grandmother used to say. There was nothing left of the patrol car, and he was glad he hadn't been driving his own Lincoln Towncar that night.

The monster went off toward Henderson; Hubbins headed the other way, toward the Boulder City suburbs. It wasn't much closer, but there would be more traffic once he reached the interstate and he would get a quicker lift to a phone. Not that he knew whom he was going to call or what he was going to say when he did.

Anyway, the military was hardly going to miss spotting this one, and he had half a mind to just hitch home and say the hell with it. Send a tow truck and a big spatula for the car in the morning. But he couldn't do that: Jack was still running around somewhere—unless the thing had stepped on him—and he probably had more questions than ever.

Hubbins was lucky. Just as he reached the highway he

spotted a pair of headlights coming his way. Then a trio of helicopters passed overhead, their floodlights illuminating the road like sunlight. He didn't bother to wave.

☆

Jack slid down the giant's calf when it stopped moving to swat at the helicopters.

The rapid cracks of fire spat from their guns as the helicopters circled the giant in wide sweeps. It seemed more annoyed than anything else, now that Jack could see its round full face.

The giant was faster, much more limber, than the helicopters could ever hope to be. Its arms were extended, keeping the buzzing nuisances at a distance when, it seemed to Jack, it could just as easily have knocked them out of the sky. The rounds hitting the giant's arms and shoulders must have stung it, at least, as it twitched and flinched at the pelting.

The battle was moving steadily away from him now, but closer to Henderson and the trailer park Jack lived in. He had no hope of keeping pace with them, but he ran anyway, holding as much ground as he could.

He was out of breath though still running when Doggart's jeep pulled up. Doggart was inside, and Janniffer and her friend—and there was also Sheriff Hubbins, who had survived the car crushing and looked red and perturbed and dirty.

Everyone in the car shouted at Jack at once but he felt no obligation to speak to any of them. He looked at Sheriff Hubbins.

"What is it?" he asked the Sheriff.

"I don't know any more than you do, son."

Jack didn't believe him. Always he felt the Sheriff knew more about things than he let on.

"You saw it!" said Jack.

"Saw what?" said Janniffer.

The giant was far out of sight now, though the helicopters could still faintly be heard in the distance.

"You'll read about it in the morning paper, honey," said Sheriff Hubbins. "Hop in, Jack, we'll take you back to our house, call your Mom from there. You know you got everybody upset again."

"We gotta try and stop it," said Jack, "It's headed right for the trailer park."

"Naw," said the Sheriff. "Never get that far, the army will stop it."

"What's headed toward your house?" Janniffer demanded.

Jack told her.

"I've seen that movie," said Doggart.

"It's not a movie," said Jack.

Janniffer shook her head.

"Ask your Dad," said Jack.

"Well I saw something, that's for sure. But I wouldn't worry about it. They're always cooking up something out there in the hills. Ninety per cent of the land in this state is federal, you know."

"That's all you've got to say, sir?"

"It's probably a giant secret weapon robot that got out of control. The government wouldn't put it here if it really posed a threat to the community," said the Sheriff.

"It's a man. Human. I touched it."

"Well then, it's a man."

"And you're not going to do anything about it?"

"Nothing with a car full of teenagers, I'm not. Tell you what, Jack: let's run you kids back to my house and you can clean yourself up. I'll get on the horn, round up my deputies and we'll come back out. Probably just be in the army's way but —"

"I don't like it, Sheriff. I don't know why you're acting this way—like all of this is no big deal. But I guess it doesn't make any difference. You're the way you are and I'm the way I am."

"Now listen, Jack—"

Jack turned his back on Sheriff Hubbins while he was still talking. He had never turned his back on an adult before.

"Jack!" called the Sheriff and Jack ignored him. He heard the Sheriff tell Doggart to pull the jeep up.

The jeep came alongside him and kept pace as he walked. They were all shouting at him. Janniffer was telling him not to be stupid. Her friend Paige was yelling at her not to be stupid. Finally Hubbins cried, "Enough!" He ordered the jeep stopped and got out.

Then he told Doggart to turn it around and take the girls home. His voice did not leave room for objections.

When the two of them were alone on the highway, Jack started walking home and the Sheriff kept pace with him, a few steps back.

Neither spoke for a long time.

"Must be pretty far from here by now—for it to be completely out of sight," said Sheriff Hubbins.

"You can still hear the helicopters," said Jack.

"You can hear pretty damn far out here, when it's quiet like this. There's nothing but dust and sagebrush, nothing at all to block a sound."

Jack turned to face him. The Sheriff was looking off into the distance and, not seeing that Jack had stopped, walked into him.

"Well," Hubbins said, "we're stuck out here now."

"Where'd it come from? What is it?"

"Your guess is as good as mine."

"I don't believe that, sir."

The Sheriff's mouth tightened. "That's too bad."

"Did my Dad really shoot himself?"

The Sheriff sighed and dropped his head. "Now why would you ask me that? You know he did. I'm sorry for it. We're all sorry for it, but it happened, son.

"Things happen," he continued. "Things happen that're just a shame, but that don't mean there's anything more to them than meets the eye. That's not fair, it don't make it any easier to accept, but there it is. Your Dad was my best friend. He was a good man. If he were still around he'd probably be Sheriff now instead of me."

"But he isn't around," said Jack. "And I want to know what happened to him. Did the government kill him?" Then he added, "Did you?"

Sheriff Hubbins suddenly looked drawn and old. "I grew up with your father, your mother. I was the best man at their wedding. And I've always looked out for you and her. John Arthur Jaffe Jr, how can you say something like that to me?"

Jack felt ashamed and cast down his eyes. "I know you cared for him," he said, without really being sure of anything. "But something strange did happen up there that night, and the giant proves it."

"A lot of rumours have come and gone about what happened and they're all bunk."

Sheriff Hubbins had told him that before, and he had heard all the rumours himself, of course: that the government had murdered his father and made it look like suicide because he had stumbled onto the test site of a new secret weapon—a weapon so terrible it made the H-bomb and the neutron bomb look like toys; or that he had come upon the crash site of a UFO, and was killed by aliens, which the government then covered up.

"It was my Dad who went up there to investigate the flash in the sky—the meteorite or whatever it was—and never came back. Then all of sudden the government fenced off all that territory."

"Just coincidence, Jack. They were probably planning the fence for months before that night. No government project in history ever moved that fast."

"The giant glows green. Just like the hills do—did. And when my Dad went up there it was the first night anybody ever saw them glow at all."

"They don't glow—that's an optical illusion."

Jack threw his hands up in disgust. "Is that what you're gonna say about your car? That it got crushed by an optical illusion? Don't lie to me anymore—that giant proves you wrong!"

"What difference does it make—it was a long time ago. Come on, it's late."

"Are you going to tell me what happened or not?"

Jack believed they had been building secret weapons out in the hills—or dumping radioactive crap everywhere. That was what the giant man was, the product of government testing. It was as silly as believing in the Incredible Hulk—but there it was. His father had stumbled into it and they killed him, then brushed everyone else off. Sheriff Hubbins could have been in on it, too. Maybe they fixed him up with the Sheriff's job. After all, he even admitted that his father would be Sheriff now if he were alive.

He told this suspicion to Sheriff Hubbins.

The Sheriff laughed a little. "Anybody who wants this job can have it. This ain't no glamour job. And I wouldn't take a job in exchange for any man's life."

"But you're hiding something."

"Look, Jim, are we gonna dance like this all night."

"I got time."

"Shouldn't you be saving the trailer park from the monster?"

Jack said nothing.

"That was the fifties—" said Hubbins. "Well, the early sixties anyway. You didn't talk out about anything and everything that happened back then."

"It isn't the fifties anymore, Sheriff."

"Maybe not for you kids, but times don't change as fast as you think they do." Sheriff Hubbins shuffled his feet on the loose gravel littering the blacktop. "Jim, I don't know what really happened up there that night—not much of it anyway. But I guess you're a man now and you should know what I can tell you. I don't believe your father did kill himself. But what's done is done and it can't be undone. Sometimes looks like there never will be an end to that business."

Jack listened. When the Sheriff paused he held his breath, waiting for him to continue.

Finally the Sheriff did. "The old highway used to run right through those foothills, and that night your Dad was patrolling and saw a flash of light. He called it in and then went up to have a look. He called in a second time.

"The dispatcher said he sounded excited and out of breath. Transcripts of the calls were confiscated later but I had a chance to read them first; your father found some kind of wreckage up there—he estimated that it spread over half a mile at least. Thought it must be an aircraft. Turned out to be a spaceship."

"A spaceship?"

"And he found a man's body. A man in a space suit. And the space suit had those old letters on it: CCCP. We sure knew what that meant."

Jack shook his head. He didn't.

"That was USSR in Russian. The dead man was a Russian cosmonaut." He paused, seeming to collect his thoughts. "I was the first officer to get there, but by that time the place was already swarming with military from the testing base. They wouldn't let me through their perimeter, so I screamed and hollered until somebody with a lot of gold on his lapel came and told me about how they found your Dad.

"They showed me the body of a dead cosmonaut. Then they brought me to your Dad's patrol car and showed me his body. There was a bullet hole in his temple. They already had him in a body bag but they unzipped it enough to show me the wound. I asked to see the rest of him and they refused. I'd be lying if I said that didn't make me suspicious.

"But there was an awful lot of them and only one of me. I just nodded and held my tongue. I swore that I would do something as soon as I got away from them—but at that moment I was in no position to start an investigation. Who's to say there might not've been two suicides that night if I wasn't careful."

"You left him."

The Sheriff looked angry. "I used my head—not my smart mouth, son."

"And you are alive."

"That's right, Jack, I am. Go ahead and hate me for it—but it won't change a thing."

Jack was speechless. His head was swimming with thoughts and resentments. He wanted to be away from there—he wanted to go and never see the Sheriff or the town or anyone he knew ever again. He wanted never to think of his father again.

"They escorted me back to my patrol car and put a couple of their boys in with me. We all went to the station and they spent a long time in private conference with old Sheriff Bailey. Everybody on the force—there were about thirteen of us back then I guess—had all been called in, and we sat in the station waiting for them to emerge from the old man's office. When they did, they had my report all written out for me and ready to sign.

"I signed it," he continued, "you bet I did, or I would've never held a state or county job again. I just sort of understood that was how it was meant to be—the way you just sort of understood things back then—without anybody having to spell it out for you. Anyway, the report was just pretty much what I had seen minus the spaceship and ..."

"And what?" said Jack.

"And one other thing I saw that they left out—they were picking through the wreckage—I saw a piece of the cockpit, or whatever you call that part of a spacecraft—the capsule. Your Dad reported finding one dead cosmonaut and I saw one body. But there were two seats in the wreckage."

"Maybe the second cosmonaut was still alive." Maybe he still was, living for years off the radiation-soaked desert and growing under the hills.

"And killed your dad."

"And the government covered it up?"

"Wars start over that kind of thing. About thirty miles from the crash site they were doing underground H-bomb tests. They put out the story that radiation was detected at the site and that's how they kept people away. Cost them a lot of money settling the class action suit a few years ago—but they couldn't change their story after so many years—and anyway all the money went right back into the community. Settlement money built your new high school gym for one thing."

"And that's worth letting everybody believe my Dad killed himself."

"I don't think anyone around here thinks less of him. Or your mother. You weren't even born yet, but the whole community came together during all that. Everybody liked your father, Jim."

Jack squinted, trying to prevent tears from coming. "Then why didn't they stand up for him? Why didn't you?"

"Maybe when you're older you'll understand—but nobody did anything that night just to hurt you or your Dad. I think everybody did what they thought was for the best."

Jack wished the giant who had murdered his father would crush the whole town under his feet. He turned from the Sheriff and walked.

"Jack." He heard the tone of seriousness in the Sheriff's voice. "Jack, don't go that way. I mean it."

Jack ignored him and kept walking the direction the giant had gone. He didn't want to think about what he might find when he got back home; he only knew that he did not want to hide from whatever was going to happen.

The Sheriff was not following him, but back there—down the road—Jack heard trucks. A flood of lights swept under his feet and he turned.

The army rolled down the highway in full force.

☆

Moments after her Dad had ordered them to leave, Janniffer began to fear for him and Jack. Jack had been half raving with his talk of the giant man, and even her father—who was never bothered by anything—seemed weird. And what had happened to his patrol car?

Paige must have picked up on her feelings because she spontaneously reached over and held Janniffer's hand. The two of them were in the back and Doggart was up front alone. He was uncharacteristically quiet—thank god.

They never got as far as home. Green army tanks and trucks were moving toward them down both lanes of the highway. Janniffer didn't know tanks could move so fast.

"What do we do!" shouted Doggart in a panic. There was no room for them on the road and the tanks weren't slowing down.

"Pull off!" cried Paige.

He swerved the wheel and they were out of the way just as the convoy reached them and suddenly ground to a halt.

A jeep slipped out of the line and came alongside them. An officer got out and motioned for them to roll down a window. He was a redhaired man who did not look much older than they were, but when he spoke he addressed Doggart as "sir" and the two girls as "ma'am" when he asked to see identification.

Paige and Doggart each showed him their driver's licenses.

"I don't have mine," Janniffer said. "I ran out of the house without it."

"I see," said the officer flatly. She could not tell if it meant that she were in trouble.

"She's Sheriff Hubbins' daughter," said Doggart. Damn Doggart. He went on: "We just left the Sheriff—he told us to go straight home and that's what we're doing."

"I see," said the officer again, "and where'd you leave Sheriff— I'm sorry what was the name?"

"Hubbins. Maybe half a mile up."

"I'm going to have to ask you to leave your vehicle and step into the jeep, sir. Ladies. There is a curfew in effect."

"Woah," said Doggart. "The curfew is not active outside city limits."

Was there no end to his stupidity? thought Janniffer.

"I don't know what curfew you are talking about, sir, but my curfew is in effect anywhere and everywhere I say it is. This is martial law, sir."

☆

Sheriff Hubbins would have been more than happy to have the Calvary arrive if they hadn't been hauling his daughter and her friends along with them.

A captain with red hair and freckles got out of the jeep Janniffer and the others were riding in. He carried an electric blue folder—the kind with a flap over it and elastic string wrapped around it. He walked up to Hubbins who didn't give him time to speak.

"Son," said Hubbins, "what do you mean by hauling them kids back here into the fire zone?"

"Which fire zone is that, sir?"

"Don't bullshit a bullshitter. I saw the thing. If you're gonna catch it you're going about it mighty slow, aren't you?"

"I have my orders," said the captain cryptically. "Please take a seat in the jeep, Sheriff."

"It's like that, is it?"

"It's for your own safety, Sheriff. I notice you seem to have misplaced your sidearm."

"You noticed that, eh?" He turned around to say something to Jack but the kid was gone, slipped off into the darkness just as the battalion pulled up.

Hubbins squeezed into the back of the jeep next to his daughter. She looked at him after the battalion started up again and the captain and the driver were concerned with other things. He watched her mouth the words, "Where's Jack?". Hubbins shook his head briefly.

For some reason the captain chose that moment to look back at them. Hubbins said to him, "You figure you got enough tanks?"

The captain got into the jeep and did not turn around again.

They drove along the road and it appeared to Hubbins they might have missed the giant entirely. Perhaps the monster had veered off the highway. Possible, especially since Hubbins could hear the whooshing of fighters jetting off into the east.

They came to the mobile home suburb where Jack and his mother lived. Hubbins himself had grown up there—lived most his life in the place until the Sheriff's job had enabled him to get a real home for his family.

The giant cosmonaut had been and gone; the area was a shambles. Power lines were down and the streets were dark. Trailers had been kicked around like Lionel boxcars. It was quiet.

The teenagers beside him were shocked speechless. It felt to Hubbins like everyone must be dead.

The captain ordered his vehicles to fan out in a crescent across the devastation. Men picked up bullhorns and called out for survivors.

Gradually a few beaten wretches crawled out from hiding places. The captain ordered them rounded up and had their names taken down. Hubbins did not see Jack's mother among the dusty survivors.

"Captain," said Hubbins, trying to sound as polite as possible, "you'll want to start digging, won't you? There must be other survivors under all this rubble."

The young officer looked at him as though the Sheriff had farted. "Thank you for the input," he said.

Once the soldiers had the survivors' names they started leading them to the transport trucks. This was no way to be doing things, Hubbins thought.

Then, perhaps for consistency's sake, the soldiers decided to move Hubbins and the kids out of the jeep and into a transport. Hubbins asked a soldier if he could speak to the captain, who had wandered away, but his request was denied. He noted a masked indifference in the soldier's thin face—an indifference that denoted an attitude with which Hubbins was acutely familiar. He had taken the same attitude himself many times in his career. It was the attitude you take toward a bothersome but powerless prisoner. Hubbins didn't like how that made him feel, though there wasn't a thing he could do about it.

Once inside the transport, the flaps were pulled down and Hubbins observed the attack survivors. There was no talk of the giant at all. It was late in the night now, and most of them had probably been asleep when it happened. The general impression was that the trailer park had been bombed.

"Bombed or strafed," said a man, an old retiree in a checked bathrobe. "I heard machine-gun fire." Others nodded in agreement.

That was would have been the helicopters strafing the giant, but Hubbins decided not to say anything—even though some of the speculating got pretty wild. There were some that believed the attack had been nuclear.

"We wouldn't be here talking about it if it was," said someone else.

"Maybe we just caught the edge of it. Maybe they're gonna quarantine us for radiation sickness."

Hubbins said, "If there was radiation danger those soldiers would be wearing special gear." And why weren't they wearing protective suits, come to think of it? That giant was glowing green. It was obviously radioactive. Maybe the soldiers knew less about what was going on than he did.

"And anyway," objected another, "why did I hear shooting? No, it had to be a terrorist attack."

Hubbins saw that his daughter was shaking. Her friends, too. "Now come on," he said, "all this speculation is getting us nowhere."

"Well, what do you propose, Sheriff?" said a balding man wearing pajamas that had swords and shields printed on them. He was missing a slipper.

"I propose we take a ride and relax."

"If you haven't noticed, this truck isn't moving," the man commented. "What do they plan to do with us?"

"They'll take us into the hospital in Boulder City, I expect. They'll check us for shock and injury and when they're satisfied we're all right, they'll set out some cots in the high school gym for the folks that can't make any other arrangements."

"I don't need any 'arrangements'. I'll set up a tent in my own damn yard." The bald man stood up in the truck indignantly. "And I am certainly not in shock." He went to the flap and threw it open. He stepped over the back of the truck—bad move, thought Hubbins. But even he had no idea just how bad.

The instant the bald man stepped onto the truck's bumper a burst of gunfire cut him to ribbons.

☆

Jack had stolen off into the desert while Sheriff Hubbins was distracted by the advancing tanks and before the floodlights caught sight of him. Fortunately, and for whatever reason, the Sheriff had chosen not to reveal Jack's presence in the desert.

Hubbins had always taken care of both Jack and his mother—though Jack now suspected it was out of guilt rather than kindness.

Still, the Sheriff had been—had tried to be—a second father to him and he felt like a traitor running away from him into the desert.

There was Janniffer to think of as well. He knew that she worried about him, feared for him. His mother, too, of course. It got demeaning, all these people always worried and looking out for you. That was why, maybe, he turned out to be a good runner—always wanting to get away.

His clothes, having been drenched in sweat, dried and drenched again, were icy and chafing. He covered ground less rapidly now, alternating wind sprints, steady jogs, and long-strided marches. Anything to keep moving. With the way the highway twisted, and the slow rate the battalion moved, he thought he might beat it to the giant with a little luck. He didn't know what he would do then.

He kept moving.

☆

The giant was easy enough to spot again; there was a faint, gradually increasing roar of fighter jets to guide him.

The giant was not able to ignore the jets as it had the gnat-like helicopters. It stopped walking and engaged the careening jets head on. They shot rockets at its massive bulk. Most missed—the giant was able to maneuver itself much faster than the jets were able to circle around for strikes. But some of the rockets found their target, drilling into the flesh of the massive torso like bullets.

It bled.

Jack heard the monstrous head shriek at its attackers in thundering incomprehensible syllables. Because of the sheer volume of the shrieks booming over the roar of the jets, it took Jack a few moments to understand that they were not animal noises—but words. Not English—but words certainly.

Now heavily wounded, the giant cosmonaut tried to drag itself from the fray. The jets kept coming. On the distant horizon Jack could see flames from two or three wrecked planes, but it now seemed as if the giant was too sluggish to destroy any more of them.

Jack felt helpless. He was caught in the midst of a deadly ballet that he could take no part in. The cosmonaut had murdered his father years ago, the military and the Sheriff's office and even the townspeople had conspired to cover it up, and it all was going to end here, all their decades of lies and deceptions. The military was enacting the final episode in the drama and he was only a bystander. Just as Sheriff Hubbins had taken the truth about his father's death and hidden it from him—appropriated it for expediencies of his own—now the army was killing the giant.

He was certain it was dying. The caked dirt over the giant's skin was awash in its own blood. It stumbled. The jets drove in, hammering the thing to its knees. The great chest collapsed to the earth, the great eyelids drooped as its head settled into the ground.

A river gushed from its enormous nostrils. The dying giant lay a quarter mile off, facing him.

Jack edged a little closer as the fighters finished pumping shell after shell into its back. Once they broke off and regrouped high in the sky, Jack sprinted across the open ground.

The giant still breathed; it opened and shut its eyes.

Jack wanted—he needed—the thing to see him.

He put both hands on the giant's eyelash and pulled. Then released and let it snap back. Both huge eyes fluttered, the giant seemed to stir, but remained unaware.

It would be dead in a moment. It would be dead and Jack would never be able to confront his father's death.

The fighters dove again.

The giant had whiskers and Jack climbed them. High above, straddling its ear, Jack whipped off his shirt and waved it like a flag at the jets. If he could get them to stop firing ...

They stopped. Perhaps it was the surprise of seeing a human being standing on the giant's ear—or maybe they realised that they had killed the monster—or maybe they had simply run out of ammo. Whatever the explanation, the jets veered off toward the base just as helicopters appeared over the horizon. These landed a few hundred yards away. That gave Jack only a few minutes at best.

He screamed into the giant's ear, trying to revive it. There was only this last moment—and if the giant could not—or would not answer ...

It moaned.

"Who are you?" Jack yelled.

The cosmonaut gave a long and garbled Russian name then stated its rank and serial number in thickly accented English. All Jack got was that his father's killer was a major.

There was no time. "You crashed," said Jack. He could see a phalanx of troops from the helicopters making their way from the road slowly, like shadows.

"Yasss," slurred the giant. "Pitched craft. Taken for prisoner. Political ..."

Jack pressed on. "You killed a policeman. A deputy—"

"Nye—no. Oszer's ..."

Others? "Did the other cosmonaut do it?"

"Soldiers," it said, "soldiers kill him."

☆

When Nikolai Petroyevich came to, the first thing he saw was a bright light—but it was not the bright light of heaven. It was a flashlight. And the figure behind the flashlight was not God, but a man—a man wearing a uniform.

The man spoke to him—and whatever he was saying it was not Russian. Gradually the haze began to dissipate and the words made sense. It was English, and he spoke a little English.

"Sir?" the man said.

"Where am I?" asked Nikolai in the best English he could manage.

"Just southeast of the base," said the man.

The base? What base? Where in the world? "What country?"

"America," said the man.

Nikolai realised there was a blanket placed over him, probably to keep him from going into shock. He had better say no more. This fellow appeared to be a peace officer of some kind, and would help him. His mission had been a secret, and this man would hardly be expecting to find a cosmonaut. He had mentioned a base—a military base perhaps? It might be better to let the man believe his flight had originated there.

"My—" he struggled for the right word, "co-pilot?"

"Let's just see about you first—help's on the way," the officer said with hesitation in his voice.

Nikolai assumed that this noncommittal answer meant that his fellow crew member was dead, and that he was alone. This would be a mess, he was thinking, but a mess for Moscow to unravel—not him. Most embarrassing for them to launch an experimental nuclear-powered spacecraft secretly and lose it on American soil. Nikolai laughed.

"Glad you've got your sense of humour, pal," said the officer. "The name's John—John Jaffe."

"Pleased." He avoided giving his own name. "I am not from here," he said, and he knew it must sound oddly redundant.

It did, and now the man called James Jaffe laughed as well.

"You're not too far from the base," the man told him.

Nikolai felt he was in great trouble. Worse than that, he felt intense nausea, a sign that the worst might have happened—the nuclear core of the spaceship may have leaked and poisoned him. His co-pilot was lucky in that case—he had died quickly.

Nikolai expected to be taken into custody but did not fear a long delay in his release. He was not on a spy mission after all, and cosmonauts like astronauts were international heroes. Nikolai closed his eyes and waited for whatever was going to happen to happen.

He was awakened by the roar of vehicles, the booming of loudspeakers and the shouts of men. There was a gunshot. Nikolai involuntarily snapped upright and his back seized into spasms. He could see the peace officer lying prone a few feet from him, and there were soldiers, sweating and cursing one another. They spoke too fast for Nikolai to follow their English, but they were clearly arguing over the slaying of the peace officer. Nikolai could not guess why they had done it—unless in a panic caused by the dark and a fear of the unknown.

A soldier noticed that Nikolai was conscious and advanced toward him, rifle raised. This will be it then, thought Nikolai. No slow death by radiation—I am to be executed by these fearful and desperate men. Perhaps they would neatly pin the murder of the peace officer on him. His troubles were at an end.

The soldier did not shoot. He merely kept his weapon trained on Nikolai and shouted for his comrades' assistance.

He was unable to control the urge to vomit and jerked his ruined body to the side to do so. The soldier ought to shoot, he thought. He shook and felt life draining from his body. He was going to die in some foreign desert and no one—not family, not friends—would ever hear from him again.

Nikolai felt a profound sympathy for the murdered peace officer. Did the man have a wife and children? If so, they would never see him again—and for what? For waiting with a dead man until aid arrived.

Nikolai quaked with pain as he thought of these things. It was a bad way to die.

But he did not die.

Though he would never find out what exactly happened next, he lost consciousness—slipped into a coma perhaps. Gradually, self-awareness returned. Or rather, a new awareness emerged: slow, dreamlike and housed in his very bones. He came eventually to understand that he had lain for years in a secret chamber in some forgotten underground facility under a vast desert—in a sort of American Siberia where the US had tested its nuclear weapons. Radiation from those tests fed his body.

Fed it and made it grow.

Though homesick and alone, Nikolai came to relish his peaceful limbo, content never again to witness oppression or deal with governments. Even here, in the supposedly-free West, his last memory was of soldiers killing their fellow countryman: the peace officer whose only crime had been to stumble across Nikolai in a downed experimental craft—merely coming to the aid of a traveler from the other half of the world.

At some point, radio broadcasts began piercing his consciousness. In time, they whispered undreamed of news: the Soviet regime that had oppressed his Russia had crumbled. Joyously, he decided to wake himself into this new world of peace.

Instead, he woke to violence.

Now, nearly two decades later I am killed by the remnants of the bipolar world for the crime of rising from the grave, thought Nikolai, watching a tiny human being shout at him and climb along his nose. Even enormous size and the fullness of time were not enough to protect a simple man from the machinations of the world.

Nikolai wondered about the small creature before him. It was hard to tell but it seemed that it was little more than a boy. What odd chain of events or quirk of personality led this boy to risk death beneath the roar of military might, to climb a giant's dying face to shout questions in his ear? He wanted to know about the man Nikolai saw murdered. He must be the officer's child then— who else would care about a single man after so long a time?

☆

There was pandemonium in the truck when the bald man died. Hubbins watched as the passengers climbed over each other like animals to get away from the bullets. But the bullets kept coming. His daughter scrambled with the crowd and he did not want to watch her die. He was thinking that he was glad he had gotten so fat in the last twenty years, as he pushed through the bodies and threw his whole bulk upon her—hoping it would be enough, yet fearing that the army would send a man or two into the truck with hand guns to finish up once most of the witnesses were dead.

She was crying and he put his hand over her mouth. "Play dead, honey," he said to her. "Play dead." To gain another second or two of life.

☆

Soldiers had killed his father, Jack had heard the giant say. So it had not been suicide.

He stood unmoving upon the ear of the murdered giant, while helicopters landed and soldiers poured out onto the desert sand. Jack wanted to kill them all, all the men who'd been there that night, all the men who had killed his father, or those like Sheriff Hubbins who had allowed his death to become a lie.

They came nearer in loping, strained gaits, laden with heavy packs of machinery and weapons. Jack knew he could easily outrun them, and probably lose them in the desert night—for a while at least. But he did not run; he had all he wanted to know about himself there beneath him, in the mountain of human flesh that was the slaughtered cosmonaut. Below him, the great dark cave of the dead giant's mouth gaped open.

☆

As she crawled through the rubble that had once been her home, Mary Jaffe was thinking only of her son Jack—she prayed he was not in the group she had just watch being slaughtered by the soldiers. She had been trying to make her way toward them with her leg all twisted, too weak to call out, when the men started firing on her neighbours. She fell and hid, watching with horror as the murdered corpses of Tom Hubbins and his daughter were dragged onto the ground. She saw two other friends of her son as well. They, too, were dead. But no Jack. All night she had prayed that Tom would find her son, and now she thanked God that He had not listened to her.

There was chaos and an officer with red hair tried to restore order. The panicky soldier who had started the firing was unconscious—the officer had butted him in the head with his sidearm. Mary tried to make herself as small as possible in case they combed the neighbourhood for witnesses.

They did not.

What they did instead seemed to her even more ghastly than what had happened already.

Quickly, his face wet and red with anger, the young officer ordered gasoline poured over the truck, and over the bodies that had spilled from it. He ordered his men back into the other vehicles and signaled for them to move out. Then, climbing aboard a tank, he tossed a match.

Mary cried.

☆

Jack slipped and slid over the giant's tongue, ducking down at the back of the throat. Evidently the soldiers did not find the prospect of pursuing him appealing or—even more likely—no one had noticed his small figure against the giant's much greater one.

He turned and faced the new world before him. South to the stomach, he thought, or north to the brain?

There was light through the nasal cavity. Jack had assumed that this was light shining through the nostrils. But then he realised it was dark outside, so where was the glimmer coming from?

The light had the faintest tint of green to it.

As Jack forced his way up through the giant's head, he considered his chances. It was the brain that was glowing green. Whatever impossible force that had allowed the cosmonaut to grow fifty feet high and to rise again in the world was still alive in that brain. Perhaps he could take advantage of that fact.

They would undoubtedly want to study the body—because of its sheer size that might take years—and as he crawled behind the eyes he saw that soldiers were already applying grappling hooks to the giant's limbs. He did not know how long he would have. If they cut right into the brain he might be caught by morning—if the body lay in storage while bureaucratic infighting led to inaction, he might have months or even years.

His own skin was bathed in green light now, and he settled into the folds of brain tissue to allow the glow to do its work most effectively. With a little luck—with a lot of luck, actually—and the willingness to embrace the patience he had never had, Jack might grow into a giant like the cosmonaut. He had no idea what the process would be like: had the cosmonaut been growing steadily for twenty years? Or did he spring up from the dead that very night in a sudden cosmic growth spurt? Jack did not know.

Through the ear canal, Jack heard the wup wup wup and the whistling of helicopters rising into the air, hauling the giant heavenward. There was green light everywhere, heating, massaging and stretching his skin.

Jack found that by touching the right nerve endings he could see with the dead giant's eyes. What he saw was the rising sun.

Morning had come.

Daqinshan

Kylie Seluka

Daqinshan—the Big Green Mountain—wore its name like an imperial jade cloak. For countless millennia it overlooked the Huang He River flowing through a picturesque valley in Central China. Then people arrived. The city of Lanzhou bloomed like invasive mugwort until it had crammed itself into the valley. All in the pursuit of progress: workshops became factories became manufacturing plants became industrial parks. Daqinshin's grand shadow disappeared in the thickening foul air. Its wondrous green cloak wore away to a threadbare dusty yellow. Such things did not perturb Daqinshan. The mountain stood constant ... as it expected it always would.

☆

Amongst the congested smog and grey concrete below the 'Big Green Mountain' lived a little man. Little by size, but not by heart. He had the heart of a giant, though no one saw it. If they noticed him at all, they saw someone smaller, thinner, and weaker than most ... in fact, all. Even his parents had called him Xiao or 'little one'.

Like every other morning, Xiao woke up and washed himself in a bucket in his closet room rather than going to the public baths—having a giant heart didn't mean he was reckless with it. He put on his faded blue tunic and oiled his thin black hair, now streaked with a forty-seven-year-old greyness. After taking two herbal tablets that promised to make him bigger, he flexed his arm. *Maybe I should take four*, he thought.

☆

"I want more congee," demanded his young nephew, Bao, banging an unruly tune on the table with his spoon.

Xiao's sister-in-law looked on approvingly as her son devoured another bowl of the rice porridge. Mingmei gave a sour glance to Xiao, "Give your nephew some money for school this morning. Don't be cheap like last time, eh?"

Xiao nodded several times, smiling, as he handed her a glass of soybean milk. His younger brother, Chen, strode in putting on his suit jacket. Mingmei passed the glass of milk to her husband

and he gulped it down.

"You should eat more. Here, have these for the train trip," she said.

Chen grinned as he took the steamed pork buns. "Work hard at school today," he said to Bao as he left.

"Yes, father," said Bao gravely.

Xiao sighed. Xiao had no family of his own; he wasn't even married. No self-respecting girl would want to marry the smallest man in Lanzhou, maybe in the whole Gansu province.

Like every other day, Xiao dragged his mobile shoe repair and shine shop down the stairs, all eleven flights. At each floor he squashed himself into the rubbish that had piled up in the corners. People queuing up behind him then shoved past as he smiled and nodded at their mutterings.

Xiao stepped outside, into a blast of noise and noxious fumes and hawked out the over-ripe reek caught in his throat. He pulled a red handkerchief up over his mouth and pushed his shop along the path. It wasn't far to his usual spot—on the side of one of the busy streets near the Longhai train station. He set up his shop and stool, smiling at potential customers. Some people stopped for a quick shine before catching the train to work. To them he was 'the shoe boy' but most just passed by and didn't notice him at all.

It was like the beginning of every other day. However, this day was not going to end like every other day.

☆

"Hey, today I can't even see the bridge!" Bing said, cigarette dangling from his mouth. He handed Xiao a bowl of steamy noodle soup from his food cart.

"Tsk, this city is not a good place to live." Xiao shook his head.

"Ha, it's not so bad—besides where would someone like you go?" said Yuan from his newspaper stand.

"Where it's green and the air is cleaner," said Xiao pensively, "Or near the sea."

"Ha, you're crazy! You'll never go there!" said Yuan.

Bing nodded. "Yes, you're always complaining. Maybe you should try doing something about it instead."

"Ha, he's not the type to change things. He's not like Deshi, you know!" said Yuan. "Now there's someone to listen to. Deshi's going to make a difference—get rid of all this bad air."

Yes, someone important, Deshi, had come up with an Idea. It had spread quickly around the city—some laughed, some lamented and amazingly some listened. The Idea was that if the mountain Daqinshan wasn't there, all the pollution would simply blow away to somewhere else. So they—being the Powers That Be—had decided to get rid of the mountain. Starting that particular day, Supporters of the Idea dutifully walked up the mountain and started digging the summit away.

Xiao had ideas. His ideas were very different—such as more parks, trees and fewer factories—but no one listened to him. He didn't like Deshi's Idea, especially as his Ancestors were housed in Daqinshan. *Maybe I better check on the family shrine*, he thought.

☆

The Ancestors didn't think the Idea was a good idea either; in fact they were quite alarmed. Surely, they thought, these people would quickly give up on such a silly idea. But they hadn't, and so something had to be done. Now, Chinese ancestral spirits aren't just mist and moaning—and these ones had a whole mountain to draw power from, not to mention magical connections to the other elements. They came up with a Plan.

Xiao started his journey, struggling up the mountain into the thick, pasty sky. People carrying down their baskets of mountaintop passed him by, smiling as they would at a young child wanting to help. Of course Xiao smiled back. Encouraged, comments started to fly until one yelled out with an uncharacteristic meanness. "Hey Chong—worm boy! Here's a rock for you to carry down if you can," and he flicked a pebble at Xiao. It was such a good joke, all joined in and he was pelted unmercifully.

Xiao continued to smile. But don't be mistaken in thinking that the constant barrage of sticks, stones and names didn't upset Xiao. They all hurt. A lot. And inside, the hurt tightened around his heart, squeezing. However, Xiao, being the dutiful eldest son, kept going.

He came to the shrine—a graceful arc of white stone. After he had swept it clean, and lit the incense bowls, he bowed. "Ancestors, I wish to honour you. Is there anything I can do to serve you?"

Pungent incense smoke swirled towards him, full of whispers and murmurs. The spicy aroma intensified around him, thick and close. The light grew dim and spun as he fell to his knees.

"As a matter of fact, there is," they replied—and drew him in.

☆

The people working on the slopes of the mountain felt a curious little shudder. But that was nothing compared to what was going on inside—for the mountain now had a soul and Xiao had disconcertingly become a mountain.

The consciousness of Xiao sat there for a while, tentatively pushing his mind out into the dark earth. Nothing happened. Finally he asked: *What now?*

"Now, you should stand up and roar. Scare those foolish people who think they can move us. Then you can sit down and we can go back to the way it was before the Idea," replied the Ancestors.

Obediently, Xiao stirred. Curves and crevices started to form as he and the mountain merged together into a kneeling little man-mountain kind of shape. An energy force welled up from deep inside. Monstrous vibrations triggered an unearthly noise as the mountain ripped itself away from the ground, stood, stretched and roared a yawn.

Silence flooded the valley. Dust settled. All living things looked up in awe for a long, still moment. Large clods of yellow earth and a few unfortunate supporters tumbled down, their movements echoing in the quiet. Then it erupted—not the mountain—but panic, mayhem, chaos. For there stood the inconceivable—a human but of mountain size and material. Some couldn't even see that, all they could see were two earthy shafts veering up to the smoggy heavens.

The Ancestors congratulated themselves, thinking that now they would be even more revered.

"Okay, time to sit down. That should do the trick," they said.

Revelations coursed through Xiao as he looked down over the city of Lanzhou. All the people looked like ants and all the buildings like picnic leftovers. He liked it. He liked it a lot.

"I am beyond huge, I am immense!" His mouth curled firmly into a smirk.

For unfortunately, while Xiao now had the body of a giant, his heart had shrunk to that of a man. Everything he had kept confined in his once giant heart escaped, bursting forth in bitter release.

"Nothing can hurt me now!" He picked up a couple of boulders with his big earthy hands. "Here are some rocks. I hope they are not too small!" he yelled as he flung them at the frenzied specks below. He stomped into the city. His footprints created deep holes amongst the fungal growths of buildings. "Here's my shoe—give me a shine!" he growled. His big earthy feet crushed all underneath—trains in particular. They crackled like eggshells.

Old wounded grievances boomed out from Xiao's mouth, now a cavernous hole. The vibrations of his ranting caused buildings to shudder, walls to crumple and glass to shatter. No one really understood what he said. His voice was deep and rumbling—hard to decipher and anyway they were all too busy screaming, running ... dying.

Xiao looked up at the funnels belching out black, toxic grunge into the air. Memories of his parents coughing up that same coal-black tar protested through him.

"No more!" He pounded towards them. Swinging a vengeful fist of earth, he smashed it down onto one coal-processing plant... and then another ... and another. Fragments the size of buses flew up and embedded themselves into his legs, but he was beyond feeling.

"Anyone want to play soccer with me now?" he yelled as he kicked over all the funnels and watched them tumble, crashing into the factories below. An explosion of dirt and debris boiled up into a grotesque cloud that hung over the city, before falling like a shroud.

Angry yellow dust and Xiao's euphoria dissipated. He was faced with the reality of his actions. It wasn't a pretty sight—smashed and smoking remnants were splattered all over the place. The train station where he and the others worked had disappeared. The Huang He River now ran grey, rumpled and creased with wreckage.

A horrible, sinking remorse billowed into Xiao's considerable stomach. *What have I done? What about all the people ... my brother and family?* He started to run, stumbling and staggering until he got his rhythm right—running far, far away from his mess.

Helicopters and planes whirred about. They became very annoying, buzzing around his head, and Xiao swatted them away with his chunky hands. The Powers That Be soon realised that it was a waste of time, resources and not to mention pilots. They considered blasting him, until someone mentioned something about devastating climatic consequences. So they tried to think of something else ... without much success.

A giant mountain man—over a kilometre high, careening through the countryside—is bound to cause some problems, mainly the squishing and squashing kind. At first, Xiao tried to avoid everything. However, as he headed south, the terrain became rougher and thicker with forests. He blundered on, trying not to think about what was happening below, particularly what was sticking to the bottom of his feet.

In his misery, Xiao didn't notice the great expanse of water spanning out in front of him until the last second and had to pull up quickly. Everything caught up with him and he proceeded to throw up a significant quantity of internal mountain bits.

"Finally we've stopped! Now ... we must go back," the Ancestors said.

"I'm never going back there!" Xiao looked around, noticing how clear things appeared. "Besides, this is nice—it's so green and the air is fresh."

"Back home is better," said the Ancestors gloomily.

"No! Just change me back into Xiao," he demanded.

"We can't do that," the Ancestors said.

"What!" Xiao churned up a cloud of dust.

"Not here," said the Ancestors, "Not until we go back!"

"Well ... I'm not going back," said Xiao defiantly.

So they sat there at the edge of the South China Sea. The light of a long and strange day faded and a sliver of a moon hung above them. A melancholy exhaustion sent Xiao into a deep sleep.

☆

Around him, tourist spots abounded. Close by, the now bustling coastal city of Yangjiang became known as 'Place of Mercy'. Everyone there had been praying madly to Kwan Yin, Goddess of Mercy, that the mountain monster would not come to the town—and it didn't. So they built a splendid temple to her that thousands flocked to, hoping for some 'mercy' of their own. If they could afford it, the pilgrims took home a speck of sacred mountain spew or 'miracle mix', as it was packaged.

It was not the only thing that had changed. When Xiao woke from his little recovery nap, about a year later, he felt different—more at peace. It was like some of the mountain's immutable spirit had seeped into him. He was no longer just Xiao but had become Xiaoshan.

He looked around stiffly, and said, "It's still quite nice here, despite all the new developments. Wouldn't it be good if this is what Lanzhou looked like?"

"It could. Maybe they fixed everything up," suggested the Ancestors slyly. "Why don't we go and see."

"Oh, I'm not sure I could," said Xiaoshan, stretching out his arms.

"Come on, they would have forgotten about everything by now!" said the Ancestors. "In fact they probably have honoured you for helping them to make Lanzhou a better place."

"Really—you think so?" asked Xiaoshan, hope rising.

"Besides, we can change you back there," urged the Ancestors.

☆

Xiaoshan grew somewhat uneasy as his massive earth-brown legs lumbered along, bringing him closer and closer to the valley. The journey back seemed to take a lot less time, and all too soon he was there. His lovely new green mantle started to itch when he saw the city sprawl before him.

"I don't believe it," muttered Xiaoshan. The place where Daqinshan had once rested was a rash of construction activity—factories and buildings swelling up like virulent boils. Lanzhou hadn't become a nicer place at all! He clenched his fists. *Lucky for them I'm not a volcano*, he thought, wondering what he could smash first. The area was deserted. He paused and looked around.

"So you want to be changed back now?" asked the Ancestors.

Millions of hiding eyes stung him from across the river and the surrounding mountains. A collective swell of fear, hate and anger rose up above him. He imagined himself, as Xiao, standing small and alone facing such a wave. "Erm, no … not yet," he said. *I have to make things different, better, before I can change back,* he thought.

Standing at the river's edge, Xiaoshan bent down and cupped water in his hands. He trickled it over the infection of new constructions and then began to flush, stir, dig and mould. A large sculpted area emerged, with a surrounding moat channelled from the river. *I was always good at making mudpies,* he thought.

"What's this for?" asked the Ancestors.

"It's my Idea. *I'm* going to do something, change things—tell them to put a nice big green forest here," replied Xiaoshan. He wrote the symbol for 'forest' with his giant muddy forefinger.

"Ho!" said the Ancestors. "Why would they do that? When you

are little Xiao, who's going to make them?"

Xiaoshan was silent.

"Eh!" said the Ancestors eventually. "Well, you need to put us somewhere. Then we can try and change you back."

"What do you mean ... try?" demanded Xiaoshan.

This time the Ancestors were silent.

"You can't do it, can you?"

"Maybe ... maybe not," sighed the Ancestors.

"So you have no power over me! I can do whatever I like—go anywhere ... and you can't stop me!" Xiaoshan turned to charge away—and bellowed.

There was Qilan—another sickly, barren hill—with the top razed off. It was happening again! Scowling, he lifted his foot, ready to stomp. But he was not the same as he was before.

"I don't want to be like them—so small and stupid," he said, putting his foot down gently.

"Yes! Yes! You can be like us," cajoled the Ancestors. "We are clever and powerful."

A contemplative moment that stretched into an hour followed.

The mountains to the North sent out a welcoming call. The river flowed away into the east, inviting him to follow her to a new adventure. The valley, choked by a pallid cloud of waste, remained mute. Another giant moment passed. His scowl sweetened into a smile.

"I know what to do. I'll *make sure* they follow my Idea," said Xiaoshan as he walked over to the unfortunate hill named Qilan. Soon he had settled down over it. *Together we will be too big for them to even think about trying their stupid Idea again—and I'll be able to keep an eye on everything.*

☆

Under the attentive shadow of Xiaoshan, the people did what he had demanded and planted a forest on the reclaimed area. They continued his Idea and cut down on coal-burning factories and implemented new environmental measures. Magnificent ancestral shrines were rebuilt and trees were planted all over the new mountain. Daqinshan once more wore the name of 'big, green, mountain' with dignity. Xiaoshan slumbered into position with a contented smile and the Ancestors congratulated themselves once more.

Time passed, fears diminished and people relaxed a little. Some said they could still see the outline of a man in the folds of the mountain—sitting and watching over the city. They called him 'Grandfather'. When the people had been particularly reverent, a sweet breeze—*the Ancestors' Blessing*—would fan away any smoke or smog.

Everyone was happy—well almost everyone. The spirits in Qilan weren't terribly impressed but they didn't mind that much ... for now.

FROM THE SEA SHALL IT RISE

JAMES COOPER

1

I have a story I am reluctant to tell. If I could avoid writing it at all, I would, but it has haunted me for several years, and the time has come to finally lay it to rest. It is not a story I am particularly fond of, but its time has come, as I always knew it would, and I sit here in nervous deliberation considering how best to set it down.

Am I a writer? No, of course not; can't you tell? I have a slippery grasp of language at the best of times and I have no idea how this confession might turn out. But it has to be told. It has to be passed on. Only then will you understand what I mean.

2

In truth, the opening credits passed me by, but this is what I heard from Old Sam Tudor, who apparently witnessed it all (though how reliable his account might be, I've never quite been able to determine to this day). From the top of Dreisler's Bluff he had been watching the sea hurl itself onto the beach, smoking his pipe and observing a handful of tourists gamely toil across the sand. It was a common feature of his day and no matter how inclement the weather, even on a bitter February afternoon like the one in question, Old Sam could invariably be found watching the winter sea roll in. He was fascinated, he said, by its raw power, its relentless erosion of the very land itself, no matter how impregnable the cliffs and the surrounding rocks might appear. Perhaps it reminded him of his own mortality; certainly Sam Tudor could rarely be caught with anything less than a perplexed expression creasing his already troubled brow. What he witnessed, however (or forever afterwards *claimed* to have witnessed) on that pale winter afternoon would have burdened the sweetest complexion in the Cove.

Even through the thin mist of drizzle that regularly descended across the bay, Old Sam had spied Walter Meredith down on the beach dusting the sand for gold. It was a recurrent source of amusement between the two of them that while one was sitting at the cliff's edge considering what the ocean might be trying to hide, the other was busy wading through the surf rummaging for what it might have coughed up. I don't think either one of them found what they were looking for, but if old men have earned anything, I guess, it's the right to be as eccentric as they please, and Old Sam Tudor and Walter Meredith had discovered in their routine a mechanism to ease them through the day. It may not be to every man's taste, but Sam and Walter seemed perfectly content with their lot, which is more than I can honestly say about most.

When Sam saw Walter, of course, he did what he always did —removed his pipe, nodded his head, and gave a brisk wave, whereupon Walter would raise his metal detector and doff his cap, satisfying another of the day's endless routines. Except, on this particular day, the acknowledgement was left incomplete, for when Walter raised the metal detector, it emitted a high-pitched shriek, the likes of which neither Sam nor Walter had heard it produce before. In fact, Sam had begun to imagine the thing to be defective, having only heard it sing for its supper a handful of times, usually when it became clogged up with sand.

On this occasion, though, the wind carried a full-throated screech that neither of them had the sense to ignore. Both Sam and Walter looked slightly bemused and Walter shrugged his shoulders, settling himself on the mound of sand over which the metal detector had plaintively squawked.

Sam rose to his feet and peered through the drizzle, trying to ascertain if Walter's frantic paddling with the spade was bearing fruit. It looked like *something* was being exposed, but it was clearly part of a much vaster object than Sam's idle imagination could construct, and he simply waited for the rest of it to be unearthed.

Walter must have dug on his own for a full forty minutes, exposing tantalising fragments of the find, before he collapsed to the sand, perspiring from labour and frustration in equal measure. He looked utterly defeated, and turned his attention to Sam to gauge whether it was worth continuing with the dig. He raised his hands to the sky and waited for some sort of signal from Sam, hoping he would advise him to stop.

But Sam had already experienced the first disconcerting lurch of reality. Walter had no idea of the vision he had just exposed, but Sam's perspective was altogether more expansive. He stood at the cliff's edge and let his pipe carelessly drop from his lips. He had a perfect overview of what Walter had stumbled upon and the terror was writ large on his face.

He let the wind make mockery of his unkempt hair and began muttering a dimly-remembered prayer. Down below, half-buried in the sand, was a vast eye as cold and sightless as the sea.

3

To hear Sam tell it, the eye was as big as a country pond, but, of course, that turned out to be false. Like a lot of stuff that came out about Hetty in the beginning, I guess, when we were all guilty of getting carried away. Still, I mustn't be tempted by the obvious detours my story presents. If I jump ahead of myself you must be patient; I have a lot to confess, and it's easy to lose sight of the path.

Once Sam and Walter had alerted the authorities of their discovery, it quickly became apparent that they had found something far more miraculous than either of them had been able to decode. Not just an ancient eye, lain dormant for years, but a fully formed husk of something unimaginable. The only problem was, nobody had any idea what it was.

But I'm tumbling forward again; let me take a breath and a cautionary step backwards, and allow Hetty the good grace to declare herself in her own time. That, after all, is what she'd done with Walter and Sam; I should, I imagine, take my cue from her.

How long Hetty had been buried beneath the Cove, no one really knows, but we certainly know how long it took to dig her out. Walter's brave scrabblings with the spade merely exposed the tip of the iceberg, and when word spread around the bay that an unnatural phenomenon had been unearthed in the sand, it didn't take long before every kook and weirdo in the vicinity had assumed a position down by the water's edge. Included in that bunch, of course, was me, along with everyone else who could be spared from the Aquarium, eager to see what new anomaly had been washed up.

Initially, the dig was overseen by the RNLI, who had dispatched a team of lifeguards to follow up on Sam and Walter's rather garbled report. What they discovered, of course, was something far beyond even their broad remit, and it soon became apparent that their limited resources would be stretched.

What was also obvious early on was that whatever monstrosity was concealed beneath the Cove, it had clearly been dead for some time. Within a matter of hours, the dig had become a full-scale exhumation and the crowd was pegged back by a hastily erected wooden fence. Inevitably, news of the story spread and both regional television and newspaper journalists were passing through the crowd attempting to filter fantasy from fact. It was escalating into a full-blown media circus with unprecedented speed and I couldn't help feeling mildly frustrated that we were unable to fully claim the story as our own.

My colleagues and I had been among the first on the scene and we were wedged up hard against the fence, craning for a better view of the creature gradually taking shape in the sand. It looked impossibly proportioned, the sand having set in gothic clumps on its frame, like a gargoyle brought heavily to its knees. I felt a thrill course through my body as I watched the thing emerge from its grave, though I was still uncertain as to exactly what was being disinterred.

It wasn't long before the lifeguards held up their hands and decided there was little more they could do. They had made significant progress, but at least half of the thing was still buried underground. We were all holding our breath by this time, because it was evident that the creature, the fundament of which was still half-submerged, was larger than any other animal previously spotted in the Cove. By my reckoning, it looked to be about twenty-five feet long, and there was clearly a biological diversity to the thing that would remain hidden from us until the sand and the detritus was chipped away.

The next hour was lost to tedious bureaucratising as the Local Council interceded with its customary heavy hand, until they landed, almost by accident, on a solution: the bobcat reserved for realigning the bay after heavy storms was dragged from hibernation and steered towards the unyielding mass in the sand. Why it hadn't been thought of before, we didn't know, but the plucky digger, operated by Harry Wainwright, accomplished more work in half an hour than the other volunteers had managed in two.

The light was fading now and the sea level had already begun to rise. Whatever happened, the creature would have to be salvaged tonight or else face exposure to elements that could easily tear it apart.

The hastily assembled crew began to work a little faster, digging down ten, then fifteen, then twenty feet in an attempt to make room for the creature's release.

Finally, as the grey sea nudged at the dark band of workers on the sand, the unknown, and as yet unnamed, creature was carefully winched onto one of Harry Wainwright's trucks. It disappeared into the night and the gaping hole from which it had emerged stared back at us, the only proof we had that any of this had taken place at all.

We were cold and left feeling sadly vulnerable, vaguely aware that the moral axis we had always been governed by had been carelessly spun out of true. Whether it would ever be realigned was unclear, but I don't doubt for one second that every one of us present felt exactly the same way. There was a change in the air and the Cove's future looked suddenly bleak.

Eventually, as the drizzle turned to rain, the silent crowd dispersed.

4

The next few weeks were a blur of media activity and bureaucratic bumbling. It was the press that christened the creature "Hetty", and though the National Heritage Society tried desperately hard to have the thing transported to the British Museum, our own lowly councilors for once proved shrewder than them all. They came to an arrangement that Hetty would remain in the Cove until the following year's tourist season was passed, thereby enabling us to benefit from some of the media fallout that Hetty herself had already begun to produce.

Once she had been cleaned up and chiseled out of her tomb of sand, Hetty was a spectacular sight indeed. My initial estimate of twenty-five-feet was not even close. She stood a proud, and dare I say it, quite aggressive forty-five-feet, with her pivoting tail extending an additional ten feet behind.

Describing her now, after all these years of reflection, is no easy task, not least because I barely possess the vocabulary to do so. Her anatomy was, in all honesty, unlike anything you or I could comprehend. The fact that I have witnessed the thing first-hand does not necessarily make it any easier either. Just cast your mind back to the time when the story broke. I know it's a cheap device, and I shouldn't be doing it, but I can't resist the temptation: if I fail to paint a sufficiently vivid picture, just remember what you saw on the news.

Not that the screen image really did Hetty justice; she was a magnificent specimen of unnatural *otherness*, with a biology that had presumably been warped by countless years beneath the sea. She had a richly textured carapace that had softened in death and now looked like an oily sheath of mottled skin, but was, the scientists reported, much tougher than any epidermal compound they'd seen. The creature had limbs of a sort, but nothing familiar to you or I, that was for sure. Its upper torso, which was slick with sand granules, had broad shoulders that deviated into twin tentacles on each side, much like those on an octopus or a squid, but significantly longer. At the tip of each tentacle, a vicious arrangement of retractable barbs suggested that Hetty wasn't nearly as cuddly as she appeared.

Most striking of all was the creature's head, which was shaped like a twisted heart. Its eyes were rimless and wide, beautifully serene, while its nose was an ugly smear in between. There was no mouth in the conventional sense, just an unsophisticated flap that no doubt occasionally trawled open for food. Directly below this was a sensitive spread of boneless digits, which lent the creature a look of wild ugliness that I instinctively felt was unfair.

Below the waist, Hetty's legs were more recognisably like our own: two vast pillars of muscle that supported all forty-five-feet of her. Instead of toes, though, the lower limbs flared out into a unique, bell-like sucker that presumably enabled it to more easily negotiate conglomerate reefs in the sea. It was all speculation, of course, but the scientists had enormous fun trying to recreate Hetty's history, piecing together information on habitat, interaction and diet, none of which could ever be recorded as fact. Indeed, it was the close scrutiny of the scientists that settled the matter of why Hetty had activated Walter Meredith's metal detector in the first place. On close inspection of the creature, Hetty was found to have traces of iron ore embedded beneath the skin, attributed by those in the know to the creature's tendency to drag its mighty body along the seabed, allowing for the natural accretion of minerals and salts. All very simple, they said, though I don't think Walter or Sam were ever truly convinced. To them, the answer was far more prosaic: Hetty's time had come, they said, and, like a siren, she had summoned them, mesmerising them with her mystery and captivating everyone in the Cove.

It was as good a theory as any, I suppose, and I much prefer the whimsy of this to anything else I heard at the time. To be frank, much of the surrounding science left me cold, especially in the face of Hetty herself, who dominated the Cove for the next six months, reminding us how little we know and, more pertinently, how insignificant we are when we're afforded a glimpse of the broader design.

More divergence? No; not this time. All of this is crucial if you're to fully appreciate the scale of what I'm trying to tell. You see, the discovery of Hetty is only a fraction of the tale. There is another story I have yet to disclose; which I dread, but whose time has now drawn near.

5

There was only one place in the Cove that could feasibly accommodate Hetty and, naturally enough, I suppose, that was at the Aquarium where yours truly happened to be employed. The main atrium was a cavernous arena usually reserved for importing rare exhibits and the occasional ecological demonstration, but at last here was an exhibit that was truly worthy of being displayed.

The customary precautions were taken, of course, but the end result was breathtaking. Hetty had been preserved in all her terrible glory reclining in a perspex case, perfectly frozen in death. Her body had suffered the most dreadful decay down the years, and I couldn't help wondering how long she had been buried beneath the sand, those great muscles slowly losing definition in the dark. She still looked beautiful though, like something we had stolen from the stars, and it would be no exaggeration to suggest that interest in the Cove practically trebled in the few months that Hetty, and the wild theories that surrounded her, graced the landscape of our quiet, unassuming town.

When something happened to take it all away, I began to wonder whether we'd brought it on ourselves; and if we had, how much of it we deserved.

6

You'd be right in thinking, of course, that so far my involvement in proceedings had been pretty limited; that there were people better placed than I who could have delivered a narration more telling than mine. All true.

But (and this is something I would genuinely have been glad to concede) the next part is all about me. And Hetty's consort, of course, who was always a part of it, and had finally been drawn to us, summoned from the depths of the sea.

7

Afterwards, they called it the Bakemono, which I think is a Japanese word meaning "demon" or "evil spirit", a designation that couldn't have been further from the truth.

I guess by rights I should have been the one to christen it as I was the one who got to see it first, though in the ensuing commotion this was quickly overlooked, for which I have to admit to being grateful.

Please don't ask why I was at the beach that night, because I have only a nebulous grasp of the reason. I could easily lie, I suppose, claim that I'd been escorting a girl home, perhaps, or night fishing off McElligot's dock, but the truth is simpler and duller, and less likely to throw me off track.

You still want to know? Fine. I was doing what plenty of people who live by the ocean like to do: I was listening to the darkness and trying to imagine the sea. Not something I'd confess to in a court of law, perhaps, but there you go, that's why I was there, and that's how I got to see it first: the Bakemono; Hetty's dark twin, flooding us with the memory of its loss.

As it approached the bay, I thought I saw a distant rippling of the darkness, but it wasn't enough to alarm me. I was used to the peculiar lament of the sea and the occasional rebellion in its belly; we all were. The sea is notorious for changing its face at a moment's notice, and it would have taken more than a playful shift in the current to set alarm bells ringing in my head.

The Bakemono, though, was an awesome sight and its appearance was impossible to disguise. One minute the moon was freely shining down on the bay and the next it had completely disappeared, eclipsed by the creature's advance.

I jumped up and caught my breath, staring at the shadow on the sea. The Bakemono had broken water at least a mile or more from the coastline and was gradually increasing in size. It was like watching a balloon expand before your eyes as the creature silently invaded the bay.

I stood there mesmerised by the dreadful sleekness of the thing's approach, becoming increasingly horrified as the creature declared itself on an unsuspecting world, dripping the pungent salt of the sea. It must have been fully sixty-five-feet tall, I realised, almost as tall as the cliffs, in fact, which were the only natural defenses we had.

If the Bakemono had seen me it was either unconcerned or too focused on its task to care, for it waded from the sea trailing an endless stream of parasites and pipefish whose company was quickly renounced.

The Bakemono stood at the edge of the bay, breathing raggedly, and sniffed at the unwelcoming air. Was it searching out its mate, I wondered? Or had I been too heavily influenced by cheap B-movies to recognise anything other than the lamest significance in every gesture the creature clumsily made?

I had no time to consider it further, for the Bakemono was on the move. It wrapped its tentacles around some of the trees on the top of the cliff and lifted itself closer to the town. I could hear its breathing becoming heavier and then it slowly disappeared behind the cliffs.

Momentarily, I was uncertain what to do, then my civic duty (or plain old curiosity) overcame me. I sprinted up the incline from the beach and followed the enormous black shadow into town.

I could barely comprehend what was happening. Nor did I want to dwell on what might happen once the Bakemono reached the lighted streets of the Cove. I had read enough melodrama in my time to construct a whole tableau of events in my head, none of which seemed preventable given the prodigious dimensions of the beast we were about to face.

I watched great swathes of water drop from its body, fascinated by how expansively it moved. It was so silent, so deliberate, so *precise*, and it was this improbable delicacy and finesse that marked its passage as it slid along the deserted promenade. Even out of the water, it carried with it a sureness of foot and an *elegance* that further made me marvel at its size. How could something so colossal be so *graceful*? How could it dominate the entire skyline and remain so perfectly *poised*?

The question didn't linger for long. As the Bakemono eased further into the Cove, stationary vehicles were almost effortlessly and randomly overturned. Some of them had horrified occupants beating at the glass inside, their screaming faces lit by snatches of moonlight, their cries for help unheard.

It wasn't long, of course, before people began lining the streets to see the silent terror for themselves, and no matter how hard I tried to urge them back, they continued to follow in its wake. Who was I to offer advice in such a situation? No one of substance that was for sure. And wasn't I doing exactly the same thing, trailing the creature directly to its source, eager to see why it had dragged itself from the charmless depths of the sea?

Inevitably, perhaps, there were casualties as people strayed into the creature's path, but the vast majority of the crowd remained undeterred. Many of them had now begun the digital pursuit of the Bakemono with a view to having their 'exclusive' footage broadcast across the world. It was a sickening indictment of twenty-first-century man, whose tragic decline could now be deemed complete. Following in the wake of the Bakemono, these people greedily consumed every single fatality on film as though they were watching some sleazy Hollywood confection designed to perplex both the intellect and the soul. This in itself was a harrowing realisation, and I briefly wondered as I ran if any of us would ever be the same again.

I stopped running as the Bakemono itself slowed down. It had dragged itself to the Aquarium and clearly sensed the body of its kin inside. It had instinctively known where to go, of course, because its mate's resting place had been inelegantly disturbed, its physical remains debased. Who's to say that we too wouldn't register a metaphysical premonition if the body of a loved one was violently displaced? The idea that we might have brought about our own destruction has never been an easy theory to accept, but the truth remains that the Bakemono possessed a clarity of vision that was disconcerting even at the time. It needs to be stated, then, for the record, that refusal to believe in something doesn't necessarily make it so.

The Bakemono gave another strangled, hissing exhalation and tried to block its eyes from the flash photography. It flicked its tentacles at some of the gathering throng as nonchalantly as we'd bat at a fly. Needless to say, those caught by the flaying barbs were instantly torn in two.

Still there was only a marginal retreat from the crowd, a reaction I'm unable to comprehend to this day. These were people I'd lived with all my life, people I'd talked to, played with, accepted as my own. Who would have imagined them to be quite so indifferent in the face of such a wantonly destructive force?

The Bakemono drew another deep and difficult breath and wrapped its tentacles around the dome of the Aquarium, pulling away the entire framework of the roof.

There was a moment of unnatural silence and then the Bakemono emitted a laboured wail of despair. The tentacles disappeared and the silence gave way to a glacial crack; when the tentacles emerged they were tenderly wrapped around Hetty's desiccated body, which had been so poorly preserved by the sea.

Wearily, the Bakemono turned back towards its natural element and began gingerly retracing its steps. The crowd sensibly parted this time to let it pass, but, like the parasites and the pipefish, immediately reassembled in its wake, hoping to acquire the rarest footage of all: images of the creature and its mate being devoured by the silent sea.

It never happened, of course. You know that by now; the story was in the papers for weeks.

The Bakemono made it as far as the cliff's edge, before it gave one final debilitated wheeze and then dramatically surrendered its life. I stood and watched it, along with all the others, as it tried desperately to reach its own environment, willing it on, wanting it to survive. But fate had already played its hand and the Bakemono, despite its resolute purpose, had fallen foul of its adverse design. The lesson was simple: no matter how invincible we imagine ourselves to be, we eventually take a step too far. We shouldn't be surprised when the ground rushes up to meet us and we find ourselves flailing at the air.

For Hetty and the Bakemono, that's exactly what happened. The Bakemono stumbled at the edge of the cliff, possessively clutching its prize, cried out in frustration and pain, and then tumbled from the cliff to the shore, where the water began lapping at its face.

We crowded round to see the unfamiliar dark shapes settle against the waves, listening for the sound of its breath. It was hard to believe that the Bakemono too was gone, its endurance and strength ultimately no match for the simplicity of the earth and the air.

Have I ever fully recovered from what happened that night? Of course not, and I never really expect to. Indeed, maybe it's something that should live in me forever, just as the connection between the two creatures spanned the depth of the ocean, a genetic attachment that nothing had the power to deny.

The truth is I still dream of it, sometimes, when the wind is full and the sea is driving across the bay, and I wonder if there's another still out there somewhere, powering through the ocean, whose love for its own kind is as strong.

THE EYES OF EREBUS

CHRIS MCMAHON

The Dark is alive.

It hums with points of red and violet. Distant places of heat that sometimes tease me with the brilliance of their demise. It is filled with the silence of dumb mass; and strands of unknowable strangeness that twist out of sight within the coldness.

... Oooo, la, la, la, la ...

There are senseless calls in the distance—the meaningless chatter of an empty universe.

I am lonely.

My lover has gone, worn down by my embrace, yet her memory remains in stone and flowering teeth of metal, vast cords of heavy basalt tied with my hard, desiccated flesh. Gifts of ice all but gone.

My eyes are vast and many, reflecting the tiny lights around me. So distant they are, yet I have seen them swell before, and as they do, my need grows apace.

I have taken many lovers, some wet, others as dry as dust, others frozen with an acid tongue, but all I take into me. None endure, nor remain to be part of me, to share this vastness.

I parted from my mother long aeons passed. The flesh between us ripped on jagged edges. I tried to call, but my voice is a small thing, and as yet I am young. Never again have I passed her in this desert sea.

The lovers fail to satisfy, although their taste is a welcome distraction. My mother will have taken many by now, perhaps she will not even remember me.

Sleep at least is an end to the longing. And dreams ... my beautiful dreams ... if only I were old enough to call as I should, perhaps then I would have my lover. Sleep ...

... travellin' down that lonely road,
Oh, lordy mamma!

I don't get no pork and beans.
Oh, honey.
I needs me a sugar-baby ...

A call!

Faithfully the signals are filtered through the shifting, swarming nodes of my nervous system. Thoughts. Feelings.

Strange. My Vendeth line has heard nothing like this before, but I am not discouraged. Each line has its own language.

Nothing more than a fragment, yet the first words since I ripped from my mother, long ago.

I search, spin and twirl, my senses reaching for the slightest trace, eyes fully open. If only I had not been asleep I would know the direction!

Excitement slowly leaches from me.

Was it nothing but a dream? Wishful thinking transforming the chatter into sense?

The lights are cold, and far away.

... and despite the health problems, Chuck."
"Yes, Bob. We could not describe Eisenhower's return to office as anything else but a landslide."
"Absolutely. What a result. Only eight holdout states ..."

There! Strange in its quality, yet words. Reaching toward me from a distant point of heat.

Does my lover wait for me even now?

This is the chance I have prayed for.

I let myself fall, swinging around one of the massive, silent giants. The tight manoeuvre has given me the speed I need.

I fix my vision on that one light in the dark.

I groan, despairing at my hunger and thirst. I hear nothing, and fear soon overwhelms me, but it is too late. I am truly in the void now. Nothing to speed me, or slow me in my flight.

One sign! That is all I ask.

My girl she knows how to roll,
O Betty!
You look's so sweet in my '50 Chevy.
Ooo, baby, ya' know how ta' jive!

There! Again. This time there can be no mistake. My sensitive ears have confirmed the target. My lover awaits! Who else could be talking such as she? Here amid the terrible emptiness of my Universe.

Soon ...

☆

"And of course, here is the man who needs no introduction. The man who saved Earth from the threat of Nemesis. Director

Matrick Keterson."

Applause filled the room, the dim, cold corners cut by bright staccato flashes as photographers surged against the red-roped barriers.

Mat stepped up from the stage onto the tiny platform to join Vice-President Linten and Hari Wottard, NASA Director of Space Sciences. His head swam with the view. The Caltech lecture theatre was packed with press, suit-clad men and women in sombre power-dress. He looked across an auditorium jammed with students, all in awe as they stared up at him on the podium. Scattered amongst them were the members of his own team. Jereece, unshaven as usual, waved laconically.

The applause became deafening as he took the lectern, and he unconsciously gritted his teeth. His hair was steel-grey, as it had been since his early twenties, neatly trimmed around a long, serious face.

He tried to smile and raised his hands to still the applause, his two lanky arms like a crane's wings fanning out beside him.

"Please ... please ..."

Gradually the applause subsided.

"Thank you. But first of all, diverting 2017KW13 was a joint effort, a team one. And equal praise must go to Director Yo Tein of the Peoples Republic of China and Vladimir Rotanski from the Russian Space Directorate." Mat turned to nod at Tein and Rotanski. "Without their help, and the help of their governments, this ... this incredible achievement would not have been possible." Tein nodded back with polite reserve, while Rotanski merely glared.

"The list of all those who contributed is just too long. Both here at JPL and throughout NASA, where I have been lucky enough to be part of this extraordinary program."

He took a breath and looked at the crowd.

"Ladies and gentlemen. This is truly an historic time for Mankind. For the first time we have been able to protect our home, Earth, from an asteroid impact of devastating proportions.

"The revolutionary NTRs—Nuclear Thermal Rockets—now installed on 2017KW13 have already pushed it out of a collision course with Earth, using ice from the asteroid itself as propellant."

Mat stopped and scanned the crowd. They were quiet, expectant. The sound of a stifled cough from the back of the auditorium filled the room.

"There were some who said the task of diverting a 123km long asteroid was impossible. But thankfully advance warning from our Near-Earth Object program, along with our NTR technology, meant that we got the crucial lead time we needed to meet the beast head on."

"We beat Nemesis!' screamed out a man in the front row.

The room broke into applause again.

The news was really months old. But now that the huge asteroid was less than one day away from its fly-by of Earth, the whole world was on watch—and the PR geniuses at NASA had judged it the ideal time for this event.

In the rush to divert the massive asteroid, no one had thought to name it, but that had not stopped the press. "Nemesis" was irresistible, and that name had been splashed in heavy black across media headlines for the last seven years.

"Ah, ladies and gentlemen, please ... please! And I must correct that gentleman in the front row, and all the members of the press here please take note. 2017KW13 is not called Nemesis. There is already an minor planet called Nemesis, 128, which bears no resemblance to 2017KW13."

"When will it be named," yelled back the man, his press-tag glistening in the lights as he rocked on his heels excitedly.

Mat smiled and looked across to Hari, holding up his palms in a silent question.

Hari whispered to the Vice-President, who nodded and flashed a bright row of Texas teeth.

Hari stepped up to the podium beside him and leaned across to the mike. "One of the announcements we have for you today is the naming of 2017KW13. Usually these things are named by the astronomer who first discovered the object, but in view of the circumstances we thought it only fitting that Director Keterson have the honour."

The room erupted in applause again, and Mat looked across to the doorway to see Jereece leaning against the sill, his eyes slightly mocking as he took in the scene. Jereece had been one of the key people on Mat's team, a team leader in the NEO program and the man who first identified 2017KW13. It seemed a lifetime ago—those heart-stopping months when they realised its orbit would swing it past Jupiter and send that massive lump of ice, carbon and rock heading straight for Earth.

Hari raised his hand to the crowd then waved at Mat, clapping above his head as the room went wild.

Camera flashes stabbed into his eyes, and suddenly the empty, blank lenses were filling his view. He felt himself staring at the beginning of a vast, unstoppable future.

"It *is* an honour, and one that should not be mine."

Calls came from the room, demanding the name.

"Very well, ladies and gentlemen ... I will keep you waiting no longer." He raised his hands once more for silence.

"I have decided to name 2017KW13 ... Erebus."

There was silence as the room took in the name, a sense of confusion, perhaps even disappointment.

"Erebus is a deity from Greek mythology—always an old favourite for planets." That had been his ice-breaker joke, but it went completely flat.

"Erebus arose from Chaos, and was wedded to the darkness of

the night, but also represented an infernal region, through which souls had to pass to reach Hades. And this—this whole project—has been a test and a challenge for Humanity. But we have passed through it, to a place where we are one step closer to controlling our wider destiny in this beautiful, but deadly Universe."

There were more camera flashes, then Mat was being ushered away from the podium, displaced by Linten, who raised his hands to the crowd and began a prepared speech that highlighted the foresight and good sense of the Yerry administration. He was soon finished and people surrounded Mat, shaking his hand, patting him on the back. Everyone was talking at once, and a dense wall of expectant eyes pressed in on him.

Mat rose onto the balls of his feet to look over the heads of the crowd. He spotted Jereece and the other members of his team and waved them over. If he was going to share this moment with anyone, it would be them. They started moving toward him, but the packed crowd was swarming toward the stage now and they were pushed back.

The reporters arrived. Microphones and cameras were pushing into his face.

"Mr Keterson, what are your plans now ..."

"Are you staying with NASA?"

"Here, Mr Keterson!"

"Mr Keterson, do you have any comment on the rumours ..."

Mat surveyed them coldly, wondering how he could extricate himself without seeming rude or aloof.

Hari appeared and took Mat by the elbow. As Director of Space Sciences he had a more public role than Mat's, and seemed at ease negotiating the aggressive crowd of TV-jockeys.

"Thank you, ladies and gentlemen. There will be more opportunities for questions after the reception," he said.

Rapid-fire questions trailed after them.

Hari nodded and four secret service agents neatly surrounded them, cutting off the press. They followed the Vice-President's entourage into an adjacent hall, which had been decked out in silver service for the grand reception. Mat was in the VIP section. By design, he and the other dignitaries were scattered through a crowd of wealthy supporters, multi-millionaires who had invested in the NTR technology. Without them, Erebus would still be hurtling toward them on its deadly course.

He dreaded the dinner, and was longing for the blessed silence and comfort of his small apartment. No doubt he would be saddled with some boorish oil billionaire whose 30-year-old engineering degree and avid reading of the *Wall Street Journal* qualified him as a space expert.

Mat was relieved to take his seat, and eagerly accepted a cool lager from the waiter, drinking it down greedily before the press of the crowd forced social niceties on him. His face flushed with heat as the alcohol began its work, and his body relaxed. He loosened his top button and tie, and was about to lounge back in his seat when he caught sight of her.

"I believe this is my seat, Mr Keterson?"

Mat almost choked on his beer, but managed to swallow and straighten in the same motion.

She was tall and elegant, her wavy yellow-blonde hair matched perfectly to her long golden dress, which shimmered in the soft overhead lights.

"By all means, allow me ..." said Mat, leaping up to make the suave manoeuvre of taking her chair out for her. Unfortunately his long legs caught under the table, sending the silver service and precisely laid glassware skittering across the heavy linen. He looked across at her, but only the merest tension at the corners of her mouth hinted at a suppressed smile. He was grateful for her tact.

"Why, thank you." Her accent was Southern, and delightfully sexy. "I am Athy Jates." She held out a soft, yet strong hand for him to shake.

"Matrick Keterson. Pleased to meet you."

She smiled, her soft brown eyes lighting up in her rounded, beautiful face, offset perfectly with shades of subtle makeup.

He felt a little foolish introducing himself—half the world must know his face—but she seemed genuinely pleased.

Mat waved for the waiter, unobtrusively straightening his tie as she turned her head to watch him approach.

She scanned the tray and looked back at the waiter. "Do you think you could find me some of that champagne?"

The waiter nodded, and Mat took another beer before he disappeared. He knew he should slow down—didn't they always say not to get too smashed at these things?—but after the stress of the last few months, he just needed to let loose.

He put down his empty glass and saw Athy smiling at him.

"You know, I have always wanted to meet you, Matrick. We were all so lucky to have someone like you in control of that project."

The waiter arrived with Athy's Moet. Mat took another beer and smiled, feeling relaxed and happy with the world for the first time in ... well, seven years.

"Cheers," said Athy, holding up her glass.

He looked right into her eyes and felt a jolt of excitement. She seemed cool and collected, but Mat could not help noticing the heave of her chest above the off-the-shoulder gown, or the slight tremor in her hand as they clinked glasses.

She smiled.

"Cheers," he replied.

The table filled up around them, but Mat did not take his eyes off Athy.

The waiter arrived once more, and they eagerly reached for the tray.

☆

Jarry Twine pushed himself carefully across the tiny cabin of the NTR control unit. Even after almost a year in the micro-gravity of 2017KW13, he was still overbalancing. It was a tiny space, no bigger than a small trailer, yet packed with electronics and process control equipment. The air was rank with body odours and the stale, artificial flavours of their ration-packs.

"Vapour flow on ejection port five sub-optimal, Ranky. I'd get on it," said Jarry.

"Roger, control," came the reply from Ranky, who was EVA at NTR#3, six hundred metres away.

Jarry felt a slight tremor under his feet.

"Oh, boy."

He raised the radio mike to his lips.

"Ranky! Tie yourself down! We've got another one!'

Despite of the analysis of 2017KW13's structure, and all the modelling, the whole rock had been shaking like a Turkish apartment block. They'd had seven tremors in the last shift alone. Big ones, too.

"Roger, Control. Going for tie-down."

Each of the EVA rigs carried an explosive spike for emergencies, allowing the operator to tie themselves securely to the deep-frozen ice and rock of the surface in less than a minute.

The floor surged up under Jarry's feet and his porta-screen shot across the room. He made a grab for it, but a drinking tube slammed into the side of his head.

"Fuck!'

Loose papers and equipment shot around the cabin, tossed like greens in a salad shaker as the thin walls trembled. Soon the whole thing was shaking, the big alloy casings of the monitors banging together violently.

Multiple alarms blared.

He tried to brace himself and access the console at the same time. It was useless. The keyboard was moving too much.

He pushed across the cabin and hit the view-port release. The hydraulics whined and the heavy shield shot back from the window.

"Holy, mother—"

The whole surface of the asteroid was rippling, waves passing through it as though it was a fluid. He could see two of the big NTR installations being literally shaken loose.

Cries for help came from everywhere.

"Jarry! I need help. I can't hold—"

"This is NTR#1, we have systems failure—"

"Control! *Control!*"

"*Oh, mother of Christ!*"

He felt one of the big mounts on the control shack break. Then another. A wave lifted him up, tilting the whole space.

The NTR#1 control unit smashed into his chest. Pain flared

from his right side.

Jarry looked out through the window.

The rough surface of ice and rock was gone. In its place was a strange, patterned expanse of bulging hemispheres, perfectly regular, as though the whole thing had been constructed by forcing dark spheres together until they joined without a gap.

A crack appeared across the middle of each bulging section.

Jarry screamed, his hands bloody as they beat at the weight of the casing that pined him.

Another ripple swept through Erebus.

This one ripped the control room apart.

Jarry's breath was sucked from him, his whole body swelling with red-hot pain as he decompressed, tumbling out into space.

The surface of each hemisphere drew back.

He tried to scream, but the greedy emptiness sucked even harder at his vital fluids. Then his eyes exploded, leaving him in agonising blindness.

☆

Mat woke suddenly, desperately thirsty, and with a thumping headache. He felt a soft warmth against his side and the night came back in a rush.

He looked down to see Athy, her naked body curled into him, her large breasts and small pink nipples pressed into his thin chest, wavy yellow-blonde hair tumbled across his shoulder. Even through the pain he smiled, remembering the fun they had had playing cat-and-mouse with the media, giving the paparazzi the slip somewhere between Caltech and Athy's suite.

But something was not right.

There was an angry rhythmic sound pulsing in his ears. It sounded like traffic. No. Not traffic.

Mat groaned and shook his head.

He delicately extracted himself from Athy, covering her gently with a sheet. Then he rummaged around in the mini-bar to find the headache tablets, washing down three with a Coke, wincing as the ice-cold carbonated mixture hit his throat.

Athy had a huge suite, and he moved into the lounge room and flicked on the television.

News.

He flicked again.

News.

Again.

News.

News. News. News.

It was on every single channel.

His eyes widened and he turned up the volume on a chat show.

" ... some are calling it incompetence, others scientific error. But all agree we have been betrayed at the highest level," said the host.

"But the thing is. How can a mistake like this be made?"

The camera swung. The man was red-faced, obviously sweating in his cheap suit. He was so angry he was almost rising from his chair as he spoke. "How can an organisation like NASA, with all the resources at their command, make a mistake like this?"

The camera returned to the host. "How indeed?" he said solemnly.

"But the real question is, where the hell is Matrick Keterson?" said an older woman.

"My God, it's Marjorie Heters," said Mat, recognising a highly respected astronomer that had worked alongside his own team.

There was a thumping on the door, growing louder.

The camera swivelled back to the host.

"Just to recap. Australian astronomers tracking Erebus have this morning confirmed the massive body is back on a course for Earth. Despite the best efforts of NASA and co-operation ..."

Mat could not take it in. The words washed over his sleep-deprived and alcohol-sodden brain, refusing to register.

The thumping on the door was violent now, and he could hear the roaring again, growing louder.

"Who is it?"

He looked up to see Athy, tying a patterned silk gown of blue, yellow and red around her as she headed for the door.

"I ..."

He realised he was completely naked, and he had time only to gather a pillow from the lounge to cover his privates when Hari Wottard burst into the room flanked by six secret service agents and three aides.

"Mat. Where the hell have you been? I have been trying to reach you since 3am."

"I ..." He had turned off his cell even before he left the reception.

Mat looked across to the clock on the wall. 4:17pm. *Christ!*

Hari pushed into the room and drew the heavy drapes, letting in the harsh afternoon sun.

"Look down there, damn you! *Look!*"

Mat stumbled toward the window, shielding his eyes from the painful glare with one hand while he held the pillow with the other. He knew nine men would be staring at his white, skinny arse.

An angry crowd, swelling by the moment, packed the courtyard and entrance of the hotel.

Mat squinted, trying to read the placards, but his eyes were still too fuzzy.

"What on Earth do they want?" asked Mat.

"Want? They want to know how the *fuck* you got it wrong, Keterson. We all want to know!"

Mat's hands went slack, the pillow dropping to the rich carpet.

He felt himself shrivel to the size of a pin-prick.

"You mean ...?"

"Erebus is still headed for Earth. *Still headed for Earth.*"

"Excuse me, gentlemen."

It was Athy, polite to a fault; and not the least bit intimidated to have ten angry strangers in her room while she was a good as naked.

"I think you should leave. Matrick will attend shortly."

"He'll be coming with us. Even if I have to drag him," snapped Hari, his face flushing red.

Athy took a small cellphone from her gown and hit a speed-dial button.

"Afternoon, Mr Kalls. Would you be so kind as to attend in the main suite with your staff?"

About ten seconds later four extremely tough-looking bodyguards moved into the room, flanking the other secret-service agents.

"I believe you are in my private quarters, Mr Wottard."

By now, Mat had collected his thoughts. If what they were saying was true, he needed to assess that data straight away. It made sense. Only the stations in Australia would be in position to track Erebus right now, but that would be changing within hours. When the US stations came online he wanted to see that data first hand.

"Wait outside, Hari," he said. "I'll be right out."

Hari glared at Athy, then stalked out of the room, followed by his men.

"Miss Jates?" said Kalls.

"Thank you, Mr Kalls. If you would be so kind as to wait outside for me. Perhaps you could keep those other gentlemen company?"

Kalls smiled, revealing two golden teeth amid a row of chipped neighbours.

"Yes, Ma'am."

As the room emptied, Matrick walked across to Athy. He stopped a few paces away, unsure.

"I have no idea what's going on, Athy. But I'm sorry to bring this down on you."

She smiled and closed the distance between them, rising up on her toes to plant a soft, warm kiss on his cheek.

"Now, don't you go worrying about me, Matrick. You just take your time. No need to rush into that shark's den out there. Erebus is still more than twenty hours away, and you know as well as I do the US stations will not be online for hours."

The smell of her soft skin and hair sent a thrill through Mat, and she smiled mischievously, sweeping her eyes down to his stirring member. She untied the front of her gown and leant in closer. He could feel the soft warmth of her skin pressed against his. She tilted her head up and kissed him passionately before pushing away and retying her gown. He had one last fleeting glimpse.

"Business before pleasure, Mr Keterson."

She took a breath, her eyes growing more serious.

"Now. You can use the other bathroom. I will have some fresh clothes brought up for you."

She smiled once more then disappeared back into her suite.

Mat felt foolish standing in the middle of the vast sitting room alone, and walked across to the other side where a set of sliding doors gave access to an unused apartment that was the twin of Athy's.

He went straight to the shower, his headache now compounded by nausea as the effects of the night caught up with him.

He needed to break down events, analyse them, but he hardly knew where to begin.

He let the hot stream wash through his hair and down his back. The citrus smell of the hotel shampoo refreshed him as he worked it into his hair.

How could 2017KW13—*Erebus*—change orbit? Every calculation, every projection they had made had been broken down and checked to the last line, the last constant. Double-checked. Triple-checked. Ratified and cleared by five teams of independent experts. They had even surveyed the huge body before installing the NTR thrusters and the automated mining plants. They knew the density, the composition. The rest was mechanics—and the basic laws of physics did *not* change. So assuming Erebus had flipped, how could it happen? Sabotage? A nuclear strike on the body itself? Some unforeseen geological event? Impossible. Nothing that small could be geologically active—not even the Moon was. Collision with another body? Also impossible. The nearby space was mapped down to objects the size of a pebble.

He turned off the shower and dried himself, marvelling at the softness of the towel. He was surrounded by luxury. Which suddenly reminded him where he was: in the suite of Athy Jates, one of the wealthiest industrialists in the USA.

He walked back into the bedroom of the twin apartment to find clothes laid out on his bed along with his personal effects. He felt mildly unnerved he had not heard anyone enter. He dressed quickly, checking his watch with concern as he pulled the expanding band over his wrist.

And what about his people on Erebus? Had no one heard from them?

"I've got to get to JPL. *Fast.*"

He combed his hair quickly, hardly sparing a glance for his drawn, ashen face in the mirror. His mind was already in hyperdrive, flashing ahead, running down alternate paths of investigation. If Erebus was headed for them, they had little time. None of it could be wasted on navel-gazing or over-analysing the errors. The effort to re-divert that monolith *must* come first.

He swept into the sitting room, ready to call a quick goodbye to Athy on his way out of the apartment, but was caught up short.

A huge dining table had appeared in the middle of the room, its gleaming surface reflecting the last, glaring rays of the LA sun as it dipped in the West. A vast breakfast, all on silver service platters, was laid out on the table.

Seated at one side, with a place set up beside her, was Athy, now in a long dress of dark grey, her hair pulled back in a single ponytail.

"Athy, I need to get to JPL."

She smiled. "Of course you do. But after you've eaten. If this crisis is as big as it looks, you may not get another decent meal for days."

"But, Hari is outside—"

"Let him wait. I insist." Her voice had taken on an edge of steel, and for the first time Mat fully registered the change in her demeanour. She had transformed herself from Southern Belle to Corporate Executive.

He stepped toward the table and pulled out a chair.

At the table beside her, until now concealed by a silver candelabra, were two top-of-the-line laptops, one of which was split into six small screens.

"I have had Dajourie scanning the airways for us. This story has gone worldwide. But nothing of substance so far, just rumours and panic. It will be more than half-an-hour before the US tracking stations are online." Athy reached over and closed the media screen.

A smartly dressed woman in a red skirt and jacket entered the room.

"Ah, Dajourie. I want you to rustle up a secure phone for Mr Keterson. I think his standard link will be useless."

"Yes, Miss Jates."

Mat cursed himself, realising he had still not turned on his cell. He pulled it out of the pocket of his coat and switched it on. Within seconds it gave an insistent *beep* and loaded with no less than one hundred and thirty-eight messages, then abruptly began to ring. Startled, Mat answered.

"Hello, erh—"

"*Mr Keterson, this is Twal Chen from* the New York Times. *Would you be able to comm—*"

Mat switched it off and laid it gently on the table. What sort of a shit-storm had he landed in?

Athy lifted one of the silver food covers, which rang with a soft *ting*.

"Greasy bacon and eggs, it's a patented hangover cure ... Well, that and these." Athy slipped two small white pills across the table to him.

He raised one eyebrow.

"Anti-nauseant and pure codeine. Definitely not over-the-counter. But, this is an emergency ..." She reached over and poured him an orange juice.

He swallowed the pills, wincing at the brief bitterness on his tongue—they were not sugar-coated, but then nothing today would be. It would be the truth, the whole truth, and nothing but the ugly truth.

Gritting his teeth, he took some of the bacon and eggs. He began eating methodically.

"Well, Matrick. The timing is hardly conducive, but I must admit to having an ulterior motive."

Mat was about to smile at what he thought was sexual innuendo, when he saw how serious she was. Any lover's playfulness had long vanished.

"As you know, the world headquarters for Jates Industries is in Hong Kong. I have strong business interests in China. That was where we manufactured most of the reactor components for the NTRs in your Erebus program."

Matrick poured himself a coffee, hardly taking his eyes off Athy.

She seemed suddenly unsure.

"Hell, Matrick. It was no accident I was sitting next to you last night. My Chinese associates and I wanted to offer you a job heading up our asteroid mining program. The Chinese have already committed heavily, with the government in as one-tenth partner. We have the full support of Director Tein, who will be giving us priority use of Chinese space assets."

Matrick felt the ground shift beneath his feet. It had seemed a carefree accident—a delightful night of magic—but was it nothing more than manipulation?

"Then, last night ..."

Athy's eyes blazed. "How dare you even suggest that! What do think I am?"

Matrick dropped his fork and rubbed his temples.

"I'm sorry ... I ... it was wonderful."

Athy took a breath and pushed her plate away from her.

"We wanted to offer you a job, Matrick, leading the program for the consortium. The rest was ... well, unplanned. I ..."

Mat wanted desperately to heal things between them. His first wife had left him six years ago, accusing him of ... how had she put it? "Being an insensitive, over-analytical robot with the tact of a NAZI". He had tried hard to improve, but it seemed he still had a disastrous talent for ruining relationships.

He looked at her hopefully, searching for any sign that he had not destroyed their intimacy utterly, but she had receded into an impenetrable corporate shell. He knew then that what they had shared was something rarely given. Something quickly withdrawn.

"I see now that ... well, with recent events it is completely impractical," said Athy.

She pushed back her chair and rose.

"Good day, sir."

She walked back into her apartments, her stiff manner the only hint at how deeply he had wounded her.

"Blast."

He turned his phone back on. It rang immediately, but this time he recognised the ring tone. He had it set to recognise Hari's cell.

"Keterson," he answered.

"Mat, finally. Look, are you coming or what? Jates's goons won't even let us ring the doorbell."

Hari sounded more relaxed.

The drugs Athy had given Mat were killing the pain, and the nausea had vanished. Suddenly he was ravenous.

"I'll be right out."

He wolfed down two helpings of the rapidly cooling breakfast, then stood, sweeping his eyes across the table setting and running his hands down the fresh, new suit Athy had provided for him.

She had been wonderful, and kind, and he had repaid her with accusations.

"Damn it!"

Dajourie appeared.

"Here, Mr Keterson."

She handed him a slim video-phone, the casing metallic and reflective.

He tapped it with his fingernail.

Dajourie turned to go, but he halted her with a light touch.

"Could you please thank Athy for me?"

Her eyes were cold and she pushed his hand away. "You can thank her yourself. Her number is programmed into the cell." Then she was gone.

Outside he pushed through Athy's guards to see Hari and all three of his aides busily talking on mobile phones.

Hari ended his call and nodded to the agents, who ushered Mat down the hall and into an elevator.

"Has the team been assembled?" asked Matrick.

"Yes, they have been working the problem, but without data ...," said Hari.

"When do we come online?"

"In twenty minutes. We should make it to JPL in fifteen."

"I would love to know what the hell is going on," said Matrick.

Hari simply stared at him, and Mat had the uncomfortable feeling he was measuring his neck for a noose.

☆

Pestilence!

Worse even than the Seekers of the cold clouds.

Parasites of hot, flaming breath, breathing radiation like a distant sun, and yet so small and cold.

I roll again to shake off the last and the wound rips open even further.

They have torn into me! Ripping the skin and stealing the frozen blood from my outer segments.

What are these biting pests? Like all Vendeth I have the memories of my ancestors, yet nothing in that blurred landscape prepares me for this.

My sleep had been long, a blissful silence to fill the years of darkness. Lost in beautiful dreams of my lover, all skin, hot magma, steam and ice.

Slowly my blood heats, my massive body still leaking a trail of vapour into space behind me. Instinct guides me; I know my course. I pump my thinnest blood through the deep, hot chambers of my insulated heart, through funnelling veins of diamond to the rigid skin of my wings.

I unfurl, even as the rock-like skin of my lids draws back across my length. At last I take my first glimpse of this new solar system.

A cool yellow sun, triumphant in its middle years, and before me, the scent of my quarry. My ears grow sensitive once more as my blood flows and warms. Jets of superheated steam build in my outer jets, the strain against my inner walls welcome after such a period of dormancy.

... like a cold stone rapper,
street hard,
I don't take no fall.
You can't take my grill,
No, sucker.
Can't take my grill ...

... and today on the Yopa Linfey show we have a special guest,
someone who has ...

... the news today, Tuesday 23 May, 2024, headlining today's
stories, are the rumours true, will Erebus ...

... Yeah, red hot!
I'll burn you, baby.
Ahhh! I gotta get this!
Got to,
Gotta, get me some ...

I scream and block my ears from the torrent of noise. It has been a trick. A ruse. No Vendeth mate awaits me. My heart tears with loss, then rage.

I am too small? My song too weak to attract a single lover?
Mother!

Before me lies my greatest disappointment, nothing but a planet. A cold planet, and yet ...

I send huge jets blasting into space, stabilising me, correcting my course, wasting vital, precious fluids; but I have no fear, no.

Even through the disappointment I feel a jolt of excitement, of lust. Many are the empty, cold lovers I have taken, yet this would be my greatest conquest.

My eyes swell with greed at the feast before me.

Oceans of precious water. Surfaces swelling with organic carbon, neatly organised into easily digested pieces by the processes of slow, gravity-bound life. With this feast, I would be mighty. My song would resound with the vast chambers of magma I could harness from this sparkling planet of blue and green.

Yes, I could truly grow.

My fins unfurl, flexing and expanding, hardening. I will need them soon, to break my fall as I surrender to the embrace of this world. This cold, mindless lover.

Oh, I hunger for your embrace.

Feel me swell ...

☆

Matrick checked his models one last time, re-running the test cases through his programs. There was nothing wrong with the modelled scenarios, although he knew that already.

The Erebus mission room was packed. His team, led by Jereece, crowded the big monitors of the darkened room, the ghostly light of the screens making their drawn, hung-over faces as pale as ghouls.

Jereece could not sit still. Wired on caffeine, he paced from one station to the next, talking rapidly. He leant down to one monitor then looked back up to Matrick, where he sat with Hari and a small team of rapidly assembled experts led by Terry Kones, a presidential advisor Mat had never seen before. He was waiting to call President Yerry, a secure cell link placed with perfect symmetry on the desk in front of him. None of the "experts" had said a word, Mat's small talk met by stony, slightly terrifying silence.

Mat had asked that Rotanski and Tein attend with their teams, but he was overruled. In less than a day his project had been turned from a shining example of international cooperation to another national security project that shut everyone out except NASA and the military. Rotanski was furious, and was downstairs with his team, periodically demanding access. Tein was already back in China.

"Three minutes to tracking feed," called Jereece.

"Let's get ready, gentleman," said Kones.

On cue, the three advisors flipped open their own heavy-duty laptops.

A dull, heavy feeling settled into the pit of Mat's stomach.

"Hari, what is going on here? I thought they were observers," said Mat.

Hari looked uncomfortable. "They *are* here to observe. Directly, for the president."

Kones looked at Mat, his eyes briefly contemptuous before becoming guarded once more. His jaw was clenched.

"We are here to observe, and to take direct control of this program," said Kores.

The other men, who were dressed in identical black suits with closely shaved haircuts, were busy on their laptops, and were ignoring the exchange.

Mat's heart began to hammer in his chest, and his hands came down protectively on the keyboard of his laptop.

"Hari?" asked Mat, his voice shaking with outrage.

"I'm sorry, Matrick. The President's own team have always been closely monitoring the program. With the current situation ... we felt a change was needed. The public needs reassurance."

"What about the Russians and the Chinese?" asked Mat.

"That is being handled at the diplomatic level," said Kones.

"But this is a scientific project ..." Then it hit him. They were not talking about another intervention. They were planning a nuclear strike on Erebus.

"Hold on a minute—" started Mat.

"No, you listen to me!" snapped Hari, his face flushing a dangerous red. "You had your chance. How you managed to fuck this up, I don't know. But you and your people are to give Kones and his team your full cooperation, understand me? They have a mandate from Yerry himself."

Mat was shaking not only with anger—but with fear. Time was running out, and the wrong move could spell the end for all of them.

"But, Hari," said Mat, pleading with his boss. "Surely you know that a full strike will not prevent impact. That thing is not a metallic body. Even with penetrators it will just shatter into fragments."

"Oh, we will smash it alright," said Kones. The men at his side laughed coldly.

Mat's eyes flashed down to the laptops they were using. Heavy duty. Military. They were inputting launch codes. This could not be happening. This was everything he and his team had tried to avoid.

"No, I can't let you do this."

Kones's eyes flickered to two heavy-muscled, armed MPs who had been standing guard unobtrusively at the door. They were behind Kones' chair in an instant.

Mat's jaw went slack and he looked across to Hari in disbelief.

"I'm sorry, Matrick. National security."

Kones motioned with his chin, and the two marine MPs returned to their position.

Jereece, oblivious to the whole thing, turned toward them and held up his hands, counting down with his fingers.

"Feed in ten, nine ..."

They all looked up to the huge screens above the room, now displaying the NASA logo.

"... three, two, one."

One of the screens flickered, went dark then filled with an actual magnified view of Erebus, coming in from their advance observation satellites. The asteroid was a tiny blip against a field of bright stars.

"Jereece. Anything from Control on Erebus?" asked Mat.

Jereece's face was grim. He shook his head. Seven astronauts. His people. Gone.

Mat's attention went to the second screen, which had a bright set of orbital schematics set against a light blue background. A heavy black line denoted the corrected orbit Erebus should have taken, while a red line showed another trajectory entirely, one with multiple, irregular changes to speed and direction. It looked like a joke. Something concocted by a team of drunken NASA scientists after the Christmas party. Asteroids just did not behave like this.

But Mat did not draw any conclusions; he was too well trained for that.

"Jereece. Feed the trajectory information over the network," called Mat.

"OK. Should be coming across ... now."

The raw data loaded into Mat's program and he initiated an interpretive scenario. The fast little machine spat the results out in less than ten seconds.

His breathing grew fast and shallow as he looked over the results. His hands began to shake, his fingers tingling with hyperventilation.

"Work the results," he muttered to himself. "Work the results."

The room was full of raised voices on the edge of panic.

He forced his breathing to slow.

"Quiet down, people. Focus on the job." His voice was stern, but controlled.

The noise receded.

"We only need the current orbit for the targeting satellites, gentlemen. Let's not waste any time," said Kones.

Mat could hardly believe the insanity that was taking place here. Any nuclear strike—however massive—would leave myriad smaller fragments to rain down on Earth. Not only that, Erebus was now too close for even the most massive of explosions to divert. He had to shut Kones out of his mind. He needed to understand what was happening.

Based on his modelling, it appeared that somehow Erebus had flipped itself, not once but seventeen times until every one of the four NTR mounts and the Control base had been dislodged, along with the automated ice-miners. Then it had changed its own orbit by applying thrust. There had been no collision; no explosion. It had been a carefully controlled orbit correction. Erebus was acting like a spaceship. A spaceship under the control of some sort of intelligence. There was no other explanation.

But the surveys? Multiple sample points, taken randomly, some at depths of up to ten kilometres below the surface. They revealed nothing but carbon, ice and rock, all mixed like a pudding across the surface of the body. The composition had been remarkably consistent—yet they found nothing that would suggest an artificial construct. Their high-energy scans of the internal structure had been designed only to determine if it had enough integrity to take the applied thrust of the NTRs without fracturing.

The secure cell on the desk in front of Kones rang. He swept it up and answered it with machine-like precision.

"Lieutenant-Colonel Kones here, sir. Everything is ready. Do we have the Russians and the Chinese on board, sir?"

Mat could hear Yerry's voice, small and mouse-like across the link, but could not make out the words.

"Yes. We have relayed the targeting information," said Kones in reply.

"Wait!" yelled Mat. "Stop! Erebus is some sort of spaceship."

Suddenly Mat was lifted from his feet and dragged away into the corner of the room, one MP on either arm.

Jereece watched it happen with incomprehension, the pen in his mouth falling to clatter on his desk. The other members of Mat's team had ceased work, some standing up from their seats.

"Get back to work! All of you," yelled Hari.

Reluctantly they re-took their seats, but their eyes were glued to Mat. Not a single one of them was moving.

"The feed, Jereece! Crank the magnification on Erebus to max!" yelled Mat.

Jereece worked his terminal furiously.

Mat did not struggle. He would win this only by convincing Hari and Kones what they were dealing with. If he was right, if Erebus was a spaceship on its way to visit Earth, then it would be shifting into position for an orbital insertion—in fact, it would be already doing so.

The tiny image of the asteroid increased in size until it filled a quarter of the screen, then magnified again.

Gone was the irregular shape, crusted with ice and debris from its long journey through the Oort cloud.

What they saw now was a long segmented form, like a string of pearls, flanked by six wings of reflective material that drew together at ninety degrees to the body like the petals of some enormous flower. Each spherical segment was faceted, like the featured surface of a geodesic dome. The wings were supported by wedge-shaped structures that emerged from the central segment, darker in colour than the bright wings themselves.

"Jesus, those sails must be more than a hundred kilometres square," said Jereece.

"They are symmetrical," said Mat in wonder. "This has to be an artificial structure. Hari! Kones! This is a ship. A spaceship."

Kones looked at the image without emotion. Beside him Hari's mouth was open, his eyes fixed on the screen.

"Is it still on a collision course for Earth?" said Kones.

"Yes," said Jereece. "It's accelerating."

No. This cannot be right.

"Jereece. Its course must be consistent with some sort of orbital insertion. Check it. Quickly!"

Jereece rapidly worked the data. He paused, shook his head then tried a different approach, then turned to Mat.

"Whatever this thing is, Mat. It will impact on its current course."

Mat could not understand. If it was some sort of a ship, perhaps driven by an automated system, was it possible that it had been damaged by their efforts to divert it? No. It's orbital corrections had been too precise. The conclusion was inescapable. The intelligence that directed Erebus meant for that thing to hit them.

The panic rose again, and this time Mat did nothing to stop it. Would could he do?

As they watched they could see jets of material shoot in unison from it segments.

"It's increasing speed."

The huge, gossamer wings fell away, leaving only the stubby support structures. The whole body was becoming streamlined, the segments drawing together and flattening out.

Kones lifted the cell link back to his ear. "The object is still on collision course and is accelerating, Mr President," said Kones. "Acknowledged, Mr President."

"Kones! Tell your men to release me," said Mat.

Kones gave Mat a level look, then nodded to the MPs, who let him go and marched back to their station at the door.

Mat took his seat and watched the screen, fighting a sense of unreality. It was as though he had left the world he knew and stepped through into somewhere else—somewhere utterly alien. He knew a nuclear strike would not avert the threat. Yet as furiously as he considered the problem, he could provide no alternative. How could he have foreseen this? *This!* Perhaps Rotanski's people could think of something.

Kones looked across to his men. "We have the Russians and the Chinese on board. Let's proceed with the strike."

"Mr Kones," said Mat.

Kones looked across at Mat, his eyes intense.

"Is there any way we could delay the strike? Get Rotanski's people in here? There may be something else we can do."

"Negative," said Kones, continuing as though Mat had said nothing.

Mat pushed his palms into his eyes, trying to stifle the impulse to scream at Kones. He had to seize control of the moment—to think of something. But it was too late.

"Gentlemen. Target locked. Satellite online. Initiate on my mark. Three. Two. One. Mark."

Kones and his team hit their keyboards in unison. Four soft taps, and their fate was sealed. Seconds later there was a series of snaps as the lids shut.

"What are you hitting it with?" said Mat.

"This has all been modelled by our own people," said Kones, reopening his laptop. "I've sent the data through your network. We have one hundred and twenty-five warheads converging on Erebus. More than a thousand megatons of firepower. Seventeen will penetrate the asteroid itself; the rest are programmed to detonate at the surface."

Mat plugged the data into his own model, but he already knew the answer. Finding those launchers at short notice was impressive. Even so. Ten years ago, with Erebus so much further from Earth, a strike like this might have made a difference, but not now. His own model confirmed his fears.

It would be more than seventeen hours before the missiles closed on Erebus. For now he needed a strong coffee, and to collect his thoughts.

He pulled out his cell to check his messages, but before he could even turn it on Kones snatched it from his hands.

"No private communications allowed."

Mat glared at Kones, but he seemed invulnerable to any protest.

Kones waved to the two MPs.

"Sweep everyone. No communications are to go in or out. The network is already sealed to the outside."

Mat looked over at Hari. "What the hell is this?"

Hari shrugged, and for the first time Mat saw defeat in his slumped posture.

"I'm sorry, Mat. They've taken mine as well. This is being controlled by the military now. Orders were to keep a lid on developments—God knows how they can hide more than a hundred simultaneous launches. Any tin-pot country with a satellite and space program must know what we are trying to do."

"And how futile it will be," said Mat.

Kones eyes swept over to lock onto his, then Hari's, his gaze determined. "I will only say this once. If we are facing a Global crises, this needs to be coordinated from the top down. The President and his staff are already secure. Other preparations are being made for the impact. Your only job, Keterson, is to tell us exactly where those fragments are going to land after the strike on the body."

Mat was roughly pushed to his feet. One MP stood by impassively while the other swept him with a portable metal detector.

He could feel the small, heavy lump of Athy's cell in his pocket, and was resigned to giving it up. But the hand-held swept over it without registering a blip. Then he remembered the sleek, metallic casing. It was shielded!

Bless you, Miss Jates.

☆

"We're getting something."

Mat jerked awake, scattering the greasy cardboard relics of yesterday's dinner onto the thick grey carpet of the Erebus mission room along with a very cold, very ugly brew of coffee that was more than seven hours old.

His head pounded and he focussed on the big display with difficulty. There were no magic pills to help him this time. He rubbed his stiff neck while he took in the images. He felt as though he had been watching that huge plasma rectangle his whole life.

The view of Erebus was better than ever. The petal-like wings were long gone now, the segmented body flattened, the six stubby support structures now woven together beneath the flattened under-surface like the wings of a hypersonic aircraft. The whole structure seemed so rigid it was hard to believe it had re-shaped itself at all.

The surface of the body comprised multiple elements, each of which now glittered like lenses. Like eyes.

Its whole structure was baffling.

"One of the forward observation posts has taken a spectral reading of the gases being ejected by Erebus," said Jereece.

Mat looked down into the central part of the room. Like the main desk above, the consoles were scattered with the remnants of takeaway meals and Styrofoam coffee cups. Yet where before—over a thousand long nights—these had been an integral part of the feeling of camaraderie within the 2017KW13 team, now they were like the remnants of prison food. The whole atmosphere in the room was oppressive.

Three more agents had joined Kones, along with five more MPs. They were in danger of outnumbering the scientists. Hari had lost his seat on the upper table, evicted by another "specialist", and had been forced to take a vacant seat in the main room below. It seemed the NASA hierarchy had been temporarily voided. No one had been allowed to contact friends or family. "Arrangements have been made" was all Kones would say.

"What have you got?" asked Mat.

"The gases are mostly hydrogen, ejected at very high speed, followed by a trail of water vapour."

The views flickered and changed. A one-minute countdown started in the corner of the screen.

"This is it, gentleman," said Kones, pointedly ignoring the four female members of Mat's team who were busily working on the floor below.

They saw an actual view of Erebus on one screen, with a schematic of the incoming trajectory on the other.

Mat's heart was hammering so violently it shook his whole chest. The headache, his aching neck—all were forgotten.

"There they are," yelled Jereece. The chemical boosters on the nukes were powering up for the final strike, standing out like a forest of fireflies before the leviathan of Erebus.

One of the women cried out, and one of the others reached across quickly to put an arm around her. At some unspoken signal, most of his team left their seats and crowded together before the screen. He should have been with them.

Then, just before impact, something incredible happened.

Erebus applied a massive thrust away from the detonation coordinates.

"Sir! Sir! All 125 warheads have missed the target," yelled one of Kones's men.

"Get control of yourself!" snapped Kones.

The picture went suddenly white, then dead. The screen with the tracking information displayed a large red "ERROR". The nuclear detonation had obliterated the forward observation posts.

Hari rushed toward Kones.

"What the hell just happened?" demanded Hari.

A marine MP blocked him.

Kones was sitting silently, collecting himself. He reached forward and shut his laptop.

"Most of the warheads were programmed to detonate at fixed coordinates. That was what blew out your satellites."

"But they missed."

Kones nodded. "Yes. But the seventeen penetrators were smart-bombs. Our own," said Kones with a touch of pride. "They will have tracked the target. Of that you can be sure."

Mat rose unsteadily to his feet.

"How can we track the debris field now?" yelled Hari, his voice breaking as he pushed against the MP. "The NASA satellites are gone. That thing was due to impact in less than four hours."

"You and your whole team are to relocate with us," said Kones.

"Where?" demanded Mat. "These people have families. They might all be dead in a few hours. They deserve their own freedom, Kones."

Kones merely returned Mat's gaze. "You will all be moved to a secure location. As for your families, they will be taken care of."

Mat stepped back, and collided with the bulky MP behind him.

God help them.

He reached down and touched the solid shape of the secure cell in his pocket.

"I need to go to the toilet," said Mat.

"We will wait for you downstairs," said Kones. "Don't worry. We won't leave without you."

☆

Pain.

Red hot, searing pain. My body has been ripped asunder.

Magma. The glowing, lifeblood of my body, splashes cooling into space, spilled from the fractured tubes of my diamond chambers. One of my segments has been obliterated, the eyes shattered.

But I am more than the sum of my parts. Each tiny cell of my outer body speaks with its own tiny song; and is a seed of rebirth. Enough of me remains to rebuild; to reform.

Enough of my mind remains to know from where those pestilential bringers of fire arose. I, at one with orbits and bodies of mass, traced their approaching vector back to their source. The dumb little comets, they were easy to escape. It is the smarter comets whose mother I need to punish.

It seems gravity-bound life can bite.

Have no fear, my lover.

I am strong.

☆

The tall glass windows of the atrium seemed to magnify the harsh sunlight as they pushed through the doors under guard.

Outside a swelling crowd was screaming for news behind a cordon of soldiers five deep, each holding a submachine gun levelled at the demonstrators.

At a command from Kones, the ranks parted.

A line of six black humvees with darkened windows awaited them.

Suddenly there was an explosion behind them.

The crowd screamed and ran as five of the big glass windows shattered with the impact, big fragments of glass crashing nosily to the tiles.

The soldiers swivelled, and a group of press suddenly pushed toward them, surrounding Kones and the rest of Mat's group of bewildered scientists.

There was confusion and shouting, and without warning the crowd surged back, breaking the ranks of the waiting soldiers.

People screamed.

Mat saw others fall, to be trampled by the mob.

A man waving a microphone seized Mat and pulled him away from the group. Mat started to struggle until the journalist leaned in toward him and whispered in his ear, "Athy sends her regards."

Mat took another look at the man. At six four, with a livid scar down his left cheek, he did not look like your regular TV prop.

He took Mat by the wrist and started pushing roughly through the crowd. Five other large men joined them, forcing a path.

Mat could hear Kones yelling orders at this men.

Within seconds they were inside a non-descript Ford and screaming through the back lots of JPL.

"You're going the wrong way. This won't get you out," said Mat.

The man who had rescued him just smiled.

Three turns later he saw a civilian helicopter sitting in a deserted rear carpark, the rotors turning with angry determination.

They abandoned the car and ran.

Mat was bundled inside, and almost fell across the lap of Athy when his long, awkward legs tangled with the cramped seating. A slight smile played on her lips, which she quickly banished. Her eyes were coolly assessing.

He sat beside her, trying to collect his thoughts, unsure about the ethics of abandoning his team, and yet convinced that Kones was leading them down a useless path. Erebus would hit them, of that he had no doubt; either the asteroid itself or the fragments left by the strike—either way the total incoming mass was the same. If they survived the plasma wave of the impact, what then? He did not want to spend years locked in some secure underground haven along with the President and a thousand hard-case military types like Kones.

"Take it up, Mr Kalls."

"Yes, Ma'am," replied Kalls from the cockpit.

"Athy, I'm sorry for my hasty words this morning," said Mat, laying a hand on her shoulder. He felt awkward talking like this in front of a cramped helicopter full of Athy's men, but time was running out for all of them.

"That is quite alright," said Athy coolly, pointedly brushing his hand away. "This is strictly business, Mr Keterson. We need your expertise."

Mat felt his heart go cold. It seemed adolescent, even infantile, to care so much about a casual affair, but the loss of intimacy between them disturbed him more than he could say. For just a few brief hours it had seemed as though the world was his. After years of awkward and ill-fated relationships, years of dedication to the Erebus project, it seemed that at last the world—and cupid—had smiled on him.

Seconds later they were racing through the sky.

LA was burning.

Whole districts were ablaze, the streets filled with people running, fighting, dying. Below him Mat could see the highways were choked to a standstill. Kones would never get out in time.

Mat swallowed and turned to Athy. "Where are we heading?"

"I have a rocket-plane at the airport, fuelled and ready to go."

"Where?"

"Gansu province. Northwest China."

"Jiuquan Space Centre," whispered Mat. "We can't be in the air when the plasma wave hits."

"We don't plan to be," chimed in Kalls from the cockpit.

☆

Mat's eyes adjusted slowly to the cavernous situation room at Jiuquan.

"This was where we centred the NTR project," said Athy beside him. "And, as you know, most of the launches were from here."

Mat nodded impatiently. "But most of the technology was American."

Athy smiled. "This is China, Mat. Do you think a few patents are going to stop them?"

Mat's head jerked around at her.

"That's right. Our syndicate has been manufacturing the NTR drives as fast as we can for five years. We already have hundreds of them up in L1."

"So the asteroid project—"

"A whole colony, Mat. That's what we were planning. A whole self-supporting community that lives off the raw materials available out there. A true space colony." Her eyes were glowing with the fire of her vision, and just for the moment, the awkwardness between them was forgotten.

"That's why we wanted you. No one alive knows the asteroids like you do, or the best way to survey and approach them. Plus you were already a leader in the application of the NTR technology."

There was a babble of excited voices, all in Chinese.

Athy walked quickly over to the terminals and interrogated a technician. Mat was shocked to hear her speak fluently in Cantonese, and was reminded yet again how little he knew about her. The seemingly innocent Southern Belle who took him to her bed was long vanished.

She turned toward him.

"Erebus is entering the atmosphere. It's still intact. There are a score of minor fragments, but they will not survive re-entry."

"But that's impossible. It was hit with ground-penetrating nukes. With its composition it should have broken up."

The technician spoke rapidly then pointed at the big screens above the room.

"This is historical footage. A fast-forward of images collected after impact from long-range spy satellites," said Athy.

Mat could hardly believe his eyes.

The massive body—smashed to pieces and leaking hot fluids into the darkness of space—slowly reformed itself, once more taking the long, streamlined form it had before the nukes hit it.

The images flickered and changed. Now there was a shaking video feed, a real-time view of Erebus itself as it plummeted through the atmosphere, superheating the air, surrounded by massive turbulence. It had flattened even further, and was coming in like an antique shuttle, heating up along the leading edges of the huge flattened underside.

"How are we getting that feed?" asked Mat.

"Tein has fighter craft tracking it."

Mat shook his head. It was suicide. Even so he could not tear his eyes away from that image.

"It's trying for atmospheric entry. I was right. It *is* a spaceship."

Athy's eyes were flickering from screen to screen as the image grew. She was shaking, and Mat knew it was not from the cold.

He reached down and placed an arm around her shoulders, and she did not protest, letting him draw her into an embrace.

All around the room, a deathly quiet had settled.

It must have been only a matter of minutes, but it seemed like they watched that massive, alien thing plummet down toward them for an eternity.

A single voice barked a command, and suddenly the room was in motion again.

Mat looked across to see Tein on the floor of the room. He nodded gravely to Mat, before continuing to work.

One of the big screens flickered again, and they could see the trajectory of re-entry. An elegant curve that would put Erebus down in the North Atlantic, less than three hundred kilometres from mainland USA.

"Oh my God ..." said Mat.

He felt Athy tremble in his arms and looked down at her, but her features were composed, her eyes focussed with intelligence.

"The East Coast. It cannot possibly survive. Not even with the aerobraking that Erebus is applying," said Mat.

He felt a guilty relief, a hidden, exultant joy, that *he* was safe. That he would survive the initial impact of this massive body.

Tein marched up to them and Athy disengaged herself from Mat, looking up at him with a mixture of longing and anger on her face.

He was more confused than ever.

"Good evening, Mr Keterson. I trust your flight over was pleasant?" said Tein in English. His British accent was strong, a relic of his Hong Kong education.

Mat gritted his teeth. Tein always treated him with excessive good manners that were aggravating at the best of times. Now with billions of tonnes of rock, ice and God-knows-what hurtling down toward them it was downright infuriating.

"Very pleasant."

"Good to hear it." Tein smiled at Athy, who turned back to the screens.

"I would like to give you a tour of our facilities—a full briefing on our proposed projects. Then I would like you to go back to the US."

"Back?" said Mat.

"Yes. If this is as serious as I fear, we will need to bring to bear all the resources of the developed world. Our government is already making diplomatic moves with the Russians and others, but we need you to convince President Yerry of the absolute need to assist us."

"Assist? With what?"

"The evacuation of Earth, Mr Keterson."

The babble of excited voices rose on the floor below.

Erebus was glowing red hot, the streamlined edges below it shining with the fires of Hell itself.

Below the huge, red-hot form they could see the ocean—a peaceful flat expanse, shimmering in the sun. It looked impossibly tiny beneath the bulk of Erebus, as though the vast Atlantic had shrunk.

Impact.

For a brief moment they could see a vast spout of water rising to the sky, then a white-hot, rushing wall of superheated gas, vapour and sediment.

The screen went blank.

Silence.

Tein gave a quick command and the feed switched to another aircraft, now heading out of the area as fast as it could fly. Its rear-mounted camera showed a wall of fire expanding from the crash site like the ring of a huge atomic bomb. A column of material rose into the sky, and yet below this the Atlantic seemed still and calm. The blast wave, and the oceanic surge that would follow, were still on their way.

Tein looked silently at the screen and chanted something in Chinese.

Athy looked at him sharply, a single tear glistening on her cheek. Her eyes flicked to Mat and she wiped it away.

"Come with me, please. We have another communications centre set up inside," said Tein. "The main control room must return to space operations now. We all have our work cut out for us."

Mat and Athy followed Tein into a small room set up with banks of monitors, each showing a different video feed.

"God, that's New York," said Mat.

The streets were filled with people, climbing over cars and trucks jammed-packed in the streets. Buildings were on fire. Bodies lay on the sidewalk amid scattered suitcases and boxes of possessions, as unnoticed as alleyway rubbish.

Mat looked from screen to screen. It was the same all across the Eastern seaboard of America, yet every city in the world seemed to have been gripped by the same panic. Everyone trying to flee, yet trapped by the sheer mass of humanity.

Mat and Athy followed Tein's lead and took a seat at the bare conference table, while an assistant brought coffee in white, chipped ceramic cups. Tein gratefully accepted a steaming cup of green tea.

Mat tried to bring the cup to his lips, but his hand was shaking so badly he spilt the hot fluid on his hand. He hardly reacted, overwhelmed by a crushing sense of guilt. If only he had insisted on more detailed surveys ... perhaps if they had used more NTRs ...

Athy watched him with cool assessment.

"You know there is nothing you could have done to stop it," she said.

Mat's reason slowly asserted itself. It was true, given the behaviour of Erebus, and the lack of effectiveness of the nuclear strike ... what could he have done?

Perhaps if Earth had a fleet of space-going destroyers armed with powerful energy weapons—maybe they could have outmanoeuvred and dismembered Erebus. Perhaps. Who knew what other resources that ... alien artefact ... could bring to bear?

Mat gave up trying to drink his coffee and used both hands to place the cup carefully on the table.

"How many hours till the blast wave hits us?"

Tein took a measured sip of his tea.

"It will hit China in seven hours, the East coast of America in less than one. The wave will have completely circumnavigated the globe in sixteen hours. But our calculations show the power is greatly diminished already. Erebus slowed its descent quite markedly prior to impact."

Tein lowered his teacup to the saucer with a soft clatter.

"So what exactly are you proposing?" said Mat.

Tein pushed his cup away from him slightly and straightened in his chair.

"The consequences for the planet will be extreme. We are facing a disaster unique in recorded history. The climate disruption will make the Greenhouse Effect look like a mild summer's day. Crop failures, agricultural impacts, storms of incredible intensity ... how many years of this can our delicately balanced global society survive?"

Mat looked across to Athy, who was calmly sipping her coffee, a quiet determination on her soft features. She looked back at him like a stranger.

"We were already preparing for the most ambitious space project in history," said Tein. "With the impact of Erebus, the stakes are even higher.

"What we want to create is a true outpost of global civilisation. Self-supporting. Big enough to survive. With a wide enough gene pool to carry on the torch of civilisation if the worse should come to pass."

"But what about food? Surely you will need to be supported from Earth? How can a project like this possibly by sustained now? It might be decades before the climate begins to stabilise again."

"The asteroid colony was already designed to be self-supporting. We have identified the natural resources we will need out in space. We have stockpiled seed-stock, agricultural supplies —" said Tein.

"You mean grow your own food? To construct a rotating colony with simulated Earth-gravity?" said Mat, incredulous. Every cost model ever run had shown how prohibitively expensive this was.

"Work has already begun on stockpiling the materials in orbit. But we will need to accelerate plans. Time is short," said Tein.

Mat sat as Tein and Athy sketched out the details of the massive undertaking. Athy become animated, her eyes aglow with the dream of space colonisation. He tried to focus as the time crawled forward. Finally, while Mat drank his now stone-cold coffee, one of Tein's assistants approached them and whispered something in Chinese.

The smile on Athy's face fled instantly.

Mat did not need a translation. The blast wave was about to hit the East Coast.

The views of New York, Boston and the other cities still showed the same chaos, as though people were trapped by those high walls of concrete.

First came the wall of superheated air, shattering windows and igniting anything that was exposed: wood, paper, plastic. Flesh.

The TV images were silenced instantly.

Tein switched to satellite feeds, and Mat watched, stunned as a massive wave engulfed New York. The buildings were buried under the huge swell, and the wave continued sweeping on into the interior—unstoppable.

Tein's aide reappeared.

"We have your plane ready, Mr Keterson."

Mat turned to Athy, hopeful that she would come back with him, but this time it was all business. Tein and she had needed him to bring in the US support, he could see that now. The feeling between them had been nothing more than a fanciful delusion, like a mist killed in the cold light of day.

He turned away and gritted his teeth.

"OK, Tein. I will talk to Yerry."

☆

"Are you sure this is safe," yelled Mat over the roar of the helicopter blades. He looked out through the window, struggling to see anything in the darkness. He had been seconded to Hari Wottard's Erebus team, and the former NASA director had insisted on this "familiarisation run".

"Our people have modelled its growth. It has been predictable. We have been to the edge of Erebus more than ten times a day since it landed," said Hari. "I may need to you to supervise some of the investigations—up close."

Mat loosened his collar.

"We will be at the edge any minute, Mr Wottard," said Captain Stephenson, their pilot.

Mat looked over at Hari, but he was looking out, his gaze riveted on the view below. He was now coordinator of the President's Erebus Emergency Panel.

"Switch on the lights, Stephenson," ordered Hari.

Mat looked down.

Miles and miles of naked seabed, once beneath the vast North Atlantic, now devoid of life—dried to dust and exposed to the bleakness above.

For so long Erebus had been just a series of images to Mat. In his mind, a massive, mindless asteroid; a challenge for him to divert from its collision with Earth, yet still nothing more than a stream of data—a transmission of zeros and ones rendered to photographs and short video images. Just a concept. Even when it came alive, shaking off his nuclear thermal rockets and its layer of dust and ice, transforming into its monolithic, segmented form, it was still nothing more than a phantom on a screen; an impossible, intelligent artefact, determined on its course for Earth; undeterred by even a massive nuclear strike.

Even the footage of the impact—Erebus, glowing red-hot as it hit the North Atlantic—and the scenes of devastation from the East Coast and Africa; the blast wave and the huge swell of water that had followed, had filled him with nothing but a sense of unreality.

This was different.

Now he would see Erebus with his own eyes.

He would see what came of his failure.

They were running over the strange, almost desert-like surface under a dark brooding sky. The only sign of the sun was a slight lessening of the oppressive dark near the zenith, otherwise they were obliged to run under lights, as though it were a night-time operation. The dust kicked into the upper atmosphere by the impact of Erebus would take years to drop out. Meanwhile the globe had been divided into hemispheres of Night and Gloom.

"We are coming up to Erebus now, sir."

Mat felt a chill on his back, even though the stuffy cabin was heated against the frigid air outside.

He had returned from China five weeks ago. As soon as he reappeared in the US he was promptly put under guard, then shuffled through an obscure string of underground military installations that no taxpayer had ever heard of. Not a single person he had seen had been inclined to listen to Tein's plan for setting up a self-supporting asteroid colony—and Mat had to admit the further he was away from it, the more absurd the whole thing seemed. It was also impossible the US could take a lead role in the enterprise, since all its major space assets had been destroyed by the Erebus tidal wave. Reports were showing a steady stream of lifts from Jiuquan. Madness or not, the Chinese and their partners were going.

The initial blast wave had been weaker than they'd feared. By the time it reached the West Coast, it was little more than a hot, biting wind that gave third degree burns to those exposed to it. Apart from the devastated East Coast, most of the US infrastructure was intact. The Mid-West was fighting fires and a flood of saltwater, surging down along the major drainage lines.

The world had been expecting Armageddon, but aside from the American continent and the East coast of Africa, it had survived the impact with little more than a scrape. In fact the panic had caused as much destruction as Erebus itself.

The long-term effects of the climate disruption would be harder to gauge. In the developed world at least measures were being taken to stockpile and preserve foodstocks, protect water supplies from contamination, even grow under artificial lights powered from nuclear, coal and gas.

"Here it is," said the pilot.

"Dear, God," whispered Mat.

Well of Darkness.

Erebus had grown from a thickening across the horizon to a vast, black wall that rose more than three kilometres above them, reaching from the dry bed of the Atlantic into the upper atmosphere.

The pilot positioned the helicopter three hundred metres away and swivelled the bank of powerful halogens toward it.

The skin was dark, the whole structure composed of cells about a hundred metres across. These individual, bubble-like cells were crowded together to form a compact lattice.

"It looks biological," said Mat, still amazed that Erebus had survived impact.

"It's grown exponentially over the last five weeks," said Hari quietly, his voice almost at a whisper, as though Erebus itself would hear him if he spoke too loudly. "It's absorbed most of the North Atlantic; the sheer mass of it now stretches from Newfoundland to the Straights of Gibraltar and from Brazil to Angolia.

"Northern Europe is freezing solid. The poor bastards. First the dust cloud, then the loss of the Gulf Stream ..."

"But it's halted its expansion at the land surface, hasn't it?"

Hari looked intently at Mat, his face drawn and pale. "For now. But its mass is still growing at the same rate."

For the first time the implications hit him. For it to have experienced that sort of growth in only five weeks ...

"We have less than a month before it takes the whole planet," said Mat. The mathematics of it was chilling.

As they watched, Erebus began to bulge outward. New cells appeared, pushing apart their neighbours. Then more.

"Damn. I've never seen this sort of growth," said Hari.

The wall quivered, then began to expand, faster and faster.

"Oh, shit!" cried Hari.

The pilot did not need an order. He turned the helicopter and accelerated back toward the mainland. Behind them the whole jostling mass was accelerating, *outpacing them.*

"Turn the lights back toward it!" yelled Mat.

The co-pilot swivelled the lights back toward Erebus.

The cells were looming closer. Each one was bigger than their helicopter, and there was thousands upon thousands of them. In one moment of horrifying clarity, Mat truly understood how massive Erebus had become.

A whole section of the cells began to outpace the others, reaching out from the main body of Erebus toward them. The cells changed as they drew near, the heavy skin rolling back to reveal a curved, glistening surface beneath. Mat saw his own reflection in hundreds of these lenses, as though they were being chased back toward the mainland by the vast, faceted eye of some gigantic insect.

"It's still coming! *It's still coming!*" yelled Phom, their co-pilot. She had turned in her chair, like Mat and Hari, and was watching the mass of cells close on them. Her hands were held out toward Erebus as though to ward it off.

Eyes.

Coming for them.

Thousands. *Thousands of them.* Mat was lost inside them, shrinking like a microbe falling backwards into a drop of water. He had no doubt now. It was alive. A single, huge entity come to take them all.

Those eyes were chilling in their blank intensity, charged with purpose, power and merciless intent. And the most frightening thing of all: it did not see them.

To Erebus they were nothing.

Never had Mat felt so utterly insignificant. His very existence was dissolving like an aspirin tablet in the vast ocean of Erebus's being.

"It's coming down!" screamed Hari.

Mat looked up and saw he was right. Erebus was flattening out, reaching toward them. Closer.

One enormous eye was so close he could have reached out to touch it. Opalescent, dull silver with no pupil or iris.

Closer.

The helicopter shuddered then spun out of control. Eyes and darkness swept around them like a whirlpool.

Mat was aware of someone screaming, and looked over to see Hari yelling, his eyes wide, unfocussed. Only then did he realise he was screaming, too.

Mat gripped the chair and bit his lip until it bled.

"Shit, this is it!" screamed Hari.

"I can't hold it!" yelled Stephenson.

Even Mat could hear the panic in the pilot's voice. That was bad. If the pilot lost it, they were all doomed.

Hari was screaming something incomprehensible, tears squeezed from his eyes as he screwed his lids shut.

"Stephenson!" yelled Mat.

The pilot looked around, his eyes were wild, flitting from point to point.

"You have to focus! You have to get us back." Mat thought desperately for a way to reach him, then he saw the writing on the US Army jacket. CAPTAIN STEPHENSON. Military. *Just push the right button.*

The whole craft seemed to be surrounded by those huge bulbous eyes. Empty. Implacable.

Mat projected his voice with as much authority as he could muster. "Do your job, soldier! Now! Get us out of here!"

Clarity flowed back into Stephenson's eyes. His training took over.

Like a miracle the helicopter slowed its hurtling flight and stabilised. Mat could see a thousand tiny reflections of the chopper. He looked closer into the eyes. Beneath the tough outer cover they were perfectly smooth, reflective, yet there was a long line through the middle of each round surface. Perhaps a second eyelid? They glistened wetly, and stank of salt—the rank, rotting smell of the sea.

"We're gaining," yelled Phom with relieved elation.

Mat let out a long breath, conscious for the first time of the throbbing pain in his lip and the taste of blood in his mouth. He forced himself to let go of the seat arms.

Phom was right. They were leaving Erebus behind. The acceleration caused by the collapse of the wall was slowing. One by one the lids were closing over the eyes. The whole thing was becoming a featureless expanse once again, nothing more than the bumpy wall of darkness they had first observed.

"Hari ...," Mat looked across at his former boss. The man was still crying, yet he was wiping the tears away from his face as though they were acid, burning his skin.

"What?" snapped Hari.

"Hari, we have got to stop that thing." Mat's voice sounded weak, at least to himself, and he cleared his throat.

"The President has authorised a full-out nuclear strike. No other nuclear power is joining us. Even with the growth, no one else wants to risk adding a nuclear winter to the climate disruption."

"A strike!' said Mat, his heart hammering. "A nuclear strike could not destroy it in space, how do you think that will help now?"

"What the hell else can we do? What can we do?" said Hari.

"There has got to be some other way. Nerve agents. Viruses. Attack it biologically. Analyse its structure."

"We've tried, Mat. We have tried it all. It's not like anything we've ever seen. It's got nothing like DNA. The whole thing is some sort of distributed nervous system. Parallel processing across the whole structure. Anything vulnerable is buried under a trillion tonnes of flesh and water. We took samples straight away. But it does not respond like Earth-bound life."

Mat suddenly knew what he had to do. After all, Tein and his associates, including his beautiful Athy, had been right. There was no way they could have known about the real threat Erebus represented, yet they had embarked on the only course that would save them. It was not a matter of saving civilisation, but of saving Mankind itself.

"Take me to President Yerry, Hari. I know what we need to do."

Hari looked at Mat suspiciously.

"What? If you have any ideas, you tell me. I will take it to the Erebus Panel."

Mat shook his head. He might have bowed to Kones, letting that military jerk bombard Erebus with nukes in space, but never again would he stand by while idiocy was given reign.

"I need to see Yerry. Straight away. In person."

Mat looked straight into Hari's eyes, saw the fear and uncertainty there, and held his ground.

"OK, Mat. You win. But you better not be wasting everyone's time. In case you haven't noticed, we have more than fifty million dead and a whole country in ruins."

Mat said nothing. Instead he looked out across the dry, dark expanse of the ocean floor back at the dark line of Erebus.

Time truly was running out.

☆

"This is your plan? *This is your plan?*"

Mat was deep inside the Nevada Presidential bunker. They had taken his blindfold off a few minutes ago. It was Cold War paranoia at its best. He could hardly believe it; after all, it was not the Russians who had flooded the Eastern sea-board from the Great Lakes to Florida, and who was slowly expanding over the bulk of mainland USA.

"Mr President. We need to help Director Tein. We need to get our best people *off* this planet. We need to move our key resources while we can. Get everything into orbit with whatever we have, then get away from Earth."

"To go where? To live in space? *With the little green men?*" screamed Yerry. Mat have never seen the man so livid. He had put on weight since he'd last seen him, the rotund belly held back by the stretched buttons of his fine Italian suit. His round fleshy face, topped with short, grey hair—so familiar from a thousand broadcasts—was bright red.

"Mr President, I think we need to consider hard options. Tein at least has the infrastructure in place—"

"I am minutes away from sending a nuclear strike into that thing out there. I am trying to defend what is left of this country.

And you are telling me to forget that? To let it just keep expanding across the mid-West?"

Yerry, almost a foot shorter than Mat, was literally jumping up and down on the spot, using his finger like a skewer to punctuate his points.

"Yes. That's exactly what I am saying. Those ICBM boosters could shift valuable material into low-Earth orbit for Tein's project. We could lift maybe another hundred of our people—people who will otherwise die." Mat was beyond any worry about offending Yerry. He could not let them waste their last chance.

"We want to *kill* the fucking thing," screamed Yerry. "That will save millions. Thousands of millions."

Mat shook his head, retaining his calm.

"Yes, Mr President, I know your intentions. But the strike will have no effect. Those weapons could not destroy Erebus in space, and now it has thousands of times its starting mass."

Yerry rubbed his eyes with his fingers then took his hands away, shaking his head sharply, as though to clear it. He turned away from Mat and motioned to his men.

"Get him out of here," he snapped.

Two aides shuffled Mat out of the office, under the implacable gaze of four secret service agents. Linten, who had watched the whole exchange, followed Mat out.

As the door shut with an angry thud, Mat heard Linten's Texas drawl behind him.

"It's too late for a change of policy now. Everyone from the Joint Chiefs down is pressuring Yerry to act. This was unavoidable."

Mat and Linten were alone in the corridor. The Vice-President motioned for Mat to follow him and they walked down the hallway into a deserted conference room that smelt of old coffee and faint solvents from the hasty construction.

"Take a seat," said Linten.

Mat was exhausted. He had not slept in almost two days. His mind had been working feverishly throughout his journey and the interminable delays as he waited again, and again, for Yerry. He'd known he would have only one chance to sway him, and yet there had seemed little he could construct in the way of an argument, little he could add to what Yerry's own advisors had already presented to him. Each appointment had been rescheduled without notice. Today he had been given one minute.

"Yerry has never been a supporter of the space program. He was elected on other issues."

Mat smiled at that. Everyone knew Yerry had been elected on a strong ethical ticket. *Moral Revival.* The Bible Belt had put him in office. The space program had been on his hit list for cutbacks, and Linten had backed him all the way.

"But there are other people inside and outside the administration who want to be involved in Tein's program," Linten continued.

This sparked Mat's interest.

"We have been in communication with Tein and the consortium in China, and I have been coordinating a group of wealthy industrialists who want to take part. It may not be government support, but resources are resources. Tein needs everything from high-tech alloys and electronics to seed-stocks and rocket fuel." Linten took a breath; his eyes were serious. "I cannot leave the President, or his team, but I need someone to represent the US in Tein's group. I want you to be that man."

Mat felt his heart accelerate. He nodded slowly, his mind suddenly full of possibilities. This was more than he had hoped for. The fact that Linten had made the offer in an empty conference room meant that it was off the record, but this was no time to quibble.

"Yerry wants you locked down with Hari and his team of advisors, but I can get you to Jiuquan in a few hours."

Linten leaned forward. His face was pale, his hands shaking slightly as he pressed them together. A small muscle ticked beneath his right eye.

"Something of us must remain," said Linten.

"I'll do my best, sir," said Mat.

☆

Oh, joy of the feast!

Sweet, sweet waters—deliciously warm—nothing like the frozen, dusty drink I am used to, with its taste of sulphur and metal.

Wonderfully digestible organics! How I swell with this carbon, but I need heat. I must dig deep to reach the hot, precious fluids of this tiny world. It is these I need to warm my inner segments, to truly gain the power I need to grow.

At last I shall reach my prime. A fully realised Vendeth of heroic proportions. My call shall reach to the dark centres of galaxies. My lovers shall come, and I shall take them into me.

But the taste of this world! It is as sweet as nectar.

Mmmmm ...

Something approaches.

I open eyes across vast sections of my Westward length.

Tiny lights. I know these. The bringers of fire. The hot weapons of the parasites. In my desiccated, starved form I feared them, but these cannot harm me now; I have grown too vast on sweet water, methane hydrates and the bounties of gravity-bound life.

What I need now, they bring.

☆

The compound surrounding Jiuquan had become a huge, complex city of tents, portable offices and hastily erected industrial buildings, their zinc coatings gleaming dully under the heavy sky.

A mass of power cables threaded through the site and emergency power had been channelled from the local grid. Huge lights illuminated every inch of ground. The nearby airstrip had been expanded, and everything from rocket-planes and passenger jets to huge, prop-driven transports were touching down and lifting off every few minutes. The pace had become frantic since the failure of the nuclear strike on Erebus.

Mat had been here a week. Tein had set aside one precinct for the American contingent, but so far they had done little but stockpile a hopelessly uncoordinated flood of raw materials, technology and fuel in the vast network of storehouses.

He was on his way back from a briefing with Tein. Many of the components were already in orbit, but they needed more, so much more, before they stood even a chance of surviving. He turned into the narrow alley formed by two towering industrial buildings and pushed through the busy mass of people, carefully stepping over a mass of cables.

He had tried more than twice a day to reach Athy, but she never answered his calls. It infuriated him that he could not control his impulse to be near her. He was being a fool. Miss Jates had finished with him—she had made that plain before he left for the US. So why could he not put this obsession out of his mind? Why did those few hours they spent together—the sound of her laugh, her eyes, the softness of her hair—keep flooding back into his mind when he had so much more to think about? When they would all soon be dead and every minute wasted was another score of lives lost?

Once more Mat pushed Athy out of his thoughts and concentrated on the logistics of the project. There was much to be concerned about, yet most disturbing was the trend that Mat was seeing.

He had expected Linten to send scientists and engineers, but what he was getting was a mass exodus of America's rich and powerful and their families and advisors, every one hoping to barter a place on the asteroid colony with badly needed supplies. It seemed Linten was busily repaying his election contributors. It was insane.

The reports from the US were bad. Initially the strike seemed to be effective. Whole sections of the advancing wall had been obliterated and Erebus withdrew—but only temporarily. It soon began advancing again, faster than ever. Soon they would have another type of refugee entirely—the politically powerful. *They* would be entirely more difficult to shut out. President Yerry and his ilk still controlled enough firepower to wipe Jiuquan off the face of the Earth.

In less than a week Erebus would have covered the whole of continental USA, a little more than that and the whole continent of America, along with Africa and most of central Europe. The mass of the thing was destabilising the Earth's spin. Every few hours brought another tremor, and major earthquakes around the globe were being reported every hour. Earth was shaking to pieces.

Mat wove through another narrow alley and walked through the huge gaping doorway of US#28, a big industrial building he had been using as his headquarters.

He could see Trill Bates, with two aides, outside the door to his office, trying to force their way past the two Chinese guards that Tein had assigned to him. Trill saw him coming and immediately set off to intercept, his men close behind.

Trill was a large man, bald now, with thick growths of wavy grey hair on either side of his shiny dome and a paunch that pushed out across his designer belt.

"Keterson. I have been trying to see you for two days."

Although probably the richest man on the planet, the software trillionaire had become just another face in a sea of self-important men and women, all trying to get inside—to be where the decisions were made, and guarantee that *they* and not the others would take their place among the precious few leaving Earth.

They all knew that Erebus was coming.

"We received all the components, and the software, Mr Bates, and we thank you. They will be invaluable."

"But what's going on? What is the schedule? My family and I have been completely left in the dark."

His two advisors, who had not been included in Bates's impatient demand for safety, exchanged a concerned glance.

"*No one* has been told. You will be informed along with everyone else when the time comes."

Mat walked toward his offices.

"Hold on a minute!" blustered Bates, his face flushing red. He reached out to grab Mat's arm, but the tall scientist easily evaded him.

The two Chinese guards instantly levelled their rifles, barking out a command.

Bates did not need to be a linguist. One look at the steely resolve in their faces was enough. Hundreds of people had been shot at Jiuquan. Without ceremony. Without explanation. Tein expected, and received, complete obedience. So far order had been kept, but Mat suspected it would get a lot worse before the end.

Bates took a breath.

"I expect to be told as soon as you know anything," said Bates, although his voice was weak, almost asthmatic as he backed away.

Mat walked past the two guards and into his office with a sigh of relief. He dumped his notebooks and slim-line reader and walked through into his communications room.

One of the concessions he had been able to wring out of Linten had been the release of his NASA team and their families. Not one of them had been happy at the treatment, but he was sure glad to have them here. Most had been dispersed through Tein's organisation—sorely needed space scientists on a base swarming with non-specialists.

"What do you have for us, Jereece?"

The astronomer looked up from his monitor and smiled at Mat. Two other women from his old team were here as well, Yath and Lane. All three were busily analysing the orbital insertion of a continuous stream of materials, as well as undertaking an overall scenario analysis of the construction in orbit. They needed to know the major problems *before* they tried to assemble the main colonies. There would be no resupply from Earth, of that there was not doubt. Whatever they got into orbit, they were stuck with.

"Erebus is still expanding at the same rate, but there is something else. Satellite photos show that it is developing cylindrical growths along its equatorial length. They look hollow," said Jereece, pointing at the screen.

Mat leant forward, concerned.

"They must be hundreds of metres across."

"And there are thousands of them."

Mat nodded. "Anything else?"

"It looks like Erebus's metabolism is starting to change the atmosphere. The good news is that the increasing carbon dioxide will offset the cooling."

"And the bad news?"

Jereece grimaced.

"At the rate the oxygen is dropping, we could not survive another month, even if it stopped growing."

Mat nodded, resolutely pushing away the slightest trace of emotional reaction. There would be time enough for that when he watched the last rocket blast away from Jiuquan.

"Oh, one more thing," said Jereece, brightening.

"What?" said Mat, cheered to see more of the old Jereece.

"You have a visitor. She's waiting for you inside."

Jereece jerked his head toward the conference room.

A few heartbeats later, Mat pushed open the conference room door to see Athy sitting alone inside, an untouched coffee on the table in front of her, busily steaming the room full of enticing volatiles. The no-nonsense outfit was gone in favour of a loose dress of light apricot, patterned with abstract shapes. A long coat was draped across the table.

The smell of coffee mixed with her faint perfume, and Mat's breathing grew rapid as he gently closed the door.

"Athy, I ..." said Mat. *I didn't expect to see you again.*

Athy turned and smiled. Her eyes were framed with dark rings of exhaustion, her face pale and without the slightest hint of makeup, as though she had been stripped down to her essential self. Her blonde hair was tied back in a single ponytail, but roughly, with wisps escaping the temporary bondage. He was shocked to see streaks of grey. She looked thin. Stress had wasted away the beautiful curves he remembered so well.

"Mat, I have been meaning to ... come and see how you are going."

Her hands were shaking, her eyes glassy.

She laughed self-consciously. "I know. I look a mess. Too many all-nighters. Too many drugs. But who is going to worry about health effects now, hey?"

The shaking in her body grew worse, until it was a tremor that shook her whole chest.

Mat was drawn forward. He took her hands, all caution thrown to the wind. "What is it, Athy? What's wrong?"

She leapt from her chair and hugged him fiercely, her body fitting neatly into his. "It's all coming apart. The future, everything ... I can't believe it's come to this."

The tremors finally gave way to tears.

"I'm sorry. I didn't want to burden you with this, but none of my family got out, Mat. My mother. Father ... I'm all that's left. I have been just holding myself together."

Mat held her, thinking of his own distant cousins and relatives, most of whom had died in the first hours after impact. They too were gone. Thankfully he was an only child, and had buried his own parents years ago. He had been spared that shock.

Athy pushed away from him.

There would never be another time to say the things he wanted to say. He wanted her desperately, for whatever time they had left.

"Athy, I love you. I'm sorry if I treated you poorly, you were kind to me."

She smiled and wiped her tears away. "And damn my Southern pride. I love you, too, Matrick Keterson." She frowned, her brow creasing with concern.

"What is it? What's wrong."

She took a breath and fished a small disk out of the pocket of her coat.

"This is the final cut," said Athy. "Tein wanted to send it with one of his aides, but I wanted to see you."

"Are we ...?" *Are we on the list?*

Athy shook her head. "I didn't look, Mat. I don't want to know. Not yet." She smiled. "Say, does that door have a lock?"

Mat was at the door in one stride, fiddling with the tiny mechanism. There was a satisfying click.

For once Mat's dexterity did not desert him.

☆

Ecstatic growth.

My sharp, tentacle roots have smashed down into the mantle now, piercing the oceanic crust and tasting the delicious magma below. It surges through my diamond veins, a flood of warmth bringing a rich soup of minerals and metals.

I take up the last of the oceans, filling the cooler chambers of my vastness; I roll across the dry lands, consuming all, taking the precious carbon into my structure. I could not grow without it.

Strange it is, this planet-bound life. How it flees before

me; myriad images flood back through my senses of it running before its own destiny. What thoughts do they have, these little parasites? Do they mourn the loss of their world? Even if they did, should I feel compassion for something so microscopic?

There are no more hot comets. But I no longer need their warmth to fuel me.

Nothing can slow me now.

This world is mine.

☆

Tein barked an order, and the bunker's huge blast-shield began to open.

"When are we being taken to the launching area?" demanded President Yerry.

Tein turned and smiled genially, but said nothing.

The room was packed with political leaders and the mega-rich of Earth, all suited for launch. The crowd looked slightly ridiculous in their space suits. Thankfully there had been a surplus of those.

"Director, Tein, I demand an answer!" shouted Yerry.

Tein's guards tensed. Even his own aide, Lieutenant Yoshi Chan, whom he prized for her self-control, reached down to the holstered pistol at her side. Tein caught her eyes and shook his head. His guards took the same cue and relaxed back to attention.

"President Yerry, I apologise for the delay. But as you know, to coordinate so many launches simultaneously is an extremely complex enterprise."

"Tein. My people tell me that the advance wall of Erebus is less than twenty minutes away from Jiuquan."

Tein smiled. "My information gives us more than a comfortable hour to launch. Please relax."

Yerry seemed convinced, but Hari Wottard, who had become the President's chief advisor on Erebus, whispered urgently in his ear. Tein had little time to spare for their feelings. He nodded to Lieutenant Chan, who surreptitiously left the room. She would be back soon.

He walked confidently through the crowd, greeting leaders and other self-important figures with quiet words of praise and encouragement.

They were in the forward launch bunker, a massive structure created in concrete and steel. Originally it had been a construction area for the old-fashioned chemical boosters, and more recently had been used for launch preparation. Its size, and proximity to the main launch field, made it ideal for his purposes.

The huge blast-shield—designed to withstand the accidental detonation of a nuclear device being sent into orbit—fell back into place with thud, giving them an excellent view of the launch field. No less than seventy-three heavy-lifters waited outside for departure.

Tein had completed his circuit of the room and was approaching the US President once more. "President Yerry. I want to thank you and your countrymen for the invaluable assistance you have given. The men and materials you provided have enabled us to meet, and exceed, our goals for the asteroid colony."

Yerry nodded in acknowledgement as Tein walked back to the main control panel. He checked his watch. It was time. This had to be timed precisely.

He stepped up onto a small platform and raised his voice.

"Through your efforts," said Tein, waving his arms to include the whole group of multi-national leaders and wealthy capitalists, "you have enabled the survival of Humanity."

There was a loud detonation, then another, then a continuous roar as one by one, the massive boosters lifted from the steel platforms of Jiuquan.

Tein turned to watch, but the light was blinding, pouring in through the big window in a blaze of chemical fire.

Behind him, Tein could hear the panic, but he shut it out of his mind. Would there be time for one last cup of tea?

"What the hell is this?" screamed Yerry.

Tein shielded his eyes against the glare and watched as Chan re-entered the room with hundreds of Chinese infantry. He held back tears as he watched his men and women. Not a single soldier lost composure.

Tein nodded to Chan, who gave an order in Cantonese.

Five hundred sub-machine guns were cocked in perfect unison. The panic in the room was replaced with a shocked silence.

Above them, disappearing like fairy-lights into the gloom of the darkened sky, were the last spacecraft to leave Earth.

Tein cleared his throat.

"All I ask for now, ladies and gentlemen, is decorum."

Yerry's jaw was slack.

"But, but ... you are remaining behind."

Tein smiled. He had read Yerry and the others like a book. They had been so sure that he would secure his own place of safety—so sure that he would insert himself in the place of another, more deserving, younger candidate—that they had allowed themselves to be blinded to the truth.

He looked up at the disappearing lights. His own nephew, Twang, only twenty-three but already a brilliant biologist, was among the chosen few. Tein would survive—at least through him. He only hoped that Twang would honour his memory.

"Mr President, T-minus thirty seconds," whispered Hari Wottard.

Through the huge window, there was a gust of rank, rotting air. Tein tasted salt on his tongue. It filled the air, stinging his skin.

Erebus had sucked up every drop of the world's oceans. It now *was* the sea of Earth, transformed into one massive, rolling wave of rock and flesh.

People screamed and pointed out the window.

A huge, dark wall was approaching them, coming fast. Within seconds it was close enough for the powerful lights of the launch field to catch on it. Tein had heard reports of it from all around the world, so he was ready when it happened.

All along its length, tens of thousands of lids opened. Suddenly the lights were reflected by a galaxy of eyes, all suspended in that wall of darkness.

Death was coming, in the myriad guise of their own reflection.

"And so we kill ourselves," he muttered in Cantonese.

"Sir?"

He looked down to see Chan at his elbow with a cup of tea.

"Oh, thank you, Chan."

Tears glistened on her cheeks as she carefully handed him his plain, yet much-loved cup and saucer. She bowed deeply.

Tein frowned. "Stand straight. You know I dislike such imperialist traditions, Chan."

"Yes, Director. I know."

They turned to watch Erebus approach.

"The eyes! *The Eyes!*"

The civilians were screaming.

Indeed the eyes were frightening, sweeping down to engulf them. But was this any less frightening than a life spent without purpose? Without moral principle?

As Tein sipped his green tea he watched the assembled crowd carefully. How very few had cultivated *peace of mind*. How easily they gave in to panic.

The saucer clattered softly as he put down his tea cup.

Erebus was closing on them.

"Wait," said Yerry. "They aren't eyes! They're *mouths!*"

All along its length, the opalescent eyes split across the middle, the upper and lower membranes drawing aside to reveal an awesome set of metallic teeth, grinding together in hungry anticipation.

Thousands of teeth, each big enough to swallow a multi-storey building.

"Fascinating," said Tein.

Then the Eyes of Erebus were upon them.

☆

Lover, feel my embrace.

☆

"Mat, we're receiving a feed via satellite."

Mat gave a gentle push and drifted across the cabin toward Jereece's workstation.

"My God."

Erebus had circled the globe. The long cylindrical tubes that had grown up all along the equator were erupting regularly now, shooting up vast sections of digested mantle and waste material.

"Do you have an analysis of those gases from the tubes?"

Jereece nodded. "Yes. They're the same as the jets we observed incoming, hydrogen and superheated steam. The whole mixture is igniting in the atmosphere. There are more than fifty-thousand launches a day. Billions of tonnes, all breaking orbit and heading out into space."

Mat snapped his fingers, the sudden movement sending him crashing into the metal hull of the capsule. He stabilised himself with a light touch.

"It's a Light Gas Gun," said Mat. Erebus was digesting the planet, flashing water into steam to super-pressurise a chamber of hydrogen and fire chunks of Earth out into space along those massive tubes. It took a light gas like hydrogen to produce the high muzzle velocity.

"Do you have anything else?" asked Mat.

"Yes, there seems to be some sort of radio communication emanating from Erebus into space. I can't make any sense out of it, but it's incredibly powerful, and increasing in strength."

Mat rubbed his tired eyes.

"Didn't the lab boys in Hari's team say something about that?"

Jereece nodded. "Yeah, that's right. It seems that it communicates with itself using various wavelengths of electromagnetic radiation. That's how it coordinates its own structure and nervous system through all those disconnected elements."

"Well, no point getting too concerned about the damn thing's biorhythms," said Mat.

Jereece smiled, but did not laugh.

The usually cheerful astronomer was subdued, his eyes haunted.

"What's wrong?" asked Mat.

Jereece tried to smile but failed. He took a deep breath, then turned back to his monitor, his eyes glued to the image of Erebus, swarming and rippling over Earth.

"I've been thinking," said Jereece. "The Missing Mass. I think its biological."

"Missing Mass?"

"You know—the missing mass of the Universe. Some cosmological models say it should be much more massive than the observed visible mass."

"Ahh," said Mat. The last few weeks, getting all their materials safely away from Earth orbit to their new base in the asteroids, had been hectic. It had been a long time since he could amuse himself with cosmological speculation.

Jereece turned to Mat.

"I think the Missing Mass is Life. *Enormous* Life. And if that's true—it makes us look like microbes ... molecules. Who knows what is out there? I mean, what eats Erebus? Where does the food chain end?"

Mat's tired brain chewed over Jereece's theory then he pushed it out of his mind. It did not matter what was out there, for now they simply needed to survive.

"Call coming in," yelled Yath from the other side of the small cabin.

Mat floated back to his station.

"Afternoon, Mr Keterson."

Mat smiled as Athy's face filled the screen. She was dressed in a grey, workman-like uniform crumpled with weeks of neglect. Her hair was greasy and unkempt, with long strands fanning out around her head in the zero-g. A knot of desire tightened low in his stomach. For a second he just looked at her, marvelling that they had found each other and survived through it all—the arrival of Erebus—the slow destruction of Earth.

"You're a sight for sore eyes," said Mat.

"How long till you reach the construction zone?" she asked.

"Only ten hours now. Time to let someone else have a turn watching Erebus."

Athy leant forward toward the video camera.

"Come home, Mat. I need you," she whispered.

His breathing accelerated, blood pounding in his temples.

"I'm on my way," he whispered hoarsely.

He smiled as he cut the link.

☆

My need grows apace. This lover, however sweet, will shrivel beneath my embrace, leaving only its hot core to power my heart.

My voice is growing stronger, the call insistent, yet I must wait. Again I must sleep, and dream.

Soon another *must* answer the call, and at last I will have a true lover. This time, a Vendeth.

Our brood will be strong, of that I have no doubt—and will awaken hungry, tearing their way free of our bodies with savage determination.

But for now I am alone, and the heartbreak is still hard to bear. I had so hoped this lover would be the one. Those strange snatches of song I first heard, I now recall like a broken promise.

Is love truly so hard to find?

CINEMA SUPPLEMENT

HERPETOCALYPSE
NOW!

ANDREW MACRAE

Hotel womb. Home suite home. Time stretched. Time spanned. On my right, a loaded gun. It was a shiny black passport, an oblivion machine. On my left, a bottle of single malt. It was a chemical salve, a nightmare shepherd.

Spiritual unity. The phrase snagged in my mind from somewhere. Freedom.

The room took a call. It was the studio. How's the draft coming?

I demurred. I delayed. One more week. It's almost ready.

I talked up the script. It's going to be the best monster story ever. The kids will love it. Number one with a bullet.

They weren't happy but what could they do? Bring in another writer/director?

I ended the call and the room lit my cigarette. A point of focused light combusted paper and tobacco. I inhaled. I looked from the gun to the bottle to the empty page. It always came back to this. Many different pathways led to the same place.

I slurped single malt.

Spiritual unity.

I've been in the monster movie business since 2009, when Arnie sold California to Sony. The US dollar had crashed. The US film industry had bottomed out. It was a tough time for white men in the monster game. I cut my teeth working as a script editor on *City Four from Los Angeles*, *Annihator*, *Rorah* and *Rorah Vs Bilaor*. Movies made on the cheap in the US to sell in Japan.

Adrift: I looked over to a battered road case stowed with my luggage. I got the shakes. The word *Monsterscape* was stenciled on the side. I slipped off the lounge and walked over to the case.

Genre wars. There's a feedback effect between Japan and America. *King Kong* and *The Beast from 20,000 Fathoms* influenced *Godzilla*. *Godzilla* boomed big on both sides of the Pacific in the mid-50s but the heyday of American monster movies was already over. The genre went off in Japan. *Godzilla* had babies. *Godzilla* spawned clones. *Godzilla* outgrew the market in the 70s but rose again.

I popped the clips on the case. The monster suit glistened in the light. *Monsterscape* was my first film as director. The suit was old and battle-scarred. It smelt of gunpowder and spirit glue.

The Americans tried to steal the genre back. TriStar released *Godzilla* in 1998. They fucked up. They mistook the map for the territory. The movie bombed. The genre was *still* going off in Japan. By 2010, with California in the bag and rich from their success at home, Sony executives wanted to try again. They dubbed English versions of their old series and repackaged them for the home entertainment market. They made *Pain Souls*, the biggest, most expensive monster movie ever. They fucked up. The timing wasn't right. The movie bombed. Monsters didn't resonate with the Bible belt. Monsters were nature spirits. They were evil. *Heathen.*

I lifted the suit out of the case. It came in two parts. I put the legs on. It felt right. I put the top on. It was hot. It was heavy. My vision was restricted to a mesh rectangle in front of me. It felt gooood. My spirit reared up inside me. I roared. I stomped. My breath came heavy and loud in my ears. I threw my smartcloth notebook on the ground.

Then came the earthquake of 2015. The West Coast got hammered, worse than anything the Big G could have done. California disintegrated. Something in the American psyche shifted. They couldn't kid themselves anymore that they controlled nature. They couldn't hit back with missiles and bombs. The timing was right. *Monsterscape* went stratospheric. The studio made money. The studio sold merchandise. The franchise was huge. It was bigger than me.

I rampaged. I smashed the telescreen. I ripped the gloves off the suit. I threw off the monster head and snatched the gun from the table. I dumped five rounds. Bullets rattled. Bullets scattered.

I spent the next ten years making the same movie over and over again. I hit on a winning formula. It worked but it cost me. I pissed myself up against the wall through eight movies. My hair fell out. My spirit shattered into a thousand shining pieces.

I spun the chamber. I bit the barrel. I tasted metal. Oil smell hit me. I screwed my eyes shut. I pulled the trigger once, twice. The hammer clicked. One, two.

Stars waxed and then waned. Our studio, the shark that ate up all the little fish in its path, was suddenly a take-over target. The heat was on to make the biggest monster movie of all time. The South Asian market was ripe: Indonesia, Hong Kong, Australia—where I grew up. The studio wanted *me* to make it. My last shot. And there I was, wearing a monster suit in a hotel room, drinking whiskey for breakfast and trying to come up with the script.

I pulled the trigger. Three, Four—BLAM. The gun kicked. I shot the empty page. It flowed like mercury.

☆

OPENING TITLES
Pixelated patterns coalesce out of the darkness. We see iridescent
blue cells spilt and divide on a red background. Cells mutate.
Patterns grow and transform: horses, clouds, a train, the lights of
a city at night. We see scaly hide. Microbes squirm. Nuclear war.
We see a sand monitor basking beside a baking desert road. We see
a thorny devil against red sand. Hazel fractal pattern. The camera
zooms out. We see an eye with a horizontal pupil. It blinks. The
camera rotates clockwise. We see the words HERPETOCALYPSE
NOW burning in atomic orange on the black pupil.

☆

The room opened the curtains onto another day. I was naked,
wrapped in a sheet. The suit lay crumpled in a corner. Broken
glass and shell casings littered the floor. The room patched
through a call. It was my office.

My assistant, Sam, said, "John? Is that you? Listen, we got Wosa."

The biggest rubber-suit monster actor of all time. And he
belonged to a rival studio.

"What?" I said, my voice hangover thick.

"You better be working on that script, because we just secured
Win Wosa to work on our film."

"How?"

"A combination of blackmail, clever contract law, and a
shitload of cash."

"Holy fuck."

"Yeah."

The room put me in the shower.

I was in orbit. If I came up with the right script, we could do it.

My shattered spirit rallied. My shattered spirit coalesced.

☆

FADE IN:
EXT. SIMPSON DESERT.
A treaded vehicle crests a red dune. On the side of its well-worn
exterior is a stencil of a sand monitor lizard.

The camera sweeps around and we see the POWER STATION.
The building is a triumph of futurist architecture. It consists of
two sets of four coils built either side of a perpendicular wedge.
It HUMS. There's a pipeline running from it in the direction from
which the rover came.

The place crawls with robot activity. Robot dozers build roads.
Transports shuttle equipment and material. Flying vehicles hover
around the station, making repairs and vacuuming dust from
external components.

INT. ROVER.
SAM has dark hair and a beard. DAVE is grey and clean-shaven.
The compartment behind them is full of computer gear, rock

samples and items scavenged from the desert. They peer out the windscreen at the building.

SAM
There it is. That's where the pipeline ends.

DAVE
Covert AI shit. Gotta be.
(taps a keyboard)
It's not on any of the maps. It only showed on the radar when we came over the hill.

A RUMBLE from outside. The rover SHUDDERS.

SAM
Shit, man, it's pretty unstable. That seismic activity's getting more intense. We're right on top of the fissure now. You sure you wanna stick around?

DAVE
Something that well-cloaked, sitting way out here? I bet there's someone willing to pay for the map reference.

Sam is tapping at sensor equipment, trying to get a reading, gather data. The Geiger counter squeals.

SAM
Radiation off the scale. Whatever it's doing, it ain't geothermal.

DAVE
Who builds a reactor on a fucking fault line?

A RUMBLING ROAR. The cabin SHAKES. Dave stares out the windscreen.

SAM
Shit. Another tremor.
(checks an instrument)
Biggest yet. Let's get outta here.

There's the sound of an explosion. They both look out. Their faces are lit by orange light from outside.

EXT. POWER STATION.
Explosions rock the station. Support vehicles and flying drones tumble away in the blasts. The earth rumbles. The pipeline bursts at the juncture with the power station. It oozes red fluid into the sand. A rent opens in the rock at the base of the station. We glimpse a gaping black hole and—a flicker of movement.

INT. ROVER.
DAVE
Almost there ...

White light from outside, brighter than anything previously.

SAM
Fucken he—

EXT. ROVER.
A wave of white flame engulfs the rover. A dark shape blocks the camera.

☆

I skipped over tangled freeways in my jumpcar, boosting from one transit platform to the next. I watched the meter. I fed tokens into the slot to maintain priority status. The script for *Herpetocalypse Now!* was on the smartcloth in my pocket. It needed editing but it would work. It would put me back on the map.

The studio loomed on the screen. I vectored in. Another boost and I was on my way down towards the office landing platform.

Jerry, the special effects director, met me at the platform. He was wearing a grin as wide as his cowboy hat.

"I love it," he said. "Some of your best work. Gonna be a bitch to film, though." His eyes gleamed.

Jerry was two years younger than me. He built rubber monster suits in his backyard even when he wasn't getting paid to do it.

"Did you hear we got Wosa?" I said.

"Yeah. I hope he's been practicing quadruped, coz this new sucker's got backwards-facing legs."

We took the stairs to the workshop. The door opened onto little-boy heaven. Teams of effects crew worked on models. We used CGI a lot for texture and to mask mistakes but nothing had depth and weight like a miniature or a prop. With a miniature, you can capture the charm of the abstraction. With CGI, the abstraction has become its own thing.

A twenty-foot-tall hydraulic waldo, construction yellow, hissed steam from its joints. On another sound stage built like desert terrain, a one-twenty-fifth scale M1 tank squared off against three remote-controlled Apache attack helicopters. A fighter jet grew armoured legs and squatted down on a section of tarmac. I felt the illusion in my gut. I itched to be back in the chair.

The crew spotted me. Work stopped. A standing ovation bolstered my ego. I smiled. I shook hands and slapped backs. They gathered round, beards and ponytails *de rigueur*.

"Well, you've probably all heard the news by now. We're going to make the biggest fucking monster movie ever."

Their faces shone. I saw it in their eyes: they loved me. I gave them the spiel. I bought them.

Afterwards, I drew the monster suit team together. They were excited. They had already mocked up clay model design concepts. I was impressed but didn't let on.

"Listen, guys. I just wanted to say that Wosa comes with his own suitatronics people, so I'm sorry. You're going to play more of a supporting role than you're used to."

"We'll still get to work with him, won't we?" Raphael said. Raphael had tried to make it as a monster actor in his own right. He didn't have what it takes. Now he specialised in suit eye and nostril movement.

"Definitely. You guys have got the local knowledge and the established teamwork. It's going to take a lot of cooperation to make this thing work."

I talked them through it. By the end, they knew they still came out in front. They would get to work on a set for the great Wosa to destroy.

☆

EXT. DESERT TRUCKSTOP. NIGHT.
The truckstop is an oasis of civilisation in the wilderness. Its neon signs light up the night. Driverless road-train transports, behemoths of the desert highway, cluster like animals at a feeding trough. Despite all the activity, we can't see any humans.

INT. TRUCKSTOP.
JAYDEN and QUYNH watch TV. They have an apartment inside the truckstop. Jayden wears a fireproof vest over a flannel shirt. An orange mesh back cap with an agribrand logo perches on his head. Quynh is fat. She's in a nightgown and has shoulder-length black hair. She's eating ice cream.

An alarm sounds a quiet and persistent tone. It takes a moment to register. Quynh drags her eyes from the TV and looks across at a control panel.

QUYNH
Problem with pump nine. Check it out, will ya, honey?

JAYDEN
(grunts).

He pulls himself out of his chair.

EXT. TRUCKSTOP.
Jayden exits the door and walks past the trucks. We see how big they are. They have four trailers connected to a mammoth prime mover. They are computer controlled and don't have any doors or windows. We can hear them howling along the highway outside, making the regular run through the Interior from Darwin to Melbourne.

Jayden arrives at pump nine. He checks a read-out and gives a puzzled grunt. From the front, there doesn't seem to be anything wrong with the truck. He walks down the side of the vehicle. Everything seems to be okay.

He looks up.

We see a huge gash running down the side of the four trailers. We see for the first time that the vehicle is a live animal transport. We see four trailers opened like a tin can.

There's nothing left of the cargo except blood and shit.

Jayden tips his head back. His jaw drops. His hat falls off.

☆

"Where the fuck is Wosa?" Sam said. It was 5.00am. She nursed a double-espresso.

"Did you call him yet today?" I said.

"Not yet. Last contact was six hours ago. I got the brush off," Sam said. She shot me a look. "He better be worth it."

I frowned. "He will be."

"We could use a stand-in. What about Raphael?" she said.

"I've been using him to block out scenes. He's not good enough. We need Wosa. No one else has the gravitas."

I walked down to the building that housed the effects studio soundstage. A miniature Melbourne had been lovingly constructed from satellite photographs and reconnaissance missions. Nothing thrilled an audience more than watching their familiar landmarks destroyed by a giant monster.

I bit down on my fear. I schmoozed the team. I enthused. I exuded confidence. I put Raphael in the suit and picked up the storyboard. We rehearsed another scene. Raphael was distracted.

"What's up with you?" I said to him.

He snapped out of it. "Well, at least I got to wear his suit."

My phone rang. It was Sam. "I just got the call. He's on his way. He'll be here in three hours."

I drove out to the airport with Sam and Jerry.

Jerry did a lot of the talking, his cowboy hat pushed right back on his head. "I can't believe I'm going to meet him, let alone work with him. It's amazing. You know, he lived with wild bears for two years to get their movement." He popped his gum.

"My friend Karma worked on his last film," said Sam. "She said he's amazing to watch. He channels the monster. She said he studied under Satsuma."

The van pulled into the car park at the local airport and we stared in amazement as an ancient 747, painted green with a scaly skin pattern, taxied towards the terminal.

"Holy shit! He doesn't mess around. That's amazing," Jerry said.

"I didn't know they were still allowed to fly planes that big," Sam said.

"Man, does he really need a whole 747 to himself? It's not like he's got to bring his own props or anything," Jerry said.

"He's got staff, technicians." The colossal antique aircraft rattled me, too, although I tried not to show it.

We got out of the van and walked over to the stretch of runway where the plane had stopped. Instead of a stairway, a bipedal forklift clumped over from a nearby hanger. We looked at each other.

A cargo hatch opened in the belly of the aircraft. The forklift positioned itself and extended a hydraulic arm. Wosa emerged slowly from the gloom. He was enormous and seated on a throne-like medical apparatus. The forklift whined and creaked as it took his weight. It braced itself with a step backwards. Wosa wore a gold velvet tracksuit. He shone in the afternoon sunlight.

Sam said, "He must weigh at least 300 kilos."

Jerry was pale. "We're going to have to rebuild the suit."

☆

EXT. DESERT. DAY.
Heat haze reflects off a straight stretch of silver-black tarmac. We see a sign: MELBOURNE 696KMS. The camera pans up and a robot drone flies over the sign. We hear high-pitched computer squeal. Titles on the screen translate:

Drone 233, head north. Follow the pipeline. Film everything and report. Acknowledge.

The drone bleeps and turns through ninety degrees.

EXT. DESERT.
We see the desert from Drone 233's PoV. Parched earth and stony sand. A digital overlay filter covers the screen and we see the pipeline. It glows red and throbs like a vein. A black shape blocks it off. The black shape sucks up the pulsing flow from the pipeline.

The overlay switches back to visible light. We see that the dark shape is a small mountain range, curved around the pipeline. The drone angles in for a closer look. Light-and dark-coloured rocks make regular patchwork patterns. There is a ridge along the spine of the range. The drone flies closer. It passes a jewel. The jewel BLINKS. The mountain range RUMBLES.

The mountain range becomes flesh. The drone squawks. The drone dodges falling rocks. It climbs hard. The mountain range climbs harder. A black claw scythes the air. It knocks the drone to the ground. A red eye-light dies.

☆

"He hasn't read it," said Sam.

"What? You mean he hasn't read today's scene?"

"I mean, he has no idea what the movie is about." She flicked her hair and looked through her fringe. "We paid him a forty-million-dollar advance and put production on hold for three weeks while we waited for him to arrive and he hasn't even read the fucking script."

I opened my mouth and shut it again. She went on.

"Shit, man, his office gave us all these guidelines about how it had to be specially formatted in sixteen point type and printed on fucking *paper*, for god's sake. They wanted it bound in *leather*. It cost us a fortune. It ended up five-hundred pages long. We couriered it to Tokyo by overnight express.'

"He hasn't read the script?" I said.

"Yeah, that's what I'm sayin'."

I looked at my watch. It was time for my first meeting with him. My stomach flipped.

I left the studio office and walked across the road to Wosa's hotel. Crowds of local retards milled around, angling for a glimpse of Wosa. They carried cameras. They had merchandise for him to sign. A guy turned sausages on a grill. His partner squeezed them between slices of white bread and sold them for $10. Wosa was the biggest thing that had ever happened here.

Security swiped me through to his door. I knocked and his room let me in. He hulked in the darkened space. The carcasses of six barbecued chickens littered the bench.

I bowed. "Wosa-san, you honour us," I said.

His translator AI burbled Japanese. He grunted in reply, leveling his gaze at me. His face was greasy from the chicken. He was still dressed in his tracksuit.

"I hope everything's okay with your accommodation," I said.

He spoke. His voice rumbled. His voice was like a landslide. The window frame shook. The translator talked: "Your name doesn't mean shit to me. This shoot doesn't mean shit to me. I just want to get the work done and get out of here."

"With respect, we must agree on the best way to get a result we can both be proud of."

Rocks tumbled against each other in his chest. The translator said: "I want more chicken."

I ploughed on regardless. "We've already done some of the matte work with the costume and the CG touch-ups of the monster's first appearance. Tomorrow we're going for the first of the miniature effects shots. You'll be in the suit, if we can get the adjustments made in time."

The translator spoke: "I have choreographed many monster scenes. You just look after the direction and I will take care of the rest."

"My assistant tells me you haven't read the script yet," I said.

"This is a monster movie, isn't it? I know how to make monster movies."

"Well, we're trying to do something different with this film. I think you should read the script. We've done this synopsis for you. At least read that to give yourself an idea of the creature's motivation." I handed him a page. Sixteen point type.

"Motivation. Ha! How can humans know or understand the monster? We can anthropomorphise it, pretend it is an expression of our unconscious, but it cannot be controlled. It cannot be known."

"All the same," I said, "the creature doesn't exist in a vacuum. The whole point of the monster movie is to place the monster in a situation. Each situation is different and it will react differently depending on the circumstances. You should read the script."

He belched. His chest boomed.

Tottoto kaburimon kisetekure, de, orewa dokowo arukya-iinda.

The translator filled me in:

"Just put me in the suit and show me where to stomp."

☆

EXT. MELBOURNE SKYLINE LOOKING NORTH WEST.
GENERIS looms above the northern suburbs of Melbourne. He moves on all fours. He turns his head from side to side. His tongue flicks and we see that he has twelve tongues. Black poison oozes from his gums.

He lumbers over roads and houses. From a distance, he appears to move slowly, a storm cloud of muscle and bone rolling over suburbia. We zoom in closer and see that relative to the ground he's moving fast. People flee as a black-clawed foot stomps the car park at Barkly Square. The K-Mart sign snags on scaly skin as he moves past.

A 20-metre claw carves a gouge in the roadway. Cars career. Generis opens his mouth to flick his tongue and we see a close shot of the twelve tongues writhing. A black drop falls from his mouth.

The city marshals its defenses at Princes Street. Battle tanks form a grid across the intersection to stop the beast's advance. They fire coordinated salvos but Generis ignores them.

Five robot-controlled attack helicopters hover into position. Rockets and missiles plough Generis's hide. He flicks his tongues at a helicopter that gets too close. The rotors snap off and the machine crashes to the ground.

A sortie of fighter jets approaches from the east. More missiles stream through the air, aiming for his eyes. They hit! Generis HOWLS. He swats with his foreleg. The planes are too fast. They arc around for another attack run. Generis is angry now. Patterns on his skin shift and change. He glows orange. The jets are on their second approach. Generis opens his mouth and a beam of white energy lashes out. The jets are a rain of falling ash.

Generis sniffs the air, picking up the scent of the pulsing pipeline. He moves towards the centre of town.

☆

We flooded the set. It was humid and hot. Insects buzzed. I sweated. Time unwound. Time came undone. Red light lit my world. I watched as a snail crawled along the straight blade of an art-knife left on a workbench. It slithered. It survived.

Wosa was in the suit. He looked good. He was *big*. He carried *weight*. He had *mass, inertia*. He moved slowly. He wasn't the monster in my script but it worked.

I was in the director's chair. I gave the orders. "Double around for another attack. Crouch low."

Wosa talked back. The set shook. The translator was sluggish. It glitched. It spoke in riddles:

"A leech rent pop sow. Sol poet nawe perch."

I motioned him to move his head to one side. He did it. The eye team contracted the pupil for a close shot on Generis's head.

Wosa's suit people sat at their console just off the stage. They were all Japanese. They didn't make a sound. I'd heard the rumours the crew circulated. They're telepathically linked to him. They're clones. They're wet-wired. They're empty cases slaved to a master.

Jerry came over for a conference.

"He's ruining our movie!" he said.

I looked at him. "He's ruining *my* fucking movie," I said. I let the anger build. I fed off it.

Jerry said, "He's saying he doesn't think the monster should be attacking the city. He says it should be protecting it from some unknown alien force."

"The monster is attacking the city because the AI buildings are tapping its energy. They awakened it," I said. "That's the point."

"He says he wants more monsters. He says he needs to fight."

"I'll give him a fight," I said.

I strode over to Wosa. He stood on the effects stage. He had taken off part of the costume. Suspenders held the leg and hip section in place. He rehearsed his next stomp. It wasn't on the storyboard. It wasn't in the story. It wasn't in my script.

"What are you working on, Wosa? The next shot calls for you to take a step backwards, towards the river."

He fixed me with a stare. "This is where the pipeline stops," his translator said. He stood impassive. Like a mountain. He rumbled some more syllables. "The seat of control of the AI buildings that built the power station in the desert. Generis attacks here."

"So now you're an expert on the script?" I said.

"You listen to me. I will tell you the way to make a monster movie," he said.

My vision clouded red.

☆

EXT. DOWNTOWN MELBOURNE.

Generis arrives in the CBD. He's following the pipeline. He takes up a lot of room in the city streets. He crushes smaller buildings, crumbling masonry and brickwork as he passes. His tail sweeps traffic islands and tram stops in his wake.

He's heading for the MULTI-FUNCTION POLIS, the tallest building in the Southern Hemisphere.

Generis approaches the tower from Collins Street. His belly scrapes the buildings either side. Debris falls. Generis crushes cars and trams underneath his feet. He reaches the bottom of the building. He lashes out with a taloned foreleg. The tower SHAKES. Generis strikes again. Claws bite into the tower. Blue glass falls in sheets. Pedestrians scatter. The tower sounds an evacuation alarm. People flee from emergency exits.

The tower SHUDDERS and GROANS. It begins a transformation. It uproots a buttress from the ground. People are still trying to escape. They tumble over mounds of rubble as another buttress pulls free from the pavement on the other side of the tower. The buttresses grow toes and knee joints. Outcropped structures form arms. Glass cascades like water. The tower transforms into a 450-metre-tall fighting robot. Generis squares off against it.

The tower braces itself. It lifts an arm and launches missiles from its fingers. They track spiral trails and explode against Generis. He ROARS. He's pissed off. He attacks with his teeth, ripping through reinforced steel.

The tower takes a faltering step. Pavement cracks under its feet. It backs away towards Spencer Street Station.

Generis BELLOWS. His skin glows orange as he readies a charge. The tower turns its exterior into a reflective surface. Generis fires. The charge reflects. The charge chars two blocks of downtown Melbourne. Smoke wafts. The tower is unharmed.

Generis is weaker, now. He falters. He crosses the river. He crushes Crown Casino as he tries to get behind the building. He stands in the river, sizing up distances and angles.

☆

My spirit flared. My anger sang. My fists balled tight. I lost it. I swung, left then right. He took it like a fly had landed on him. He looked away, over my shoulder. He SWELLED. He moved towards me. Model buildings died. Jerry shrieked.

I backed down. My spirit retreated. I was suddenly awkward. I sidestepped, one foot at the intersection of Swanston and Bourke, one foot at Finders and Elizabeth.

Wosa said something in Japanese. The translator glitched: "Placebo when presto."

He swung a punch at me. I dodged it.

Jerry stood aghast. Raphael jumped between Wosa and me. Raphael's eyes were wide. He fixed me with his gaze. "No, you don't understand! He's a genius," he said. "You've got to listen to what he's saying."

I pushed Raphael in the chest. He fell over, crushing Swanston Street to Victoria Parade, diagonal. Jerry flipped out. He took off his cowboy hat and jumped on it.

Wosa spoke. He pointed at me with a monster-taloned finger. His translator worked. "Wait. You must play the tower. It's the only way."

Some of the locals had made it into the studio. They cheered Wosa on. They snapped photographs and gawked at the atmosphere.

"This is my movie," I said. "I'll end it my way."

☆

The tower stands firm, bracing itself. Generis deploys his tail attack, whipping his body around, lashing the tower with his tail and knocking its legs out from underneath it. The tower topples. Two city blocks erupt in dust and debris. Generis ROARS, victorious, turning his head from side to side.

The tower lies prone. One arm is extended above its head. The arm opens up. Coordinated movement shuffles between Spencer Street Station and the arm. A section of mag-lev track extends from the station, forming a rail gun up the tower's arm. Generis notices the movement and stops gloating. He moves towards the building to try and beat the attack but it's too late.

A mag-lev train carriage at the end of the track shoots up the arm at tremendous velocity. It rockets through the air and smashes into Generis's head. He is bleeding and leaking black poison from his mouth. He is shaken.

The tower climbs to its feet, taking a part of the station with it, now as a permanent and deadly attachment. It moves towards Generis, going in for the kill. Generis is wily. He slinks back across the river, luring the tower onto soft ground.

The tower realises too late what has happened and loses its footing in the river. It falls face first onto Southbank, crushing arcades and apartment buildings. Generis presses his advantage and crawls to the tower. He crushes the array of sensors on the tower's penthouse head and smashes the rail gun.

☆

The locals were going ape-shit. They chanted Wosa's name. I was face-first on the ground, in the tower suit. I lay across the miniature Southbank. My breath came in gasps. I could hear Jerry ordering people around on-set but it was still my movie. I was going to take Wosa out. Fuck the sequel.

I rolled to my left. I crushed houses and cars. The tower suit was damaged. Movement was difficult. The suit was lighter than the one from *Monsterscape* but it was still heavy. I looked through the cracked visor. I smelt my own fear. The air was thick with it. Sweat stung my eyes.

Generis loomed in my field of vision. The locals droned, "Wosa, Wosa." I staggered to my feet.

"That's great, John," said Jerry. "Keep going."

I got my balance. Wosa moved towards me, almost like he wanted it. I rushed him. The suit's toes bit model pavement. I shoulder charged. We fell together onto the set. Squibs ignited. Charges flared. Flame gouted. Black smoke billowed. It choked me. Wosa/Generis was underneath me. I drew back my damaged rail gun arm and slammed it into Generis's head over and over again. Teeth smashed. Tongues writhed. The tail flopped. The tower killed Generis.

"Cut," I said.

The crowd was shocked into silence. Jerry clapped. The crew whooped. Wosa moved underneath me. He groaned. His translator garbled.

☆

The film was in the can. It was big. It was *bad*. It was the last film I would make. My spirit guttered. I drove out to the airport to see Wosa off.

"We couldn't have done it without you," I said to Wosa and meant it. I watched as his suit team were packed into crates and stored in the cargo hold.

"Thanks," his translator replied. "You're not such a bad guy, you know? The film is good," he said.

I don't know how he knew it. He hadn't even seen the rushes.

"Yeah," I said.

"Come and visit my monster dojo sometime. You're good. With some training, you could act."

I smiled. "I'm finished with monsters. Thanks anyway."

Wosa was lifted into the cargo bay.

The plane taxied for takeoff. I thought about the global promotional tour ahead of me. My spirit cried. My spirit bled. An endless round of appearances, interviews, cocktail parties and signings. Hotel rooms. The gun. The bottle. *The horror.*

CONTRIBUTORS

Lyn Battersby has a dozen sales to her credit to date, and has won Western Australian SF Achievement Awards for both her writing and editing, including issue 11 of *Andromeda Spaceways Inflight Magazine*. In addition to being a writer, she is a qualified massage therapist and a full-time mother. Her desk looks much cooler than her husband, writer Lee's. "The Memory of Breathing" was her second story sale, and is currently being developed as a feature length film. Lyn's website can be found at http://battersby.com.au and she maintains a regular web journal at http://battblush.livejournal.com. She blushes with unbelievable ease.

By day, **Michael Boatman** acts, professionally. He galvanised himself in the television series *SPIN CITY, ARLI$$* and *Gray's Anatomy*. He's devoured scenery in films like *Hamburger Hill, The Peacemaker* and *The Glass Shield*, and can be glimpsed in the upcoming films ... *And Then Came Love, American Summer* and *My Father's Will*. His stories lurk in the anthologies *Lords of Justice, Until Somebody Loses An Eye, Sages & Swords, Dark Dreams II* and *III, Badass Horror*, and magazines such as *Horror Garage* and *Red Scream*. His short story collection, *God Laughs When You Die*, will be published in October 2007 by Dybbuk Press. He haunts the desolate wilds of suburban New York along with his mate and four enormous children. He blogs at www.michaelboatman.blogspot.com.

David Bofinger became a nuclear physicist in the confident expectation that a radiation accident would give him super-powers. When this failed to eventuate he found employment with the Department of Defence, hoping to take out his frustration repressing mutants. He now works in amphibious warfare, which turned out to involve far-fewer-legged dolphins and gilled soldiers than he'd hoped.

Michael Canfield writes about monsters, superheroes, couples, bank robbers, babies, astronauts, paranoids, hobbyists, and other people. His first dozen or so stories have appeared in *Strange Horizons, futurismic.com, Black Gate, Talebones, Flytrap* and *Realms of Fantasy*, and the anthologies *From the Borderlands* and *Fantasy: The Best of the Year 2006*, on the podcast *Escape Pod*, and other places. He lives in North America and keeps a blog (with links to free stories) at www.michaelcanfield.net.

James Cooper lives in Nottinghamshire with his wife and son. His first novel, *The Midway*, was published by Crowswing Books in 2007. His stories have appeared in many anthologies and magazines, including *Cemetery Dance*, *Postscripts*, *All Hallows*, *Midnight Street*, *Not One of Us*, *Cold Flesh* and *When Graveyards Yawn*. He has also edited the anthology *Dark Doorways*, published by The Prufrock Press, and is currently at work on a collection of interviews with some of today's leading practitioners of dark fiction, entitled *In Conversation: A Writer's Perspective*. His debut short story collection, *You Are The Fly: Tales of Redemption and Distress*, will be published by Humdrumming Books in August 2007. You can visit his website at www.jamescooper.org.uk.

Shane Jiraiya Cummings is a Ditmar award-winning West Australian writer, a graduate of Clarion South, and a member of the US and Australian Horror Writers Associations. He has published more than fifty short stories in Australia, USA, and Europe, with many of these stories collected in *Shards: Forty Short Sharp Tales* (Ticonderoga Publications) and *In the Heart of Midnight*. Shane is the managing editor of *HorrorScope: The Australian Dark Fiction Web Log*, and editor of several anthologies including *Australian Dark Fantasy and Horror* 2006 edition and *Shadow Box*.

Darren Goossens has published fiction in *Aurealis*, *Andromeda Spaceways Inflight Magazine*, *Orb* and *All Hallows* and a small handful of other places. His drawings have appeared in *NFG* and an Australian physics textbook.

Robert Hood is a writer of horror-fantasy and SF, with stories appearing in magazines and anthologies worldwide. His work has been collected in *Day-dreaming on Company Time* and *Immaterial: Ghost Stories*, as well as *Creeping in Reptile Flesh*, a collection of old and new stories (Altair Australia Books). He is the author of the *Shades* series of supernatural thrillers and the novel, *Backstreets*. He edited *Daikaiju!: Giant Monster Tales* with Robin Pen. His website is at www.roberthood.net. He likes cats, zombies, and giant monsters, though he considers it's best to confine the last two to the imagination.

MP Johnson hangs out in Wisconsin and Minnesota, puking up stories about monsters and weirdoes. He is the mastermind behind *Freak Tension* fanzine, which focuses on punk rock and things that eat brains. Find out more about MP Johnson at www.freaktension.com.

TP Keating's "Happiness, or the Cash Equivalent" appears in the US anthology *Small Crimes* (Betancourt & Co), while his "Killer Heels Kill Twice as Dead" appears in the US anthology

Murder In Vegas (Tor Books). His short story "One Sick Vampire" was nominated for the James White Award. His first novel, *Bleeding Hearts: The Diary of a Country Vampire*, is available from www.lulu.com. Many further stories are available online, including on Rutger Hauer's personal website. The author's website is at www.tpkeating.com.

Maxine McArthur lived in Japan for 16 years and has a particular fondness for the daikaiju in the *Ultraseven* series, as they acted as babysitters when her sons were small. She now lives in Canberra and writes science fiction. Her last novel, *Less Than Human*, is set in a near-future Japan and features a gaijin, robots, and a neo-Buddhist cult.

Andrew Macrae is a member of the SuperNOVA writers group in Melbourne, where he lives with his partner. His stories have appeared in *Orb*, *Aurealis* and *Agog! Ripping Reads*. His hobbies include obsessive blog surfing and typewriter art. He loves email. Look him up on Google.

Winner of the One Book, Many Brisbanes short story competition and dedicated tea drinker, **Chris McMahon** currently works as an engineer in the development of alternative fuels and energy sources and has worked extensively in the environmental and greenhouse fields. Chris's fantasy novel, *The Calvanni*, was published in Australia in April 2006, and his short work has appeared in various publications including *Orb Speculative Fiction*, *Aurealis*, *Redsine*, and the anthologies *Fantasy Readers Wanted — Apply Within*, *The Devil in Brisbane* and *Fantastical Journeys to Brisbane*. His short story "Within Twilight" was shortlisted for the 2002 Aurealis Award in both the SF and horror categories. Self-confessed movie and video addict, Chris also enjoys martial arts and music. www.chris.mcmahon.com

Jason Nahrung works as a newspaper journalist in Brisbane, where his work covering the Australian speculative fiction scene won him a William Atheling Jnr award for Criticism or Review. A member of *Vision* writers group and the *Writers on the Edge* critique circle, he has had several short stories published. His debut novel, *The Darkness Within*, is out now through Hachette Australia. The supernatural thriller is based on a novella written with his partner Mil Clayton by email when they were living three states apart. www.jasonnahrung.com

Robin Pen is a founding editor of the prestigious Australian science fiction and fantasy literary magazine *Eidolon*. He is the author of *The Secret Life of Rubber-Suit Monsters*, a book of humorous criticism aimed at fantastic cinema. He has received four Australian Science Fiction Ditmar Awards for his writings.

Tony Plank was born in the UK, but soon became an Australian citizen. Fifty years later he was awarded a Seniors Card and got to ride on trains free. As a writer he has over 90 publications in such publications as *Wicked Mystic*, *Antipodean*, *Eldritch Tales*, *Aurealis*, *Specusphere*, *Fifth Dimension*, *Jackhammer*, *Agog! Fantastic Fiction*, and *Australien Absurdities*. Born in the same English County as Charles Dickens and the same town as Jane Austin, he hopes some of their talent has rubbed off on him. When not reading or writing he runs the "Inkspillers" website at www.inkspillers.com—a site of such importance that it would undoubtedly have been mentioned in the *Doomsday* book were it still in existence.

Kylie Seluka resides in Canberra. She writes and teaches. Recent stories have appeared in the anthologies *Fantastic Wonder Stories* and *The Outcast*. She confesses to taking some liberties with Daqinshan's story but not with the Idea.

Todd Tennant has been drawing and creating his own stories as long as he can remember. Starting out as an architectural illustrator, Todd took to illustrating giant monster stories in 2000 and continues to do so today, with several ambitious projects on the boil, especially in the graphic novel print media and the world of comic art. In 2006, Todd began creating a (fan-based) American Godzilla '94 online graphic novel, taken from the Rossio/Elliott screenplay that was rejected by Tri-Star for the proposed Hollywood remake. It is available on his website. Todd currently lives in Northern Alabama with his wife and his son. His Kaiju-art can be seen at his website, American KAIJU: www.american kaiju.kaijuphile.com/main.shtml.

Paul A. Toth's novels *Fizz* and *Fishnet* are available now. His third will be published soon. Short fiction credits include *The Barcelona Review*, *Night Train* and *The Mississippi Review Online*. His multimedia work has appeared on the *Iowa Review Web*, *Drunken Boat* and other sites. See www.netpt.tv for more information.

☆

www.ingramcontent.com/pod-product-compliance
Lightning Source LLC
Chambersburg PA
CBHW020837260626
47169CB00003B/1025